Redemption

DAWN WILLIAMS

To: Nancy
Thank you for
your support!
Dawn
Williams

First Edition

PAGE PUBLISHING, INC.
New York, NY

First originally published by Page Publishing, Inc. 2014

ISBN 978-1-63417-061-1 (pbk)
ISBN 978-1-63417-062-8 (digital)

Printed in the United States of America

Acknowledgments

To Kimmy, my sister and best friend all wrapped into one, words cannot express the inspiration you have been and always will be to me.

To Patty, any chance of putting down *Fifty Shades of Grey* and reading your little sister's book?

To Jamaile Parker, Ashley Sells, and Jennifer Johnson, your enthusiasm for this book inspired me to *Believe*.

To my husband, Dave, thank you for your unwavering support and all you do for us so I can write. You found the light at the end of the tunnel and I'll forever be grateful!

To those not listed here, you know who you are and how very dear you are to my heart. You have my heartfelt thanks.

1

It was a race against time.

The piercing, insistent beep streaming from her pager jolted her awake. She scrambled to sit up, ignoring the aching protests from her body for lying on the hard, unforgivable bench in the physician's locker room. She brought the pager closer to her sleep-deprived eyes, seeing a nine-nine trauma code indicating a very critical adult patient was due to arrive in the trauma center.

She glided her feet into a pair of shiny black clogs, tossed her stethoscope around her neck, and with long purposeful strides, headed toward the trauma center. Her honey-blonde hair tumbled carelessly down her back as she carried herself confidently, aware of the appreciative glances.

Summer was admittedly happily married to her profession. She loved the energy, the excitement, and the teamwork at Regional Medical in Jacksonville, Florida. Every day was different where she cared for the sickest, most severely injured patients.

It was the first Saturday in June.

A day promised to keep her winded and worn out gliding from one patient to another just as it had the night before because on nights and weekends, people had the tendency to wreck their cars and stab or shoot one another.

She made quick work changing into fresh scrubs, donning her protective gear, and then scrubbing intensely.

Her nurse, Mariann Haley—a petite bouncy, short, spiked redhead with level blue eyes that could turn deadly serious one moment and laughing the next—greeted her with a grim expression as she stepped inside the brilliantly lit trauma room, a frigid sixty degrees.

"Dr. Benson, our young lady will be arriving any minute."

Suddenly, the double doors wrenched open as two paramedics rushed her patient through on a wobbly stretcher.

All eyes were on the deathly pale female lying before them covered with a snow-white blanket. Broken glass sparkled in her lush auburn hair, upswept elegantly with pearl pins. With a few deep scratches across her right cheek, her patrician features showed little of the real danger lurking.

A resident whipped back the white blanket to reveal the slender patient wore an off-shoulder elaborate lace and crystal embroidered wedding gown.

A beautiful bride.

Her team consisting of residents, nurses, a respiratory therapist, an x-ray technologist, and an anesthesiologist swarmed her patient. While the residents cut away her gown revealing even more injuries, the team listened to the report.

"Two car accident. Twenty-eight-year-old female. Distended abdomen, possible leg fractures, and internal bleeding."

"Where did the impact take place and where was she?" Summer asked.

"Passenger side on both. Her father has some minor injuries and should be released today. The DUI suspect is down a couple of bays and has a facial laceration."

Summer's mind swirled with questions. Was she breathing on her own? What were her current vital signs, her respiratory rate? All too soon, those questions were answered as her team transferred her patient onto the trauma cart, started lines, and connected hoses to her. Within seconds, monitors beeped and hummed, giving her the most vital information to save her patient's life.

Mariann stepped beside her and frantically worked to find an intravenous access in the patient's forearm. Her first attempt was successful, and the IV fluids funneled through.

"Was she trapped in the vehicle?" Summer yelled, glancing over at the resident.

"Yes, for twenty minutes and ten minutes in traffic."

"Thirty minutes left in our golden hour, team." She pointed to the patient's bruised abdomen along the site of the lap portion of her seat belt and indicated to the resident. "I want to see what's going on in there."

"Blood pressure?" Summer shouted.

A resident shouted out, "80/52."

Summer proceeded to shoot orders at her team.

"Start the blood. We've got to get her stabilized."

In response, Mariann whirled around, grabbed a bag of blood from the coolers, and administered it through the IV.

"Respiratory rate?"

"Twenty-eight," responded the respiratory therapist.

"Get the ventilator going," Summer ordered.

The technician worked quickly, snaking the tube down her patient's throat. Within moments, her chest started to rise and fall as the ventilator breathed for her, seventeen breaths per minute.

Glancing up at the screen, Summer grimly noted the sonogram results. Her patient's abdomen was filling up with blood.

A quick look over at the anesthesiologist and receiving his nod signified he already administered the medications to paralyze, sedate, and take away any of her patient's pain.

Summer took her position at her patient's side. Magically, a razor sharp scalpel appeared on her right gloved palm. She made an incision to the abdomen's upper right side. Seconds later, she became fully aware of the faint thumping against the toe of her right boot, her patient's blood dripping, splattering from the trauma cart. Even with her mask on, the scent of copper, heavy metallic, stung her nose.

As soon as Summer pulled back the skin, opening the abdomen wide, she and the entire team knew how bad it was. Blood was everywhere. Precious moments were wasted but were very necessary to try to rid the abdomen of blood so she could see where to work. When the real damage was revealed, it was shocking.

A deep laceration ripped apart her liver.

Sitting behind the liver sat the inferior vena cava, a major blood vessel carrying blood from the lower half of the body into the heart's right atrium. Angrily, it defied her every attempt to staunch the bleeding.

Summer looked over at the fair-headed anesthesiologist. "You realize you're going to have to be my hero today?"

He gave her a quick nod.

Bottom line, she knew if he couldn't drive the fluids into her patient to keep her stable, her effort would be in vain.

Feverishly, she worked to repair the laceration with large compressing stitches, stopping the worst bleeding, but not completely and not for long. Blood oozed here and there, reminiscent of a water balloon riveted with pin-size leaks. The faster she worked, the more the leaks sprung, the more the bleeding became uncontrollable.

"Her blood isn't clotting," her resident grimly noted.

The anesthesiologist nodded toward the monitors. "I'm pushing every available fluid into her, but she's slipping."

From their observation, the patient was dying on the table right before their very eyes, and there was nothing they could do to prevent it.

She refused to give up and worked frantically to halt the bleeding, glancing up every few seconds to gauge the monitors.

All around her, the sounds of the room seemed to magnify. The steady humming, beeping, and swooshing sounds of the machines, people's voices turned to roaring—insistent, rapid, and deafening. She continued for the next forty-five minutes trying to defy the monstrous odds against her.

Perspiration beaded her forehead. It was sweltering hot in the room with nine people hovering over a two-feet section combined with the overhead lights and bedside machines. She turned her head so Mariann could swath her forehead. Summer looked into her eyes with blurred vision from her tears her protective glasses failed to conceal. Her mask covered her runny nose. She swallowed the large lump suddenly forming in her throat knowing her efforts were futile.

She looked down at her patient's unconscious face and simultaneously felt her heart burst for her. For too many minutes, the young bride laid trapped in a car, slowly hemorrhaging to death on her wedding day. She was sure when her patient left her home to travel to her wedding, the last thing she thought would happen to her would be being involved in a car accident.

She paused to look down at her blood-soaked hands enveloped into her patient's body to her elbows. Her blood loss sent her into irreversible shock. They were keeping her alive by a massive transfusion, but it was a matter of minutes before she died.

Summer watched her trauma team go through the motions, under no illusion how grim the situation had turned. Death hovered in the room, waited eagerly at any and every opportunity to claim his prize.

He would certainly gain a prize today.

With a heavy heart, she began closing her patient, albeit with nerve-wrangled, jerky hands. She was grateful when two residents stepped in beside her and quickly took over.

Walking out into a changing room, Summer quickly stripped off her boots. The yellow smiley faces recently painted on the toes of her boots by her staff were no longer visible, drenched with blood. She looked down at the front of her scrubs. Blood splotches bled through the material and made her nauseated. She disrobed quickly, walked over to the sink, washed up, and scrubbed her skin so vigorously, it glowed an angry red.

She changed into clean scrubs and donned her white coat.

Her coat of armor.

She wore the coat when she had to give patient's families the most dreaded news they'd ever hear. This coat supposedly represented a trained medical professional who could easily tune out a wailing mother's scream upon being told the young daughter she gave birth to, bandaged her bloody knees, held her hand through the first day of kindergarten all the way to college, and beyond had died on her wedding day.

Summer, the anesthesiologist, and Mariann escorted her patient to the Intensive Care Unit to place her in a proper room where her family could visit with her one last time. It was indeed a somber journey while a curtain of silence hung between them.

Advised of the hopeless situation, the ICU nurses gazed sadly upon the young patient as she was wheeled into a room. Summer knew the range of their thoughts, the helplessness they felt because they were her own. This patient was far too young to die, and inside they struggled with the concept of having to stand aside and watch her vivacious life slip through their fingers.

"Let's clean her up a bit so her family can visit her privately and say good-bye," Summer advised.

"She's a beauty," a nurse commented.

"Today was to be her wedding day," Mariann divulged to the nurse, her voice broke with emotion as she gently plucked a few remnants of glass from the patient's hair.

Mariann rarely got emotional; she was a true professional, yet times such as this cracked the thick armor she and many other healthcare professionals built in their persona so they could perform their job efficiently and without mistakes.

"Lisa!" a male's anguished roar and fast heavy footsteps resounded from the lengthy corridor.

Somberly, Summer stepped out into the corridor and watched a very tall, dark-haired young man dressed in a midnight-black tuxedo approach. He came to a stumbling halt before her, his chest heaving.

"Are you Lisa Thomas's fiancé?" she asked, gazing up into his red-rimmed, tearful eyes.

"Yes! Take me to her!" he demanded hoarsely.

Summer looked over her shoulder to see the nurses dim the light in Lisa's room.

"Sir, Lisa's condition is grave. She—"

The man ignored her, shouldered himself around her, and strode quickly into Lisa's room. He skidded to a stop halfway in the room, look startled, shocked, taking in the hum of the ventilator and the incessant beeping of the machines attached to his fiancée's body.

Summer joined him but kept a respectful distance.

The man reached for his fiancée's limp hand. "Lisa, they'll get you all fixed up. We'll get married as soon as you're out of here. I promise you," he whispered against her forehead, placing a lingering kiss there.

The man looked up fleetingly to see the last nurse file from the room. He whipped around and angrily demanded, "Where are you going?" The nurse stopped hesitantly, looked over at Summer, and receiving her subtle nod, quietly left the room.

Summer stuffed her hands deep in her coat pockets and walked over to stand at the foot of Lisa's bed. "Her injuries are grave, sir. We were going to give you some time alone with her," she replied as she glanced at the monitors. Lisa's blood pressure was dropping rapidly, her heart rate slowing.

Misunderstanding, he replied, his hands clenched white knuckled against the bed rails. "I'll have plenty of time alone with her, but first, you have to help her!"

"I'm sorry, there's nothing more I can do. She suffered a lacerated liver, and the bleeding couldn't be controlled."

Confusion was etched on the man's face.

A long shrill buzzing from the monitor permeated the room.

She was dying.

Harsh reality struck him. With disbelief etched across his face, he whirled around. Nurses stood motionless in the doorway. Then his furious eyes landed on Summer.

"You're just going to stand there and let her die?" he screamed incredulously. His eyes became dark with indignation when no one rushed forward. "She's dying, God damn it! You've got to save her!"

"There's nothing more we can do, sir," Summer said quietly again. "I'm so very sorry."

"Sorry? Like hell, you're sorry!" His face reddened with fury, cords strained from his neck, and his hands fisted at his sides. "You're letting my fiancée die and not help her!"

"We couldn't stop her bleeding, and her body went into irreversible shock," Summer explained, once again trying to make him see reason.

Tears slid unheedingly down the man's anguished face. He suddenly turned and bolted out into the corridor and snagged a young startled blonde resident and dragged her into the room.

"Please help my fiancée. They won't help her," he said as he shoved her toward Lisa's bed and gave Summer an accusing stare.

The resident looked over at Summer. "Dr. Benson?"

Summer answered with the barest shake of head.

"I'm sorry, sir," the resident replied and cautiously backed quickly out of the room.

"No!" the man bellowed, his face etched with disbelief. "What's wrong with you people? You're letting her die! I want to speak to whoever is in charge!"

Summer stepped forward and said softly, "I'm in charge."

He pointed at her, jabbing his finger in the air.

"You're a killer and not fit to be in charge of anyone!"

The anesthesiologist stepped forward. "Sir, Dr. Benson's a very talented trauma surgeon, and if your fiancée's life could've been saved, she would've been the one to save her. We'll leave you alone with her for a few more minutes. There was nothing more we could do. I hope you understand."

"I don't understand!" he roared and walked back to her bedside. He leaned over and kissed her cheek tenderly.

As Summer and the anesthesiologist stood back by the door, the man whipped about, looked at her, his features snarling with ill-reputed fury.

"So help me, you'll pay for letting her die!"

His words sent an icy shudder up her spine.

As others came to her defense once again, Summer waved them off. She walked across the room and came to stand at the bedside with him. "I'm very sorry."

"Get out of my face, bitch!" he growled, grabbing her shoulders, shoving her violently back against the bedside tray stand.

Summer, the tray, and its contents toppled over with the water jug splashing, a glass exploding, shattering across the floor. She landed hard on her back in a pool of water and glass shards, momentarily stunned.

"Call Security!" the anesthesiologist shouted and tore across the room and went down on his knees to help Summer sit up. Crimson snaked through the arm of her coat and down her fingertips.

The anesthesiologist examined her hands and looked at Summer with relief. "You've got a nasty gash on your forearm, but your hands are okay."

He ushered her quickly to her feet and into the corridor flooded with nurses, doctors, and residents. Three security officers rushed toward them.

Summer stepped forward, blocked the entrance to the room, ignoring the exasperated officers.

She believed he deserved some privacy. She looked over her shoulder to see him slide to his knees, his anguished cries echoed around them. She dropped her head sadly, felt his pain.

After fifteen minutes, the man walked to the doorway and looked directly at her, gave her a gesture with his hand as if pointing a gun at her head and pulling the trigger.

A large man with a military stance bearing walked over to her. "I'm Officer Havilan, chief of Hospital Security. They tell me he assaulted you." His eyes flickered to her coat sleeve drenched with blood. "Would you like to press charges?"

"He's grieving," she defended, hoping he'd drop the subject.

"They said he was violent," Officer Havilan countered.

"He just lost his bride. Imagine how you'd feel. I won't press charges," she said adamantly.

"Dr. Benson, I'd take this situation a bit more seriously if I were you," he warned and gave her a card with his contact information. "Call me when you leave today, and I'll escort you personally to your car, whatever you need."

"It'll be just fine, but thank you anyways." Summer stuffed his card deep down into her overflowing coat pocket of papers, pens, a pager, and her stethoscope.

"Be careful," the security guard warned then spun on his heel and left.

Everyone departed soon after.

Summer walked back to the bedside and looked down at her patient, her face so serene. All the while, a huge lump grew in her throat, threatening to choke her as she placed her fingertip along her patient's neck feeling for a pulse.

No pulse.

To stand aside and watch her patient take a turn for the worse went against everything she believed in. Yet, when surmounting circumstances such as this occurred, it was simply out of her control and in a much higher power's hands. She wished she could've made the young man understand. She lived in her own hell, faced her demons every single night when she closed her eyes to sleep. Inevitably, the patient's faces who lost their lives on her watch haunted her, made her question her split second decisions, question her worth as a doctor.

Her young patient, Lisa Marie Thomas, had hopes and dreams earlier in the day. Now, she would never marry and say her vows, the one milestone every woman dreamt of, anticipated in her lifetime.

She lifted the white blanket and covered her face.

Entering through the nearest stairwell, Summer slumped down on the third step. Emotionally and physically exhausted, she pressed her face into her hands and sobbed.

Suddenly, the door burst open and just over her shoulder, large and looming, stood Dr. O'Malley.

Quickly, she wiped her tears against her sleeve.

"I just heard," he simply said, his eyes narrowing on her.

She stared down at her feet while her body trembled.

He said nothing as he quietly walked down the steps and reached for her, snatched her off the steps, and held her in his arms for a long moment.

His hug was comforting and endearing.

"You should've let me take the call, Summer. You didn't have enough rest in you to handle this situation."

Her mind tried to unravel his words. She untangled herself from his arms and looked up at him. Shock yielded quickly to fury. "I beg your pardon?"

"I just wish you'd ask for help when you need it," he said exasperated.

She took a step back from him, her face burned with indignation. "I have you know I have my patient's welfare first and foremost on my mind. I would have never taken the call if I believed even for a second that I was too tired to work the case. I'm always one hundred percent committed whenever I walk through those trauma doors. How dare you question my actions! I was in there, you weren't. She was trapped in her car for twenty minutes and another ten minutes in traffic. She slowly bled to death before I even touched her, a grade four liver injury. The worst possible scenario as you very well know, but that didn't deter my team from trying to save her life when the odds were already stacked against us."

"You can't admit it when you're wrong, can you?" he said, slicing his fingers through his hair in agitation.

"I wasn't wrong in my actions. I'm very methodical and did everything I could to save her, and you can read it on the record if you'd like. Or perhaps, it just might occur to you, Dr. O'Malley, that some of us are just as talented as you. The difference is, we don't let our egos get in the way."

She stomped up the steps. Over her shoulder, she flung the biting words, "Shall we compare our patient's mortality rate? I think it's safe to say my patients far outnumber yours walking this earth today." She wrenched open the door and stormed out, leaving him standing there.

"Now that hurt." He laughed sharply, shaking his head as he stared at the door.

She was feisty as hell.

Three hours later, she arrived back at the doctor's lounge after rounds in ICU. She collapsed onto the bench in front of her locker.

The worst day of her life.

She cradled her head in her trembling hands, closed her eyes, took a deep breath, and tried to relax for a moment.

The death of her patient broke her heart.

She was only human after all.

It was all she could think of while doing her rounds. She could barely concentrate. She dismissed the residents who dogged her every step because she couldn't answer their questions, her mind became too fogged, too distracted, too devastated.

Dr. O'Malley insinuated her actions were illegitimate against her patient, yet she knew better. If she had to do it all over again, she'd do the same, but for him to insinuate…

She made enemies by the hour today. She lost the confidence of her favorite colleague. Not to mention, her patient's fiancé believed her fully responsible for his loved one's death.

In the past, she had threats levied against her and even on occasion been stalked by outraged, disgruntled, and grieving family members. She, like many other doctors, experienced threatening or harassing behavior including telephone calls, unwanted approaches. It was part of the job. You took those threats in stride and prayed they'd never act upon them. The thought held true with her patient's fiancé.

In the foreground, she overheard doctors chatting, laughing, opening, closing their lockers, and then it turned quiet and peaceful. She opened her locker, peeled off her white coat, and shrugged on her sweater. As she pulled her hair back into a ponytail, she heard a metal click behind her head.

She froze.

Her hand hovered above head, too terrified to move.

Suddenly, she was wrenched around and her back slammed painfully up against her locker. She looked up at a familiar face.

Her patient's fiancé.

He clamped his hand over her mouth and stifled her scream as he pressed the cold hard steel of his handgun painfully against her forehead.

She was going to die today.

2

Summer wondered why in God's name she didn't learn those self-defense techniques her brother so desperately wanted to teach her.

A question she'd have to answer another day if she lived long enough to tell it.

Right now, she looked into fathomless eyes staring back at her with such hatred; sheer black fright swept through her. She wanted to look away but made herself remember every detail about him to identify him to the police.

His stature, the breadth of him, was larger than life. His hair was dark, glistening with gel, short and spiked on the top. His eyes were cold and black as midnight. His features reminded her of an Indian with proud high cheekbones, broad nose, and forehead with a squared jaw. His lips were hard-pressed with rage. Had she seen him outside this situation, she would've thought him a very attractive man.

Dressed in a dark business suit, he could've easily been mistaken for a doctor or another healthcare professional as he walked the hospital corridors. However, this man had no good intentions. The look in his eyes was vicious and ruthless, and he meant business.

He rested his warm cheek against hers.

"I want to kill you right now. I even brought along a silencer," he ground the words out between his teeth, still applying pressure against her forehead with the barrel of his gun.

Summer stayed motionless, but her heart thundered, roared in her ears like a heartbeat while his voice remained level and calm. It almost made her believe he'd done this before. The way he confidently held the gun in his hand, how he stealthily stole in the doctor's lounge without a soul noticing, like a ghost.

"Then again if I kill you right now, you wouldn't have suffered properly," he remarked, tempering his fury with amusement.

He released the gun from her forehead, uncocked it, and warned her, "Let this be a lesson. I can appear from nowhere, and you'll never see me coming. Just know your days are numbered, killer. When *you* die, I'll be the one standing over you just watching, doing nothing to help you. Now, turn back around and face your locker."

Summer obeyed and listened for his footsteps to fade away, listened for the sound of the door opening and closing while her heart thundered in her heart and in her ears.

He disappeared in thin air.

She dropped to the bench. Her legs gave out from under her.

Seconds later, the door opened and shut again; Summer's eyes snapped wide open. She looked over her shoulder and held her breath wondering if the man decided to return and fulfill his deadly promise.

She sighed with relief seeing Dr. Phillip Chamberlain, a vascular surgeon in his midfifties. He always had a smile on his face, but right now, as he came to stand before her, he frowned down at her with concern.

"Summer girl, you look like you've just seen a ghost. Are you okay?"

She swallowed hard and bit back tears as she stood on wobbly legs. "Long day," she replied hoarsely.

"Yeah, I know. I heard about your young patient and I'm sorry. That's dreadful," he said as he walked just around the corner and opened his locker. "These people drive like a bat out of hell when they leave their homes and bars not giving a care what's in their path. When is society going to…"

Summer walked numbly out of the lounge, not hearing him finish his tirade against foolish, reckless drivers. She had other things on her mind like as soon as she got home pouring herself a good stiff drink. Then again, she'd have to wipe the dust off the bottle first.

She tossed her coat over her arm and skirted quickly down the corridor praying she wouldn't run into her patient's fiancé.

The glass doors to the parking garage slid open and the sounds of distant car doors opening, shutting, the shuffling of footsteps and voices made her body flinch with dread. Perhaps she was too hasty in declining the security officer's offer to escort her to her car. Before, she never paid attention to anyone around her or the cars pulling in or out in the garage while she fished around the bottom of her purse for her car keys.

Now, being cautious took on a whole new meaning.

Not a moment too soon, she spotted her freedom.

Her car.

Parked just around the bend and in a dark corner, she berated herself. She'd never take such chances again! Hurriedly, she walked to it, counting every step along the way, eating up the pavement as fast as she could. Her hands shook so violently she dropped her car remote twice on the concrete before she could push the unlock button. Quickly, she slid into the leather seat and roared the powerful engine to life. She squealed her tires, leaving the parking garage, allowing her car to devour the distance quickly taking her away from the hospital toward a small sanctuary she called home just ten minutes away.

Large rain droplets splattered against her windshield then another and another. She turned her windshield wipers on. The wind picked up, ruffling the leaves of the tall palms lining the road.

Not a moment into the journey, her heart resonated, threatening to explode from her chest. Her breathing stifled in short gasps. Her eyes clouded with tears and slipped heedlessly down her cheeks.

She'd never get used to the idea of losing a patient. After her sobs subsided, she punched the button to turn on her car phone.

"Call Kyle."

The phone rang until the voice mail came on, her brother's comforting voice, "This is the Bensons. We're not home right now, but leave us a message, and we'll call you back."

She sighed, exhaling a shaky breath, thoroughly disappointed to hear the answering machine turn on.

Suddenly, she heard a child giggle in the message's foreground.

Her nephew, Sam.

She smiled.

She hit the disconnect button, not leaving a message; besides, what would she say? Would she reveal to her brother a crazed lunatic held a gun to her head and threatened to kill her today?

She would not.

If she divulged, he'd send the Navy SEALs after her.

Literally.

Times such as these, she dearly missed her parents having lost them in a tragic accident several years ago. As a result, she wished her brother and his family lived closer than the Navy SEALs Coronado training base in San Diego, California. She wished she could drop by and steal one of his comforting hugs without him having to know the real reason and worrying about her.

The hospital consumed her life, and therefore, she wasn't alone much to contemplate what her brother insisted as of late she missed.

A family.

Now, his wife, Sibella, was expecting their third child; and as much as she'd like to weep on her brother's shoulder about today's events, she refused to worry him. When her brother laughingly told her he meant to keep his ravishing wife barefoot and pregnant, he meant it in every sense of the word. They met, fell madly in love, and married within two weeks.

They shared a very unique love story. She was a relief worker in Afghanistan and was taken hostage along with a host of other workers. The conditions were deplorable and many became sick, including Sibella, a diabetic. Kyle's SEAL team was called in to rescue them.

Kyle rescued Sibella and then decided to keep her.

Her brother told her living on the edge all his life taught him one important thing. When you find your soul mate, grab him, hang on for dear life, and don't let go.

He was right. He and Sibella was a perfect match.

Her thoughts inevitably veered back to her patient and her fiancé. Did she feel that way about her future husband, set to spend the rest of her life with him?

If that was the case, how must her fiancé feel having fate intervene, rip their lives asunder? The resentment he must feel right now at the situation, dear God, at her. The same question kept running through her mind as it did all day. Did he really mean to harm her? Surely to God not! But then again, he seemed to believe with all his heart and soul she allowed his fiancée to die. As in her days of being a young, fresh-faced resident, she found herself questioning her actions, wondering what she could have done differently, wondering what Dr. O'Malley would have done differently.

They say in medical school when they are preparing you for the outside world that there are certain patients you never forget. Undoubtedly, the patient she lost today captured a piece of her heart, not only because the extraordinary events surrounding her, but because her patient resembled what could've happened to her today in the doctor's lounge, her dreams shattered in a blink of an eye or, in her case, with a bullet.

Perhaps she should've played it safe and became a cosmetic surgeon or delivered babies. Then again, she knew where she thrived, right in the center of a chaotic crisis, saving lives, thinking fast on her feet, using her critical thinking skills. Nothing gave her more satisfaction than to snatch her patient away from death's door and give them another chance at life. Many of her past patients returned and thanked her personally, and that's when she reaped the rewards, seeing them in good health and having fulfilled her doctor's creed.

Days like this today, however, offset the joy. Thankfully, she never experienced many of them. Her heart couldn't take it.

The sun set rapidly since she left work.

As she turned down her long driveway lined with pine trees and hidden shadows, she suddenly hated the seclusion, which was what she loved most about her home. Her imagination was in overdrive as her hands, white knuckled, clenched the steering wheel and her eyes darted from tree to tree wondering at any given moment if her patient's fiancé would spring forth and point a gun at her head for the second time in one day.

She maneuvered her car into the dark garage and paranoia set in as she wondered if someone hid inside. She took a deep breath, pushed aside the scenarios, quickly got out of the car, and purposely walked over to the workbench and picked up her hammer for protection.

Quickly, she strode through her white tiled corridor leading from the garage into a brightly lit kitchen wrapped in white cabinetry and stainless steel appliances and dropped her messenger bag on a nearby chair. She made her way to her bedroom dominated by dark furnishings and glanced over at her sleigh bed covered with a fluffy white comforter. She sighed. She couldn't wait to slide between the sheets, but first she needed a shower. She walked into her master bath, turned on the shower, and undressed. Gently, she peeled off the bandage around her forearm to assess the damage. The two-inch gash resembled a red angry welt.

She stared at her reflection through the mirror. She gasped and peered closer.

The center of her forehead bared a perfectly round bruise from the barrel of the handgun.

She went to step inside the shower when she hesitated and looked for her hammer. She'd left it on the chair in the kitchen. She wrapped a towel around her, walked into the kitchen, and retrieved the hammer. That's when she saw the back door ajar.

A chill ran up her spine.

She turned the light on, stole a peek into the garage, and saw nothing out of the ordinary. She did the same as she walked through the house and saw nothing. Perhaps she forgot to shut and lock the door. It put such a fear into her she forfeited the idea of a shower. Instead, she chose to wash from the basin, too afraid she might not hear an intruder.

A long night ahead of her, she decided to indulge in that stiff drink after all.

Almost midnight, Summer lay on her bed staring up at the ceiling just as she'd done the past three hours, unable to sleep watching dark shadows filter across her bedroom walls. Her nightlight was on. She refused to turn on her ceiling fan for fear she couldn't hear any alarming sounds. Tonight of all nights, the wind rustled her chimes on her front porch and made the branches from her hydrangea bushes tap against her bedroom window. It rattled her nerves to no end.

A quick glance at her clock announced midnight. Next to it, her eyes flickered over to a brushed silver picture frame. She reached over and picked it up, a photograph of her brother and his SEAL team. Taken five years ago, the SEALs were dressed in flat dessert khakis, assault boots, hats, and dark sunglasses. They held their weapons close to their bodies as they sat upon a hilltop in northern Afghanistan. They were an extraordinary group of men who strapped one hundred pounds of gear on their backs daily and acclimated to travel in any type of weather conditions, whether searing desert heat or temperatures hovering below zero. Since their faces were fuzzy, her brother identified them by name and told her of their heroics. She felt like she knew them even though she had never met them. One in particular she desired to meet was Storm to thank him for saving her brother's life.

Her phone rang.

She reached over and picked up her phone from the nightstand.

"Hello," she said with a smile in her voice, anticipating it was Kyle checking on her. Many times, his free time from home and work came around midnight, and they would enjoy a peaceful conversation. She smiled down at the photograph and waited for him to speak.

No reply.

The color drained from her face.

"Hello?" She tried to listen for any background noise.

Complete silence.

Was it *him?* Was this one of the many ways he'd terrorize her? She hung up the phone and glanced down at her hammer leaning against her bedside.

Her stomach suddenly lurched, rolled, and heaved. She tossed the photograph aside, jumped out of bed, and barely made it to the bathroom where her body jerked forcibly as her stomach heaved. The stress of the day had finally taken its toll.

She forgot to eat.

There were no more phone calls.

When she returned to bed, she fell into a deep exhaustive sleep.

3

The week went by without incident.

To her relief, she received no additional threats. No one stalked her and no mysterious phone calls.

However, what occurred during the week was Lisa Thomas's funeral and the outpouring of sympathy from the community.

Front-page news.

Photos appeared of her coffin being carried out of a Catholic church and down sprawling steps by six black-suit-clad men. The next photos were taken at the cemetery surrounded by mourners. One particular mourner, Lisa Thomas's fiancé, Mark Malone wore dark sunglasses and a black suit, his face ravaged by grief. Now, she knew the name of the man who vowed to kill her.

This particular morning, Summer walked down her driveway to pick up her newspaper and was met by her elderly neighbor all dolled up in her black silk robe, matching silk slippers, and her salt-and-pepper hair wrapped tight in curlers. Vivid red lips clutched a long cigarette, its tip overgrown with ash threatening to break off while she unraveled her newspaper with slim, knobby fingers bearing overly long red fingernails and smelling heavily of the mixture of floral perfume and cigarette smoke. Worse, the widow still weaved from obviously imbibing in too many spirits from the night before.

Summer bent to retrieve her newspaper from her driveway and had a ready smile on her face for her neighbor when she turned around to face her and had to stifle a laugh. Her neighbor's fake eyelashes were missing on her right eye. "Good morning, Mrs. Parker."

"Good morning, Summer dear. Your cousin came to see you yesterday afternoon. I told him you normally don't get home until late, and you were off today. You've undoubtedly spoken to him already, Sugar?"

Summer stiffened, her heart dropped to her feet.

"Yes, thank you. Have a nice day, Mrs. Parker," she told her and jogged back up her driveway. The problem was she had no cousins. So now, he knew where she lived, so much for having a blocked address and phone number. Maybe she hadn't imagined her back door ajar after all.

She took a deep, shaky breath, cast her newspaper aside, and spent several hours keeping busy trying to forget her grim situation.

When that didn't work, she relieved the surgeon on call during early evening, too terrified to be home alone after dark.

After finishing rounds in ICU, Summer wandered into the hospital coffee shop.

"Coffee, decaffeinated please," Summer ordered from the young, dark-haired girl, wearing a black French cap. The first lesson a student of surgery learned was to avoid caffeine drinks before surgery; it caused your hands to tremble. She turned around and glanced at the newspaper stand in the corner.

The bold words stretched across the *Daily Herald*'s headline taunted her: *DUI Suspect Missing.*

Distractedly, she paid for her coffee and newspaper. All the while, her eyes remained glued to the article as she walked over to a sitting area, and sat down at a secluded corner table.

Jacksonville police say suspect Greg Allen was reported missing by his family just one day after posting bail. Currently, he is facing vehicular manslaughter charges after driving under the influence and killing Lisa Thomas.

Her heart pounded fiercely against her chest. The news signaled a foreboding. She firmly believed Malone was responsible. He was coming after those he believed responsible for Lisa Thomas's death. She was next.

Her pager went off.

When people sat down for their dinner was when Summer's night began.

She walked briskly through the trauma center all the while trying to shake her fear, thankful for the distraction. She arrived at the last bay where a young black man laid trembling and bleeding in his abdomen area.

Mariann greeted her, handing her the patient's chart.

"This young guy needs a miracle. He'll be in the trauma room in less than two minutes."

Summer's eyes quickly scanned the chart.

Twenty-six-year-old male, victim of a drive-by shooting, shot in abdomen by an AK-47. She frowned. People shot anywhere in the body by an AK47 spelled bad news for the simple reason when the bullet entered the body, it fragmented and most often times couldn't be removed because of the risks involved. Not to mention the obvious, it brought on a slew of destruction to the internal organs. She was in for a long night.

As she turned to leave and go scrub, the young man reared up, winced in pain, and asked, "Am I going to surgery? I've never had surgery."

She walked over to his side having to first side step a pancake-sized puddle of blood. She gently pushed him back into a lying position as the technicians crowded around him cutting his clothes off his slim body. "What's your name?" she asked.

"Jacob Howard," he said weakly.

Amid the shouting and chaos around them, she barely heard him.

"Jacob, just relax. Yes, you're going to surgery. We'll take good care of you," she coaxed and then once again she turned to leave.

Yet, young Jacob was persistent and once again asked, "Excuse me, nurse, where's the guy who's doing my surgery? I'd feel better if I met him," he trailed off sluggishly, laid his head back down on the pillow with a thud, his eyes drifted closed.

The medications started to work.

She never bothered to correct her patient about her status; it was needless. All that mattered was saving his life.

He tried but couldn't lift his head off the pillow, so he reached out his hand to her.

She grasped it.

"Where is he?" he persisted sleepily.

Some of the residents chuckled under their breaths.

She leaned back over him. "It's me," she sighed. "I'm doing your surgery."

His frightened bloodshot eyes snapped open suddenly. "You look younger than me, and you're a woman. Oh god, I'm going to die," he groaned and stared up dismally at the gleaming ceiling.

She paused and looked down into his frightened eyes. "I'll do whatever I can to help you," she promised.

There were times when she believed the outcome would be good, yet the patient died beneath her hands and vice versa. Everyone knew that once you encountered a life-threatening situation, the outcome was out of your hands the moment surgery began. Having the skills to keep the patient mechanically alive was all and well, but if the patient didn't have the faith he could make it and gave up, it normally sealed the deal.

Jacob Howard never responded. Instead, he fell into a drug-induced sleep not having any faith in her ability. She would prove him wrong. She had all intentions of saving his life.

She was scrubbed and waiting for him as soon as they wheeled him into the room under a blaze of stark lighting, high-tech gadgetry, and trays of stainless steel instruments.

As it was in Lisa Thomas's surgery, time was of the essence.

She took her scalpel and made an incision just below his sternum to just above his pubic bone.

He bled profusely, gushed like a neglected water hose left turned on. The team made a very determined effort and stemmed the blood flow. Five exhausting hours later, Jacob lost three feet of his colon and his right kidney to a bullet. She removed many bullet fragments, however not all because some were lodged in dangerous places where the risk was too great to remove them.

She stepped away from the table drained. Her right foot tingled, threatening to go to sleep. Her throat was dry, parched, and hoarse from shouting orders to her team.

She craved a bed.

Mariann followed her to clean up.

"Tell me what you think, doc. Will he make it?"

"I don't know. I certainly hope so," Summer said, stepping out of her boots and removing her mask.

"I bet he will. He's only in his midtwenties after all."

"Yes, but I wish he was more like sixteen because kids that age are pretty indestructible." Summer sighed.

"You saved his life tonight. He'll pull through this," Mariann reassured, giving her a wink as she removed her gloves and mask.

"He's not entirely out of the woods yet. I'm still concerned with his blood loss, organ death, and infection. God help him if he gets pneumonia. Plus, this is just one of many surgeries he'll need."

"No worries, he'll pull through just fine. Hey, I heard the documentary will be shown at the hospital gala next week and then shortly after on television. It's going to be strange seeing you on TV."

"You forget. You're standing right beside me 90 percent of the time, so you'll not just see me, but yourself as well."

Mariann gave her a knowing smile. "Yeah. But, girlfriend, you were the star. Those camera people gushed over every word you uttered. They snapped picture after picture of you."

Summer shook her head in response, tugging off her scrubs.

"You hate the attention, don't you?" Mariann asked as she got them clean pairs of scrubs from the closet.

"With a passion," Summer admitted with a cringe as she looked back over at Mariann slyly. "I think you ended up getting a date or two out of one of those cameramen, didn't you?"

"I did," she sighed. "It was a nice candlelight dinner, but nothing more as usual. It wouldn't have gone any further."

They both stepped in shower stalls and took a quick shower.

As soon as Summer got out, she looked over at Mariann as she toweled dry. "Just curious, why do you say it wouldn't have gone any further?"

Mariann hesitated as she pulled on her scrubs. "Well, because I'm in love with someone who doesn't know I exist," she confessed barely above a whisper.

Summer glanced at her, saw the forlorn look on her face, and couldn't help sympathize.

"Mariann, you're a strong, confident young woman. The man you love needs to know you exist. I suggest you go after him, seek him out."

Mariann gave her an impish smile. "You're much worse off than me. How long has it been since you've had a date?"

"Awhile," Summer replied, grimacing as she pulled on her scrub bottoms. "Let's see. It was about a year ago and with an egotistical pharmaceutical rep who couldn't seem to stop touching his hair."

Mariann went into a fit of giggles.

Summer laughed with her. Her love life was too comical and ridiculous to get upset over especially since it was nonexistent.

Sadly enough, her career consumed her every waking moment with little time for anything else. Her highlight when sharing call rotation with Mariann was hearing about her latest dating experiences and those normally had her bowled over in laughter.

Summer leaned against the locker and watched Mariann towel dry her hair. "About the documentary, Mariann, the public needs educated on what we have to offer them and our need for funding to help the community."

Mariann gave her a knowing smile through the mirror.

"Save your political response and give it to someone who wasn't there. I witnessed how extraordinary you were saving lives while the cameras rolled."

"I'm hoping it will bring in some wealthy donors for us," Summer muttered. "We'll need all the funding we can get to turn this hospital into a Level I trauma center."

"Personally, I think it made our ego-minded docs around here pretty jealous these past months watching the cameras fawn all over you. By the way, please tell me you finally applied for the chief of trauma position?"

Summer nodded. "I did, just yesterday morning."

Mariann sat down next to her and slipped her sandals on.

"I can only imagine this documentary will work wonders for your chances to snag the position."

"I sincerely doubt I'll get a serious consideration considering I'm up against Dr. O'Malley and a few other docs who've been here much longer than me."

Mariann stood and removed her purse from the locker. A smile lit her lips teasingly. "I'd love to see the expression on Dr. O'Malley's face when he hears you've applied. Especially since he believes the job is already his because of his family's money and connections."

Summer stood, snapped her pager on her waistband, and laid her stethoscope around her neck. "Dr. O'Malley may assume correctly. I realize my age may once again be a deterrent factor."

Together they walked out into the corridor. Mariann shook her head, disagreeing.

"The outgoing chief endorsed you. What more could one ask for? I also think it's the coolest thing ever, a lady surgeon in this male-dominated field who kicks ass, takes names, and getting much deserved recognition through this documentary. I'd love nothing more than for you to become the chief."

"It doesn't really matter either way to me. I'd love to have the position because I have ideas to promote the hospital and give better patient care. Nevertheless, if I don't, I'll still be here."

"You're so dedicated," Mariann said. "Are you going home now? You look exhausted."

Summer paused, looked at her watch. Ten-thirty. Normally, she'd be in bed already.

Fleetingly, she thought how nice it would be to have a husband to come home to. Yes, a guy would come in very handy about right now, in more ways than just for protection.

Mariann looked at her curiously. "Is everything okay?

"Perfectly fine," she lied. "I think I'll wait until Jacob's settled in ICU."

"Are you worried about that bride's fiancé? I don't like how he threatened you. I understand he was grieving, yet he looked at you like he wanted to kill you," she said with a shudder.

"Thanks for reminding me. He was upset, rightfully so. I just hope he forgets about me."

Mariann gave her a doubtful look.

"You didn't do anything wrong, Summer. I guess when you're distraught you can't think straight, but to levy threats against a person is totally different. I think you should file a police report."

"It'll work itself out," she muttered, mostly to herself. God, she hoped so. She wouldn't dare confess to Mariann that the man actually held a gun to her head.

They said their good-byes, and shortly afterward, Summer checked on Jacob in ICU. Swathed in bandages, he slept peacefully in his bed despite the steady hum of medical equipment surrounding his bed monitoring and controlling nearly every aspect of his existence. She prescribed a block to paralyze him and sedation to control his pain. His body didn't need further thrashing; it needed plenty of rest and time to heal. She ordered fluids to keep him hydrated, yet they bloated him. When he arrived at the trauma center, he weighed around 160 pounds on his five-foot-ten-inch frame. Now, he tipped the scale at around two hundred and ten pounds. She frowned as she walked out of his room, troubled by his elevated heart rate.

She returned to her small call room, the size of a broom closet accommodating a twin bed, which she gazed at longingly hoping to take full advantage. She sat down at the small desk and checked patient labs and entered orders.

An hour and thirty minutes later…

"Dr. Summer Benson. Dr. Summer Benson," the hospital's overhead announcement system droned.

She jerked awake and glanced at the small alarm clock on the nightstand.

Midnight.

Hearing her name announced on the hospital overhead speaker system made her wary. In today's world of cell phones and pagers, it usually meant all hell had broken loose some place.

Her first thought was of Jacob.

She called the hospital operator who placed her on hold.

Hospital security came on the line.

"Dr. Benson, this is Officer Havilan. Do you drive a white Mercedes Benz?"

"Yes, I do," she replied cautiously, wondering if he was set to tell her it was vandalized, stolen.

"There's a problem with your vehicle," he informed her.

"Problem?" she stammered in bewilderment.

The officer evaded her question. "Can you meet me in the hospital lobby right now?"

She paused.

"I'd like to escort you to your car if you don't mind."

She swallowed with difficulty and found her voice. Why would he insist escorting her to her car? Suddenly, she felt terribly uneasy.

"Yes, of course."

She grabbed her messenger bag and her coat since she was finished with call. Her left cheek stung as she reached up and felt the indention of computer keys against it.

As she approached the lobby, she saw Officer Havilan pacing in front of the oval-shaped water fountain.

In silence, they walked down a long winding corridor leading to the deserted parking garage. As she approached her car, parked at the very end, she heard hissing, crackling sounds. To her disbelief, spirals of white steam floated from the hood of her car toward the roof.

Why in God's name was her hood steaming? Her stomach did a somersault as she looked up at Officer Havilan's grim face.

"Acid," he reported. "Someone poured acid on the hood of your car and wrote you a message."

She took a closer look.

The word *KILLER* was scrawled across her hood.

She gasped and was thankful there were no bystanders.

"Do you know who's responsible for this, Dr. Benson?"

Of course, she knew. Beyond a shadow of doubt, Mark Malone was responsible. He hadn't forgotten her as she'd hoped and now resumed his hell-bent mission on terrorizing her.

How could she forget? Today was Saturday. One week ago Lisa Thomas died. Shock, anger, and hopelessness filled her.

"No, I don't know who did this," she lied distractedly.

The officer's eyes narrowed on her.

She was a terrible liar and was sure he saw right through her.

"Can I lend you protection, Dr. Benson, while here at the hospital?"

Her pager went off.

Another trauma patient.

"No, sir, but thank you anyways." She rushed out, pointed back toward the hospital.

She jogged back through the trauma center doors with tears stinging her eyes.

In trauma bay two, her next patient awaited her. A young girl with enormous brown eyes, waist-length chocolate silky hair approximately ten years old battled for her life because her deranged, drug-induced mother stabbed her in the chest.

4

Around seven o'clock in the morning, she arrived home and never bothered to check every door and window. Exhausted, she made her way to her bathroom, turned on the shower, stripped off her clothes, and stepped inside the glass shower stall. Her whole day was engulfed in weariness and despair.

Under the constant band of warm water, her world came crashing down around her. Icy fear twisted around her heart and threatened to choke her. She leaned against the shower wall and sobbed so hard she could barely breathe.

When the water began to run cold, she stepped reluctantly from the shower and toweled dry.

If her life ended today, her biggest regret would be not hearing her brother's voice one last time and telling him how much she loved him.

She picked up her cell phone and dialed.

On the fifth ring, he answered.

"Hey, Sunshine, I'm glad you called," he said, out of breath.

"Kyle," she sighed. It was his voice, solid and steadfast, that comforted her when she was happy or sad. It reminded her of the days she'd sit in the stairwell at Johns Hopkins and endlessly drone about her worries over her studies while he listened so intently, so very patient with her. Over time and distance, he encouraged her, cheered her, gave her confidence, and in her darkest hours let her sob on his shoulder. He picked her up and dusted her off, gave her the strength to keep her chin up, no matter what obstacles faced her.

"I'm sorry I didn't call you back earlier in the week. It's been hectic around here, but you were on my mind."

"There's no need to explain. So what are you doing?" she asked, trying to swallow the lump in her throat.

"Sam and I are watching cartoons and eating cereal. Are you at work?"

"No, I just got home from the hospital, a busy night," she said, clenching her hand around her phone.

"You okay?"

She paused, swallowed hard.

His voice brought forth a rush of emotion. Inside her, all her nerve unraveled. She couldn't hide anything from him. He knew the very secrets of her soul.

"Sunshine, talk to me."

She clamped her hand over her mouth to quiet her sobs.

"What's wrong?"

Her brother's normal, cool, collected voice became concerned with a hint of franticness.

"I'm fine, Kyle, just a rough week at work. I wanted to hear your voice."

"What happened at work?" he asked persistently.

"I…I lost a patient," she cried softly into the phone and clenched the towel tighter around her.

"I'm sorry," he sighed. "Who was the patient?"

"A young bride on her way to get married."

He sighed again. "You tried to save her. You did everything you could to help her," he consoled.

"Yes, I did, but…" She trailed off with a ragged sigh.

"But what?"

"Nothing," she cried with a shaky sigh.

"Why don't you take a vacation and come see us? Just jump on a plane and come to California. Do you ever think you're going through burnout? After all, it's been almost five years without any break whatsoever."

"No," she replied. "This isn't a good time." Especially since a lunatic was hell-bent on terrorizing her, threatening to end her life at any given second. He could follow her there and terrorize her brother's family. She'd never take such a chance. Instead, she'd face the problem alone and get it resolved.

"You need to find a husband," he said, trying to take her mind off her worries. "I don't like you being alone. You need to settle down and have babies. You're hitting the thirty mark soon."

"Twenty-nine, I beg your pardon. The only man I'm interested in meeting is the man who saved your life."

"Storm. Yeah, I need to introduce the two of you, but right now, he's got some stuff going on I'm afraid. How about someone else in the interim, someone to take your mind off work?"

"No, you're not. I won't settle for just anyone," she interrupted him with a laugh.

"I'm not so sure he'd be a good influence on you. He'd eat you up as a snack."

"Well, he's the only guy I want to meet, no substitutes. He looks handsome in his fatigues even though I haven't seen a good picture of him without his sunglasses or his helmet."

Kyle laughed under his breath.

"What's funny?"

"You don't need a picture."

"So what exactly does Storm look like?"

Long pause.

"Well, you've got to remember he's been through a few wars. It does a pretty number on your body after a while. His body isn't what it used to be with his leg injury and the loss of his right eye."

"Kyle?" she interjected.

"I've not shown you a recent picture because he's pretty beaten up. You can imagine being a SEAL for fifteen years," Kyle explained.

"Okay, let's start with the basics. How tall is he?"

"Height shouldn't be a factor. This man is worth his grain of salt even though he's been gaining a bit of weight and losing his hair. He's solid and trustworthy."

"Oh my god," she muttered. "How tall is he?"

"A solid five foot, four inches."

"That's my height, Kyle!"

Kyle continued, "He hated his red hair so it doesn't bother him that he's losing it. However, now he worries what affect it'll have on the ladies. He's dying to meet you. I'll arrange a meeting soon since it's the least I can do. I've lost you to him a few times in some card games back in the day," he admitted ruefully.

"Seriously?" she asked, appalled. Her fantasies of the man who singlehandedly faced down three terrorists carrying bombs and threatening to blow up a shipload of people didn't fit the description her brother just laid before her and not the guy awarded the Navy Cross for his bravery and going beyond the call of duty. She had nothing against shorter men, but in her mind, all these years, she envisioned a courageous man larger than life, indestructible.

Red hair? That brought to mind childhood memories of a young bully she experienced in first grade. To this day, she could picture his pale chalky skin, freckles bleeding over every inch of his skin. Mentally, she shuddered and breathed out a shaky laugh.

"Nice to hear you laugh," he said softly.

His comment brought to mind the real reason for calling. Her brother always had a quirky way of making her laugh when she least expected it, making her forget her problems. His voice calmed her from the vast miles between them, and she loved him dearly for it.

"You always make me laugh, which is why I love you so much," her voice broke again.

"Want to tell me what's really going on?" he prodded. "Is someone harassing you? I'll kick their ass."

"It'll be just fine," she assured him.

"Sunshine, tell me right now what's going on," he ordered.

She clamped her hand tightly over her mouth because his nickname for her brought forth a rush of tears remembering a time when things weren't so complicated before her life got so busy and hectic.

"Tell you what. I'll get on a plane tonight and tear down your goddamn door. Now, tell me what's going on!" he bellowed.

"My patient who died, her fiancé is very angry with me," she rushed out. "He blames me for her death, for not helping her when he thought I should, but she hemorrhaged and was too far gone for me to save her. I couldn't seem to make him understand."

"Did he threaten you?"

"He's devastated as you can imagine," she defended in a sob.

"He threatened you? That son of a bitch, I'm coming!"

"Kyle, it'll be okay, and no, you're not coming here. I've been threatened before…," she trailed off. But then, she'd never had a gun held to her head, a first for her.

"I don't like this one bit," Kyle grounded out.

"Eventually, he'll see reason. I didn't call to upset you. I called because I can talk to you. You always make me feel better."

"That's why I'm here. Either way, I don't like it when you're upset. I know how strong you are, and this guy must have done a number on you. Want me to talk to this guy?"

"No, it'll be okay," she gulped. "So tell me," she said, hoping to change the subject. "Are you being nice to those baby seals?"

"Sis, I hate when you call them that. They're trying to become Navy SEALs."

Laughter escaped her.

"It's Hell Week, so you can just about imagine. I'm not supposed to be nice. The shiny bell has been ringing steadily all week." He laughed. "It's midweek, and we are at about 70 percent dropout. They haven't figured out that it's 90 percent mental and 10 percent physical, but then again, I'm not going to tell them that. They'll have to figure it out on their own. They'll be more dropping out," he grimly predicted.

"Either way, go easy on them, remember when you were in that hell," she reminded him.

He laughed in response. "Oh god, don't I remember."

"How are Sibella and the kiddies?"

"Sibella's great, getting fat and sassy, and ready to deliver the baby. Sam and Elise keep bringing insects in the house as pets, and it's not working out so well."

She laughed. "Give them my love, will you?"

"Of course."

"I best be going. I'm so happy I got to talk to you. Thank you for the pick-me-up."

"So you're heading to bed now for some rest?"

"Not quite yet. I'm going to grab some breakfast at Birdies and then take the car to the dealership."

"What's wrong with my beauty? She's practically brand-new."

She hesitated. Obviously, she couldn't tell him the truth. "Just getting some service and then I'll be back home to sleep my day away."

"Will you call me later today, Summer? I want an update to see how you're doing."

"It's not necessary. I'm much better now having talked to you."

"Summer, if you don't call me, I'll be calling you," he warned. "I love you, babe."

Again, she clamped her hand over her mouth to stifle her sob. What if something happened to her and she didn't get to tell her brother how much he meant to her?

She took a deep breath, swallowed hard as she tried to find her voice.

"Kyle, you've been the best brother a sister could ask for. You've made so many sacrifices for me. I'll never be able to repay you. I love you too, very much," she said then hung up the receiver before he could respond and before she gave a way to heart-wrenching sobs.

Kyle Benson frowned down at the receiver he clenched in his hand. Summer never made a habit telling him she loved him every time they spoke on the phone. It was always there, unspoken. Yet today, she was more revealing, pouring her heart out to him as if she believed she might not get the opportunity again. He experienced the same emotion before when on a mission with his SEAL team and the odds were stacked against them. He recognized the signals all too well. He had a feeling a lot more had happened than she let on.

He boiled inside.

No man would harm his little sister. They'd have a death wish on their hands. He hesitated only three seconds before he punched a speed dial on his cell phone.

The phone rang several times.

No answer.

Storm's answering machine turned on.

The warm breeze from the Atlantic whistled through the massive windows of the master bedroom, bellowing the white sheer curtains as the blazing sun began to climb into the cloudless blue sky over Amelia Island.

The scene could've been construed as peaceful and serene had it not been for the German shepherd's harsh, sharp barks piercing the quiet air.

Nick "Storm" Maddox's nude body was sheened in sweat as he rolled onto his back and stared up at the beamed ceiling. He blew out a harsh, shaky breath as he clutched the pillow against his chest.

Finally, his nightmares released him, but he also knew they'd relentlessly return the next time he closed his eyes, just as they had every day for the past two years. Every dream the same, the face of a beloved ten-year-old child, her long hair the color of a shimmering pale moon, smiling up at him with trust shining through her sky blue eyes.

The child he failed to protect.

He flung the pillow aside and rolled onto his side and, in turn, received a wet, hot lathered lick against his cheek.

Apollo.

The dog's ears perked, and his tail wagged; he bounced on his large paws while his chocolate eyes danced with devotion as he stared expectantly into his master's eyes. Another pierce bark erupted from him.

Storm sighed as he reached over and softly patted Apollo's broad head and ruffled his pointed ears. He was a highly trained working military dog who for the past five years had been with him through a firestorm of bullets and dogfights as they marched through the deserts of Afghanistan and the streets of Somalia sniffing for bombs, booby traps, finding false doors, clearing houses, and doing searches. This dog had done and seen it all and had his own set of baggage to prove it, a limp from a shrapnel injury to his hip forfeiting him into early retirement.

Regardless, the guilt ate him alive, tore at his gut, and crushed his heart.

Today was the day.

Apollo read his thoughts. He whined and nuzzled his nose under Storm's hand and licked his fingers. Again, he barked as if to say, *Just one more day.*

He just couldn't.

"I'm sorry, fella," he said wearily as he sat up, displacing a whiskey bottle, tumbling from the bed onto the hardwood floor with a heavy thud. He stood, nudged it under the bed with his foot, and heard it clank against the rest of the bottles.

He cringed.

Each night he drank himself into oblivion, passing out on the beach or in the beach house some place but never in his bed. It would be fitting he'd sleep his last night in his bed.

His phone rang; the ringtone muffled under the covers.

He ignored the phone call, the insistent beeping. It represented someone wanting something from him he didn't have the energy or the strength to give. He was weary, worn out, and the life sucked from him.

He got out of the bed, walked into his bathroom, and peered at his reflection through the oval mirror above the sink. The haggard, drawn face staring back at him with smudged rings under his eyes was a stranger. He'd become another person who dreaded the sunrise and sunset as it was fraught with unpleasant memories.

As he pulled on his swim trunks, his answering machine kicked on.

"Storm? Pick up if you're there, man."

Storm hesitated. "Reaper, what the hell do you want with me," he muttered under his breath. Kyle was also a recently retired SEAL, another who had traveled across many a foreign land with him dodging bombs and bullets. He didn't have the heart to say good-bye to his best friend and decided to ignore the call.

"Storm, I have a problem. It's Summer."

Storm's heart lurched as he turned his back on his answering machine, his life, his buddy, and quickly skimmed down the staircase and bolted out the door with Apollo, defying the backward glance beckoning him to see what he was leaving behind.

He stopped at the newly installed wooden post next to the front door, hunched down, picked up the rope lying on the sand, and motioned for Apollo.

The dog stood back several yards away, refused, barked at him, and looked back at him with liquid soulful eyes. Nervously, he pawed the ground since it was the first command he ever refused to obey from his master.

Storm swallowed the lump in this throat. It threatened to choke him. He had to hurry before he lost his resolve. Through the window, he heard his best friend pleading him to call him back to help him. Apollo laid down, whimpered.

"God damn it, I said come here. Now!" he shouted at the dog, pointing to the ground, and instantly regretted it. Never had he yelled at Apollo in such a tone. He never had to because the dog was completely loyal, never questioning his orders.

Until today.

Apollo crawled on his belly in the sand, coming to lie submissively before him as he waited for Storm to tie the rope around his neck.

"It's for the best, you know," he said to Apollo as he looped the rope around his thick neck. "I can't have you chasing after me and doing something foolish. I haven't been good for you the past few years as I should've been and I'm sorry. You deserve better, buddy. You've got plenty of food," he said motioning to a mixer-size bowl heaped with dog food next to the post. "The cleaning lady will arrive this afternoon. I left her instructions to call my parents and then you'll go stay with Reaper. He'll take good care of you. He has kids too. You'll have a family now."

Still, Apollo whimpered.

He bent low, kissed the dog's head.

"You know I love you, and I'll never forget you," he said as he gave him one last loving stroke against his fur. He turned on his heel and jogged across the beach. The heat from the sun warmed his face and feet. He realized he'd never feel the simmering heat of the sun against his skin or the gritty sand between his toes nor hear Apollo's bark now turning ferocious and urgent.

His plans after retiring from active SEAL duty were to just sit back and relax. He'd seen enough action to last him a lifetime. Yet all that changed when he agreed to protect a young girl in Venezuela from her wealthy father's enemies. The money was outstanding and supposedly only short-term until the family relocated to Greece.

It never happened.

Fate dealt him a set of dirty cards changing his life forever.

He closed out the world with regret as he dove into the rolling tumbling waves and swam, his powerful arms slicing through the murky chilling depths. Quickly, he became winded, having foregone his disciplined exercise regimen, which disgusted him even further; but it wouldn't stop him from carrying out his plan.

Apollo twisted wildly against the rope, yelping, barking frantically. He wiggled, clawed, chewed against the rope as he tried to maneuver it off his neck. He lunged and lunged, using his full body weight against the post, choking himself and the rope biting further into his neck, rupturing his skin now oozing with blood. Yet he never gave up, never took his eyes off his master, fading into the shadowy waters.

One last ferocious growl and one powerful lunge was all it took and he was off, the discarded post trailing after him across the beach, kicking up swirls of sand until finally the rope broke away freeing him to leap wildly into the sea.

Storm swam until he realized he no longer heard Apollo's bark. He treaded water, looked back toward the beach, and saw to his amazement his dog paddling fiercely toward him. The dog was so damn loyal. He knew Apollo would kill himself trying to save him. He swore under his breath. He felt torn, yet knew he couldn't face another tomorrow ripped to pieces with guilt. He stopped treading and allowed the murky depths to swallow him whole. He had the uncanny ability to be able to hold his breath under water for several minutes. He prayed his life ended a lot sooner.

He had no fear of dying only sadness for the hurt he'd cause his loved ones he left behind.

The sea showed no allowance for the weak. It didn't care why you chose its world to end your life. Given the opportunity, it would take you in a heartbeat and snatch the life right out of you.

He chose the sea to end his life because it was his passion since before he could walk and because he never wanted to be found. He wanted to disappear into oblivion, remembered for the man he once was, a Navy SEAL, not the shell of a man who now lacked confidence and whose hands shook violently because of his lack of drink and a cigarette.

His life flashed before his eyes.

He envisioned his parent's weathered faces, his young sister, and his SEAL team brothers who stood shoulder to shoulder with him in fiery combat across the world.

Breaking through those memories was Calypsia's horrific screams as he frantically tried to rescue her. Words couldn't describe the devastation he felt when she died in his arms. He'd never forgive himself for not being there for her. He failed.

Then there was Reaper, his best friend over the past twenty years and one of his SEAL brothers, sharing a lifetime of memories in the navy. On assignment, they saved each other's asses numerous times. He would miss him. It jolted him suddenly he was leaving his blood brother in a time of need. He'd never heard him sound so desperate. He felt a twinge of guilt. He owed Kyle, really owed him. The thought of Summer being in trouble, now, that nudged him.

As a Navy SEAL, he was taught to never focus on himself but of his team. Yet he turned his back on his blood brother.

Apollo's barking seeped into his subconscious. The damn faithful dog wouldn't allow him to die in peace. He and Apollo were like two peas in a pod; they only had each other.

Perhaps he wasn't ready to die yet.

One more day.

He broke surface, gasped for air, his lungs burned and his head felt like it could explode at any given moment. He looked for his dog.

In the distance, he saw Apollo paddling the waves with all his might. He slipped under the water twice and was going under the third time when Storm reached him, diving under the water, and pulling him above surface.

"Yes, another day, buddy," he said as he hugged him tightly against him. The dog's tail wagged intensely. He swam sidestroke with his dog in tow.

They stumbled ashore and lay sprawled on the beach. The warm sun glistened off their water-beaded bodies as seagulls squawked noisily overhead.

Apollo stood, shook his coat with fervor then staggered over, licked Storm's cheek, and trotted off.

Storm tried to catch his breath while staring up at a large fluffy white cloud trying to push back the sun's rays. As he lay there, the realization hit him how selfish he'd been avoiding his loved ones phone calls.

Yet in knowing all this, he still tethered on the edge wondering how to deal with the all-consuming guilt threatening to consume him, eat him alive.

He stood, brushed the sand from his body, and jogged back to his house. On his way, he tossed aside the discarded wooden post and rope and made a mental note to burn them. He walked inside with Apollo following, picked up his phone from the bed, and called Reaper.

Reaper answered on the second ring.

"Reaper, I'm sorry I missed your call," Storm said and he paused, waited for the fury to ignite his receiver.

He wasn't disappointed.

"I've called your ass ten times this past month. Why haven't you called me back? The guys have called me worried about your sorry ass. Don't be surprised if they walk up on your doorstep any day now."

Storm drew a deep ragged breath. "I've been busy," he lied. "I'm sorry."

"Busy doing what?"

Storm couldn't find the words.

Reaper sighed. "I know you like no other, man. I know you're hiding on that island of yours and getting sucked into the guilt."

"It is what it is. I can't seem to forget that," Storm breathed out.

"You're wrong, buddy. It wasn't your fault. You can't be every place all the time. It's the worst possible scenario and those risks come with protecting someone, as you well know. Hell, it's not as if you danced away from this situation. You were shot in the back, so let the past stay in the past and start living, Storm."

"That's easier said than done," Storm replied, clenching his phone in his fist.

"You can't bring Calypsia back. I wish like hell you could, but you can't. It's fate."

A long silence filled the air.

"So what's going on with your sister?" Storm asked.

"She's got a problem with a guy. The fiancé of her patient who died last week. He's putting some heat on her."

"Is he threatening her?" It was automatic, the fury surging through him at the very idea of someone causing Summer Benson any kind of pain, distress, or heartache.

"She wouldn't elaborate. I had to drag it from her, yet she was disturbed enough to call me. So yes, this guy has rattled her cage somehow. God damn it! I hate I'm in California and she's there, and I can't help her."

"What hospital is she working at?"

"She works at Regional Medical in Jacksonville."

"I'm only thirty minutes away. I'll find out what's going on," Storm promised.

"If you think she's in any danger, promise me you'll watch over her, protect her until this situation is under control."

"You want me to do what?" he shouted through the phone incredulously. "Knowing my record?" Storm started pacing across the room. "No, this isn't a good time. I'll find out what's going on, but you'll need to find someone else to watch over her," he said adamantly.

"Storm, I trust you like I trust no other, man. It's my sister we're talking about, and there's no other man in this world I'd trust with her life more than you," Reaper pleaded.

Storm sighed heavily.

Fuck!

"She doesn't want any interference," Reaper warned. "I believe she's naive thinking this man will just let it drop. But I don't have a good feeling about this."

"The last picture I saw of her was when she was twelve. What does she look like now?"

"When you see her, you'll see my resemblance just a bit more eye catching." Reaper laughed under his breath.

"I guess I could also identify her by the butterfly tattoo on her left ass cheek," Storm added teasingly.

"If you get that far with my sister within the first few minutes of meeting her, then I should probably start heading that direction, if you get my meaning."

"Fine, fine, fine. She's safe from me. I'll drive over this morning," Storm trailed off laughing.

"Storm, keep her safe with you in every way if you catch my drift," Reaper ordered.

"Okay, I'll try not to get her drunk and seduce her. Scouts honor."

"You were never a scout," Reaper countered without humor.

"I wondered if you'd catch that," Storm said, smiling into the phone.

"She's at home right now but mentioned in the next hour going to Birdie's Restaurant just down the street from the hospital. I appreciate it. Be discreet, just check her out, and call me to let me know what you think. She'd skin me alive if she knew I sent you. I'd go myself but my baby is about to pop and it's Hell Week, and I'm knee deep in training."

"No problem, I'll let you know what I find out. Give Sibella and the kids my love."

"Storm, I really appreciate it," Reaper said soberly.

"I know. You'd do the same for me."

"In a heartbeat."

Reaper would love nothing more for Summer and Storm to meet, become a couple; yet on his sister's behalf, he knew it a high improbability. She abhorred any man who willingly placed himself in the line of danger. Obviously, she saw the flipside having to mend their broken bodies. Yet in Reaper's mind, Storm was exactly what Summer needed. Her life was way too orderly and full of schedules, too organized, and not a helluva lot fun. And Storm knew how to have fun, or at least he used to know how to have fun. He was a cause for concern as well.

Storm hung up and paced the long corridors of his home coming to look out onto the Atlantic to see lances of sunlight pour through patches of cloud and onto the ocean. What mess had he gotten himself into again? This was how his last fatal assignment began, a fellow SEAL asking him for a favor to take over protection of someone.

However, this time, he'd treat this situation much differently. He wouldn't allow his heart to become involved in emotions he had no energy to deal with. He wanted to find the son of a bitch who terrorized Summer and take care of business. Patience wasn't one of his virtues. He faced danger, never ran from it; that's what being a SEAL taught him.

He ran upstairs, took a five-minute shower, and changed clothes. He put a salve on Apollo's neck in hopes to heal it quickly.

"I owe you," he said, leaning down and kissing the top of his head.

He discarded his end-of-life instructions for the housekeeper. Before he walked out the door, he gave a quick look over his shoulder to see Apollo sprawl his lean body down on the wood floor smack dab in a puddle of sunshine. In the next minute, he snored soundly.

"I'll be back, buddy," he said softly, closing the door behind him.

Summer pulled into Birdie's Restaurant parking lot. She maneuvered her car into the far corner, away from prying eyes. Heaven forbid if someone saw *killer* written across the hood of her car. It stunned her someone hated her so much to commit such an act against her.

The restaurant was hustling yet not completely full. She walked across the parking lot and noticed a tall man walking toward her. It was eerie. Suddenly, he was right behind her when she opened the restaurant door. She took a seat next to a wide bay window feeling edgy and suspicious of the man.

She had just ordered her glass of orange juice and reached for her newspaper when she glanced out the window to see a guy with a breathtaking body walk quickly across the parking lot drawing short, quick puffs on a cigarette as if it were his lifeline.

Bronzed by the wind and sun, his face was swallowed by an unshapely dark mustache and beard while his eyes hid beneath dark sunglasses.

The smoke curled around his face as he walked, like an illusion. He ran a distracted hand through his dark windblown hair that brushed his shoulders. His chest and arms were packed into a tight black T-shirt that stretched taunt across his broad chest. She swore the thread was unraveling in the seams from the pressure of his every movement. Black jeans hugged his slim hips and the long length of his muscular legs, showing his history of athleticism. Scuffed black boots completed his ensemble.

Intrigued for some unknown reason, Summer hid behind her newspaper, peeked over the top, and followed his every move as he strode his towering frame into the small restaurant. His broad shoulders slumped forward, his body tense as a spring threatening to recoil at any given moment. He raised his midnight black sunglasses revealing startling zinc colored eyes; a lustrous bluish-silver and looked directly at her, probing her wearily with a brooding gaze.

Storm picked up a discarded newspaper from the counter, scanned the patrons sitting at red and chrome tables as he walked across the restaurant, and slumped down at a table in the corner with his back protected against the wall, an old SEAL habit. He saw only three women who looked in their late twenties as Summer Benson. One lady had midnight black hair, one with pale blonde hair, one with honey-blonde hair, all comely women. He wished one of them would've worn the obvious scrubs to easily identify. Although he tried, he couldn't see Reaper's features in any of them.

Hell.

He barely noticed the young waitress dropping off his coffee, and he couldn't remember what he ordered because he was focused heavily on the honey-blonde who sat by the window.

She caught his attention.

She looked wary, tense, constantly looking around the restaurant at the customers, out onto the parking lot. It just so happened when she looked tentatively over her shoulder at him, he was juggling his coffee cup like a babbling buffoon because his hands shook so pathetically. God, this was not how he wanted his first meeting with her. Still, he couldn't make the connection if she was Summer. The other two women stared openly at him, their eyes more than friendly. Which one was she? He had no energy to play games.

His breakfast arrived about the same time as the honey-blonde's, and he found himself closely watching her as she picked at her food. Occasionally, she looked uneasily across the room at a man sitting in the center of the restaurant stabbing at a large steak and eggs.

The same man Storm noted had arrived only a minute before him, the same man he caught staring at her when he walked into the restaurant. The man, tall and lanky, wore black jeans and a black T-shirt. Aged mid to late forties with a crown of thinning hair, his face was deeply lined under his eyes and hollowed cheeks. The man bared two scars; jagged scar on his left temple and straight cut under his right jaw. He wore round silver-rimmed eyeglasses and no wedding band.

His left hand was his dominant hand even though he ate with his right hand as evident by how loosely he held his knife and sliced his steak.

These observations were made from the time Storm walked in the door until he walked by the man. A past, but not forgotten trait being a SEAL, making those quick assessments normally saved his ass more times than could count.

Storm's eyes traveled back to the honey-blonde. Her face looked uneasy as she observed the man.

If he were a betting man, he'd bet she was his lady. He smiled. She was supposed to be his lady, the sister of his best friend he'd never met. Ever since he'd known Reaper, it was an inside joke he would marry Summer. After all, she was his prize whenever he beat Reaper at chess and cards. Yet sitting right here, right now, he knew there was no way in hell he'd even contemplate hooking up with someone, not even with Summer Benson.

And if his gut was right on and she was Summer, her suspicious demeanor told him that she hadn't disclosed to her brother the full extent of her dilemma. Something had shaken her, her vulnerability shown in her eyes. He watched her push a full plate of food away and stare out the window.

Her phone rang.

He watched her answer it and immediately her face lit up as she turned away and looked out the window.

Suddenly, there was a commotion at the table where the suspicious man sat. He began coughing, low at first and then it subsided. He drank some water, and then his coughing became more forceful, louder.

"Shit," Storm muttered quietly under his breath. He was in no shape to save a man's life today, just the thought exhausted him, but he'd do it if he had to.

The man was obviously in distress. He jerked to his feet and grasped his hands around his neck, choking. The restaurant quieted, and the patrons sat there and curiously eyed the man unsure how to help him.

A young bouncy redheaded waitress walked up to the man's table, her eyes wide, horrified as she looked at the patrons, waving, pointing toward the man. "He can't breathe! Can anyone help him?"

Just as Storm rose, the honey-blonde sprang into action.

Dr. Summer Benson.

Now, he understood why Reaper never divulged a more updated picture of his gorgeous sister with his closest friends because he knew he'd have hungry hounds pacing at his door. Yes, she was his best-kept secret, he smiled inside, chagrined.

As he approached her, her beauty became very evident. She was a natural beauty. She and her brother shared the same blue eyes, but Reaper's hair was strawberry blonde. She was petite with honey-blonde hair lying in waves past her shoulders down the middle of her back. Her face was sun-kissed with a few freckles sprinkled over the bridge of her straight nose. She didn't look a day more than twenty-one years old, although through Reaper, he knew her to be in her late twenties. Her dreamy bliss-blue eyes were almond shaped and her lips… very kissable blush-pink lips that were full and lush and every time he looked upon them, every clean coherent thought fled his mind and in its place forbidden erotic images. She wore skin-hugging jeans and a white fitted blouse outlining her hourglass figure to mouthwatering status. It felt criminal looking at her considering he was seven years her senior. Yet his mind fantasized, thinking all the places on her lovely body he'd love to explore with his mouth. The pledge he made to Reaper about not touching her suddenly seemed like one helluva monumental undertaking.

Instantly, she appeared at the man's side, trying to determine his injuries while he clawed at his throat. He tried to speak but couldn't. His face took on a bluish hue.

Summer stepped behind the man, leaned him forward, and gave him quick blows between his shoulder blades with the heel of her hand. God help her, with every blow she gave trying to save his life, she wondered if someone paid him to take hers.

Regardless his intentions, she was a doctor first and foremost.

Next, she attempted the Heimlich maneuver on him, wrapped her arms around his middle, and gave him a number of deft inward thrusts to dislodge whatever blocked his airway. It didn't work and, when the man lost all unconsciousness, lost his footing; Summer tried to catch him, but he was no match and slipped from her grip.

Storm caught him.

She was already leaning over his body feeling for a pulse before Storm could lay him on the floor.

"Call an ambulance," she yelled out without looking up.

Storm kneeled beside the man, looked up, and winked at the waitress. She immediately shoved her hands in her apron pockets and produced a cell phone. Her fingertips dipped in midnight nail polish deftly punched in the emergency phone number.

"I'll have to perform a trache," she said without looking over at him.

Suddenly, chairs scratched against the floor and the patrons formed a wide circle around them, their necks craned, strained to get a good view, their voices rushed out in whispers.

"I need a quarter inch tubing, a straw, a pen, and I need it now!" she yelled over her shoulder.

The waitress thrust a straw into Summer's face, all the while her hand shaking like a leaf.

Storm reached into his front jean pocket for his folded pocket-knife. His hands shook like an almighty as he tried to clean the blade with a napkin. He laid it in her open palm.

She positioned the tip of his knife against the hollow of his throat. "Hold him still."

Storm held the man's shoulders down against the floor.

The waitress leaned over them. "You're not going to cut him, are you? He'll start bleeding and—"

"Or he'll die," Summer muttered under her breath.

A rather large, rotund bald man wearing a grease-stained white apron wrapped around his middle plowed through the onlookers coming to stand at the foot of her patient.

"Young lady, you stop right there," he ordered, pointing at her. "You're responsible if this man dies. There's a law about this."

Summer paused. The knife hovered against the man's neck.

Storm leveled a glare on the man, making him slowly back away.

Summer caught the look he gave him, shuddered to think of the consequences had the man been persistent. Undoubtedly, she'd have another patient to work on.

Loud gasps abounded across the restaurant as Summer made the incision and blood oozed down his neck. She tucked the straw in the slit and packed napkins around it to stop the bleeding. She glanced over at the man who assisted her.

His hands trembled.

"Rough night?" she quipped gracing him with bleach-white teeth and an electrifying smile.

"You have no idea," he returned. His eyes pierced her and gave her the opportunity to see through the mask of sadness.

"Do you mind checking the man's pockets for some identification?" she asked.

"Of course," he said almost distractedly, drowning in her hypnotic eyes.

"Money and some car keys, but no billfold or ID," he said, lifting the keys from the man's pocket and handing them to her.

Their hands brushed and her eyes flew up to meet his. This man disturbed her in many ways for some unknown reason.

"I'll be right back," she said, scrambling to her feet with the car keys. "Keep applying pressure," she ordered.

She was met by a burst of applause.

Uncomfortable with the attention, she merely smiled and skirted through the patrons and out the front door to arrive in the parking lot.

Sirens blared.

An ambulance careened into the parking lot. Two white coat gentlemen tore from the ambulance and made quick work removing the gurney from the back and headed into the restaurant.

She clicked the remote button and a few chirps sounded from a silver SUV parked by the roadside. She jogged over to the vehicle and opened the driver side door. The interior was spotless. A quick glance over the front and back seats showed no billfold in sight so she checked the door pockets, the middle console, and the glove compartment and came up with nothing. She reached her hand under the driver seat and her fingertips grazed several objects, but what interested her most was a cold, metal object. She dragged it out onto the floorboard.

A gun.

Cold grey steel.

Alarm riveted through her and she took a deep, shaky breath and tried to remain logical. Many people this day and age carried a gun and held a permit for protection. Yet it was still alarming. She leaned down and peeked under the seat. Her breath caught. A sheathed knife, a roll of gray duct tape, and a spool of rope stared back at her.

One by one, she pulled out each item onto the floorboard and a chill shot up her spine. What in God's name was this man doing with these items under his seat? It was a recipe for abduction in her mind.

Did he mean to harm someone?

Did he mean to harm *her*?

Panicked, she took a step back and came up against a solid wall. A terrifying scream tore from her lips.

Storm's hands shot out, reached for her, and steadied her. He turned her around to face him with his hands planted squarely on her shoulders. Their eyes locked for a long moment; it made her breathless. Whether or not he realized his actions, his thumbs softly caressed her shoulder. The heat emanating from him seared her as if he touched her bare skin. It felt electrifying, comforting, an unfamiliar feeling.

"I'm sorry. I just came to see if you needed my help," he explained, his forehead creased as he looked down at her deathly pale face. Her eyes were wild with terror.

She clutched her hand against her chest, felt her heart riot. "I'm sorry I'm normally not so jumpy."

Her fear, choking and stifling her just moments before, incredulously vanished as soon as he touched her.

He caught a glance at the items littered on the floorboard. It looked like the man could've possibly meant to kill her after all, a hired killer; the man she just saved. He really wanted a word with the man now.

His eyes flickered at her. She seemed much more composed. He glanced over the roof of the SUV to see the ambulance personnel step out the rear of the ambulance and shut the door.

Deftly, he sat her aside, shut the door of the SUV, took the keys, and locked it, leaving her standing beside the vehicle. He pointed at her, ordered, "Don't leave."

Summer noted the man seemed completely at ease giving orders as if he'd done it all his life and confident his order followed. She watched him angrily stride toward the ambulance. He took a quick glance inside and got in the back of the ambulance.

Summer didn't obey him; instead, she strode quickly back inside the restaurant and paid her bill.

Storm took a seat on the bench next to the gurney and looked down at the man.

The man's eyes stared up at him, wide, frightened.

"Look, man, I don't know what your intentions were today against that young lady who just saved your life, but let's make one thing clear. You try to harm her, and you'll have to go through me first, and rest assured you won't walk away. They'll never find your body because it'll be in too many pieces if you get my meaning. Take that warning back to whoever hired you or whoever plans to come next. I'll be waiting."

He just became her bodyguard.

Summer looked around for him, and still he hadn't returned from the ambulance. Again, she couldn't help wonder the story behind the stranger. She couldn't seem to forget his dazzling slate-grey eyes encompassed with sadness. A part of her wanted to know more about the mysterious man, then again, something told her he was more than what she bargained for, hence, a perfect time to make her exit. Quickly, she tucked her billfold in her bag and practically ran out the door.

Yes, she was running away.

Again.

As she walked to her car, she mused how she played everything safe all her life. Then again, her life was anything but usual growing up, always focused on academics and virtually no retreats with exception to attending medical conferences and lectures, caring for patients and endless call rotations.

It was by choice.

She lived in a protective bubble for as long as she could remember, never taking chances that could interfere in her orderly life, a profession consuming her entire being with no room for extracurricular activities—*men.*

In two weeks, she'd turn twenty-nine, and it felt like it was her fiftieth. Her life was almost halfway over and nothing to show for it on her personal side. She yearned for a husband to share her life with and she wanted children, even a pet.

She walked to her car and noticed a sleek black chromed motorcycle sitting next to it. It winked at her, beckoned her.

For the first time in her life, she looked beyond the *murder cycle* as she and her colleagues often called them and wondered how it would feel to ride such a machine, having the warm summer's breeze blow through her hair and having not a care in the world.

And just as quickly, she shuddered at the thought. She saw firsthand what happened to a person riding the heap of chrome who was at the wrong place at the wrong time.

Mangled bodies.

Sometimes the bodies were beyond repair, but her job was to piece them back together and work a miracle.

She reached for the door handle of her car then stopped, turned around, and looked at the motorcycle again. Everything about it screamed fun and freedom. She gave a fleeting look toward the restaurant windows.

No one would see you. Be daring!

She knew she completely lost her mind when she dropped her messenger bag onto her car seat and walked over to the motorcycle.

Without a second to lose, she tossed one leg haphazardly over the seat, a difficult feat. Once she climbed on, she scooted up on the seat, reached out, and grabbed onto the handlebars. She never felt such exhilaration. It screamed power, thrust, and excitement. If only her colleagues could she her now. The very thought wrenched a giggle from her especially since she was a great opponent of the *murder cycle.*

Suddenly, the unthinkable happened.

The bike's alarm shrilled loud enough to wake the dead!

She couldn't get off the bike quick enough, never mind her clog was stuck. She whirled around on the seat, tethered on the edge, and nearly fell off the bike had it not been for a set of capable hands catching her, spanning her waist, setting her securely back on the seat.

The intriguing, brooding guy.

She cringed as he pulled his remote out of his pocket and clicked a button ceasing the alarm. She tried to peer through his sunglasses and couldn't read his eyes even though he stared at her with obvious curiosity.

She was speechless. Of course, he owned the *murder cycle.*

Chagrined, she squeaked out, "Your bike?"

He nodded, unsmiling.

"So," he asked, "do you like motorcycles?"

"Oh no, I hate them," she spouted out.

His eyebrow rose under his sunglasses.

"Then I won't have to worry about you stealing my bike?"

"Steal your bike?" she asked, abhorred.

He nodded once again and pointed to her sitting on his bike, trying to hide his smile.

"Oh, I was just curious." She laughed ruefully.

A warm breeze blew at his back, and she breathed in the tantalizing scent of fresh soap and aromatic cologne, a heady, delectable combination.

"Have you ridden before?" he asked.

She shook her head.

"Then how can you hate motorcycles if you've never ridden on one?"

"I guess you could say I've experienced the aftereffects and that's about as much excitement as I can bear."

"Want a ride?" he asked, watching her unconsciously squeeze the bike's handlebars.

"Oh no," she stammered, laughing in spite of herself. "I have no idea why I got on your bike, perhaps a momentary lapse of my senses."

"And here I thought it was because you wanted my phone number," he teased, giving her a crooked breathtaking smile.

She looked flustered.

He flashed her a gorgeous white-teethed smile. She wished she could see his eyes. Dratted sunglasses!

He liked the way her cheeks turned hot pink.

"It's okay, really. Sit there as long as you'd like," he invited. He looked over at the sleek white Mercedes convertible. He tilted his head over at it. "Your car?"

She barely nodded, suddenly feeling very anxious. Her mind was consumed with the idea he saw *killer* written across the hood of her car and wondered what he thought about it. Nervously, she ran a hand through her hair.

"Fun ride," he acknowledged with a low whistle.

"Thanks. I only drive it back and forth to work," she admitted, giving it barely a glance as she watched him, wondered if he would make a comment about her recent artwork.

Storm looked over at her car again, his eyes barely flickering over the hood. Good God, he never noticed her hood when he pulled in next to her. There was no way Reaper knew his sister was being terrorized because if he did, he'd fly in, armed and ready to confront the man. He had to call him. He had a right to know.

He looked back at the white Mercedes with new appreciation. It screamed for an open endless highway, low profile, chrome wheels, and dual exhaust.

"My brother chose the car," she confessed.

Storm laughed. Of course, Reaper would pick out such a gorgeous car, knowing the head-spinning effect she'd have on men sitting behind the wheel of such a sleek and powerful car. The car wasn't needed, oh no, not at all.

He thumbed back at the restaurant.

"Pretty impressive work you did in there, by the way. I thought the man was a goner."

She shrugged nonchalantly. "It's all in a day's work. He'll probably remember to eat a bit slower next time," she said, trying to make light of the situation.

"Are you all work and no play?"

She was thoughtful for a moment, "Yes, I suppose so."

"That's a shame. You could take your first step to adventure and take a spin on my bike," he said, trying to convince her.

"Yes, but knowing my luck, I'd be the statistic you'd read in tomorrow's newspaper."

He shook his head slowly. "Not with me," he said confidently as he lifted his sunglasses to sit on his forehead. His mesmerizing eyes narrowed on her. Close up, his eyes were stunning.

"I better not," she said breathlessly, falling easily under the man's charm. He seriously threatened her sensibilities, and she needed to escape. She tried once again to scramble off the seat.

He stepped closer. "What are you afraid of?"

She laughed suddenly and made the mistake of meeting his gaze again.

"Well, three things actually. I've never ridden on a motorcycle. I don't know your name, and I just got off call and would probably fall asleep on the back of this bike and fall off."

"Nick Maddox," he said, giving her a firm handshake, leaving out his nickname for secrecy purposes.

"Summer Benson," she returned, momentarily speechless as his warm hand held hers with no effort to disengage from her.

"You're safe with me," he murmured, his eyes sending her a private message.

She stared into his smoldering eyes, tried to read more into his expression, yet it closed just as fast as it came. He released her hand.

Bemused, he countered, "Although, it's me who should be wary considering you tried to steal my bike."

Her eyes suddenly sparkled with humor.

Ruefully, she shook her head, laughed to herself. "If my brother saw me right now…"

He laughed quietly and prompted, "And if he did?"

"He wouldn't approve." She sighed as her eyes took in his powerful, dangerous presence. This man represented all the things bad for you—cigarettes, alcohol, and caffeine, basically everything she avoided most of her life.

"Why wouldn't he approve?"

She looked at him for a long moment. "Because I'm having a difficult time turning you down and it should be automatic."

He nodded, smiling. Unbeknownst to her, he would be spending time with her in the near future and have her on his bike by the end of the day. He walked over and swept her up in his arms and lifted her off his bike as if she were a feather. He led her over to her car and opened her door for her. He glanced at her hood again.

His concerned eyes flashed over to meet hers.

"A secret admirer." She grimaced.

"Anything I can do to help?"

He stared at her in waiting silence.

Thoughtfully, she gazed at him. He would be a great protector if it weren't for the fact he looked exhausted and shook like a leaf. Everything about him was huge, broad, bulky, and rock solid.

"I'm afraid not," she sighed.

He nodded and shut her car door.

She put on her seat belt, started the car, and gave him one last wave before pulling out of the restaurant parking lot feeling his eyes follow her. A part of her kicked herself for not taking him up on his offer for a bike ride. Yet it was probably for the best. The whole ordeal in the restaurant exhausted her so she headed home. She would take the car to the dealership later. She stared blankly out the windshield thinking about the stranger she just met. She had to make a serious effort to banish the man from her thoughts and stop smiling.

Storm looked up to see the door of the restaurant burst open and a young waitress running into the parking lot waving at Summer's car as she turned out of sight.

He jogged over to her.

"I found her driver's license on the floor," she said breathlessly in between loud chomps of her gum chewing.

"Thank you. I'll make sure she gets this," he said as he plucked her driver's license from her.

"Great. Thanks!" she said, giving him a slow appreciative smile before returning to the restaurant.

If he were a killer stalking Summer, the waitress just provided the information to get to her.

He shuddered at the thought.

Storm turned around to head back to his bike when she stopped him.

"Tell her what she did today was amazing!" she exclaimed.

Storm nodded, got onto his motorcycle, released the kickstand, and revved the powerful engine to life.

His destination was 143 Highland Avenue.

And yes, she was amazing.

Summer arrived home and tossed her bag and newspaper onto the kitchen counter. She walked through her dimly lit living room and headed straight to her bedroom.

Longingly, she stared at her bed, so inviting with the cool, crisp white covers. She stripped down to her panties when suddenly, deafening silence.

The electricity shut off.

Panic ran swiftly through her.

She ran across the bedroom, her bare feet padded softly against the thick white carpet and opened a mini blind to look out. She couldn't tell if any other homes lost their electricity.

Suddenly, the back door hinges creaked, leading from the garage. She whirled around, felt her heart lurch, and a sick feeling pit in her stomach. She started shivering.

Someone was coming after her.

Taking a deep shaky breath, she grabbed a heavy Chinese vase from her entertainment center, ran back and planted herself, and waited for her intruder.

She wouldn't go without a fight. She gave a quick glance down at the vase she held. "Oh god," she muttered under her breath. She picked up the wrong vase. It was a gift from a patient.

Storm walked up to the garage door. It was ajar. He walked in, glanced around, and saw the door leading into the house was also ajar. He stepped into the dimly lit kitchen. Suddenly, he became alarmed.

The house was deathly quiet.

As he rounded the corner and walked through the living room heading into the corridor leading to what looked like a bedroom, a wrenching guttural sound erupted, and out of the corner of his eye, something hurtled toward his head.

He deflected the vase with his forearm. It exploded against the wall. A shard gashed his cheek. Through the shadows, he saw a half-naked willowy figure run frantically across the room.

"Summer! It's Nick!"

Suddenly, the lights came back on, as did the steady soft hum of the appliances.

Instantly, she stilled and turned around to face him.

"Oh god, it's you!" she gasped in relief to see a familiar face. Then she frowned suddenly. "How did you get in here?"

"I walked through your open door," he said, thumbing behind him. "The waitress found your driver's license on the floor."

"I'm sorry, I thought you were an intruder," she trailed off, exhaling a harsh ragged breath. She felt lightheaded suddenly, all because of the way he looked at her. His gaze was riveted on her face, and then slowly and seductively, his eyes slid downward.

He forgot to breathe.

Her body was mouthwatering.

Their eyes locked as their breathing came in unison.

"Let me get something for you," he said, turning around to find something to cover her up.

Suddenly, she realized what held his attention.

She screamed, covered her breasts with her hands, ran into the bathroom, and slammed the door.

He dropped his head as he stifled a chuckle, shoved his hands into the front pocket of his jeans, and tried to forget the image of her seductive pink lacy panties hugging her slim hips.

In the bathroom, she paced back and forth. She leaned over the sink and splashed cold water onto her scalding cheeks. It was positively mortifying what just occurred. How could she stand before him half-naked and not realize it? She tied the sash of her robe tighter around her waist. She opened the bathroom door slowly, peeked around the corner. The broken vase no longer laid on her floor crushed. He'd cleaned up the glass. She tiptoed out to the corridor.

He remained where she left him.

She avoided eye contact. "Thank you," she said, looking down at the floor, "for picking up the mess."

"No problem. Are you okay?" he asked gruffly.

She nodded, keeping her gaze fixed everywhere but his face. "I'm sorry about that."

He smiled, thinking about it. "I'm not."

Her cheeks threatened to ignite once again. She lifted her eyes to meet his, offering him a small, shy smile.

He sent her a heated look that sent her pulse racing.

Her eyes landed on the bloody gash on his cheek. It brought to surface the seriousness of her situation, how frightened she was that someone was coming to kill her.

"I'm so sorry," she whispered as she took a hesitant step closer to him.

"A scratch," he said, shrugging indifferently. "I've been hurt far worse before. Plus, I'm sure you've seen worse."

Her cool fingertips prodded his cheek while her eyes anxiously scanned his wound, her lips pursed.

She quirked her finger at him, motioned him to follow her. She led the way into the bathroom and rummaged through cabinets.

He glanced over at the glass shower stall and couldn't help envisioning her inside naked as water glistened, rained down her shapely body; wet, frothy with soap, her long hair wet, sleek down her hollowed back. He smiled to himself as he watched her shuffle through the drawers, tossing white small packages onto the countertop, scissors, small jars. She began ripping open gauze packages, unscrewing the lids off a few bottles.

Wordlessly, she pointed to a nearby stool.

He walked over, straddled the stool, and sat down.

She stood between his legs and laid the cool liquid gauze against his cheek. Her hand trembled.

He reached up and cradled her trembling hands inside his.

"Everything all right?" he asked low, careful as he looked at her anxious expression.

She swallowed the lump in her throat and looked away from his probing eyes. "Yeah," she said, trying to keep her voice indifferent. He was way too perceptive.

From the side view, he watched a tear roll down her cheek.

He stood then, looked down at their hands clasped together, his hands dwarfed her small cold, clammy hands.

"Sometimes people's hands shake because of adrenaline, but I have a feeling that's not why your hands are shaking," he challenged, staring down at her with obvious curiosity.

"I could say the same about you," she countered just as curiously. "Why do your hands tremble?"

His expression suddenly became unreadable. "We're talking about you, not me."

She frowned up at him, tried to keep her expression under control, yet her eyes once again welled with tears. "It's been a very long week."

"Would this have anything to do with someone writing *killer* on the hood of your car?" he pressed.

It was extremely difficult to create a coherent thought while he looked at her the way he did despite the seriousness of his probing questions.

When he released her hands, she reached up and gently wiped the alcohol-laced gauze across his bloody cheek and tried to keep her expression controlled. "Perhaps, but it's only a misunderstanding."

His expression was skeptical when he asked, "What else has happened if you don't mind me asking?"

"Just my imagination running wild," she said, exhaling a shaky breath as she returned to the counter and picked up another piece of gauze.

"Like what?"

"Like believing someone cut my electricity, believing I locked my door when I didn't, thinking I received a prank phone call when it was just the wrong phone number." She laughed under her breath as she cleansed the wound on his cheek and affixed a bandage there.

"Or not," he said quietly. "Like the artwork on the hood of your car or the gash on your forearm? Or the guy at the restaurant whose life you saved had the arsenal in his SUV to make you believe it could've been meant for you?"

"Possibly." She exhaled another shaky breath and looked up at him curiously. "Why did you get into the ambulance with that man?"

He paused before answering. Obviously, he couldn't tell her he threatened his life.

"I returned his car keys to him and then discussed the situation with a police officer on sight. Do the police know about your car?"

"Hospital security filed a report, but other than that, I haven't officially talked with them."

His face was thoughtful, and after a moment, he said, "I'm sorry. I don't mean to pry, but you don't want to take this situation too lightly. Want me to take a look around to be sure everything's secure?"

"I'm sure it is," she said hesitantly.

"You wouldn't mind if I did anyway?" he said, his lips lifting into an alluring smile making her heart zip an extra hundred beats.

"Of course not," she said and watched him walk out of the bathroom. He had no weapon on his person, and for some reason, she didn't believe he needed one.

She was in the kitchen making coffee when he returned.

He was shaking his head.

"The verdict?"

His face was thoughtful as he considered her question, a teasing smile lit his lips with yet another shake of his head.

"Out of fifteen windows you have in this house, only five were secured. Plus, you have three windows where the locks don't function. Your garage doesn't lock either. Someone could easily lift the door, and they're in. Your front and back door locks rattle when you touch them."

"Just a little," she countered sheepishly.

He laughed. "Just a little, just enough that someone could take a bobby pin and get in."

"Fine, I'll get those taken care of, but first, would you like some coffee? It's decaf."

"Yes, but I don't want to keep you from your sleep."

"I can't sleep, so please have a cup," she said, handing him a cup and saucer. It had nothing to do with sleep. She didn't want to say good-bye to him for the second time in one day.

The fragile cup rattled against the saucer and threatened to tip several times as he followed her to the sofa.

She glanced humorously at him over her shoulder.

He sat down next to her yet kept a respectable distance.

"So you're a doctor?" he asked as he balanced the cup and saucer on his knee.

"Yes, at Regional Medical," she replied, sipping her coffee. His face was expectant, absorbed as if desiring to know more.

"There's really nothing exciting to tell, other than I've spent the last five years inside Regional's hospital walls without a vacation," she said. "Recently, I realized I haven't had much of a life, and I need to pursue my dreams before it's too late."

That translated to him she had been threatened on more than one occasion here recently. "What dreams?" he asked curiously.

"Marriage, children, you know, happily ever after."

"Ah, I see."

"Okay, your turn," she prodded.

She sensed his hesitation.

"You don't have to tell me anything," she replied.

"Go ahead, shoot." He laughed skeptically.

"Where are you from, Nick?"

"I was born on Amelia Island."

"Amelia Island," she said thoughtfully and felt her lips climb in a smile. "I've never visited there but my brother has."

She chuckled softly.

"Tell me," he said.

"My brother was on leave from the navy and accompanied a fellow airman to his family home on Amelia Island where he attended a rather large party. To make a long story short, his friend saved his hide from being arrested for public indecency at three o'clock in the morning. His friend had ties with the local authorities evidently."

He hid his smile. Reaper obviously left out the major pieces of the story to avoid scorching his sister's lovely ears.

He wore no wedding band. Was he divorced, married? Yes, he had to be married. If not, he definitely had a girlfriend. No, make that plural.

"Okay back to you please," she insisted, giving him a compelling look.

"I left the island when I turned seventeen," he said.

"To do what?"

"To join the navy." He hoped she didn't make the connection between him and Reaper just yet.

"I could've guessed as much seeing how fit you are," she said and couldn't help sweeping her eyes appreciatively over his lithe body. "My brother joined the navy at seventeen too. It was a good fit for him. Perhaps you've heard of him?"

He rose suddenly, walked over to the window glanced through the blinds to see the clouds trying to push back the sun.

"Kyle Benson?" she said quizzically.

"I've heard of that name a time or two," he said and wondered if his reply considered construed as lying.

He hated to lie.

She leaned her head back against the cushion and closed her eyes, feeling very lethargic.

He walked back over and sat beside her on the sofa. They sat several minutes in silence and he believed her asleep when suddenly she asked, "What did you say you did in the navy?"

After a moment, the teacup on her lap rattled.

She fell asleep.

He exhaled with relief as he plucked the teacup from her, set it on the coffee table, and looked over at her.

God, she was beautiful. He had been in a constant state of arousal since he walked into the restaurant. He didn't want to leave her just yet so he rested his arm behind her on the cushion. Within seconds, she leaned over and laid her head against his chest. Obviously, she wouldn't have done so if she were awake. Not saying he was taking advantage of the situation by any means since he'd always dreamt of being in close quarters with Summer Benson, but the situation was too good to pass up. She was frightened even though she tried to appear strong, and he was there to support her. He pulled her snugly against him and laid his head back on the cushion.

It felt like heaven.

It felt like déjà vu.

Within minutes, he slipped into a dreamless, peaceful sleep.

Four hours later, they awoke to the doorbell ringing.

9

Through the haze of her dream, Summer heard the faint chime of her doorbell. It began as a high-pitched buzzing sound fading like an echo in her dreams. She didn't want to wake up. She was warm, comfortable, and felt safe. A feeling she hadn't felt in quite some time, if ever.

Storm woke with a start and rose to his feet, walked over to the window, and raised the blind louver. He looked over his shoulder at her. "Recognize a guy in a black BMW, short dark hair?"

She walked over, peeped around his broad shoulder to see her visitor, looking his usual stunning self in a blue custom-made shimmering suit, red tie, and white crisp shirt.

"Dr. O'Malley," she said, running a ragged hand over her disheveled hair. She frowned, recalling their last conversation and not looking forward to another confrontation.

"You don't have to talk to him if you don't want."

His words were comforting. "No, it's fine."

"I'm around the corner should you need me," he said, scooping up their teacups and carrying them into the kitchen.

She retied the sash on her robe and opened the door.

Dr. O'Malley gave her a lazy appreciative smile as his eyes fleetingly drifted over her.

"Hi, Summer. Is this a good time to talk with you?"

She paused for a moment trying to gauge his mood. He seemed friendly enough and not confrontational.

"Of course," she said and opened the door wide.

She waved toward the sofa, but he declined with a shake of his head. She felt relieved. She wanted to return to her current guest, the one hiding inconspicuously in her kitchen and whose arms she slept in so peacefully.

Dr. O'Malley cleared his throat and looked at her warily. "I just wanted to apologize for the other day. I had no right to call you on your actions."

"So why did you?" she asked curiously since he'd never confronted her before.

"Well," he said, folding his arms over his chest. "I saw you asleep on the bench in the locker room, a sign of exhaustion undoubtedly because you work eighty hours a week. I believed your call of judgment would have been impaired, but I was wrong."

"Why the change of heart?" she asked.

"Because I realized you would do nothing less than work a miracle if it were in your power to do so."

"Thank you," she said, smiling up at him.

"I also heard about your car and came by to see if you need anything."

She grimaced and imagined everyone else at the hospital knew too. "Thank you, but I'll be just fine."

"The man seems a bit off his rocker so be careful."

She nodded.

He smiled at her then, giving her that knee-melting smile that made many women's hearts at Regional Medical skip a beat or two, hers included.

"You've applied for the chief of trauma position," he said, a statement, not a question.

Ah, the real reason why he stopped by.

"I did," she said hesitantly.

He reached out and shook her hand. "Good luck."

"Thank you and same to you."

He turned to leave and then paused at the door, turned around. "Do you have any idea what you're getting yourself into applying for the chief position? You're awfully young to take on such an endeavor."

"You don't think I have the experience it takes, Dr. O'Malley?"

"Of course. However, this position requires much more than just showing up for surgery. It takes years of experience on how to handle different situations you've never been exposed to."

"Showing up for surgery?" she asked aghast. "That's all you think I do?"

"That came out wrong," he sighed, shaking his head.

She took a deep breath.

"I have more ideas, hopes, dreams for Regional Medical than *you* could ever imagine," she informed him angrily.

"I realize you serve on plenty hospital committees."

Incredulously, she glared at him. "It's not just about sitting around a table wrangling about policies and procedures. It's about turning Regional Medical into a Level I trauma center and that means coming up with donor funds to pay for it. Which, I don't recall you being part of, other than to add your negative opinions. Or is this visit just about your bruised ego because I've applied for the job?"

His shoulders dropped, he exhaled deeply. "It seems whenever you and I talk about our work it gets crazy. We're both so passionate about Regional Medical. You and I are the same." He paused for a long moment as he searched her eyes. "The real reason why I came today, I have a confession."

"Confession?" she asked, bewildered.

"I've fought against how I feel about you because we work so closely together, but I can't hide it anymore," he declared.

He read her denial on her face and held up his hand. "I know about your rule, every male in the hospital knows it. I'm hoping you'll make the exception. I'm in love with you, and I think I can make it well worth your while," he said.

Blood rushed to her face.

"I'm sorry," she stammered, grasping for words. Her harmless flirting was obviously far from harmless in his eyes. Oh no, she made a muck out of things, thinking he'd take their teasing, flirting with a grain of salt. Good Lord, it all backfired.

Suddenly, he reached for her and pulled her into his arms, up hard against his chest. He lowered his mouth, crushing his lips forcefully against hers. She planted her hands against his chest to ward him off, but it felt like moving a stonewall.

"No, please," she rushed out as he tried again to slant his hot mouth across hers. She turned her head, tried to dodge his kiss that landed lopsided against her jaw.

Storm's fury erupted.

Stealthily, he walked up, reached around, and grabbed Dr. O'Malley by the throat, kicked his feet from under him, and slammed him ruthlessly to the ground.

Summer watched the scene unfold with disbelief. It happened so quickly, like a blur. This stranger wasn't winded, and his temper explosive.

"The lady said no," Storm growled as he leaned down and glared at the doctor, his boot causing pressure against Dr. O'Malley's neck, threatening to cut off his breathing.

Dr. O'Malley's face was blotchy red. He tried to get up, yet each time, Storm pushed him back down, pinning him back to the ground using his boot as leverage against his neck.

"No, Nick!" Summer said, rushing forward, seeing the blood spew from Dr. O'Malley's mouth. "Let him up!"

Reluctantly, Storm removed his boot and stepped back.

Summer assisted Dr. O'Malley off the floor. He adjusted his jacket, whipped out his crisp white handkerchief, and wiped off his bloody lip. He glared at Storm leaning nonchalantly against the doorframe. "Who the hell are you?"

"Your worst nightmare should you touch her again."

Dr. O'Malley leveled a malicious look Storm's direction then strode angrily out the door without a backward glance.

"What have you done?" Summer asked slowly, carefully trying her hardest to control her anger.

"I protected you from that jackass's unwanted advances!"

"I don't need protection," she snapped defiantly. "You could've harmed him. He's a surgeon!"

He stared at her incredulously, his eyes sparked with indignation.

"What the hell? He forced himself on you. Did you really expect me to stand aside and watch? Could you have fought him off if you were alone with him?" he asked, quirking an eyebrow at her.

Obviously, he was dead on, but she couldn't admit that to him just yet. "That's not the point."

A romantic would undoubtedly applaud Storm's actions against Dr. O'Malley as a knight in shining armor saving her from unwanted advances. However, she saw it as a major problem because she and Dr. O'Malley worked so closely together on cases, and he was known to hold grudges; and luckily, she'd stayed under his radar.

"What exactly is the point?" he snapped, exasperated. "Or, maybe you never wanted my interference?"

"He's a surgeon," she countered. "What if you injured his hands? His life is in his hands, just as mine are."

"I believe I took that into consideration already. He's lucky, I normally don't give concessions."

Could this day become more bizarre? She raked her fingers warily through her hair.

Her cell phone rang. She welcomed the distraction.

Kyle.

"Hi, Kyle," she answered, sighing with relief.

"Summer, we need to talk," he said firmly.

"What about?" she asked, alarmed by his furious voice. He'd never raised his voice at her like this.

"It's about the man who's at your house right now."

She whirled around and looked at Nick who stood before her living room window, looking out, watching Dr. O'Malley speed down the driveway kicking up dust.

"What? How do you know Nick?" she asked, bewildered.

"Nick is Storm," Kyle confessed.

She dropped the phone.

A second later, she dove, scooped up her phone with a shaking hand, and clutched it tightly against her ear.

"What's going on, Kyle?" she hissed accusingly. "I thought you said he was short and fat with red hair."

"Well, I lied. We'll discuss later. Right now, I'm really pissed. You've neglected to mention to me some serious threats this psycho has levied against you."

"He called you?" She sighed, scowling at his retreating back as he walked quietly out the front door, his hands shoved deep in his front jean pockets as he strolled lazily down her driveway.

"Yes. Thank God he did. It was no accident he met you at the restaurant this morning. I asked him to call me with his findings. He's agreed to watch over you for now."

"No, this will blow over."

"By God, it's not going to blow over. As of this very moment, you *are* under his protection. You *will* obey every order he gives you. Understood?"

"Is it understood I'm twenty-eight years old and I can make my own decisions? By the way, have you seen your friend lately? He looks like hell, like the walking dead and shaking like a leaf as if coming off a binge."

"Summer, he's gone through some very tough times lately so be easy on him. He's doing us a favor. Storm saved my life, and he may very well save yours."

"This is Storm the same guy who saved you in Afghanistan?" she asked in disbelief. She'd always wanted to personally meet the guy who saved her brother's life, meet the guy responsible for so many heroic actions within his SEAL Team Five unit, yet by looking at him right now, it was hard to imagine. He seemed so distracted, preoccupied, and weary. Yet he handled Dr. O'Malley like a walk in the park, she reluctantly admitted to herself.

Storm walked back through the door carrying her mail consisting of a few letter envelopes and her newspaper. He laid it on her glass coffee table and sat down on the sofa's edge.

"He's staying at your place," Kyle informed her.

"Here? No!" she refused adamantly. Then again, if memory served her right, hadn't she always wanted locked up in the same house with this guy?

Kyle's stern voice brought her from fantasy mode.

"It's just a matter of time before this man becomes more aggressive. So the way I see it, there's no need to discuss this further. Storm will be with you at work and home. Now, when I get off the phone, I expect you to enlighten Storm, leave out no details, and give him the name of the man responsible."

"Kyle, I'm not trying to be difficult, but I don't need to be followed at work when I have people around me. This man wouldn't harm me with people around."

"Don't count on it. Besides, I'm not taking any chances," he informed her, brooking no argument.

"Well, there's a substantial problem you've not thought of."

"And what would that be?"

"Nick can't get hospital clearance before four-thirty tomorrow morning when my call starts. It's a long drawn out ordeal, probably not for at least another week," she added, hoping he'd defer her need for a bodyguard at least temporarily.

Kyle laughed. "Taken care of. He goes by Storm."

"Storm it is. You're mistaken, Kyle. They just won't let anyone inside a surgical suite. Besides, if this guy is gunning for me, Storm can't protect me through a glass window, which is as far as they'd allow him. I don't want him harmed. Therefore, this idea of him being here with me won't work."

"It will, Summer, don't worry about it. I'll get with Storm, and we'll get everything worked out. Or you could take a short leave until we have this guy nailed down."

"I can't just walk into the chief's office and tell him I have to take time off. It's hard to find coverage, and it's very busy. And no one will dictate my life," she said, defiantly, her eyes coming to land on Storm as he got up and walked out the door with his cell phone. "I plan to keep working."

She listened to Kyle with half an ear as she watched Storm through the window make a call. A few seconds later, she saw his lips move then his entire face light up with a breathtaking smile revealing brilliant white teeth. She couldn't imagine having such a seductive smile aimed directly at her. It nearly knocked the breath out of her considering the most he'd done since they met was frown at her. Curiosity killed her as she wondered whom he spoke with, perhaps a girlfriend or a family member. Then his face suddenly became somber, and he turned his back on her and paced down her driveway.

Storm was her bodyguard.

"Summer, are you there?" Kyle asked.

"Oh, um, yes," she replied a bit breathless and distracted.

"I bet you're looking at your new roommate as we speak," he drawled humorously.

"Do you have eyes through this phone or what? He's outside."

"You were, weren't you?" Kyle teased.

She chided him, "By the way, I still can't believe you lied to me about the way he looked. I swear, when I see you next—"

"You're so gullible. I couldn't resist." He laughed. "I need to talk to Storm."

She watched Storm walk up the driveway. "He's coming back inside, just a minute."

"Summer?"

"Yes," she said distractedly into the phone watching Storm walk through the door.

"I love you, brat."

"I love you, too." She sighed, handing her phone to Storm.

She walked into the kitchen and eavesdropped as she removed dishes from the dishwasher, careful not to clink the glassware so she could hear. After all, it had everything to do with her.

"I got clearance. It's all set. Okay. Later."

She couldn't believe her ears. How could Storm easily circumvent the system? It was impossible unless he knew a high-ranking official at the hospital. He was a retired SEAL, yet to have clearance to shadow her every step and overhear possible confidential conversations between herself and her patients was another matter.

After Storm hung up, Summer walked over to him. "Storm," she said, testing his nickname, "exactly what kind of clearance do you have at the hospital?"

"Wherever you go, I go," he replied nonchalantly, folding his arms across his chest.

She quirked her eyebrows letting him know his answer was far from satisfactory.

He clarified, "I'm with you wherever you go,"

"Even in the room with me?" she inquired.

He nodded. "Whether five feet or an inch away from you."

An inch.

He gave her a slow smoldering smile.

Her cheeks threatened to combust from the heated look he gave her. He knew exactly her train of thoughts.

She finally found her voice. "Who do you know at the hospital to get such clearance?"

"It really doesn't matter, now does it?"

"What do I tell my colleagues and my patients about you?" she asked, exasperated. She thought she'd have more time to adjust to the idea of a bodyguard. She wished he didn't look so mouthwatering.

"We'll think of something. If things become sticky, we'll have to inform them. As of now, the hospital administration is aware of these measures."

She groaned and shook her head, her patience clearly thinning.

They scowled at each other in silence.

"You don't want protection, do you?"

"I'm very busy." She shook her head. She walked over and pulled her planner from her bag, flipped through several pages; coming to stand before him, she handed him her schedule for the next month.

Storm stared down at her monthly calendar and the numerable entries. It was mind-boggling. He looked back up at her questionably. "What the hell is this?"

"My responsibilities we'll have to work around," she informed him as she picked up the planner and started rattling off her call rotations, medical conferences, teaching at the nearby university and lectures.

"You've got it all wrong. I'm not working around *all* your responsibilities. It's damn impossible with what you've got going on here," he said, incredulous.

"How many students do you lecture at the university?"

"Close to seventy, three nights a week."

"No, that's not going to work. What about these medical conferences?"

"What? I'm not teaching? I have to."

"No, you don't. And no, you won't. What about these medical conferences?"

"Seven o'clock each morning."

He shook his head. "No, you can't do anything repetitive. We don't want anyone to know where you're going to be at specific times. Your only allowance will be your call rotations and nothing else, and even then, it will be hard to protect you with emergency patients having access to you. This poses a huge threat because he could easily access you this way."

She put her hands on her hips.

"You're telling me of all those things on my calendar, the only thing I can do is call rotations?"

"That's exactly what I'm telling you."

"That's not going to work!" She nearly stomped her foot in frustration.

Their eyes locked in open warfare.

"Okay, forget it," she said, tossing her hands in the air. "I'm not doing this. My life cannot be held to a standstill!"

"Your priorities are all jacked up," he said as he reached into his jean pocket, pulled out his cell phone, and started dialing.

"What are you doing?" she demanded.

"Calling your brother," he replied sharply.

"Stop!" Her shoulders slumped in resignation.

His face was livid when he ended the call.

"Oh yes, I see. Your medical conferences and teaching is much more important than your life. Even after your brother begged you to accept my protection because he's worried about your safety, you still don't believe it necessary. You think you're safe and secure there at the hospital, here, at your home?"

"Yes," she replied frigidly, raising her chin up a notch.

"Open your newspaper," he instructed, pointing at the rolled paper lying on the glass coffee table between them.

Her eyes flickered down at the newspaper then back at him.

There was a reason why he wanted her to open her paper. What news lurked inside for her to read? Was it news about Mark Malone hurting another individual or more news about the DUI suspect? Her heart slammed against her chest as she reached down and hesitantly picked up the newspaper. Slowly, she unraveled the tight rubber band down the length of the paper.

10

The paper crackled in her hands as she slowly unrolled it. Across the newspaper's headlines written in blood, the word *killer* stared back at her.

She gasped.

The newspaper floated to the floor.

She wasn't safe anymore.

"I'm sorry, I didn't want to show you," he said, grimly glancing at the newspaper, "yet somehow, you've got to take this seriously."

She slumped down into the wingchair facing him.

"So this person knows where you live now," he stated the obvious.

"He already knew." She sighed, feeling her throat restrict, felt a lump form there. She gulped, tried hard to push back the flood of tears, yet they came anyway.

"What?" he demanded.

"My neighbor said my cousin came to visit me. I don't have a cousin," she explained.

"You think it was him?"

"Yes. I mean, who else if not him?" She shrugged.

"Good question," Storm said thoughtfully.

He leveled his gaze on her.

"Someone is trying to get to you. It's up to you to take the threat seriously. Now, he may be a smart killer or a dumb killer. He may only toy with you, terrorize you at his whim, or he may initiate more serious threats. You need to be protected until we track this guy down. What's his name?"

She stared at him anxiously.

"What happens once I give you his name?"

He gave her a hint of a smile. "I'm going to have a chat with him."

Something told her it would be a lot more than just a chat.

"Listen," she said as she sat forward, "if he really wanted to hurt me, he would have. This man is very capable of killing. I read it in his eyes in the doctor's lounge later that day when my patient died. Thankfully, he spared me."

"What did he do?"

"He put a gun to my head."

Storm muttered an explicit under his breath.

"He said he wouldn't kill me right now because I hadn't suffered enough."

"Tell me what happened earlier in the day before this when his fiancée died."

She sighed, wrapped her hands around her knees, and stared down at the floor. "As you can imagine, he was devastated. He saw her in ICU virtually dying before his eyes believing no one helped her. I tried to explain she had a lacerated liver and her bleeding was uncontrollable. However, he wouldn't listen. He saw it totally different like I stood by and let her die."

To her dismay, her voice broke slightly.

"I'm not so certain you should work now. This is a problem," he advised gravely.

"I'm not leaving my job. No one's going to scare me away. I know to take his threat seriously. However, I believe this man is lashing out singularly because of his grief. No, I don't approve how ugly he's become, but I believe with all my heart he'll finally come to his senses and leave me alone."

"You're the most naive woman I've ever met in my life," he said disbelievingly, shaking his head. His tone was cutting. "Would you listen to yourself? You're making excuses for a guy who is completely disrupting your life, who may even kill you. Your brother is very worried about you and, from what you've told me this far, has every right to."

She glared back.

His voice was filled with derision. "You're all he has besides Sibella and his kids, and you're everything to him since your parents have passed. I feel like I already know you because how much your brother talked about you. He was always so proud of you and the good head you had on your shoulders. Right now, I question your logic. I'm here to protect you because of your brother, not because of you. However, I'm not going to sit here and beg for the job. I've got my own life to live."

She really pushed his buttons now.

It all came out in a rush.

"I never told Kyle because I didn't want him to worry. He has a baby coming and a lot on his plate. I don't want to inconvenience you either, but I already have. You had to bring my ID, and in turn, I cut your cheek. Plus, you had to rescue me from Dr. O'Malley, and now, you're stuck with having to watch over me. And God only knows if the man at the restaurant was actually sent to abduct and kill me," she added clearly exasperated. "Don't you mind being placed in the line of fire? I certainly don't feel right putting you in there."

He shrugged indifferently. "All in a day's work."

She shrugged too. "Okay, we'll do this. However, I honestly don't know how this will turn out—"

He interrupted her.

"Well, I'll tell you how it's going to work out. I'm going to keep you alive, and you're going to follow my ground rules."

"Ground rules?" she asked, fuming and expectant.

"Yes, for starters, you're not to go anywhere without me. Don't answer your door. Don't pick up your mail. I drive you wherever you go. This means you stay inside the vehicle until I know it's safe and then I'll escort you."

She laughed darkly while her lips curled in a secretive smile. "Escorting me is one of your duties, you say?"

He nodded and looked at her suspiciously.

"Then you'll escort me as part of your bodyguard duties to the hospital's foundation gala next week."

He raised his eyebrow at her warily.

"A gala to view a recently filmed hospital documentary before it's released to television for airing," she explained.

"It sounds painful," he admitted ruefully.

"More than you can even imagine. I don't want to go, but the hospital president demands my presence. I feel for you. But then again, you are my bodyguard, and I can't go anywhere without you, right?"

He grumbled something incoherent.

"You'll have to wear a suit," she confessed.

"I can handle it," he muttered, leaning back against the cushion linking his fingers together behind his head. He couldn't resist his eyes straying down her lithe, curvy body.

"And you'll have to endure a shopping trip with me to find a gown," she said hesitantly, sure she pressed her luck.

"I can handle that, too."

"So does this mean you dance?" she asked teasingly.

"No," he replied abruptly.

"Then what use are you to me if you won't dance with me?" she sighed, frowning at him.

"Maybe you might just need me to save your life? I'd probably become useful at that point, you think?" he replied sardonically.

She sat forward in her chair, her eyes resting on his lounging body. "So you'll open my car door for me? I don't think I've ever had a guy open my car door for me."

"Yes," he growled.

"How sweet."

"Sweet? It's not about being sweet," he clarified soberly. "My job is to protect you."

"Would you take a bullet for me?" she asked playfully. She tried to get a rise out of him, enthralled with the way his eyes smoldered at her when he was annoyed. She imagined she'd see a lot of that particular trait before it was over. She'd give him a couple of days, and he'd probably want to shoot her himself.

"Yes," he said without hesitation. "Your brother took a bullet for me," he said then switched topics.

"Now, I want his name."

Again, she hesitated.

He exhaled. "You realize I can have this man's name at my fingertips in less than five minutes? I'm asking you to be cordial. It matters not to me."

"Mark Malone," she breathed. "He was the fiancé of my patient Lisa Thomas who just recently passed. A real tall guy almost your height and build, dark short hair, military guy if I had to guess."

"I've got to go pick up a few things," he said suddenly, rising from her couch, walking around her end table.

"Okay," she said nonchalantly.

He stopped, looked at her expectantly. "You'll need to accompany me to my home to grab a few things."

"I don't need 24/7 care, and you had a life before today."

"I insist," he said quietly.

"Okay," she said, "I'll have to change."

Fifteen minutes later, she returned wearing too tight jeans and a pink blouse seemingly stretched too snug across her breasts and could easily become a magnet for him if he wasn't careful. She strapped on her tennis shoes and jauntily walked by the kitchen island snapping up her car keys.

He looked at her questionably, his brow rose.

"I forgot. I ride with you. I'd hate anyone to see my car with *killer* written across the hood. I'd scare the pedestrians."

His laugh was marvelous, catching.

Together they walked outside into the sunshine and then she remembered.

Her step faltered.

The *murder cycle* sat in her driveway.

He eyed her curiously.

"This morning, you looked exhilarated sitting on my bike."

Still, she hesitated.

He crooked his finger at her.

Her legs abandoned her and took off heading his direction without her. She wondered if he realized just how enticing his little gesture was.

He opened a side compartment, lifted out a black bag, and pulled out a shiny black helmet with a clear shield.

"Storm, do you realize we see almost thirty-five hundred patients a year at the trauma center?"

He reached a tentative hand toward her cheek, smoothed away a few wisps of her hair. "Is that so?"

"And a recent study showed motorcycle crashes, amongst car accidents, falls, and pedestrian accidents…" She trailed off as he situated the helmet on her head, fastening the strap under her chin, effectively cutting off her lecture. He swept her up in his arms and sat her on the back of his bike.

"Was part of the 75 percent of those patients," she advised him in a muffled voice.

All the while, his lips threatened to break into a smile as he got onto the bike. He turned the ignition key. The powerful engine roared to life. He kicked aside the stand and looked at her over his shoulder, giving her a breathtaking smile.

"Put your arms around me," he ordered over the roaring hum of the engine.

Her eyes widened and her heartbeat thumped like a drum in her ears as she contemplated his request. Unbeknownst to him, that's all she'd wanted to do since he walked into the restaurant, was to touch his hard muscled body. Reality settled in, he asked this of her so she wouldn't fall off the bike, for safety reasons only.

Then it dawned on her what she contemplated: taking a ride with Storm who lived life on the dangerous side, wearing no helmet, and undoubtedly ignoring speed limit signs.

She wrapped her arms around his waist and hung on for dear life.

He felt her legs hug his backside, squeeze him while her cheek pressed against his back. He closed his eyes, easily imaging her legs wrapped around his waist as he—

Storm shook his head derailing those thoughts. Oh no, it couldn't happen. He wouldn't even think about it.

As the bike thundered beneath them, she clenched her eyes shut once she felt him release the clutch and accelerate the bike forward down the driveway. Her arms tightened around his waist. She felt his chest rumble.

From laughter.

A quick glance over his shoulder showed her eyes squeezed shut through the helmet visor.

He drove at a snail's pace, and she knew this was only for her benefit. She finally felt enough ease to open her eyes and look around at the cars, people, buildings, and gorgeous landscaping rush past her.

It was exhilarating.

She let out a squeal of delight.

The warm breeze ruffled the ends of her hair and her bare arms. She glimpsed up at the tall buildings she drove by at all hours of the day and night without really seeing them.

Towering hunks of glass, brick, and stainless steel soared toward the heavens were awe-inspiring. The green-glassed multistoried building was an insurance company. She never noticed before the glass changed from a jade green color to a hint of deep blue with each sweep of the sun's rays. She stared up at the art museum, the four-storied gray-bricked building, and never noticed the intricate concrete scrollwork placed just below the roofline. Nor had she noticed the large tulip urns overflowing with concrete fruit at each roof corner.

She no longer felt so exhausted but anxious to see more, to do more. She wasn't sure where his home was located, how long it would take to get there. For the first time in a long time, she enjoyed herself. Only here and now was all that mattered to her. Was she really on the back of a motorcycle with Storm, and was he really coming to stay with her, protect her? It seemed surreal. Maybe she was dreaming of him again. Yet his hot skin felt very real under her fingertips.

Unconsciously, she moved her fingers and reveled in the feel of him, specifically, the concaves of his stomach muscle. The breadth of his broad shoulders blocked the wind from her. She could only imagine him without his clothes. Why, he'd give Adonis—the young Greek god known for his handsomeness—a run for his money.

He came to a rolling stop at the light and laughed under his breath. Did he just imagine her feeling him up? The way her fingertips traveled across his belly and ribs sent shivers down his spine. Yet many women had touched him in his lifetime, and he discarded their touch so easily. What was so different about her? Maybe because he spent the past ten years waiting to meet her?

Her arms weren't wrapped as tightly around him, signaling she was more relaxed and trusted him. That made him smile, much better than the terrified look on her face when he slid the helmet over her head. She looked like a bird about to take flight.

"Enjoying yourself?" he asked.

"Immensely," she returned. "Thank you."

The light turned green, and they were off once again with her leaning against him snugly. And she remained so until they reached Amelia Island and pulled into his driveway.

A glass house.

It was three stories of magnificent towering glass with front balconies stretching across the perimeters giving breathtaking views of the ocean, the type of house you'd see thumbing through a luxury magazine. It was three times the size of her modest home and certainly not the type of home she pictured him living in. Nothing could've surprised her more, especially one supposedly living off a navy pension. She pictured him in a small apartment, perhaps a townhouse. The location wasn't surprising considering she heard of his love of the ocean from Kyle.

A garage door lifted upon their arrival, one of four. He drove the bike into a stall next to a vehicle covered with a light gray cloth concealing everything with the exception of its shiny chrome wheels and low profile tires.

He swung easily off his bike and watched her remove her helmet. She struggled to get off the seat, her effort futile. He walked up and effortlessly scooped her off the bike and set her on her feet. He breathed in the scent of strawberries from her hair.

"Can we take a quick walk on the beach first?" she asked, her voice hopeful.

He grinned at her. "Sure."

Together, they walked from the garage where he stopped and raised the lid of a slate gray box attached to the garage wall. He planted his palm against a glass plate. The door sailed down so quietly, she barely heard it shut.

As they walked down the beach, he looked over at her, watched her long hair blow about her as she looked out onto the ocean. The look on her face was priceless as she tilted her face to the sun. Evidently she hadn't been on an excursion in some time.

She rushed forward and scooped up a snow-white seashell. Her face was ecstatic and oblivious as she gazed down at the seashell in the palm of her hand, unaware a wave was about to hit her full force.

He hooked his arm around her waist, setting her back several feet.

Excitement glittered in her eyes.

"Thank you," she said breathlessly, looking up at him. "I never saw it coming."

"I know," he said, smiling down at her.

She felt a sense of peacefulness walking down the beach, a calmness washed over her as she listened to the tumbling tides rush in and retreat into the ocean. Above her, the seagulls fluttered, flying up high in the sky. She could taste the salt in the sea spray and smell the seaweed. She gazed out into the ocean and saw two sailboats afloat with their bone-white sails bellowing wildly in the breeze while distant water skiers chased after a sleek white speedboat.

"Have you ever wondered where a seashell has traveled once it's washed upon the beach? Like how many beaches in foreign countries it's landed?" she asked, raising a quizzical brow.

"Probably a staggering amount," he said, nodding.

As they approached an ice cream vendor on a three-wheeled bicycle, he pulled out his wallet.

"Ice cream?" he asked.

"You're getting ice cream?" she asked surprised.

"I love ice cream. I'm a bear without it," he admitted with a sheepish grin.

"You don't look like you indulge in much ice cream."

He returned with a smug smile. "Ice cream is an indulgence and also my weakness, hard to resist."

She chose a drumstick while he chose an ice cream sandwich.

"So you're retired?" she asked.

"Yes," he said, not elaborating further.

"How do you spend your time?" she asked as she nibbled on the nut topping of her drumstick.

"I swim, go boating, fishing, snorkeling, have a barbeque some nights on the beach," he said as he took a bite of his ice cream sandwich.

Have haunting, hair-raising nightmares.

From her brief conversations with Kyle, she knew over the past year Storm had fallen off the radar and was working through some problems. She never knew the details, never asked. But now, she was more than curious.

"Do you work?" she asked.

He laughed suddenly.

"I've traveled the world as a SEAL, and I'm almost thirty-seven years old. I'm okay with what I'm doing now," he said as he looked over at her. "Perhaps you might take the same advice and enjoy yourself more often."

"I enjoy myself," she defended half-heartedly.

"You said that with about as much conviction as a goat."

"You're right," she said, smiling over at him. "I guess I need to work on that part." She changed the subject swiftly. "Do you have any siblings?"

"I have a sister six years younger than me," he replied, glancing over at her. He groaned inwardly, sucked in his breath as he watched her swirl her tongue around the tip of her ice cream cone, lapping up the vanilla ice cream.

"Are your parents still living?" she inquired.

He coughed. Once again, he witnessed her lick her ice cream cone enthusiastically. It was nothing short of erotic.

"Yes, they're both enjoying their retirement to the fullest and making up for lost time."

"How romantic," she said wistfully.

He stopped, popped the rest of his ice cream sandwich in his mouth, and chewed on it while she devoured her sugar cone.

She wanted to learn more about him, but now wasn't the time. He spent a great amount of effort trying to evade her questions with vague answers.

"Okay, back to your house," she proposed, licking her fingertips.

Her small gesture just about did him in. He was happy to return to his house so he could keep himself occupied and not think about what he was missing.

They walked silently across the beach toward his home, coming to arrive again at the garage. After he gained entrance, they walked through the garage's side door. He swung it wide and motioned her to walk before him as only a true gentleman would.

A sharp bark resounded on the other side of the door.

She stepped back hesitantly.

"Apollo," Storm supplied. "He knows I'm bringing him a snack," he added with a chuckle.

He opened another door for her where she stepped onto a glossy wide-planked floor stretching endlessly leading off into several corridors. Across the room, she looked upon a handsome German shepherd who sat obediently on his hind fours, looking at her curiously, his tail wagging and sweeping the floor around him.

"Apollo, come," Storm ordered softly.

Apollo cautiously walked up and sniffed her feet; his tail wagged furiously while simultaneously getting a ruffle against the ears from Storm.

"Come here, you pretty boy," she urged as she hunched down before him where he promptly gave her his paw while he sniffed her hand. He was satisfied as indicated by his tail wagging and his eyes sparking with approval.

"Apollo is a military K-9 dog, a great guard dog. I'd like to bring him with us if you don't object."

"Yes, of course. He's beautiful. Plus, he'd help me keep you in line," she teased.

"He's a loyal dog. He'd never betray me over a mere woman."

"Not even for a tasty steak?"

"You'd have to do much better than that," he challenged. "I'll give you a hint. Grab a ball and walk toward the beach, and you'll have a friend forever. Oh, he does like chocolate chip cookies even though it's not good for him."

She laughed then hugged Apollo against her. "Your master loves chocolate chip cookies, doesn't he?"

Apollo barked in agreement.

She stood then, her eyes lifted up to the empty stark white walls.

The house was empty.

He read the expression on her face and realized bringing her here was a mistake. It would bring forth questions, albeit innocent questions, but questions he was unprepared to answer.

"How long have you lived here?" she asked him.

"A couple of years."

"Did your interior designer abandon you?" she asked teasingly.

"It would seem," he said warily as he turned on his heel and walked toward the staircase where Apollo followed, taking two steps at a time.

His whole demeanor changed, and she realized all too late that there was a reason why his home looked as it did, and she had no right to ask questions about his private life.

She glanced over at the twelve-foot windows covering the front of his home, facing directly out to the ocean. Long white sheer curtains framed the bank of windows.

As they walked up three flights of stairs encased with frosted glass, she became engrossed with the frosted glass etchings of sea life that stretched with each flight of stairs. She turned around to see him walk down a long corridor that led to a very large room.

His bedroom.

His massive bed was parked against the far side of the wall facing the ocean. She eyed it enviously, picturing herself snuggled under the deep golden coverlet, the color of rich honey, and falling asleep to the rhythm of the waves.

He walked across the room into a large walk-in closet with the floor-to-ceiling cabinetry. The room was large enough to house another good-size bedroom. He pulled out a large black leather duffle bag and tugged shirts and jeans off hangers, quickly folded them, and stuffed them inside.

"You really don't need to stay with me," she said, suddenly feeling like she was causing him a ton of inconvenience.

He shook his head at her and humorously suggested, "Or we could stay here," he said, glancing around the empty bedroom carrying the echo of his voice and footsteps and the soft roar of the ocean.

She laughed under her breath. They had the same situation regarding sleeping arrangements, only one bed available at her home.

It dawned on her, and she comprehended the knowing, teasing look he gave her.

They had to share a bed.

Oh my god!

Blood rushed to her cheeks, making them explode with heat. She pushed the thought from her mind for now yet couldn't escape the butterflies fluttering inside her belly.

"I like your place better. It has such massive potential, but then again, you know this, don't you?" she asked over her shoulder at him as she walked over to stand before the windows. A large cruise liner floated at sea like a speck on the horizon, the waves crashed, rolled in as the seagulls flew overhead. "Especially the view you have from here. It looks like a post card, surreal. I'd never want to leave this place."

"Yeah, I like it," he said softly, glancing out onto the ocean as he zipped his bag.

"And I must say, very clean for a guy," she said, laughing under her breath.

"Her name is Rosalinda and she cleans the place once a week," he confessed with grin.

"Ah, a maid. The secret's out."

She sauntered over to the only other piece of furnishing in his bedroom, a long slim table containing a small oval photograph of a young girl with the ocean and the sun shining over her shoulder, her pale blonde hair braided with a few loose strands peeking out with a blemish of wet sand against her right cheek. Her baby blue eyes sparkled, relaying her adoration for the picture taker.

"Who is this lovely little girl?" she asked curiously. She picked up the picture frame and realized the photograph was taken in front of his home.

She glanced over at him and saw the sudden torment in his eyes, saw his face close, shut down all his emotions. In its place, cold, hard, dead eyes. He came to stand behind her and looked at the picture frame she held in her hands. The very same look she saw in his eyes earlier today at the restaurant. Unintentionally, she brought back some very painful memories for him.

His voice was gruff. "Her name was Calypsia."

"Was?" She flinched. "I'm sorry."

Her face sobered as she looked back down at the photograph. "Who took this picture if you don't mind me asking?"

"I did."

"I thought as much," she mused.

"Why?"

She laughed softly. "You seem to have persuasive advantage over the female population no matter their age."

"We were celebrating her learning how to swim," he offered.

"You taught her?"

"I did," he added with a slow nod.

She sensed regret in his voice but never probed further. She replaced the picture frame back on the table.

He slung his duffle bag over his shoulder and stormed from the bedroom.

Obviously, the child and swimming was a connection to the grief-stricken look on his face. She wouldn't pry. She scrambled to follow him down the staircase, a not so easy a task by the way he glided effortlessly down the many steps. As much as she wanted to explore his home, there wasn't an opportunity as he and Apollo entered the door leading to the garage.

He walked over to the far side of the garage and pushed open a door revealing a hidden access into another room.

She never followed him. She waited.

A few moments later, he carried out two large briefcases.

She never questioned their contents. Now wasn't the time as she watched his irritated jerky movements. Next, he walked over and whipped off the cover of a vehicle.

Her eyes widened at the car's beauty.

A sleek black-on-black BMW.

She wouldn't have pictured him in such a car, instead a truck or SUV perhaps, or even a tank for that matter, but not such a lustrous-looking vehicle. It seemed too formal and definitely went against his ruggedness.

He filled the trunk with the briefcases and his duffle bag before coming to the passenger door and opening it wide. He stood there expectantly.

She jumped to attention. She slid into the seat enveloping her like a glove. The interior smelled just like him—rich leather, spicy, earthy. She inhaled the ambrosia.

He let Apollo in the backseat and then slid into the seat next to her, reached up, and pushed the button on the garage door opener. The door behind them rose swiftly. He roared the powerful and throaty engine to life, blazing a trail of colorful lights across the dashboard with the speedometer needle making a full half-moon swipe as he shifted the car into gear and pulled out of the garage. He accelerated out of the driveway onto the roadway.

Tilting her head to one side, she stole a slanted look at him. He drove with one hand on the steering wheel and the other lying fisted against his leg; he stared straight ahead, anguish clearly outlined on his face.

"Storm, I'm sorry, I never meant to pry."

A part of her wanted to reach over and hold his hand, give him the comfort she knew he so desperately needed, yet she refrained, not sure how he'd react.

Storm was exasperated. Why couldn't he just tell her about that part of his life? Then again, he knew why, because it was the blackest part of his life, when he was another person so blinded by revenge he ate it, breathed it, and lived it while it consumed him whole. He made decisions he didn't regret. How could he explain the actions of his black heart to a woman with the purest of hearts, a woman who actually saved the life of the man who had all intentions of possibly killing her without her being repulsed by him?

He couldn't.

They drove in silence.

11

He took her house key from her, unlocked the door, and ushered her inside with Apollo following, his wet nose in the air smelling the different scents.

"You look exhausted. You should go to bed," he suggested.

She nodded with a wry smile. "Four-thirty in the morning rolls around pretty quickly."

Inwardly, Storm cringed. When was the last time he woke up at four-thirty in the morning? He couldn't remember. "May I grab a shower?"

"Of course, I'll lay out some towels for you," she offered, leading the way to the master bath. She reached into the linen closet, grabbed the towels, turned around, and caught his reflection through a large mirror. The towels, suddenly forgotten toppled onto the floor.

He had taken off his shirt and unsnapped his jeans when he saw her reflection through the mirror.

He was *huge.*

His tanned upper body bulged with bunched muscle with every movement of his arms, back, chest, and shoulders. His chest had a V-shaped pattern of dark fine hair trickling down his stomach.

He was breathtaking.

She stepped closer to him, coming up behind him. Along the lines of his exquisite beauty was also a battered, war-torn body riveted with scars for God and his country.

Tentatively, she reached out a fingertip, touched his burning hot skin. An electric current jolted through him, seared him with her touch. His body jerked involuntarily.

Gently, she traced a jagged scar across his top left shoulder blade—a knife wound. Next, a dime-sized puckered scar; a gunshot wound located halfway down his back missing his spinal column by less than a few inches and could've easily rendered him paralyzed. He was lucky. Her fingertips feathered deliberately across yet four other gunshot wounds then onto a host of other scars as she reveled at his resilience, knowing his past heroics and number of times he'd laid his life on the line for his country. Also, what it took on the part of a surgeon to fix yet only imagining the pain he endured. Her eyes flickered up past his shoulder where their eyes met and held through the reflection of the mirror.

His eyes smoldered, his hands fisted at his sides.

She watched him, still staggered by his beauty.

Storm was on fire.

He willed himself to fight the urge to grab her and take her to bed and give her an experience she'd never forget. He had to remember his real purpose here. He had to keep his emotions tapped down, keep her at arm's length. When emotions got involved, it was a recipe for mistakes.

But God, he wanted her. He wanted her bad.

Deliberately, he stepped away from her. "Thank you for the towels," he said softly. He stripped the belt from his jean loops followed by a loud snap.

His voice stopped her at the door.

"Do you think you can manage to stay out of trouble while I take a shower?" In the back of his mind, he nearly laughed, whom was he fooling? She was a magnet for trouble and had been most of her life so he learned from his many conversations with Reaper.

She rolled her eyes, never bothered with a reply. Obviously, Kyle highlighted her youthful escapades to Storm.

"Don't leave this house. Don't answer your door or your phone unless it's your brother," he ordered sternly.

She frowned. She hated being ordered around.

He unzipped his jeans and started tugging them off.

That sent her careening out the door, his laughter trailing after her.

She walked into the kitchen with weak knees and a heart zipping wildly as she pulled out a frozen macaroni and cheese dinner tray and put it in the oven. She hoped he liked macaroni and cheese, a household staple. Then she made her way to her bedroom and stretched out on her bed.

Apollo followed and lay down at the foot of the bed.

How very odd. As she lay in bed, she felt nothing like she felt just the day before, apprehensive and scared out of her mind. She felt safe because of *him*.

The phone rang.

It has to be Kyle, she thought as she answered the phone with a smile in her voice.

"Hi, Kyle."

"I'm starting to like the game we're playing," the man said in a low, quiet voice.

Her breath caught and her heart danced its own jig. She never paid attention, just automatically assumed it was Kyle following up on his promise to call her later.

Finally, she found her voice. "I'm not playing your game. Who is this, and how did you get my phone number?" Oddly enough, this man didn't sound like Mark Malone. God, she couldn't believe she picked up the damn phone. White knuckled, she clenched the phone while the earpiece trembled against her ear.

"Yes, you're playing right into my hands."

"Who is this?"

"I'm not quite finished with you, but soon, your time will come, and then I'm going to kill you," he said in a deadly calm voice.

She slammed the receiver down on the hook with trembling hands. She swung her legs over the side of the bed, sat up, and held her head in her hands. The walls started closing in, the floorboards raised, hovered, and drifted. She closed her eyes and willed herself to stave off the black shroud threatening to envelope her. She took several deep breaths.

For several moments, she sat and stared out the window watching the hydrangea flowers weave in the gentlewind. She could almost smell their heady fragrance.

Resentment started to build inside her. She wouldn't become a prisoner in her own home nor be intimidated.

She grabbed her scissors and tore out the front door. Minutes later, Summer walked back through her foyer carrying a crystal vase full of daisies, roses, and hydrangeas. She caught her reflection in the oval gilded mirror.

Exhaustion and tension etched her face as if she hadn't slept in a week or more, and technically, she hadn't. But then again, who could sleep when their life was in such turmoil? With her free hand, she rubbed the back of her stiff neck. She was more upset than she wanted to admit over the chilling mysterious phone call she just received.

The door to her bedroom suddenly opened.

She whirled around in surprise.

The crystal vase slid from her hands and onto the floor with an explosive crash sending chards of glass splintering against the white tile, water splashed, and flowers lay in a heap at her feet. And still, she couldn't take her eyes off the vision before her.

Storm.

Gone were his long locks of glorious tumultuous hair along with his thick beard and mustache, and in its place was a very different-looking man. He wore black shorts, a thin white T-shirt, and was barefooted.

She was enthralled.

Apollo greeted Storm, wagging his tail uncontrollably.

Storm rushed forward. "Are you okay? What happened?"

"Just a slight accident," she said breathlessly as she got down on her hands and knees and began picking up remnants of the broken vase.

Storm dropped down beside her and gently plucked up the jagged glass she held in her hands.

"I'll get this. We can't chance your hands getting pricked now can we, Dr. Benson?"

She shook her head, exasperated as she looked down at his hands, long fingered and strong. "Thank you, but I can take care of this."

"Well, not today. What happened?" he asked, looking over at her.

With his face just inches from hers, she stared openly at him. Their eyes met and held a few seconds longer than they should have.

Without the camouflage of his beard, the planes of his face were more angular and gaunt. His hair was cut short, neat, and overall gave him the persona of a guy who modeled for a men's style magazine.

He raised his eyes to find her watching him. She looked at him with dreamy eyes. Pausing, he gazed at her speculatively. She dropped her eyes then.

"Why don't you have a seat on the couch," he said, nodding across the room to the sitting area. "And while you're sitting there, think about how you're going to explain to me how you got these flowers," he said tightly, picking up the soaked flower petals off the floor.

Her mouth formed an *O*.

He walked off, and she could swear she heard him mumbling under his breath about women being pains in the ass.

She watched him retrieve a mop and pail from the kitchen and mopped the floor. When he finished, he returned them to the garage. Before she could gather her wits, she realized yet another rule she broke.

Her mouth formed another *O*.

"God damn it!"

She heard his muffled expletive bellowed in the garage. Again, she sighed heavily.

Another rule she broke.

Then the door opened and closed in the kitchen firmly with snap, nothing like the crashing echo from the garage door, just enough to announce even more his displeasure.

She closed her eyes, laid her head back on the cushion of the couch, took a deep breath, and waited. She had a feeling she'd break plenty of his rules before it was over.

His heavy angry footsteps announced his approach along with Apollo's soft padded feet as both came to stand before her.

She made the mistake of laughing, just a chuckle. She couldn't help it. Her entire situation felt unbelievable and surreal to her. In less than a week, her life had been turned upside down nothing short of chaotic. Her normal routine busted up like pieces of a puzzle falling where they pleased with her having no control. Her freedom disappeared and in its place many sleepless days and nights full of anxiety. She never felt so disorganized, so apprehensive, constantly questioning her actions at home, at work. Now, her bodyguard stood before her, about to read her the riot act because she disobeyed his rules about going outside. In her mind, he should be happy she remembered to close the doors! It was laughable and maddening at the same time.

"Please," she whispered her plea and looked away from him. She had no desire or the energy for a confrontation. She was fresh out.

He stared down at her, his body tense with fury at her lack of obedience in keeping her doors locked especially knowing her life was in danger. This was only a sign of things to come. She was going to drive him to a straitjacket.

When he saw a lone tear escape and trickle down the side of her cheek, all the bluster left him.

As soon as she reached out to him, touched the warmth of his outstretched hand, she felt safe.

The next minute, she was in his arms.

He was warm, hard yet soft, as she laid her head against his chest and listened to his heartbeat rioting against her ear. Being in his arms was the most exhilarating, comforting feeling she'd known in a very long time. Suddenly, her problem no longer seemed so large and looming, threatening to stifle her. Warm, protective, safe arms wrapped around her and kept her snug against his tall, lithe body.

"You're in so much trouble," he growled low with surprisingly, a hint of laughter. Cupping her chin, his eyes searched her upturned face, seeing her vulnerability. He hated seeing her like this. "The only thing saving your ass right now is I smell food, and I'm starving."

She felt his lips brush against her hair, sending a rush of molten heat through her veins. Completely insane and ridiculously impulsive, she had the strongest urge to kiss him. She looked up into smoldering gray eyes darkened with desire.

The next instant, he stepped away from her, held her by the shoulders. His breathing was as ragged as her own when he swiped away her tear.

Apollo stepped between them and looked up imploringly at Storm. When he didn't get his attention, he gave Summer a big lathered lick on her ankle making her giggle. She reached down and petted him, thanking him for making her laugh.

The oven timer went off. They sat down on stools at the kitchen island and ate quietly. All the while, she waited for it.

The lecture.

He didn't disappoint.

"Where did you get those flowers, Summer?" he asked with his fork hovering over his plate.

"In my backyard," she replied with a serene smile.

"Your doors were unlocked."

She acknowledged with a nod.

He looked over at her with disbelieving eyes as if berating a ten-year-old child.

"Yes, I know. I broke your rules," she snapped. "I'm not used to someone trying to kill me or someone dictating my every move."

His shoulders dropped, his patience skating on thin ice. "I can't impress upon you the seriousness of this situation. The man knows where you live, and therefore, you can't go out there alone without me."

"He also knows my phone number," she confessed.

He gaped at her. "He called here?"

"Yes," she replied. "Just a few moments ago, I thought it was Kyle calling me back."

"What did he say?"

"I was playing into his hands, and my time was coming for him to kill me."

He glanced down at her trembling hand holding her fork.

"Are you scared?"

She shook her head.

He knew better.

"He's not going to touch you," he promised as he reached over and covered her hand with his.

"The man didn't sound like Mark Malone."

"Duly noted," Storm replied thoughtfully. If it wasn't Mark Malone, then who the hell was it?

"This is the best macaroni and cheese I've ever ate," he confessed, trying to turn to a more lighthearted conversation.

"It's frozen, and I practically live on it," she said as she got up and put the dishes in the sink. She jerked open the freezer door dramatically and waved toward shelves stockpiled with all flavors of ice cream. "I also live on ice cream."

His eyes brightened. "A woman after my own heart," he sighed.

Later that night after eating ice cream and watching television together, she fought sleep because she didn't want the night to end.

He picked her up in his arms, carried her to bed, and tucked her in. He went to return to the couch, his makeshift bed, when she stopped him at the door.

"Stay with me," she whispered. "I hope you don't think it's inappropriate. I'd just feel safe if you were close by."

No! his gut screamed.

The sweet heady scent of strawberries drifted toward him as he slid between the sheets, giving him a potent reminder of the danger involved. It was equivalent of someone dangling a thick steak before a hungry, heavily aroused lion. No rest for him tonight; he had to stay on his side of the bed no matter what.

God, it would be hard.

"Thank you," she whispered as she rolled onto her side facing away from him yet feeling the heat radiate from his body.

After tossing and turning numerous times, she fell asleep with her hand resting on his forearm.

It could get complicated.

He hated complications.

12

Just before dawn, he heard a faint banging sound, perhaps a door swinging back and forth in the gusty wind. He opened his eyes to shadows with streaks of lightning flashing across the room. Rain pelted hard against the windows, perfect sleeping weather. He had no desire to get out of bed on this night. He was warm, comfortable, and free of nightmares. His dreams were peaceful, dreamless, just the way he preferred it. He blinked his eyes several times trying to clear the deep fog of sleep, feeling somewhat disoriented as he looked around the unfamiliar bedroom.

He was hard as a rock this morning, not surprising, he was every morning, but this particular morning, he was thoroughly aroused, throbbing with a need for release as fiery heat surged and swept through his loins.

Suddenly, cold toes rubbed against his calf, making him suddenly realize he wasn't alone. Then, a slim, shapely arm flung itself across his stomach.

He jerked in reaction.

Her.

She lay on her side facing him, plastered against him. Her blonde hair lay in disarray across her face and some on his shoulder. She slept soundly, her face peaceful, her lips only an inch from his arm.

Just then, an attractive shapely thigh slid from beneath the white sheet revealing itself as it climbed seductively up his leg, parting her robe, the very heat of her lay intimately against his leg. Being asleep, she had no clue the conflicting, turbulent emotions she wreaked on him. He concentrated hard to dispel any emotion, but what happened next left him breathless.

Her hand slid slowly down his stomach, coming to rest against the length of his cock; the only barrier, his trunks.

He sucked in his breath, and his body visibly jerked. He took several long, deep breaths and knew he had to get the hell out of bed. He couldn't withstand the torment. Gently, he reached for her hand to lift it off, but instead, she squeezed and then began fondling him.

In her sleep.

He was going through pure hell, experiencing a forbidden pleasure knowing the last thing he wanted her to do was to stop. He stole a glimpse of her shapely curved hip and itched to glide his hands over her. Her robe gaped open where he saw her breast nearly spilling out. He wanted to reach in, massage it, take it in his mouth, swirl his hot tongue around her nipple, and suckle it. She had a heart-stopping body that haunted him from the first moment he met her. Not to mention, he couldn't have dreamt of a better scenario to be with Summer Benson, ripe for the taking.

He squeezed his eyes shut and felt his control wavering. His urge was herculean strength to roll her onto her back, sink deep inside her, ride her with abandon, and have her scream his name in ecstasy, all without having to acknowledge the consequences.

But he refused to allow it to get that far.

Summer immensely enjoyed her dream. The faceless man intoxicated her senses as he shoved a fist in her long hair and rocked his hard body against hers. She felt his hand glide up and over her hip, then down the length of her thigh, sending shivers up her spine. A warm hand fondled and cupped her breasts while a wet hot tongue swirled around her nipple. She moaned into his mouth as she caressed him with her hand.

"Stop, please," he whispered his plea through gritted teeth, resting his hand atop hers.

She heard a man's voice and realized she wasn't dreaming.

She stirred.

Her eyelids fluttered open to stare back into a set of blazing gray eyes.

Storm's eyes.

She swallowed a startled gasp.

Her sleepy eyes popped open wide with disbelief as she realized where her hand had found a home, her leg thrown over his, for that matter where her entire body landed, virtually on top of him. She was half-naked. Mortification finally dawned when he lifted her hand off his cock. She shot up in bed, her body covered in a sheen of sweat. Her chest rose and fell with each harsh breath she took. She scrambled away from him quickly to the other side of the king-sized bed.

That dream felt so real!

"Oh god, I'm sorry," she squeaked out as if she swallowed a frog. She wrapped her robe tightly around her.

She stole a glance at him.

His face and body was coiled with tension and so was something else she noticed when her eyes dropped below his waist.

Rigid, hard, and lying against his stomach.

She could see the outline of him perfectly through his trunks. It pulsed like a heartbeat.

Her eyes met his and held for an indefinable moment until he spoke, his voice, gruff and barely above a whisper, his breathing as harsh and ragged as hers. "We can't."

"No, we absolutely can't," she repeated in a stammer. Yet the feeling of him in her hand burned in her memory. She shuddered. "You have a girlfriend," she stated not really asking the question, but assuming.

He shook his head. "No girlfriend," he confessed. "Dr. O'Malley?" he asked her.

"Oh no, just a coworker," she stammered.

Why didn't he want her? The question suddenly crept in the back of her mind, along with it a whirlwind of insecurity that crawled around and planted itself firmly in her subconscious.

Maybe she wasn't his type, perhaps not as tall as he'd like, as big breasted, the wrong hair color, or maybe he liked platinum blondes. She remembered all too well her reflection in the mirror earlier tonight. Or maybe it wasn't about her appearance but about her career. She intimidated some men, specifically other physicians, and never clearly understood why.

Or maybe he wanted no involvement because he believed it would influence how he protected her. Maybe he was right. Or was it about her brother? Either way, he planned to keep a respectful distance by either his own will or Kyle's insistence.

"Next time, I'm going to have to charge you," he said humorously, trying to make light of the uncomfortable situation. He rolled easily out of bed and reached for his gun lying on the nightstand beside the bed.

"Don't worry, it won't happen again," she informed him, making herself busy situating the covers around her. Anything to avoid his gaze now leveled on her. What an awkward situation she'd placed them. This would go to the top of the list of everything she'd ever done to embarrass and humiliate herself.

He sighed as he watched her. She took his rejection personally. "It's for the best. It's nothing personal," he replied, walking around to the foot of the bed.

He was a basket case.

He was rejecting *her* advances. The single woman he envisioned these past years walking into an operating room wearing nothing but her doctor's coat and red high heels, wrenching her coat apart, shearing off her buttons as she straddled him on a trauma cart. Yeah, he envisioned that hot little number for many years, having full-blown sex in the middle of an operating room with lights blazing. It sounded kinky and ridiculous yet countless nights he pleasured himself with that very image in his mind.

Beyond his fantasy, she was too good for him, all pure and innocent, while his soul was the blackest. He was reckless, volatile, and took what he wanted when he wanted it and asked questions later. She had her life all in order and his was in chaos. He'd keep his distance from her in the future and save them both from unnecessary heartbreak.

Lying on the floor beside her bed, Apollo suddenly got to his feet and followed Storm, coming to rest at the foot of the bed. He looked up expectantly at Storm, wagging his tail slowly.

Storm looked down at him and then pointed to Summer in bed. "Guard," he ordered.

"Where are you going?" she asked alarmed, seeing the menacing handgun he carried at his side.

"Don't get out of bed, stay here," he ordered. "I'm just going to go check something out."

"Be careful," she rushed out at his retreating figure. She listened for him as he walked across the corridor, across her home, and couldn't hear him. She heard her barn door stop slamming up against the side of the barn. She really needed to have the door hinge repaired. When it quieted, she knew he secured the door.

A moment later, he appeared back at her bedroom door without a sound. He was soaked through, his hair dripping wet, curling at the ends. Raindrops glistened off his body.

She forced herself to look away, made herself forget how much her body craved a soft caress. She wouldn't allow herself to contemplate the magical spell his fingertips could easily weave on her body.

The look of longing she gave him made him breathless. He needed a cold shower, but glancing over at the clock told him it was only one-thirty in the morning.

"If I could grab a pillow, I'll check out on the couch," he suggested.

"That couch isn't the most comfortable couch to sleep on. Besides, I'd feel guilty sleeping in such a large bed, and you having to sleep on a couch too short for you." She waved to the other side of the bed. "There's plenty of room for both of us, and I promise I won't disturb you."

He grinned at her. "This really isn't a good idea, believe me." Behind his smile, the warning was real, and he hoped she took him seriously.

"It will be perfectly fine," she assured him as she tightened her robe more securely around her. She laid back down, faced the opposite wall, and covered herself completely, bringing the blankets up and tucking them under her chin.

She listened to him quietly walk into the master bath and then minutes later return to bed. The bed dipped slightly under his weight, making her all the more aware what she was missing, feeling the heat radiate from his body no matter how hard she tried to ignore.

So why was Storm different? Why was he so hard to ignore? She was perfectly fine two days ago without any intimacy, yet he made her want him with a passion, creating an intensifying need threatening to erupt with the barest contact with him. Compared to the few men in her past and Storm, there was a world of difference. Just from meeting him one day, she could only imagine he wouldn't think twice about ravaging a woman's body on the beach, on a boat, in the backseat of a car if he wanted her. He'd be ruthless, flinging caution to the wind and taking her. Her past acquaintances were nothing but proper. Proper was nice, but proper was also boring.

Storm wasn't proper.

Perhaps she needed to think proper thoughts and stop fantasizing about him. This was about him protecting her from a psychopath—nothing more, nothing less. He had no interest in her in a romantic sense and best kept that way.

As she closed her eyes, she fought desperately to forget how wonderfully peaceful it felt to sleep against his warm body feeling protected.

She sniffed her pillowcase. It smelled like him, like the sun and rain with a hint of husky spice. It was heady and intoxicating and guaranteed her no peaceful sleep for the remainder of the night. She flung it to the floor and could have sworn she felt his side of the bed rumble with his laughter.

She sighed wistfully and sank into oblivion.

It felt like she'd just closed her eyes when her pager beeped shrilly. At first she thought it was her alarm clock, but when she glanced at the time, it was only three-thirty in the morning. She reached for her pager and saw the nine-nine trauma code. Immediately, she got out of bed and dressed. Within five minutes, she was ready to walk out the door. She walked to his side of bed. He slept so soundly, so peaceful lying on his side. She'd never seen a man look more inviting in bed. He was simply breathtaking.

She didn't have the heart to wake him since she was the reason why he spent such a restless night. She would drive straight to the hospital, just minutes away, but so not to alarm him, she'd leave him a note behind.

13

Morning came all too quickly.

She snuck out to her car like a thief in the night.

The moon was like a ghostly-silver orb in the lonely sky. Its beams spilled across the turnpike, silvering the road like rippling aluminum.

Summer glanced at her dashboard and watched the minutes tick by. Then she glanced at the speedometer—thirty-five, forty-five, sixty—it swirled upward with the barest pressure against her pedal. She eased up on the accelerator having no time for a speeding ticket.

Lights suddenly flashed into her rearview mirror. What appeared as truck lights came from nowhere and approached her quickly from behind. From the moon's shadow, it looked like an old faded black truck. It surged forward and passed her, crossing back over into the lane in front of her. She shot a glance in her rearview mirror to see another truck with brilliant square lights eating up the road behind her. Evidently, she wasn't the only one in a hurry today.

Then panic suddenly gripped her.

A few minutes past three-thirty in the morning, she traveled on a dark road alone with two speeding trucks driving dangerously close. Now the truck behind her charged up on her. She gripped the steering wheel tightly as the truck in front of her accelerated. She wondered at the driver's intention, but either way, it looked suspicious.

A raindrop splattered against her windshield.

Then another until suddenly it became a torrential downpour.

In the haze of her thoughts, she saw the blur of red brake lights blaze against her windshield. The truck in front of her slammed to a crashing halt. She smashed her brakes to the floor. The tires skidded, squealed against the wet pavement.

Her bag slammed against the dashboard and met with a heavy thud against the floorboard. Her cell phone slid off the dashboard, acted like a bullet grazing her cheekbone and meeting her with an immediate painful throb.

Thank God she hadn't rear-ended the truck.

Another quick glance in her rearview mirror saw the truck behind her gaining speed, obviously ignoring her brake lights. Her mouth went dry. He was going to hit her. She leaned over to see no oncoming traffic, clenched the steering wheel, and wrenched it across the centerline to pass the truck, but the truck blocked her.

Sandwiched between two trucks, a sickening dread of foreboding filled her.

Storm rolled over in bed. He was beyond exhausted having barely slept with his keeping a conscious effort to keep Summer at a safe distance from him. He rubbed his tired, burning eyes and tried to adjust to the room's shadows. An almighty throbbing ache pounded his temple as if someone took a sledgehammer to him.

Apollo's fierce bark rang out cutting through the silence.

He glanced over at her side of the bed.

It was empty.

He jerked upright simultaneously reaching for his gun on the bedside table. The house was stone silent. He jolted out of bed, yanked on his jeans, and slammed his feet into his boots. He grabbed a T-shirt, whipped it over his head, and bolted out of the bedroom.

"Summer! Summer!" he bellowed.

The house sat in shadows from the moon's beams seeping through the slats of the wooden blinds. He rounded the kitchen island coming to a halt seeing a note.

Paged to hospital early. You were sleeping too peaceful to wake.

"God damn it," he roared as he grabbed his keys.

She left the house unprotected.

Nothing was ever simple with the woman, like following one simple rule: never leave the house unprotected. God he wanted to kill her, well, not really kill her, but she was in dire of discipline before she got the both of them killed.

He pulled his car out of the garage and sped down the driveway all the while blistering rubber. He turned on the turnpike driving toward the hospital. Without a moment to lose, he gunned the accelerator and let his car devour the asphalt.

Minutes later, he rounded the broad curve. What he saw through his rain-splattered windshield horrified him.

She was being ambushed.

In the distance, he saw her car sandwiched between two large trucks driving excessively close and gaining speed. The outcome wouldn't be favorable for her against those monstrous trucks, their obvious intent.

He gripped the steering wheel as he slammed the pedal against the floorboard and careened around the deep corner, his powerful car fishtailing on the pavement.

Son of a bitch!

Summer watched the truck in front speed off and round the approaching bend only to disappear from her sight.

She had only a second to brace her body before the truck behind her rammed into the rear of her car.

In milliseconds, the impact thrust her head forward, nearly hitting the steering wheel. Crumbling metal thundered and echoed throughout the car stifling her screams as she tried to gain control on the slick pavement. The truck pushed her toward the pitch-black tree-laden embankment while her foot remained smashed on the brake pedal. Her tires roared and squealed, peeled against the pavement. Her ankle throbbed in acute pain, yet she couldn't let up; she had to stop her car. The stench of burning rubber and heated metal curled around her inside the car. She squeezed her eyes shut. She couldn't bear to watch her fate, like her parent's, unfold before her.

Storm rolled down his window, emptied four bullets into the back of the truck, hitting one rear tire, blistering the tailgate, and two shots exploding the back window.

Her car resembled a torpedo as it sliced through the dark forest, metal grinded, twisted around tree trunks, and glass shattered. The car dipped downward, gained speed then slid sideways, threatened to flip when it finally landed on all fours coming to rest against a thick tree trunk with a loud thud. The tree's branch catapulted through the passenger side window.

Blood trickled warmly down her forehead, over her nose. Eerie quietness greeted her, save a limb snapping here and there. She was afraid to open her eyes, afraid to move. She opened her right eye and felt her long eyelash brush against the tree limb shaped like a wishbone now sitting in her front seat. It pinned her chest and neck against her door.

Her first thought was she broke Storm's most important rule, never leave without him, and now she reaped the consequences and undoubtedly his fury.

Storm watched the two trucks barrel down the highway, too far for him to catch or see any identifying marks—all tinted glass and no license plates, only his bullet holes.

Hired guns.

He wanted to chase after them and kill them; his rage was so great, but she was his first priority. He called the accident in and then skidded to a halt on the roadside. He tore from his car with a flashlight, his car still rolling, feeling as if his heart would burst fearing for her safety.

Reaper left her in his care, and if something happened to her, he'd never forgive himself. Surely to God this wasn't happening for the second time, surely he could redeem himself and save Summer unlike he failed to save Calypsia.

With no windshield to protect her, she felt the steady fall of raindrops plaster her face and chest. From the corner of her eye, she watched smoke bellow from under her disfigured, oddly angled dashboard and out the windows. The pungent smell of burning rubber stifled her senses. Frozen with fear, she tried to catch her breath. Tentatively, she moved her hands and feet and felt a piercing ache in her ankle.

A man's voice filtered hazily through her mind. Was it the killer returning to ensure the deed done? Yet the man's voice sounded vaguely familiar through the hazy fog in her mind. He shouted her name. His voice echoed around the walls of the trees and undergrowth, yes, definitely her name.

She heard footsteps running toward her, crunching sticks and overgrowth. She stifled a scream when suddenly a light flashed across her face.

"Summer? It's Storm. Are you okay?" He held his breath, waiting for her answer. When his flashlight flashed across her bloody face and he saw the tree limb pinning her against the door, he almost lost it. His body shook all over from a mixture of rage and fear.

She saw the outline of Storm's face through the dark shadows and the windshield opening. She never felt such relief.

"I'm okay," she assured him. "I'm so sorry I should have waked you," she cried.

After several attempts, he finally managed to pry open the driver door. He brushed away broken glass from her lap and then hunched down beside her. He made quick work freeing her from her seat belt. She watched him, transfixed as his quick, intelligent eyes assessed her and the situation.

"Help is coming, just hang tight," he said roughly.

"Don't move around too much. We can't afford the car to slide. There's a lake down there," he noted grimly.

She nodded, giving him a relieved smile, thanking her lucky stars he found her so quickly. She'd do whatever he asked of her just as long as he got her out of this horrific situation.

"Where do you hurt?" he asked as he pulled a handkerchief from his back jean pocket and gently wiped the blood from her face then dabbed softly at her mouth and chin. Her forehead was scratched, not deep, thank God.

"My ankle," she replied with a grimace.

"Tell me the places I can't see," he ordered.

"There's nothing broken," she whispered.

"Good. Now, I have to go to my car. I'll be right back."

She shook her head not wanting him to leave.

"I'm coming right back," he assured her and quickly exited her car.

She listened to his fading footsteps. He was running. Paranoid, her mind suddenly worried the killers would return and hurt him. She'd never forgive herself. Relieved, she heard the welcoming sound of sirens.

It stopped raining as soon as daylight crept over the horizon. She got a sneak peek at the extent of damage.

Firemen, policemen, and emergency medical technicians surrounded her car.

Storm came back to her and hunched down beside her. "They've braced your car so it won't slide any further, but the ground is slippery. They'll need to move you quick. Can you manage that?"

She nodded.

He reluctantly backed away from her as two firemen came to her door. She looked over their shoulders to see Storm, his face wary, concerned.

"No, please," she said, nodding to Storm. "Him, I want him."

The two firemen stepped aside.

Storm maneuvered the door open wider and hunched down beside her, his eyes fierce.

"You ready? This has got to go fast," he told her, his voice uneven as he reached tentatively toward her.

"I'm ready."

He reached for her then and snatched her bodily from the car. As soon as the car felt the weightlessness, it shot forward about twenty feet, barely enough clearance to escape.

She wrapped her arms tightly around his neck and leaned her head against his chest. He carried her up the steep ravine to the edge of the road. She sighed with relief, comforted by his presence, knowing he'd protect her. She inhaled the scent of his skin and breathed him deep in her lungs. He laid her gently on the white-sheeted gurney awaiting them with medics standing by. She clung to him. He had to reach up and unlock the death grip she had around his neck.

He leaned down, his face just inches from hers, and she could've sworn he intended to kiss her, but something flickered in his eyes. Instead, he rose, squeezed her hand, and walked away.

She watched him converse with the medics. Seconds later, they wheeled her toward the ambulance and loaded her. They simultaneously swarmed her inside the small confined area. She felt light-headed, dizzy. Next, she saw Storm speaking to two uniformed police officers then they laid her down on the gurney, and she couldn't see him anymore and couldn't seem to contain her disappointment.

She waved off the medics, trying to find her voice.

"I don't need to go to the hospital. I don't have any broken bones, just bandage my ankle." The two medics looked at her skeptically, undoubtedly noticing the blood snaking from her forehead down her cheek and various stinging cuts feathering her face, arms, and hands.

The medic on her right, a young man she guessed late twenties of Asian descent, looked down at her hesitantly.

"I'm a doctor. Really, it's just fine," she assured him.

He reached for the bandages and started working while the young blonde lady on her other side reached over and placed an oxygen mask over her face. She held Summer's hand, giving it a gentle squeeze of reassurance.

Summer had always been on the other side delving out reassurance, yet this time she welcomed it.

Several minutes later as the medics bandaged her many cuts and wrapped her ankle, she stared up at the ceiling of the ambulance and wondered what Storm was doing.

Then the ambulance doors swung open wide, slowly and quietly. She knew without looking, without a word spoken, the identity of the person who stood there blocking out the sun's rays.

Storm.

The presence of him, large and looming, laid a protective shadow over her, making her feel instantly safe. The fear trembling throughout her body and gripping her heart all dissipated because of *him*.

She could feel the tension coiled within him, ready to leap, spring. His eyes were on her, assessing her, and she could picture the smug look on his face screaming, "*I told you so.*"

When the medics finished with her, they lifted the head of the gurney into a sitting position. She avoided his gaze and instead stared down at her hands. Her cuts bared numerous bandages while the many faint scratches resembled angry welts recently swabbed with alcohol.

She glanced down at her turquoise scrub top stained with blood and dirt splotches. Her clogs were missing. Her ankle looked twice its size swathed in a thick bandage. She tested it, giving it a wiggle, and winced. A light sprain she guessed.

Her fingertips feathered along her jawline where she felt the sting of a few cuts.

Her temple started to throb.

It could've been much worse.

Much worse if it hadn't been for *him*.

Her bodyguard.

Her life was completely out of control. She hated it.

She started shivering uncontrollably, her teeth chattered. Her body picked a fine time to go into delayed shock.

The medics quickly piled blankets on her to warm her.

She felt the heat of his stare burn into her. She was sure he regretted his decision to protect her, and she couldn't blame him. If he decided not to protect her, she could well understand why. Every step of the way, she made it difficult for him, flinging his rules back in his face while she threw caution to the wind, not thinking of the consequences that left him picking up the pieces. If he decided he no longer wanted to protect her, she'd need to find someone else because she finally realized her need for protection.

But she only wanted *him*.

Him, who stood less than three feet away.

She took a deep breath and slowly lifted her eyes from her hands, coming to land on his jean-clad legs leaning against the back bumper of the ambulance facing her. She seemed a bit transfixed and couldn't move beyond the rip in his jeans, just above his knee showing ample portion of his tanned muscular thigh.

She swallowed hard trying to dismiss the way her heart jerked as her eyes skimmed past the bulge lying behind his zipper focusing instead on his black braided leather belt, simultaneously swallowing a gulp. A snug white T-shirt was tucked within the waistband clearly outlining a flat stomach, a heavily muscled broad chest, and carved shoulders. His sinewy tanned arms bunched with muscle, now folded across his chest, flexing with the barest movement.

Her eyes continued to climb, coming to rest on the visible pulsing against his neck.

His heartbeat.

Slow, steady, and calm.

While hers raged wildly from the effects of her slow appraisal of his mind-numbing body. She felt hot and lethargic as her eyes lifted to his square chin coming to land on his sensual lips. Her heart took flight then raced as her body exploded with desire.

Her imagination ran wild as she tried to imagine how he would kiss a woman. Something told her it would be a wild, hungry kiss filled with reckless abandon. An explosion of passion because he was the type of guy who would use his hands to explore a woman's body simultaneously while he kissed her, pouring every depth of emotion into his skillful hands as they rounded the curvature of a woman's hips. He'd delve low across her bottom, tiptoeing up the hollow of her back to steal his hands around her rib cage where he'd give a gentle but firm squeeze. His hands would glide, climb inch by inch to cup, massage her breasts, cuddle them against his chest, pressing his heart against hers and feel totally turned on by how madly her heart pumped against his and how she trembled in his arms seeking unspeakable pleasure she knew only he could give her.

The type of passionate kiss she never experienced. Her experience included lukewarm kisses she'd received from her dates in the past, including the very recent depressing kiss from Dr. O'Malley thankfully interrupted by *him*.

He was a constant reminder just how long she'd been without intimacy.

Four long years.

The blasted shivers continued ruthlessly.

She took a deep breath and focused back on his lips, now set in a grim, straight line. He was frustrated with her. She frowned. She refused to have a confrontation; she felt beat up enough to last her a lifetime.

Glancing up at his cheeks, his face was shadowed by a day's growth, and still, she couldn't believe the transformation when he shaved his beard and trimmed his hair. As a result, it thrust her body into sexual overdrive even though she used every bit of willpower she possessed and then some to ignore the sexual prowess he emanated, the undercurrent of tension between them. She avoided looking at him, the wonder of *him*.

She saved his mesmerizing liquid gray eyes for last, his most breathtaking feature knowing all too well the effect they had on her sensibilities when cast her direction.

The time neared to look him in the eye and admit she was wrong, give him a formal apology, and ask for another chance.

Their eyes collided.

What she saw rocked her foundation.

A dozen emotions flickered across his face, and she recognized the one emotion she expected, exasperation. However, there were more. Weariness, pure agony, and torment imprisoned there. Thinking back, the same haunted look he had the first time they met at the restaurant as if something had truly aggrieved him. Suddenly, he shut down his emotions, slammed the door on her as she tried to maneuver into his mind, discover his feelings buried so deeply within him.

Now, his chest rose and fell unsteadily, the pulse against his neck throbbing at a maddening pace.

Her shivers finally subsided, only giving away to a shudder ever so often.

"We're done, Dr. Benson," the young male medic reported, interrupting her thoughts. "I'm thinking you'll need crutches," he said, looking pointedly down at her wrapped ankle throbbing to the beat of her heart.

"I'll take her," Storm said, stepping forward.

He climbed inside the ambulance. His eyes were careful as he probed her for a long moment, scanning over every place he saw a bandage as if to ensure she was safe for him to move.

"You should go to the hospital and have someone check you out," he said soberly.

She shook her head and reassured him. "I'm fine, really." Yet her voice broke despite the confidence she tried to instill in it.

The grim expression on his face changed; it softened as he reached for her hand and enveloped it between his hands. Warmth surged through her, soothing her instantly.

She frowned at herself, mostly to hide the embarrassment now staining her cheeks and gave a shaky exhale.

He waited silently until she looked up at him and gave him a tentative smile.

"Are you sure you're okay?" he asked.

"I am now," she said, squeezing his hand.

He reached for her and gently lifted her off the gurney effortlessly. His breath blew against her cheek, making her shivers restart with a fury. Carefully, he stepped from the ambulance, lifted her high in his arms, and carried her to his car. She laid her head against his shoulder and discovered all too quickly if she moved her lips just an inch, she'd kiss his neck, a tantalizing thought.

A police officer held the car door open for them as he placed her in the passenger seat and belted her in.

Minutes later after they pulled away from the scene, she glanced over at him.

"You're upset with me," she admitted in a whisper. "And I don't blame you."

He swallowed hard as if not trusting himself to speak. Then after a moment, he cleared his throat, his jaw clenched as he stared forward. "Upset doesn't quite sum up how I feel right now, Summer. You broke a major rule. How can I protect you when you defy the rules I set to keep you alive?"

"I was paged early—"

"I don't care. You can't imagine how I felt waking up and finding you gone. I'm sorry I wasn't there to protect you," he replied gruffly. "But I want to know why. Why did you leave alone? Are you trying to make me old before my time?"

"It's a call I can't easily ignore! Besides, you arrived and scared them away," she reminded him as she saw him clench the steering wheel, white knuckled.

He exhaled sharply, slammed his fist against the steering wheel, his face murderous as he looked over at her.

She jerked.

"I could've lost you today, and by God, that's not an option!" he bellowed.

She stared out the window and watched the beads of rain slide down the window as they drove. She glanced back over at his troubled face while he kept his eyes on the road.

For several minutes, they drove in unbearable silence. There was so much she wanted to say yet couldn't. Her mind froze, reeled while her thoughts tumbled into a jumbled mess. Finally, he turned into her driveway and parked in front of her garage door. He leaned his head back against the seat and stared up at the ceiling of the car. His face was tight, tension filled.

"Are you okay?" she asked.

He looked over at her, caught off guard. "You were the one hurt and you're asking me if I'm okay?"

"Yes," she whispered. "I care about you. Plus, I have a feeling you're thinking of going after those people in the truck."

The look he gave her indicated she was right on target.

"Please don't," she rushed out in a whisper. "I couldn't bear if something happened to you."

He looked over at her again and smiled softly.

"Nothing is going to happen to me, but I refuse to wait for Malone to make an attempt on your life."

He reached over, picked her hand up from her lap, and brought it to lie against his heart. With his hand pressed against hers, he held it there.

She believed she'd feel a steady, soft heartbeat, but that wasn't the case. His heart thundered against her hand as if he'd just sprinted a mile.

She looked at him and was met with a chagrined smile.

"You successfully scared the hell out of me today," he confessed. "Considering I'm a SEAL, that's quite a revelation."

"I know," she whispered.

He got out of the car, came around to her door, opened it, scooped her up in his arms, and carried her inside. He never stopped to pluck her down on the couch as she half expected. Instead, he took her straight into her bedroom and sat her down on the edge of the bed while he pulled back the covers.

Again, those blasted shivers announced themselves. Her body shook the bed.

He frowned down at her. "I'll be right back."

He came right back and thrust a glass of water in her hand, motioning for her to open her mouth. She never questioned the medication he gave her, only hoped it would send her directly into oblivion so she could block out the outside world and get some rest.

Storm rummaged through her dresser, pulled out a pair of pink silk pajamas, and laid them beside her.

"Storm, I was due for a trauma case this morning. You can find my nurse's phone number on the side of my refrigerator. Her name is Mariann. Can you tell her I won't be in?"

He nodded. "Do you need help changing?"

She shook her head.

"I'll give you some privacy," he said softly and walked out, closing the door softly behind him.

She made quick work stripping out of her clothes and crawled between the sheets.

Not a minute later, Storm returned, peeking around door.

The pink pajamas still lay on the bed untouched. He walked further inside the room his fingertips brushed across the silky material as he came to sit beside her on the bed, simultaneously tucking the comforter close to her body. The shivers worsened and now her face was flushed.

He reached over and felt her hot cheeks. He wouldn't think for a second about her being under those damn covers naked.

Focus!

"How do we get you to stop shaking?" he asked.

"You can't help me," she said solemnly as she brought the comforter up under her chin.

"Why can't I help you?" he asked with his hands on his hips.

"When you have accidents where trauma is involved, your body goes into shock and then into survival mode. While it tries to rid the body of shock, body temperature is affected. Hence, why I'm now going back and forth between shivers and burning up. Now, I'm freezing to death," she replied, her teeth chattering. "Eventually, it'll go away."

He measured her with his eyes as he kicked off his boots. Next, he peeled his shirt over his head, never taking his eyes off her while he unzipped his jeans.

"I'll have you warmed up in no time," he promised.

Good God. She wished she weren't drugged right now so she could fully enjoy the experience of being so close to him. She willed herself to void her mind of sexual thoughts, but they roared through her mind anyways.

He peeled back the blankets and, without warning, tucked his arm around her waist and pulled her back up against his hard body, an unbearably hot body. She squeezed her eyes shut as his legs came up against the back of hers. It was unbearable, sweet torture. It'd been so very long since she'd experienced a man's touch. What little experience she had was nothing close to how she felt with this man's hands on her body. She could easily stay like this forever. She glanced at him over her shoulder.

"Don't leave me," she pleaded with him.

Their eyes held and suddenly the room felt charged with an unspeakable electric current. Her eyelids were suddenly very heavy, the more she fought to keep them open, the more she felt paralyzed and no longer able to fight the euphoria washing over her.

He was no saint.

With her soft body against him, he throbbed hard and had to take several deep breaths to calm his body.

A good thirty minutes passed and still she shivered.

He rolled her over onto her back and sucked in his breath seeing the buffet spread before him. Her breasts, firm and round dotted by rose pink nipples, begged him to lavish his lips upon them. He groaned, avoided eye contact with the rest of her as he covered her, tucking her limbs into the center of his big body until he covered every inch of her skin, keeping most of his weight on his forearms.

He touched her face wordlessly.

God, his mother would be proud of him right now. His buddies on the other hand would be laughing their asses off saying it was about time he got a payback. He was actually being a gentleman and even he couldn't believe it. It had to be that way, no option. His place was to protect her at all costs, do whatever it took to keep her safe and because this young lady was different from any other.

Yet the hot-blooded part of him teased, tormented him, and made his blood boil. He moved only slightly against her and realized the way his body folded into hers, the parts and pieces almost neatly lined up; all he had to do was barely nudge her legs apart, and he'd slide in at home base in two seconds. He gritted his teeth and counted to ten.

To twenty.

To one hundred.

Until his eyes became blurry.

The last thing Summer remembered was the bed rails shaking and her wishing it was because he made love to her.

He tucked her head below his chin, pressed himself more against her, sinking her further into the bed to warm her quickly.

How blissful. Never mind her body felt like a train wreck. She never wanted it to end, feeling completely safe and knowing no one could get to her because he'd protect her. Her mind grasped the gravity of the situation. Someone tried to kill her today and almost succeeded.

"They tried to kill me," she sobbed in her sleep.

"Go to sleep, baby," he whispered, his hot breath feathering her cheek.

His warmth and those few choice words sent her into a peaceful oblivion.

He placed his lips against her temple and promised, "I'm going to find them and kill them."

14

Storm wanted to kill someone.

Less than an hour later, she slept soundly.

He left her in bed snoring so loud she could've blown the roof off the house, precisely why he gave her the sleeping pill.

As for him, he still shook with fury as he dressed. He sliced a hand through his tousled hair. All he could think about was her trembling in his arms with fear, only to stop when she finally drifted off into a medicated sleep. He never felt so helpless, unable to relax her. He sat down on the bed's edge and jerked his boots on, his hands shaking with such growing ferocity he could barely lace his boots.

Apollo woke up, walked over to Storm, and leaned into him. Getting no response, his final effort to get Storm's attention was to duck his head under his hand.

Storm sighed, feeling his fury slowly dissipate and took a minute to ruffle Apollo's neck and, in return, received a swift lick across the top of his hand. Apollo took up position at the foot of the bed.

"You know exactly what I need you to do, don't you, buddy?"

The bed moved.

Storm gave a quick glance over his shoulder to see she gravitated onto his side of the bed.

Again.

She curled into a ball facing him with the covers pulled up to her chin. Her forehead creased as if she battled an onset of nightmares. Something tugged his heart seeing her so vulnerable. He leaned over and placed his hand over hers. His reward; a slow smile pulled at the corners of her mouth and she sighed.

He could only shake his head when a smile broke out involuntarily across his lips. She would turn him gray before this ordeal was over. He got up and stood before Apollo, pointed at the bed. "Guard her. If she gets out of the bed, bite her."

Apollo's mouth opened wide for a yawn, not taking his order seriously. He hunched down on all fours and laid his head down on his paws with a resounding thump.

Reaper didn't take the news well at all when Storm called him. As expected, he chomped at the bit to check things out for himself even though Sibella was in full tilt labor a few weeks early.

Storm soothed things over the best he could and gave Reaper his reassurance he'd find those responsible and deal with them.

Those responsible for today's events would see unimaginable fury and swift justice brought to their doorstep. What happened to Summer wasn't an accident. When he called the hospital about her page, he was told she hadn't been paged, indicating she had been set up. He shuddered to think what really could have happened. Her life nearly ended in a blink of an eye, and he wasn't there to protect her, only a bystander.

He gave his watch a quick glance as he headed to the garage. He expected a visitor, the second person he called while at this morning's accident scene.

Right on time, a knock sounded from the garage door then another two additional taps.

Storm opened the door wide with a ready smile.

In stepped Derek Knight. He was in his early thirties with a pale, freckled face. He was a tall, lanky guy with hell-fire red hair standing on end. He carried with him his life link, a battered briefcase that looked like it had been through an explosion or two.

A highly talented computer guru, Derek had the unique ability to hack into any software program. The National Counter Terrorism Center had tried for years to recruit him as an analyst because they didn't want him going against them, but Derek declined; he liked his own bit of freedom. He was the man you wanted when you needed to find out the most intimate information about someone, information such as their last known addresses, family members, past relationships, recent purchases, their mode of travel, any transactions on the Internet, phone records, and conversation, even the name of their last sexual partner if needed to get down and dirty.

"Hooyah! Good to see you, man," Storm said, smiling broadly. He pumped Derek's hand and slapped his shoulder.

"Anything for my brother, or I should say brothers since it involves Reaper too," he said, giving him a grim smile. He walked over to the workbench and promptly opened his briefcase and pulled out his laptop. He rubbed his palms together, cracked his knuckles, and then let his fingertips roam intimately across the keyboard.

"What I'm about to tell you is something you're not going to want to hear," Derek forewarned him.

Storm came to stand behind him and watched him maneuver through programs so fast it made his head spin.

"So give it to me straight." Storm crossed his arms over his chest.

"Malone isn't your average guy, and the reason why I say this is because up until recently, he served in the Special Forces. Meet Sergeant First Class Mark Matthew Malone, a Green Beret and a past recipient of the Silver Star."

Storm watched the computer screen flash across a picture of Malone. His eyes looked intense.

"His last mission was in northern Afghanistan two months ago to eliminate a high value target. Just last month, they shipped him back to the states for 'unacceptable behavior' befitting a Green Beret. Disciplinary measures are forthcoming. However, he's got a history of disciplinary problems and known as a hothead and very aggressive."

Storm walked across the garage, opened his car trunk, and pulled out two large briefcases.

"You need to be careful, Storm. This guy is not dealing with a full deck, and considering this mess in Afghanistan and his fiancée's recent death, it may have sent him over the edge."

"Exactly, which is why I've got to get to him before he gets to Summer," Storm said as he unsnapped his briefcase and removed two handguns—a nine millimeter and a forty-five caliber—and ammunition. He loaded the guns, put the safety on, and then walked around to the passenger side of the car, opened the door, and placed the weapons and extra ammunition on the seat. He proceeded to secure a holster around each thigh, a holster that fitted his handguns and the other holster a deadly razor knife. He donned a bulletproof vest and sunglasses then opened the garage door.

Derek scribbled down information on a piece of paper, walked over, and handed it to Storm as he got into his car. "Be careful."

Storm tossed the latest address for Malone on the passenger seat. "Apollo's inside, probably in her bedroom guarding her. You have your gun?"

Derek tapped his vest over his heart. "I never leave home without it."

Storm drove to the outskirts of Jacksonville, Malone's latest address. The property was secluded. He turned down a long driveway with a thick forest of pine and palm trees encroaching upon the fringes leading around a bend opening to a pond surrounded by fertile green grass and willows.

Upon a small hillside sat a two-story white house. What caught his eye was the side yard in front of a large white barn.

A large target.

A chair sat at the opposite end.

Storm drove right up to the windowless two-car garage, parked his car, and got out.

His heart hammered and revved his pulse as he walked up to the house. He knew the feeling well, the last time he felt such adrenaline, he and his men were dropped from a midnight sky onto a snowcapped hilltop in the unruly mountains of Afghanistan, knowing all the while the threat could materialize just like Malone at this very moment could be waiting for him.

He had no right trespassing on Malone's property. The only thing he could prove against Malone was his threatening Summer at the hospital with a gun. The rest was suspicion he hoped to clear up today.

Storm walked up to the open-sided porch and knocked on the door. He paid particular attention to the two windows framing the front door, putting his hand on his gun.

No answer.

No sound emanated from within the home

Again, he knocked, louder this time.

Still no answer.

He unsnapped his holster and pulled out his gun and took off the safety and carried it down at his side as he walked over and hopped off the side of the porch, walking along the house's perimeter then around to the barn where he peeked through a window seeing mowers, boxes, ladders, nothing out of the ordinary. He then came to stand by the chair facing the target.

He wanted to send Malone a strong message. He aimed his gun at the target and fired.

Bull's eye.

All six shots.

He reloaded his gun, gave a quick glance at the house, and saw a curtain move on the second floor.

Purposely, he strode back to the house and pounded on the front door.

"Malone, face me like a man. You and I need to have a discussion before someone gets seriously hurt."

Silence.

"I can kick the front door down, and when I do, there won't be any talking," he warned.

Then suddenly, he heard running inside the house, going the opposite direction, toward the back of the house.

Storm jumped off the porch and rounded to the back where a young man bolted out the back door and ran frantically toward the barn. He knew without a doubt from the picture Derek showed him he wasn't Malone; although from a distance, he could see a resemblance, just a younger version, possibly early twenties.

"Shit!" Storm muttered under his breath. He dug in his heels and sprinted after him. He could hardly believe he was the same man who could run a six-minute mile not all that long ago. His lungs felt on the verge of exploding.

The young man suddenly changed direction after clearing the barn, heading toward the driveway to escape.

Storm cut him off as they approached the pond where he put the safety back on his gun and dropped it on the embankment. He leapt on the young man's shoulders, sending them headlong into the pond with a resounding splash. Storm broke the surface first while the young man wrestled frantically underwater trying to escape but couldn't because of the strong arm Storm had around his neck.

Storm let his head surface long enough to gasp for air.

"I'm not after you. I want Mark Malone. Now, are you ready to answer my questions or not?"

"I don't know anything," he sputtered in a wet gasp.

"We can do this the easy way or the hard way. I've got all day and plenty of ways to make you talk," Storm growled. "Now, who are you?"

"None of your business."

"Okay, it's the hard way," Storm gritted out as he pulled him back under the water and held him. He tried to wrestle his way loose; however, he quickly realized his efforts futile and ceased his struggle.

Again, Storm brought him up to surface.

"My patience is near the end," Storm warned.

"I'm Mike. Mark's brother," he coughed.

"Where is he?"

"I don't know," he said as he wiped the water from his eyes.

"When did you last see him?"

"About a week ago. Why do you want him?" he asked, looking up at Storm with wide, fearful eyes.

"He threatened someone close to me, and I'm not taking it too kindly," Storm said as he assisted him from the pond.

"Threatened who?" His young face crunched up in confusion.

"He's terrorized a young lady doctor."

"Mark wouldn't do that," he defended, shaking his head in denial.

"Well, sorry to burst your bubble, but he did," Storm said as he walked over and picked up his gun and slid it in his holster. "So who else would know where I can find him?"

The young man swiped his wet hair from his eyes. "I don't know. We've been looking for him. He's had problems lately with his fiancée dying, and he's not thinking straight."

"Give your brother a message when you see him next. Tell him if he threatens her in any way again, I'll hunt him down and kill him. Got it?"

He gave him a jerky nod.

Storm headed back to his car.

This wasn't how Storm wanted his visit with Malone to go. He wanted to get answers and put the fear of God in him. Malone was in hiding and could be in the throes of planning even more mischief where Summer was concerned, maybe even possibly with the DUI suspect still reported missing per the newspaper or perhaps dead for all he knew. The very thought made him apprehensive.

He never believed for one instant Malone was responsible for the ambush or for the car acid. A Green Beret would've killed her by now and wouldn't hire out such trivial means to terrorize her. Malone wasn't his only target now, but someone who knew Summer's routine, knew intimate details about her, a very dangerous person. She had no social life, and with her life revolving around the hospital, it had to be someone from the hospital.

Driving back to Summer's house, he contemplated the best way to protect her. His obvious choice was to take her away and keep her out of the public eye, but he knew she'd revolt because she doesn't want to be too far from the hospital. For now, he'd do it her way, but if and when it got to the point where he felt like he couldn't protect her, she'd go away with him whether she liked it or not.

He pulled into her driveway. He desperately needed a shower since he was still soaked through from the dive in the pond.

Suddenly, the front door burst open.

Summer hobbled on her sore ankle toward him dressed in too tight white shorts and a too tight white blouse, barefooted, her hair bellowing out behind her, her forehead creased.

And she was spitting fire.

He barely had enough time to raise his sunglasses before she began her rant.

"Are you completely demented?"

He raised his eyebrow.

"You could have been killed today. Malone is a complete lunatic and probably wouldn't hesitate killing you to get to me."

"Do you honestly think I'm going to let a situation such as this pass? Either way, I'm here now, unharmed."

"Thank God."

She threw herself bodily against him, into his arms, hugging him fiercely. Her arms crept around his neck.

"I was so worried about you," she breathed against his neck, her voice cracking with emotion. "When I woke up and you weren't here, I knew what your intentions were."

Taken aback, he had no choice but to wrap his arms around her and hold her. She smelled of fresh soap. He inhaled a little bit of heaven.

For a long moment, he just held her. Obviously, a sign her armor was beginning to crack and showing signs of stress. She held it together much longer than he anticipated.

"Did you find him?" she whispered.

"No, only his brother," he replied guardedly.

"You didn't hurt him, did you?"

"No."

"I'm glad. He's not responsible for his brother's actions," she murmured and swiped away at her tears.

She tightened her hold on him. Her body trembled and in turn made him feel a twinge of guilt not being up front with her about his intentions today, yet at the time, he thought it for the best. He felt her lips feather innocently against his neck. It did wild crazy things to his body, making him instantly catch on fire, down low. He took a deep breath and counted to ten.

Admittedly, he found her welcome gratifying seeing the relief and excitement on her face when their eyes met. Yet if he had to be honest with himself, he was anxious to get back to her as quickly as he could. It unsettled him being away from her, and he wouldn't even speculate on his reasoning because it had nothing to do with protecting her.

Finally, she lifted her head, splayed her hands against his shoulders, and scanned his face anxiously.

He looked into red-rimmed, teary eyes still heavy lidded obviously having recently awakened from her nap, a much too short nap in his opinion. The blasted woman removed all her bandages. The cuts on her face, arms, and hands were now exposed.

"Summer, why did you remove your bandages?"

She smiled at him impishly. "So I can doctor them myself."

He guessed that sounded reasonable since she was a doctor; he couldn't really argue with her.

Obviously, this was a very poor time for his mind to wander, but he loved holding her in his arms, loved how she clung to him unwilling to release him. Secretly, he yearned to carry her straight back into her bedroom and imprison her with him for seven long days and nights of nothing but pure sexual gratification. Wishing and doing were two different things. She was forbidden fruit, and he really needed to remember that.

"You're dressed for combat. The only thing missing is your helmet. I was so worried about you," she reiterated.

"Why would you be worried about me?" he asked incredulously.

"For one, you're not invincible."

"Your lack of confidence in me is appalling."

"You know what I mean. I know you can handle yourself, I just worry."

"Don't worry about me," he ordered her sternly.

"Why ever not? You worry about me."

"I don't worry about you," he lied. "Your brother worries enough for the both of us," he reminded her grimly.

"Yes, you do worry about me. I saw it in your eyes this morning."

"You have a vivid imagination, Summer Benson."

"Actions speak louder than words. You're still holding me in your arms," she informed him all too sweetly.

Storm immediately set her down gently on her feet.

She automatically reached for his hand, entwined her fingers with his. "You're wet, Storm," she mentioned the obvious as she gazed up at him and then down at her wet blouse and shorts, clearly outlining her hard nipples.

He could barely carry a single coherent thought. Her actions took him so off guard.

"I wish you would've told me where you were going. I panicked when I couldn't find you."

"You didn't do anything to Derek, did you?" he asked as he looked past her to the front door to finally see Derek walk up and give a slight wave, a knowing smile on his face. Just great, he was going to catch all kinds of hell from this little scene.

"Well," she said, giving a hesitant smile over her shoulder at Derek, "I chased him around the house with my hammer until he explained himself. You caused me a lot of unnecessary worry," she said, jabbing her finger against his chest.

"It was necessary. I had hoped you'd sleep a lot longer," he said, distracted by the way her thumb made slow caressing circles against the back of his hand.

"I bet you did," she said, looking at him suspiciously. "What exactly did you give me?"

"It was just a mild sleeping pill I sometimes take when I can't sleep."

"You have problems sleeping, Storm?" her brow ruffled with concern as her eyes narrowed on him.

He shook his head, avoiding her question. "Would you stop asking me twenty questions so I can grab a shower?"

"Sure, I'll help you," she said, tugging him along.

"No, I don't need your help," he said, tugging her back toward him where she stumbled up against him. He took her shoulders and set her away from him.

"I only meant I'd lay out your towels," she explained.

"It's best I get my own towels," he informed her, still unable to forget how affected he was by how compassionately she touched his scars the last time she helped him with towels.

She turned to walk away then spun on her heel and faced him. She gazed up into his eyes as she tenderly brushed a damp tendril off his forehead. "I'm sorry for leaving without you this morning. Thank God you came along when you did. I'm so glad you're safe and at home with me now."

"Summer," he sighed, exhaling an exasperated breath. "What happened to you today was my fault. I should've been with you."

Her eyes widened with confusion. "I don't see it that way."

"It could've all gone very wrong, Summer, and I would have only myself to blame."

"But it didn't," she argued as she placed her palm against his chest.

"Don't...please," he begged her as he cupped her jaw. With his thumb, he softly brushed away the trace of her fallen tear. "You can't imagine how hard it is, and you don't make it easy for me. We can't do this," he said, gently removing her hand. "I can't protect you the way you need protected if my mind is elsewhere. How about you go and lie down. You look exhausted."

Disappointment and rejection flitted across her pale face.

Damn it to hell!

He wished the circumstances were different. He wished he was actually coming to take her on a dinner date, something normal couples do, because above all else he couldn't deny the intense attraction hovering between them like an electric current since the moment he met her, something he'd never experienced before.

Unfortunately, the current circumstances were far from normal. He held her life in the balance of his hands, every single moment critical; and try as he might, he found his focus wavering because he couldn't stop thinking of her literally every second of the day. Worse, he started to lose his objectivity being in such close confines with her. The lines between them blurred more and more by the minute. He had to be stronger around her, a challenging feat because her charms were lethal.

God help him, he'd rather go through Hell Week again than to see the disheartening look on her face, knowing he caused her pain.

Summer brushed past him up the steps and through the front door Derek held open for them. She walked straight to her bedroom and shut her door.

"She had nightmares," Derek whispered over to Storm as he came to stand inside the door. "She was hysterical when she woke up and you weren't here. She paced every inch of this house and knew where you went. I didn't have to tell her."

Storm shook his head.

The alarm clocked shrilled.

Four-thirty in the morning came rather quickly. She rolled over expecting to find Storm, but his side of the bed was empty.

She sat up, swung her legs over the side, fished her feet into her house slippers, and walked out of the bedroom.

He walked through the front door dressed in dark jeans and a black shirt with Apollo in hand. He looked appetizing.

"You're up. Did you sleep well?" she asked hesitantly.

He looked at her curiously and laughed darkly. "Yes, pleasant dreams." She obviously didn't remember anything.

"I didn't hear you come to bed," she said. Yet she sure dreamt of him, dreamt she ravaged his body in her wild dreams.

She motioned Apollo forward and petted his neck.

"Ten minutes and I'll be ready," she said.

"Are you sure you're well enough to go to work?" His eyes wandered over her cuts, coming to rest on her ankle. She looked bruised up, beat to hell.

She nodded and charged into the bedroom.

Minutes later, they walked out the door together with Storm walking closely by her side, his arm occasionally brushing against hers. She went to get inside the passenger door when he intercepted her, motioned her around to the driver's side of the car where he opened the rear door.

She frowned. "I have to sit in the back seat behind you?"

He nodded.

"But I don't want to sit in the backseat. Let me sit in the front with you. Please?"

"Too risky," he said, shaking his head.

"Not if you're sitting beside me," she countered.

He exhaled. Who could reject such mesmerizing blue eyes? "You're lucky this car has bulletproof windows," he muttered as he opened the front passenger door.

They arrived at the hospital parking garage without incident. Having no emergencies at this time, they went to the hospital coffee shop to eat breakfast.

A couple hours later, Storm's phone rang.

He looked at the phone number and looked hesitant to answer.

"If you need to grab that, go right ahead," she said.

Storm rose, stepped away from the table, and took the call. A minute later, he returned and looked over his shoulder as if looking for someone.

Soon after, a man in a pale blue suit with snow-white hair and tanned complexion strode confidently down the corridor. Upon seeing Storm, his face turned radiant and his smile broadened. Storm walked up to greet him. Instead of shaking his hand, he hugged him.

Storm spoke to him for a few minutes and then they walked toward her. The resemblance could only mean they were father and son, and it gave a telltale sign of what Storm would look like in his elderly years, still vibrant and handsome.

Summer hurriedly wiped her face praying she hadn't left a trail of blueberry muffin crumbs on her mouth and chin.

The man stopped at the table's edge and leaned forward with his hand outstretched.

She stood and shook his hand. "Hi, I'm Summer Benson."

"I'm Storm's father, Calvert Maddox."

"Are you *the* Dr. Calvert Maddox?" she asked, surprised.

The man merely nodded and smiled down at her.

"I'm pleased to meet you. I've read about your inventions of several ventricular assist devices. The survival rate is quite remarkable."

Dr. Calvert Maddox was renowned internationally for his cardiovascular research specializing in heart failure. His device was designed to specifically take over the cardiac function and require the removal of the patient's heart. He traveled to hospitals all over the world teaching them how to enhance and strengthen their cardiovascular research.

"Thank you, Dr. Benson," he replied. "I've also heard of you, a highly skilled surgeon." He leaned closer to her, whispered, "Should you ever decide to leave this hospital and seek other opportunities, please contact me."

She nodded. "You bet I will."

Storm's father looked upon him with concerned eyes. "You've lost a lot of weight since we've seen you last. You okay, son?"

"I'm just fine, Dad."

"Your mother's thrilled to have all the family together. We want you to arrive a few days early so we can catch up."

Storm looked very uncomfortable.

"You plan to attend, don't you?"

"Yes, I do," he said as he shook his father's hand and watched him leave.

"Now I see how you got your clearance," she chuckled. "So tell me, where are you expected next week that you clearly don't want to go?"

He laughed under his breath and sat back down. She was way too perceptive.

"My parent's fortieth wedding anniversary party."

"Those aren't so unpleasant to attend," she said, finishing her muffin.

"You think not?" He raised his eyebrow at her. "I guess we'll find out, won't we?"

"We?" she asked, chuckling.

He nodded, sipping his coffee.

"I'm thinking you owe me for taking you to this gala thing, a trade off of sorts."

She laughed inside. She wouldn't make it easy for him. "So you need a date?"

Again, he laughed confidently under his breath.

"No, I don't need a date per se. It's just a get together. Plus, I wouldn't necessarily call going to my parent's anniversary party a date."

"Why ever not?"

"Because I can do better than that," he replied confidently.

"Can you?" she asked, intrigued.

"Yes, I can," he said, grinning at her.

"Well, I'm waiting." She leaned back in her chair, crossed her arms over her chest, and looked expectant.

"Waiting for what?" His brow rose humorously.

"For you to ask me to be your date at the anniversary party," she said, praising herself for keeping her voice unaffected because inside she was dying laughing.

"You want me to ask *you* to be *my* date?" he scoffed. "You never asked me to be your date for the gala. I think you gave me an order."

"You don't have much practice asking a young lady out on a date, do you?"

He tossed back his head and gave her a throaty laugh.

He replied smugly, "I don't normally have to ask."

"Ah yes, I've heard rumors about your exploits with women, particularly how it wasn't unusual to see you walking away with a girl on each arm, sometimes more, at the end of the night completely thoroughly envied by your buddies."

He felt his face blush.

"My younger, fearless days," he muttered.

Two hours later after having completed rounds in ICU, Summer received a page for a trauma code.

"It's time to go," she told Storm, silencing her pager.

Never would there be a time when her heart didn't skip a beat, adrenaline spiral, rush through her veins when called to assist a victim knocking on or walking through death's door. It wasn't about assuaging her ego when she saved lives but keeping a loved one with their families for just a little bit longer.

Storm practically had to run to keep up with her. They weaved their way through the corridors between other doctors, nurses, patients, and visitors and grabbed the nearest elevator to take them to the trauma suite on the first floor.

They were alone in the elevator.

Storm walked over, pushed her playfully against the elevator wall. She messed around with the king of seduction and now he was about to show her who was in control. He closed in, his lips whisper close against hers as he captured her eyes with his, grabbing her full attention.

"Will you do me the honor of being my date, Summer?"

Her mouth dropped open.

"Yes," she breathed and stared back at him.

The bell rang having arrived at the first floor.

Storm reached to hold the elevator door for her when he looked back over his shoulder to see her leaning against the wall, a silly smile on her face.

She could still feel his heated breath on her lips. Completely, utterly mesmerized, her legs turned to mush.

"Get your game face on, Dr. Benson," he said as he reached and grabbed her hand and propelled her from the elevator.

"You win," she sighed.

Summer was scrubbing when Mariann bolted into the scrub room and stopped dead in her tracks.

"Dear God, Summer, are you okay? I heard what happened. It's a wonder you weren't killed."

"I'm okay. So what do we have?"

"The patient is set to arrive within the next five minutes. One of four victims of a shooting spree at an insurance company, and that's all I know. Before he gets here, I need to tell you something." Her eyes widened upon seeing Storm.

"Who's he?" Mariann whispered, curiosity lighting her face.

"His name is Storm and he's observing," she said, hoping to evade Mariann's innocent yet probing questions.

Mariann leaned down and whispered in Summer's ear, "Just who does he plan to observe, you or the patient?"

Summer glanced over at Storm who stood by the door. Perhaps he felt her stare because he glanced over at her and gave her a wink accompanied by a slow wicked smile revealing a set of glistening white teeth. The combination sent her headlong into a deep blush and made her drop her scrub brush, recalling his seduction scene in the elevator. It awoke the butterflies in her belly, now dancing wildly inside her, accelerating her heartbeat and making her mouth suddenly dry. She was putty in his hands and probably a situation she'd do well to avoid, yet as much as she reminded herself, she couldn't forget how it felt to sleep beside him and wake up with him, like déjà vu.

"Yeah, just what I thought," Mariann teased, catching the interaction between them and handing her a new scrub brush.

She focused back on Mariann. "What exactly did you want to tell me?"

Mariann leaned in close to Summer. "It's off the record, and you never heard this from me, please."

"What is it?" she asked, drying her hands.

"Well," Mariann whispered, "Dr. O'Malley has a tremor in his right hand."

Summer's eyes widened in surprise.

"His dominate hand if I'm not mistaken. When did you notice this?"

"The past three times I happened to assist him in surgery over the past two weeks," Mariann said as she assisted Summer into her protective gear.

"How serious is the tremor?"

"Very serious considering his last three patients died from him accidently nicking arteries. His hand normally doesn't start trembling until ten or fifteen minutes into surgery. Gradually, the longer he operates, the worse it gets, or I should say the more agitated he gets. I wanted you to know in advance."

"Agitated?" Summer asked.

"Just about anything sets him off. As of late, his temper is explosive. He yells at us in surgery, making us uneasy. The other day, he berated a young nurse until she was in tears and threatened to walk out."

Summer gave her a grim smile. "Great. I'm not Dr. O'Malley's favorite person right now either so this should prove interesting."

Marianne sighed. "I hated getting you involved, but you're the only one who'll go head to head with him. I know the other surgeons, technicians, even the residents noticed yet they're too afraid to speak for fear of jeopardizing their jobs if they spoke against him."

"There's a lot at stake. The patient's life is foremost." Summer looked over at Storm, her smile fading. "It might get a bit rowdy inside there. Promise me you won't do anything. If I need you, I'll tell you."

Storm didn't like the sound of that and felt his body tense.

As soon as the doors swung wide and Summer and Storm stepped through, Dr. O'Malley looked up from reading the patient's chart. His face reddened with fury. Summer felt the stares of her team boring into her, wondering of Storm's presence, but she ignored them.

Dr. O'Malley slammed the chart down on the stand and confronted Summer.

Storm stepped in front of her.

Dr. O'Malley looked around Storm's shoulder at Summer. "What the hell is he doing in here? He's not a doctor, and I want him out of here. Right now!"

"He stays," she said. "He's got clearance."

"Like hell he does!" Dr. O'Malley barged out the doors, ripped off his gloves, and reached for the phone.

Summer exhaled. This wasn't going well at all. She looked over at Storm.

He winked at her.

A chuckle escaped her. He had the damnest effect on her.

"By the way, don't lock your knees or I'll have to scoop you off the ground," she said and tossed him a humorous look over her shoulder as he stationed himself next to the door.

Within hearing, she heard a female technician reply quietly to another technician, "I wouldn't mind scooping him up." While the other replied, "With pleasure."

Their comments didn't necessarily surprise her or bother her, she could well understand his magnetism and how it affected the female population. She observed it earlier firsthand walking down the hospital corridors, seeing many young women's heads turn his direction, easily capturing their attention with his stealth-like walk, graceful yet predatory, always aware of his surroundings. While he claimed it necessary they walk so close, she saw it as tormenting and glorifying teasing with the barest brush of his hand at her waist, the brush of his arm. It was one-sided, her imagination running wild, because he had no interest in her whatsoever. If he knew how he affected her, he'd undoubtedly laugh at her whimsical musings. Especially her dreams, all consumed with him—from the heat of his skin to his warm breath against her cheek to his strong hands touching her most intimate parts. Yet even in her dreams, he pushed her away.

Storm watched her walk across the room and converse with the nurses.

Scrubs. Limp pieces of cotton and linen wrinkled and a size too big, not appreciating or acknowledging the curves underneath their wearer.

But Storm certainly did.

The dazzling image Summer provoked when she thought he was an intruder wearing only lacy panties and seeing the bare firm roundness of her breasts burned in his mind. This morning when she walked beside him and innocently brushed her hand against his leg, his arm, he had to grit his teeth to quiet his heart jumpstarting with a kick against his ribs. His raging desire to take a detour and ravage her inside a vacated stairwell was great. Now, as he looked toward the empty trauma cart sitting sheeted and in the middle of the room under blazing lights waiting for the patient, he imagined her once again ripping the buttons off her doctor's coat revealing her heavenly body and them rocking the wheels off the cart.

It was all one sided obviously. She had a career path, was highly focused, and way out of his league. Then again, he never had a high level of commitment to any particular woman. Now, he began to count the number of days he'd been without sex.

Too many to count.

It wasn't just about sex when he thought of Summer Benson. For almost twenty years, her name conjured such words in his mind as a respectable lady of quality who any man would be proud to call his wife and the mother of his children. The woman he imagined himself married to, a farfetched dream of his.

In short, he wasn't good enough for her, too rough around the edges; not to mention, he courted his own set of issues around his neck. It seemed like a lifetime ago when he tried to end his life and now thanked God his bid was unsuccessful.

Last night, she'd promised to stay on her side of the bed, but she broke her promise. He woke up with her cuddled softly against his side three different times and each time he almost reached for her, indulged, yet he resisted no matter how many times she whispered his name in her sleep.

The only way he could resist her was by physically getting out of bed. He paced the floor at the foot of her bed, watched her sleep, and contemplated a cold shower but didn't want to wake her. When that didn't work, he pulled his bottle of whiskey from his bag, took three hardy sips, went outside, and smoked two cigarettes. He got himself in a predicament. Summer not only needed protected against Malone, but from him. He'd make it his mission to find the guy terrorizing Summer as soon possible for the most obvious reason to protect her but also so he could leave his heart intact. When he thought it safe to return to bed, he dreamt of her—wild, erotic, and restless dreams. When he woke for the last time, he felt more exhausted than he did before he went to bed.

He had to deny their physical attraction because if he touched her, it would be all over, no stopping him. She had a magnetic pull on him, and it tugged at him and ate away at his defenses so many times since the first time he saw her. It wore him out emotionally and physically.

A minute later, Dr. O'Malley barged back into the trauma room and, from across the room, pointed at Storm threateningly.

"I don't know whose strings you managed to pull but don't get too comfortable."

Summer watched the exchange.

Storm returned a nod to him, and if Summer had to decipher the gesture, it meant he was open to discussing the matter with him anytime, anywhere.

"Oh this could get pretty ugly and very interesting," Mariann said quietly in her ear as she also witnessed the exchange.

Suddenly, the doors burst open with two emergency technicians pushing a middle-aged man on a gurney while simultaneously trying to subdue him. Blood poured from the center of his chest and seeped from his mouth.

Quickly, they transferred him to the trauma cart and began ripping away his clothes.

Storm's fantasy just turned into a bloody nightmare.

"He's going to kill me!" the man wheezed, his words coming out in a breathless rush through his oxygen mask. He ripped the mask aside and coughed up blood, large droplets with a mixture of blood clots.

Summer watched the nurses work on the patient, placing leads on his chest, running IVs, and lines while x-ray technicians worked alongside them.

"Report!" Summer yelled over at one of her residents.

"Fifty-two-year-old male, penetrating injury to the chest wall, gunshot wound by thirty-eight caliber, possible lung collapse, right side with severe blood loss."

"He's suffering from subcutaneous emphysema," Summer noted to Dr. O'Malley as he cleansed the two wound areas. The patient's neck veins were distended like thick cords and every grueling breath he attempted sounded like a grizzly sucking sound. His body swelled with nearly every breath because air seeped from his lungs and into the space outside his chest cavity under the skin.

Suddenly, the patient raised his head, gripped Summer's forearm, and rasped, "Don't let him find me," he begged.

"You're safe," she assured him as she glanced toward the doors and couldn't help but wonder if in fact someone might seek revenge. If that occurred, it would place them all in danger. One quick look at Storm who stood next to the door automatically soothed her nerves. If a situation arose, he'd protect them, but she prayed it never came to that.

When her eyes flitted over to him, he looked at her so intently as if looking through the window of her soul.

The very next minute, Dr. O'Malley wrenched the patient's hand forcibly away from Summer's forearm and slammed his palm against the patient's forehead, slamming his head ruthlessly back down on the table.

"Dr. O'Malley!" Summer shouted, feeling her temper flare. She was abhorred by his actions as was everyone else who stopped in their tracks and stared at him.

"For God's sake!" Dr. O'Malley growled. "Would someone please put this patient to sleep?"

The nurses worked securing the chest tube and putting the patient under, but Summer still reeled in shock at his behavior. She glanced at Storm under her lashes. He looked at her, his gaze unwavering.

She had no time to analyze Dr. O'Malley's erratic behavior since the x-rays showed two bullets lodged just millimeters from the patient's heart. She quickly opened the patient's chest, and they both started working on removing the blood from the chest cavity.

Dr. O'Malley advised, "You take the bullet on the left, and I'll take the one by the heart. It doesn't look like he has any blood vessel damage."

She glanced over, the instrument in her hand stilled as she watched him, watched his right hand in particular.

It trembled, very unsteady.

"His blood pressure is dropping dangerously low," a nurse informed them.

Summer leaned over to Dr. O'Malley, whispered in his ear, "I don't think you're in any condition to finish this. I can handle it from here."

"I'm perfectly fine," he countered. He continued working dangerously close to the heart. She worried for her patient's safety, worried he could meet his demise as the others by a nicked artery.

"Dr. O'Malley, please, you're not fine," she said quietly, not wanting to call him out in front of the team.

He turned, glared at her, and resumed working.

She was furious now.

"Let's get something straight, Dr. O'Malley. He's my patient, and I'm in charge. I won't allow you to jeopardize the life of my patient."

He continued to ignore her.

"Dr. O'Malley, do you understand me?" she asked exasperated.

"Mind your own business," he said, gritting his teeth.

"If you don't leave, I'll have you forcibly removed. Is that understood?"

"You wouldn't dare," he growled, glaring over at her. His face twisted with rage. Mariann was right; he wasn't acting like himself.

"I wouldn't hesitate," she replied quietly. "You've got five seconds to step back from this table."

Furious, he whirled around and crashed his fist down onto a tray of steel instruments scattering the entire sterile contents onto the floor in a loud clatter. He barged past her, slamming hard into her shoulder, almost making her lose her balance but two nurses caught her. As he careened around the patient's table, he nearly knocked to the ground a startled young resident. "We're not through with this," he said as he leaned back and kicked open the door. The door slammed against the wall like an explosion, and he walked out.

"Back to work, everyone," she said quietly. She tested her shoulder and winced.

She felt Storm's eyes on her and was tempted to look at him yet not wanting to see his renewed fury at her for her not allowing him to intervene. Reluctantly, she lifted her eyes to meet his.

Fury settled on his face. He raised his brow at her. His eyes flickered to her shoulder.

She rotated her shoulder. A soft gasp escaped. Her shoulder felt unhinged and throbbed like an almighty. She glanced back over at him and saw him shake his head.

For the next several minutes she worked frantically to remove the bullet lodged close to the patient's heart, and even with her concentration highly focused and her hands steady, she struggled steering clear of his arteries.

With her hemostats, she scooped up the bullet and was in the process of lifting it from the patient's body when the unthinkable occurred.

The trauma doors burst open.

"Stop! That man killed my wife," a tall, thin elderly man yelled and pointed his gun at Summer.

She threw her body over the patient.

What happened next was slow motion, like a blur.

Across the room, Storm tackled the man and then there was an explosion, a flash of sparks while the pungent smell of gunpowder rent the air.

She rose up to see the room in chaos and knew she needed to get her team gathered back together; however, she couldn't concentrate beyond the burning, searing pain.

Her upper arm was on fire.

The same side Dr. O'Malley slammed into her shoulder only moments before.

Her world suddenly became cloudy.

She felt someone touch her arm and glanced down to see blood snake through her scrubs, turning them crimson, and drip down her arm and hand. Her eyes traveled back up to see Mariann's horrified look. The next minute, Summer clutched at the trauma cart trying to keep herself upright. A scream echoed across the room, and she realized it was her own.

Then she saw Storm.

He was running toward her.

16

Storm caught Summer before she fell to the ground.

Residents hurriedly took over and cared for the patient while hospital security guards removed the lone gunman. Emergency physicians and nurses exploded into the room and lent assistance. Meanwhile, Storm ran with Summer cradled in his arms to another trauma bay with Mariann following.

Mariann pulled the curtain for privacy then patted the trauma cart and waited for him to lay her down, but he held onto her, squeezed her against his chest, his face anguished as he stared down at her pale face.

"Storm, I need to see the extent of damage," she said, indicating again for him to lay her down on the trauma cart.

Reluctantly, he lay Summer down gently with his hand cradling her head.

Two residents rushed to Mariann's side to assist as she cut away Summer's top.

Mariann looked up at Storm. "You can step out, and we'll take it from here."

Storm shook his head as he looked down at Summer's pale face. "She's not leaving my sight." Storm couldn't forget Summer's secondary threat who could easily be someone from the hospital.

"Okay, have it your way," Mariann replied and kept working.

Summer tried to open her eyes but couldn't; they felt like lead weights. She felt something warm and numbing snake its way through her left arm.

Then she remembered.

She'd been shot.

Panic welled inside her.

"Storm!" she strangled out a scream.

Then suddenly she felt his big strong hand envelope hers. His voice, shaky and distracted, whispered against her ear, "I'm right here."

She peeled her eyes open, needing to see his face just to ensure he was okay. "You didn't get hurt, did you?"

"No, I didn't," he told her.

"I'd never forgive myself if you were." She sighed with relief.

Mariann leaned down and looked at her. "You're one lucky girl, Dr. Benson. The bullet grazed your arm. We're going to get you all patched up. Just relax."

She laid there while they bandaged her and watched a mirage of expressions cross Storm's face. He looked saddened, furious, regretful, and anguished. She squeezed his hand, and he gave her a small smile, nothing at all like the brilliant smile he gave her earlier when she scrubbed.

"Who shot me?" she whispered.

"Evidently, the man you operated on denied the gunman's wife insurance coverage for a cancer treatment doctors believed would have prolonged her life."

She frowned. "There's always a story behind every patient and how they end up on my table."

"And now you are the story," he said gravely and shook his head as he looked at the cut on her forehead, abrasions on her cheek from the car accident, and now this. Slowly, his hand slipped away from hers so they could finish bandaging her.

They assisted her to a sitting position and replaced her scrub top.

Storm got off his cell phone and headed toward her.

She tried to stand in part to show him she was perfectly fine, but her legs decided to fail her.

His hands shot out and grasped her, easily settling her back on the cart. He pointed at her. "Don't move."

For fifteen minutes, they sat in silence while technicians and nurses cleaned the room.

"What are you thinking?" she whispered.

"Just about what happened today," he replied distractedly.

"We normally don't have gunmen prowling the hospital. What happened today was a rare occurrence. If it weren't for you, I'm not sure how the rest of us would have fared, so thank you."

"You're thanking me for not protecting you?" He laughed harshly.

"You got the gun away from him, and you protected us. So yes, I'm thankful you were there."

He shook his head, disbelieving.

She reached for his hand. "He could have easily fired off more than one shot, killing one or all of us. Now, let's get out of here. I need to go to the chief's office and talk to him."

He nodded and gave her his arm, and together they strolled from the trauma center to catch the nearest elevator to the third floor.

Storm was leaning against the wall waiting for her when she left the chief's office. He reached for her, gently rubbed her sore shoulder, steering clear of her bandage.

"Are you okay?" he asked, his face barely containing his anger as he watched her grimace with pain.

"Just fine," she returned lightly. "I'd pay a million dollars for a shower right now."

"A million dollars, you say?" he asked with a chuckle. "I think I can make that happen for you."

"I've been officially sent home to recoup for two days. I say we run from this place as quick as we can before someone finds work for us. What do you say?" she asked with a teasing smile.

His hand was strong, firm, and protective as it rested against her middle back as he escorted her to the parking garage.

He opened her door and gently assisted her into the seat especially when her arms and legs were unwilling to move in unison; they felt a bit like rubber from the medication. She watched him round to the driver's side where he opened the door and was about to get in when he hesitated.

She glanced over at him to see what caught his attention.

Dr. O'Malley.

Tension crawled up her neck and down her spine as she watched Dr. O'Malley walk to his car just a short distance away.

This was going to get ugly.

"Storm," she said, reaching for him, but too late, he already closed the door on her plea and walked decisively toward Dr. O'Malley.

She saw Dr. O'Malley look over his shoulder, and when he saw who it was, she could have sworn he tried to run to his car. She couldn't blame him. Storm's stature was intimidating. From where she sat, it looked like Dr. O'Malley's head barely reached Storm's shoulder. She would've laughed if not for the fact she worried about the outcome, wondering if it would result into physical violence. She had to prepare herself for the distinct possibility of Dr. O'Malley being her next trauma patient.

She held her breath as she watched the exchange.

Dr. O'Malley rushed to get inside his car and tried to slam the door on Storm, but Storm caught the door, pried it open a little wider while he leaned down to talk to him. She couldn't see Dr. O'Malley's face, and it worried her even more. Was Storm choking him? She craned her neck to see and couldn't see anything because of the car's tinted windows.

"Please don't do anything, Storm," she whispered fervently.

Face-to-face with Dr. O'Malley, Storm glared at him. He wished for nothing more than to jerk him from his car and give him an ass kicking he'd never forget. What held him back was the lady in his car who undoubtedly watched his every move, and he knew how upset she'd become if he did anything. Since he'd crawl to the ends of the earth to avoid upsetting her, he'd let her feelings sway him just this once, but his patience skated on thin ice.

"You again," Dr. O'Malley snorted at Storm.

"You know why I'm here. The next time you see my face, you'll look up at me from the ground while trying to figure out how to gather your body parts. Don't ever touch her again, not in any way. If I see you so much as brush her arm, I'll break your arm. I'll hurt you so bad you'll wish you were dead, is that understood?"

"Are you threatening me?" Dr. O'Malley challenged.

"Yes. I'll make good on my promise too. You can count on it. I'm itching for an excuse to sink my teeth into you, you sorry little pansy ass."

"I'll press charges!"

"Not if you're dead," Storm returned and slammed Dr. O'Malley's car door so hard it rocked the car.

"Oh my god," Summer muttered and slid farther down into the seat as she watched Storm walk back toward the car, his face still unrecovered from his fury.

Storm got into the car and sat there for a moment, obviously trying to regain control of his temper. He looked over at her.

"I can take care of myself," she said quietly as she watched Dr. O'Malley peel away. *At least his hands and legs were intact*, Summer thought humorously.

"Did you honestly think I'd let that incident go?"

She felt the heat of his stare and kept her eyes focused straight ahead. "One could only hope," she squeaked.

"I won't tolerate someone treating you like that."

"Thank you," she sighed. "But I have a feeling Dr. O'Malley and I aren't over, especially when he finds out I went to the chief about him."

She couldn't help but feel regret regarding Dr. O'Malley's situation with the tremor in his hand. His career as a surgeon may end a lot sooner than he ever anticipated.

"Don't worry about it," he said and started the car.

He sat there a moment longer. "So there's nothing between the two of you as far as a personal relationship? I recall him confessing his love for you."

"Of course not. He's a colleague and nothing more," she replied indifferently and stared out the window. Dr. O'Malley's impromptu visit with his confession was an incredibly awkward situation.

A soft chime echoed in the car.

In her musings, she was caught off guard when he suddenly leaned over and reached around her to grab the shoulder harness of her belt restraint.

She'd forgotten to buckle up.

Her breath caught.

His face was within mere inches of hers.

She felt the rush of his heated breath against her cheek, smelled his mint fresh breath from him popping a mint into his mouth just seconds before they entered the garage.

Her eyes fastened on his slightly parted lips—sensual, full, and so inviting.

She fully expected him to move away from her, keep her at arm's length; instead, he turned a bit toward her, the leather seat creaking in protest, and pressed his index finger hesitantly against her bottom lip where his eyes was completely focused, mesmerized. He ran his finger softly across her bottom lip, stopping at the corner of her mouth. He reached, softly cupped her cheek as his eyes, drugged and hooded, bored into hers as if he spoke to her, and implored her.

Her breath caught and held.

His hand came to rest against her neck where his thumb found her erratic throbbing pulse. He swirled his thumb against it as if teasing, tantalizing it further, seeing if it could race quicker.

It worked.

The sheer force of his eyes beckoned her to him. She inched forward, testing his resistance and then stopped abruptly when she heard his breath catch.

He swallowed hard as his eyes flickered down to her lips. He dropped his head in defeat.

"Damn," he groaned.

His fingers tensed along her neck as he fought for control.

She felt hot all over, yearned for the taste of him.

"You shouldn't be so damn tempting," he breathed in an anguished whisper.

"I could say the same about you," she confessed with a ragged breath.

Hesitantly, she reached up and cupped his jaw, feeling the roughness of a day's shadow.

"It's okay, really," she urged.

He laughed harshly. "Not okay," he warned her.

"I'm a big girl. I realize it is purely physical between us."

With that statement, she took matters into her own hands. She leaned forward, held his face in her hands, captured his lips hungrily as if in the middle of a desert; and he was the only way to quench her thirst.

And that was all it took to ignite a simmering fire into a full-blown explosion.

He reached for her then.

Sliding his seat back with a flick of a switch, he brought her to lie across his lap where he took control.

He cradled her in his arms gently so not to hurt her bandaged arm. He greedily plundered her lips, slanted his mouth across hers hungrily over and over again while his tongue dipped into her mouth, swirled, teased her tongue into joining the wild rhythm with his as he tantalized her with his mint. He slid it under her tongue then sucked it back out of her mouth. He was quickly losing control, about to teeter off a ledge.

She clutched his shirtfront and moaned. She wanted to get closer to him and get inside him. There was something incredibly erotic sharing a piece of candy while they kissed. She gasped into his mouth as she felt the heady sensation of his hand snaking under her top blazing a scorching path across her belly and up her ribcage where he hooked his thumb under her bra and grazed the curve of her breast.

God, she prayed he didn't have the impression she freely offered up her body for just anyone. She trusted him, and if she chose to explore the delights of heaven, she'd want someone who would guarantee a good time. And he proved his worth, educating her fully on what a real erotic kiss felt like.

She moaned into his mouth.

He closed his eyes and dragged his mouth off hers.

"Damn," he gasped as his chest rose and fell. His eyes were wild when they looked down at her. It was too much; he felt like an inferno wanting to get inside her and explode and seek relief from all the built up tension. He stroked her and felt through the barriers of her clothing, her heated wetness. She clutched his shoulders and delivered feverish kisses against his neck. It was what she did next that sent him headlong off the ledge.

She touched him, the throbbing center of him, ran her hand down his long length now clearly defined inside his jeans. He clenched a fistful of her hair, turned her face aside, and captured her throat, suckled her with his lips and tongue, hungrily nipping her flesh with his teeth as if on a feeding frenzy.

"I…want you…so bad," he rushed out in a whisper.

He threatened to burst, pulsing wildly against her hand with every teasing, slow massaging stroke she gave him. He wanted to rip her clothes off, get her under him so he could ride her with abandon. He trembled with need as shivers curled down his spine, making his hands quiver and his forehead break out into a cold sweat.

Son of a bitch!

He knew she'd feel this good, likening the wondrous feeling of floating on air. He never experienced anything like it before with another woman, even more reason why he had to cool the situation off quickly before it got very out of hand.

He was thankful they were in a car and nowhere close to a horizontal surface. He would have taken her and nothing could have stopped him.

His hand stilled.

"Please," she begged, "don't stop."

"I…we…can't," he broke off, exhaling harshly.

She sighed, leaned up, and placed her hand on his chest feeling his heart pound wildly under her palm. She gave him a tentative smile. "I'm sorry."

"Why are you apologizing?" he asked her, gazing down at her swollen lips, feeling suddenly like a heel. He took advantage. It didn't matter if she were willing or not. He should've known better.

She shrugged.

He leaned forward and gave her a lingering kiss on her forehead. "I can't…won't let this happen again," he promised.

She sighed with regret and positioned herself back into the seat next to him and buckled herself in. She never felt so vulnerable in her life. She'd gotten a taste of him—wild, tumultuous, reckless—and she hungered even more for him only imagining how mind blowing the experience would've been. It was going to be pure hell having him in such close confines and unable to touch him.

What had she gotten herself into?

She stole a glance at him. His profile was rigid, stiff, and full of tension as he drove. He even leaned away from her toward his door as if to ward off the temptation.

"Storm," she said hoarsely as she gazed out the window ten minutes into the drive home. "I release you. You don't have to protect me. I can find someone else."

His head whipped about as he looked at her, but she avoided his stare. "Why would you do that?"

"Because it's going to be awkward now between us, and I feel like I've caused you enough problems the way it is."

"I'm not going anywhere," he said fervently. "You need me."

I need you.

17

As soon as they arrived home, Summer went to shower. She needed to clear the fog of medications from her mind and time to sort out what just happened between her and Storm.

A simple kiss.

Far from simple, their kiss was a fierce windstorm of pent-up anger, insecurity, loneliness, and need. The sheer force of the memory made her unconsciously reach up and touch her swollen bottom lip, feel the tenderness while wishing he was with her right now kissing her senseless.

She walked into the bathroom, slipped off her clogs, peeled off her socks, and scrub bottoms. She tried to maneuver her scrub top over her head yet every position caused pain to shoot up her arm now with the medications wearing off. Thank God, the bullet only grazed her skin and not any tendons, which would have required surgery. Standing in the middle of the bathroom wearing only her panties and her top, she was in a predicament. She could easily call for Storm, but she refused to put him in another awkward situation with her. No matter how much she enjoyed the kiss they shared in the parking garage, he seemed regretful and adamant for it not to happen again.

She looked around her wondering what to do.

Then it came to her.

She walked over to the cabinets, opened a drawer, and lifted out a pair of scissors. She entwined her fingers into the loops of the scissor handles, it felt awkward, and she couldn't get a very good grip.

Twice, the scissors slid from her hand and clattered loudly against the tile floor.

"Damn it!" she hissed. She stooped down once again to pick up the scissors and found herself slipping like a feather to her knees. A light sheen of sweat cast over her forehead. Heat flooded inside her, the lingering side effects of the pain medications. Time wasn't on her side. She knew any minute Storm would check on her and find her pathetically on her knees in the middle of the bathroom floor. She felt like she was in the throes of recuperating from the worst hangover imaginable.

She disliked feeling helpless, disliked the lingering numbness, cloudiness in her mind. She was always in control of her actions and now faced with the possibility she may have to swallow her pride and ask for help. The only person she ever asked for help was from her brother.

Again, she reached for the scissors, one last attempt, and instead grasped the blade. It stung like an almighty.

"Oh!" she gasped, jerking her hand back. Blood flowed freely from her index finger, over her wrist.

"Summer!" Storm knocked none too softly on the door. "Are you okay?"

Startled at his voice, she jerked.

"Perfectly fine," she replied, trying to keep her voice steady and light.

"What are you doing?" he asked curiously. "I thought you were taking a shower."

"I thought I was too," she whispered miserably to herself as she watched blood drip off her hand onto the tile. She had to get up, but everything now seemed fuzzy and her legs suddenly felt like lead weights.

"Why isn't the shower going?" he asked suspiciously.

"It will be soon," she promised in the most even voice she could muster. She glanced enviably over at her walk in shower. She may have to crawl into that walk-in shower. At this very moment, even that seemed like a monumental task.

The doorknob rattled.

"No!" she gasped, realizing she forgot to lock the damn door. If she had the strength, she would've raced across the room and locked it. "Don't come in here," she pleaded.

She swiped the back of her hand across her forehead to wipe the thin veil of sweat running into her eyes. Her stomach started revolting.

Another forceful knock came at the door and a muttered curse.

The blasted man ignored her. He barged right in on her.

She brought her legs up and laid her forehead on her shaky knees after she saw his horrified expression. She could only imagine what she looked like.

Storm couldn't get to her quick enough.

Blood.

Blood was smeared across her forehead, down her cheek and neck, and all over her right hand. His eyes drifted down to the floor speckled with blood droplets.

Scissors.

His eyes landed on the scissors lying beside her and all kinds of thoughts swirled in his mind. Did she accidently cut herself, or did she do it on purpose?

With a wet cloth in hand, he carefully dropped down in front of her, his heart thudded like a drum in his ears as he prayed it wasn't intentional. He worried about her emotional well-being.

Gently, he reached out and, with a fingertip, lifted her chin.

Tears streamed down her face.

He gently wiped the blood from her face and hands.

He discovered just then how very protective he was of her. He would do anything to get her to smile and his urge to fix anything and everything to get her back to her normal self, overrode everything else.

"What's wrong, Summer?" he whispered as he gently brushed the back of his hand against her flushed cheek.

"I can't get my top off," she cried softly. More tears of frustration streamed down her face.

"The scissors?" he asked, suddenly relieved.

"I was going to cut it off," she confessed.

He chuckled despite the situation. He really needed to give her more credit. Reaper always said she was made of tough stuff, yet she was a woman and their feelings were tender.

"Why wouldn't you ask for my help? You think you have to do everything on your own, don't you?"

It startled her, his assessment of her. He was dead-on.

"I've been a burden to you," she whispered.

"No, you haven't," he sighed, examining her sliced finger, a small slice no longer bleeding yet would undoubtedly be tender for a few days. "Can you stand?"

"I'm not sure. My legs are weak, which is how I landed in this heap of a mess," she said, glancing around her at the floor smeared with blood.

He came behind her, wound his arm around her waist, and lifted her effortlessly off the floor.

She tried to pull down her scrub top to cover her panties.

He laughed softly at her shyness.

"I think you're a bit too shaky for a shower," he noted, seeing her legs tremble.

"No," she replied adamantly. "I've got to get this blood off me."

He glanced over at the walk-in shower then over at the bathtub then back at her. "Which do you prefer?"

"Shower," she said weakly and found herself clutching his arm trying to steady herself. His strong arm wrapped around her waist never faltered, just having him near made her feel secure.

"If you could just get me in the shower, I'll hold onto the rails," she suggested.

He walked around to stand in front of her and looked down at her incredulously. He tightened his hold on her waist. "And what if you fell, you'd bust your skull open. I'll help you. Time to get this top off," he said and gently lifted her arms.

"No, you can't help me," she stammered.

"I can and will help you. Don't make me cut this top off you," he said teasingly, but inside, his gut told him to be very careful. He lacked control around her.

She looked away and laughed under her breath. "This is embarrassing."

"Why is it embarrassing? This is no time for modesty," he said, shaking his head playfully at her.

"It's not embarrassing for you?" she countered, looking into his wickedly amused eyes.

"Not in the least," he replied. "Is it me? Are you uncomfortable?"

"No, of course not." She waved off the ludicrous thought. "I know I can trust you."

"What's the problem then? You're a doctor. I thought all shyness flew out the window the first day of medical school."

"You'd think, plus I'm twenty-eight years old." She paused. "I normally don't strip in front of men," she confessed shyly.

For some reason her admission made him feel oddly relieved.

He got eye level with her. "Okay, here's how it's going to go down. I'm going to undress you."

Her eyes flew wide open.

"You can leave on your panties. Then I'm going to undress," he said, receiving another startled look from her. "I'll leave on my boxers and then we can get you a shower." He glanced over at the sink then. "Or I can wash you from the sink," he offered, praying to God she'd adhere to a sponge bath instead because the thought of running water racing down her fine-looking body was a bit much for him to bear.

She exhaled. "I desperately need a shower please."

He made himself start counting. God, he was completely out of his element here. He undressed women, worshipped their bodies, took full advantage of the situations, but he couldn't this time, not with this lady. He'd be nothing less than a gentleman.

Holy shit.

He planned to make this the quickest shower she'd ever have because the thought of her standing before him in all her glory would undoubtedly send him over the edge.

Slowly, she raised her arms and grimaced with pain.

Deep breath.

He peeled off her top and simultaneously swore he wouldn't look at her breasts. He knew it would ensure his downfall if he did. Yet no more than a second later, he came face-to-face with her bountiful creamy flesh encompassed in a pale pink silk confection. Her soft luscious curves successfully robbed him of his senses.

He walked behind her to unsnap her bra. Could he have just unsnapped her bra while he stood in front of her? Yep, in an instant, blindfolded, one handed, with two fingers, and thoroughly inebriated. He knew how to get through any lady's contraption. Yet for his own peace of mind, he chose not to face her, it was best to keep her breasts out of his view. Another reason too, she was modest. He wanted her to feel comfortable around him, feel safe.

When he saw the goose bumps raised on her arms, he halted his bid to unfasten her bra. “You’re cold,” he said as he leaned over and opened the shower door and turned on the shower for them.

“No,” she lied as her teeth begun to chatter.

He flipped on the switch for the sunlamp. The luminous light and heat flooded down on them.

One, two, three…

He counted as he looked back down at her shapely, hollowed back. Her panties rode high on her slim hips. Her skin felt like the smoothest silk. The counting kept him under control but only lasted for so long.

Take a deep breath.

With shaking hands, he reached for her bra fastening, hesitating, willing himself to keep his emotions under control.

When his hands stilled, she glanced at the mirror above the sink and saw his reflection. His eyes were closed, and his lips were moving.

Was he praying?

She quickly looked away. What she saw told her he recognized the chemistry between them and he had difficulty being in such close confines with her. They were both feeling the pain. Inwardly, she smiled.

His warm fingertips brushed her back as he carefully unhooked her bra and slid the straps over her arms.

She covered her breasts with her hands to shield herself. She never felt so exposed. Butterflies raged inside her, fluttered inside her belly at the thought of them showering together.

Behind her, she heard him unsnap his jeans.

She closed her eyes, exhaled a shaky breath.

Next, he unzipped his zipper in one quick fluid motion then the rustle of his jeans as he tugged them off. She heard him take off his shirt and smelled the heady scent of his cologne float around her, numbing her sensibilities.

“What should we do with your bandaged arm?”

“I’ll rebandage it afterwards.”

He looped his arm gently around her waist, assisted her into the shower, and placed her directly beneath the warm, steaming water. He stepped behind her and watched her bow her head, allowing the water to rain down on her for a few minutes. Her hair laid around her like a webbed sheen down the middle of her back.

The vision of a blonde mermaid popped in his mind.

While fantasizing, he happened to notice her shoulders shake.

Oh hell, was she crying?

He swallowed hard.

"Storm, I'm thankful you were with me today. That man could have killed all of us," she cried.

All his carefully laid out plans and rules about keeping his distance suddenly flew out the window. Without hesitation, he turned her around, laid her head against his chest, and held her tightly against him.

"It's okay," he whispered against her hair. "I'm here and I'm not going anywhere."

She released one breast and laid her hand on his shoulder.

Holy Mary, Mother of God.

He felt the imprint of her breast against him, the pillow softness, and the hardness of her nipple. He gulped. He had to keep his hands busy to keep his mind out of the gutter.

"Okay, time to get you cleaned up," he said as he reached for the washcloth and drizzled foaming soap on it. The sweet scent of strawberries swirled around them.

She stepped back, once again cupping her breasts, and looked up at him when he tried to hand her the washcloth.

"I don't have enough hands," she whispered, her face taking on glowering shades of red.

Inwardly, he groaned, and his mouth became dry.

This could only spell trouble.

He cleansed her face, neck, and shoulders, leaving a trail of foaming bubbles. Down the length of her arms and her hands, he painstakingly washed each finger, wrenching a giggle from her.

Laughing together, the washcloth in his hand came to land at the center of her chest where he halted.

She closed her eyes.

His chest rose and fell in a jerky movement as he watched the water run, foaming bubbles slide between her cleavage.

The washcloth slipped from his soapy hands, easily forgotten, and landed with a thud at their feet. His hands skimmed her incredibly soft shoulders and up her neck to her face where his thumbs caressed her cheeks drawing a smile from her.

And a moan.

Downward, his hands slid and feathered alongside her breasts.

She gasped when he turned her around and brought her back up against him. She dropped her hands from her breasts, now fully exposed for him to see just over her shoulder, and planted her palms against his muscular thighs, feeling the flex of his muscles.

His hands slid under her arms to the underside of her breasts where she overflowed in his hands. He cupped her, massaged her, while his fingertips feathered across her nipples, teasing them relentlessly and turning them pebble hard under his ministrations, wrenching a deep throaty groan from him.

Her body instinctively bowed against his, molding her cheeks against him, feeling his cock rigid and firm as it pressed and throbbed against her lower back. Her mouth fell open while she breathed out short hard gasps. She leaned her head back against his shoulder and let him take full advantage.

He was on fire.

His hot mouth clamped tightly against her neck as his hands rounded down over her ribs and over her hips where he pulled her back tightly against him so she could feel the heat of his arousal.

"Don't stop," she begged.

Her words suddenly clicked, and his mind became engaged. He dropped his hands from her body as if she scorched him.

God damn it!

"Oh no, no, no," he swore vehemently as he quickly stepped back from her.

"I'm sorry. I don't know what came over me," he confessed in a whisper over her shoulder.

"Storm, it's okay," she said as she turned around and faced him, covering her breasts again.

"It's not okay," he muttered. With shaky hands, he reached for the shampoo, practically wrenched it off the wall, drizzled some over the top of her hair, and slowly massaged her scalp.

She sighed with pleasure and tried to make light of the situation.

"Do you realize that when you're aroused your eyes turn the most intense gray, like a gray blue," she said softly, tilting her face up to his.

"Actually, no," he sighed heavily. "I've never noticed, but thank you for the compliment. I'm going to get out of here and make us dinner," he said distractedly as he finished rinsing her hair.

"Thank you. Dinner sounds wonderful," she said, staring up at him for a long moment.

"Feel better?" he asked as he toweled-dried off then set to the task of cleaning the blood off the floor.

Soon after, he reached around her and turned off the water. He opened the shower door and quickly reached for a towel to cover her, more for selfish reasons than anything. His control was lessening by the second.

"Much better," she said, smiling up at him while she secured the towel around her.

What she was about to say was contrary to how she really felt. She had to block out the image of him standing before her in snug black boxers showing the very outline of him, block out water trickling down his body stacked with hard muscle, and forget how his hands and lips felt on her body less than two minutes ago. She wanted him, plain and simple. It was difficult for her to rein in her desires, but for the sake of his friendship, she would.

"Storm, we're friends, right? If we couldn't be anything else, I'd want us to be friends and not just because you're best friends with my brother."

He sighed, gave her a soft smile, and gazed intently in her eyes. "Yes, we're friends because I've known you much longer than a few days but for more than half your life. Even before I met you, I felt protective of you. Reaper would confide in me about how much it bothered him that you were taunted by others because of your young age in medical school, about those horrendous men you dated while in your residency program, and so many times I wanted to arrive on your doorstep and protect you."

"The day I met you, you looked less than thrilled at the prospect of protecting me," she reminded him.

"You grew on me," he told her as he reached up and pushed aside a curtain of her wet hair from her cheek. If only she knew what really happened with him on that day when he almost ended his life. "We'll always be friends, no worries. Now, do you think you can handle it from here?" he asked as he laid his towel over his shoulders.

In her mind, he conjured up a tantalizing picture of him walking out of the ocean, his body glistening with beads raining down his body, the sun shining down on his glossy wet hair.

"Yes, thank you," she said.

Storm quickly skirted out of the bathroom and closed the door behind him. He leaned heavily against it. His heartbeat thudded hard against his chest and could've easily vibrated through the door.

He let out a deep breath.

Fuck!

How long had he been holding his breath?

Another lapse of his willpower nearly had her up against the wall while he gave her his all. She obviously wasn't aware how many times her chastity was in real danger with him every step of the way during the shower. He convinced her they could be just friends. Now, he had to convince himself.

He pushed himself off the door, wiped his forehead free of the sheen of perspiration with his towel, and headed to the bedroom to dress.

Minutes later, he headed to the kitchen to ravage the cabinets to make them dinner.

Summer bandaged her upper arm, tested it; it was still a bit tender and achy. She could easily seek relief with pain medication but wanted no part of it. She needed to have a clear, level head around Storm.

She felt envious of his willpower and his ability to ignore the heightened sexual tension between them. Now, she was thoughtful as she stood in her walk-in closet. If the circumstances were different and she was alone this evening, she'd grab her standby silky lounge pants, her threadbare favorite University of Florida T-shirt, and pull on a pair of soft fuzzy socks. But because Storm was here, she had to put a little more effort into her dress.

She wanted to look pretty yet wear clothes signaling comfort yet dressed up better than normal yet conservative and not too revealing yet carefree as if she never pondered what she wore because she had no one to impress. She laughed under her breath at her ridiculous argument; no one to impress. Yet the very reason why she stood before her closet a full fifteen minutes in contemplation.

He wouldn't notice her if she walked out wearing nothing but a pair of shorts as evident by the shower they just took together.

He was made of cast iron.

She knew no other man who could shower with the opposite sex wearing only panties and nothing else and remain utterly unfazed. She believed she got under his skin but for him to pull back took incredible willpower. She had no such willpower. He remained a gentleman, and unabashedly, she wished he hadn't.

Her wicked side suddenly revealed itself. She laughed as she weeded through the very back of her closet, obviously for clothes she rarely wore, and peeled her choices off the hangers. She consoled herself with the fact it wasn't fair she was the only one hot and bothered. If he was in fact the hot-blooded guy she got a taste of earlier, it was going to be fun watching him get a bit hot under the collar.

She tore back into her bathroom, brushed her teeth fiercely, simultaneously hiked her leg into her sink bowl, lathered on shaving cream, and gave her razor a run for its money. She tossed her hair, slathered on some good smelling lotion, and hurriedly dressed.

A delicious aroma of Italian food drifted from her kitchen stopped her dead in her tracks. She groaned. Not only was he gorgeous and an enthusiastic well-honed kisser but a fabulous cook to boot. She loved a multitalented man.

Before she walked from her bedroom, she hesitated and looked at her reflection one more time in the mirror. She never tried her hand at seduction before, never dressed or done anything to turn a guy's eye toward her. She was completely out of her element. Yet she couldn't help giggle and couldn't wait to see his facial expression.

Knowing him, he'd probably order her back in the bedroom to change just like her brother. She would if he requested her to do so, but if she were right about him, he'd go into overdrive trying to ignore her this evening while she had the time of her life watching him avoid the eye candy specifically displayed for his eyes only.

Soberly, one objective brought itself into the forefront of this evening.

No sex.

She pledged this evening would be in the name of fun only, maybe even playful and downright dangerously exciting, but no sex because she didn't want to overstep her boundaries with him.

Along those lines, she was fully aware she'd be the one seeking a cold shower tonight.

She took a deep breath and walked out.

18

Oh hell!

He did a double take over his shoulder when she walked out of the bedroom.

This was going to be one fucking long night.

She wore a white lace tank top with spaghetti straps showing ample mouthwatering cleavage, buttoning up the front with a row of miniature pearl buttons. He calculated at least twenty. It fell midtorso and exposed a generous portion of her skin down to her belly button met by a low riding white skirt, giving a whole new meaning of a short skirt. Her legs were shapely and tanned, leading to cute small feet.

She was breathtaking.

He instantly hardened, felt excruciating pulsing making him yearn for immediate gratification. He gave her his back and pretended to stir the spaghetti sauce, pretended the earth hadn't trembled beneath his feet. Or his knees just turn to jelly.

She looked like the cat that swallowed the canary.

Wine. Wine was the one necessary ingredient for the recipe of Storm's seduction. Wine had a way about seeping through your veins, warming you up, making you feel good, and uninhibited in what you say, think, and what you do. It made you hungry. For some people, hungry for food; for others, sex. It also gave you energy.

She was for all of the above.

Minus the sex part.

And just the ammunition she needed against Storm so she could learn more about the man who swore to protect her with his life, haunted her dreams for years, and highly successful keeping her at arm's length.

A bottle of red wine sat on the kitchen island. She smiled. The only problem, there was only one glass. She felt confident within minutes he'd reach for his wine glass for the sake of saving his sanity if nothing else.

She walked up to the island, plopped her elbows down, leaned over the edge, and watched him stand before the stove cooking, his back to her. His black tank top stretched taunt across the broad expanse of his back; and with every movement, a muscle bunched, tapering down to his slim waist where he wore cut-off jean shorts and was barefooted. He conjured all sorts of sexual images in her mind. Yet she also couldn't ignore how his body looked incredibly tense.

He felt and heard her every movement behind him. Mostly, aware of the emotional rip tide they encountered on this day alone, both knowing it could've ended much differently with her killed. Now, they knew they'd be infinitely linked from this day forward.

She tried to put him at ease. "I thought I was in the wrong house when I smelled the aroma coming from my kitchen."

He barely glanced over his shoulder at her. "Is that right?" He chuckled, pretending to stir the sauce.

"So what's for dinner?" she asked.

"Spaghetti."

"I love spaghetti. I don't get to make it often since it's only me."

He never heard her, too preoccupied with sending prayers heavenward she'd keep her distance.

"What are you stirring?" she asked yet another question trying to get him to turn around and look at her.

"Spaghetti sauce."

He heard her walk slowly, methodically around the island toward him. He kept his head down trying hard to concentrate on the sauce.

"I don't cook often," she said, her arm brushing his and looking into the pot of sauce, "but I can only imagine if you continue to stir that sauce so frantically it's bound to turn into puree."

He barked out a laugh under his breath and slowed his stirring. "How's your arm?" he asked, again avoiding eye contact.

"Sore and achy."

He literally sprinted across the kitchen to the countertop and grabbed her pain medication, already prepared a glass of water for her before she could waylay him.

"No, thank you. I don't want any medications tonight."

"Sure?" he asked over his shoulder, careful, only glancing at her face and not an inch below her chin. He wanted to put her to bed, tucked safely away from him so he wouldn't be so damned tempted.

And boy, what she served up was tempting.

He rifled through a bottom cabinet for a pot to boil the spaghetti.

When he rose and turned around, she was right there, leaning back against the counter, watching him fill the pot with water and set it on the stove. The ceiling fan circulated a heady sweet floral scent from her filling the room and intoxicating him.

He reached up and grabbed two plates from the cabinet. The plates clattered loudly against each other; they barely made it to the island in one piece.

His hands trembled.

She tossed a smug, confident smile his direction.

Try to resist me now.

Inwardly, he cringed at his current situation. He was at a loss on the best way to handle this scenario. He lived the majority of his life as a soldier, well versed in strategic scenarios, calculations of risks and the odds of how quickly and safely he could complete a mission and get his men out in one piece. But right now, he wanted to throw his hands up in the air and surrender. He was simply no match for her deadly charm. He'd rather sever his losses but couldn't; instead, he pledged to keep his distance.

God, it was going to be hard.

"I found some red wine. Would you like a glass?" he asked in a voice sounding a bit high-pitched and not at all like himself. He walked over to the island and opened the bottle. With his back to her, he took his time unscrewing the cork, all the while his mind churned wondered what she was thinking. He poured her a glass and slid it across the countertop to her.

"Won't you have some wine with me, Storm?"

He hesitated. The first rule in the book when protecting another, never indulge in drink in case a threat presented itself. Well, the threat did present itself, and it stood right beside him. And he damn well needed a drink. He was no lightweight but a seasoned drinker and knew wine wouldn't have much effect on him. Besides, he was a nervous wreck.

She smiled as she watched him take out another wine glass and fill it to the rim. She reached for her wineglass and took a good gulp of the sweet-tasting red wine hoping it would give her the courage to go through with her plan.

He did the same, except he gulped down the entire contents in one swig. Maybe she had gotten under his skin already. He poured himself another glass. She reached up and touched his arm.

He flinched.

She laughed under her breath. "May I have a taste?" she asked. Her eyes seductively dropped down to his lips.

He stared at her wide-eyed.

"The sauce," she clarified and watched his shoulders sag with relief. She nearly burst out laughing.

Together, they walked over to the stove where he picked up a fresh spoon, dipped it into the sauce, blew on it to cool the food. He went to hand her the spoon, but she opened her mouth and closed her eyes, waiting in anticipation.

Hesitantly, he slid the spoon through her lips, into her mouth. She clamped her mouth around the spoon. When it came time for him to pull it out, she tightened her lips around the spoon until she gradually let him pull it out a bit at a time.

It was almost his undoing.

They both took long drinks of their wine.

Was she trying to get him drunk by chance, he wondered, smiling to himself.

"I'll slice the strawberries," she offered, taking another gulp of wine before sitting her glass down.

She tumbled a carton of strawberries onto the chopping block and started slicing

"So, Storm, do you have a girlfriend, a significant other?"

Behind her, she heard him pause.

"No," he replied softly.

"Did you ever have a true love?"

He contemplated her question and then admitted sheepishly, "I did have a true love when I was ten years old."

"Who was this incredible woman?"

"Her name was Starr Morgan, a neighbor. She was a tomboy. We played with military toys, and she was quite strategic. She and I traveled many a mile together on foot and explored."

"Pretty?"

"Not really. However, when I think of her, I recall her having a pretty smile."

"So what happened?"

"She moved to Hawaii because of her father's job."

"How did that make you feel?"

"I was crushed, of course. I fell hopelessly in love with her for three solid days. She was the first girl I ever kissed. For a number of years, we corresponded up until she married and then we lost contact."

"Surely you've had more than just one love?"

He chuckled as he dropped the spaghetti into the boiling water.

"No, actually I haven't. Being a SEAL, I traveled to foreign countries with someone trying to kill me at least two hundred and fifty days out of the year and the remainder of that time I trained, which never left much room for romance and marriage. Although I've known many SEALs who have tried. The only couple I've seen make it work was your brother and Sibella."

"She's a wonderful sister to me."

"So what about you, Summer Benson, any true loves on your front?"

Her knife stilled from slicing as the realization hit her. She never had a true love.

"No one actually," she replied forlornly. Unless she counted all the years dreaming of a faceless battled hardened SEAL, Storm.

Storm stopped stirring the sauce, turned around, and leaned against the stove. He reached his hands out to her hesitantly but then pulled them back.

"I'm twenty-eight and never been in love," she whispered to herself.

"That doesn't mean men haven't fallen in love with you," he countered.

He could be one of them.

"Yeah, they're lined up at my front door, can't you see? I have no such experience," she replied wistfully.

"Oh yes you do," he laughed under his breath.

She glanced over her shoulder at him curiously.

"Don't you remember your anatomy lab partner in med school?"

Her knife clattered against the counter.

"Oh my god!" she shrieked. "How could I forget? Yes, he followed me around like a puppy. One day, he presented me with an elegant pink gift-wrapped box, and thinking like any young woman, I thought it was chocolates. So imagine my surprise when I opened the box to find a real heart inside belonging to our donor's body. How very strange," she said, shaking her head.

"And your date with him," he urged her to continue her story. He was nearly in hysterics laughing behind her. His laughter was melodious, and she committed it to her memory.

"You mean the one single date I had with that freak. He wouldn't take no for an answer, so finally, I agreed to go to the movies with him, but that's not what happened. He drove out to a deserted country road where he locked the doors and acted as if it was open season with me. He had me smashed up against my door and acted like an octopus with his hands crawling all over my body. It was funny at first because I couldn't believe the audacity then it turned serious when he ripped the front of my blouse. He became very aggressive and infuriated, and I tried not to think about the inevitable, him raping me."

She shuddered and turned around to glance up at Storm to see a murderous expression cross his face then just as suddenly disappeared.

"My saving grace was his cell phone ringing. He answered it because it was his mother, and I was able to escape. Around and around the car he chased me. I swear it felt like musical chairs until finally I was able to jump inside his car. I drove off and left him on that pitch-black country road. I called Kyle as soon as I got home because by that time,

I realized the seriousness of the situation. Strange, but three days later on the following Monday, he transferred to another school. I never saw him again after that ridiculous date and never felt quite so relieved actually." She returned to slicing strawberries and heard a smirk behind her.

Once again, she looked over her shoulder at him. "What's so funny? I think you've laughed enough at my expense over that situation."

Suddenly, uncontrollable laughter rippled from him, floated in the air between them. It made her smile. She realized then just how much she enjoyed being with him and didn't want the night to end.

When he continued to laugh, now in hysterics, something dawned on her as she watched him clutch the countertop. Somehow, she knew her brother was involved in her date's sudden switch of schools. And he wasn't the only one.

"He didn't!" she exclaimed.

"Oh yeah we did," he confessed, smothering his laughter.

"We? What exactly did you guys do to him?"

"He needed a comeuppance," he defended, still laughing under his breath.

"Oh my god, who else was involved?"

"Me and your brother," he said hesitantly, obvious he was a terrible liar.

"And?" she said, placing her hands on her hips.

"Well, our SEAL team, but they just came along for the ride."

She shook her head in disbelief. "Please tell me you didn't kill him."

"Of course not," he scoffed. "But I must say, your brother, had he been alone with him it may have turned out much differently."

She motioned him with her hand, waiting to hear the rest of the story.

"We hitched a ride in an Apache helicopter and visited your boyfriend," he said, grinning.

"He wasn't my boyfriend!" she adamantly replied then saw his smile and knew he only tried to get a rise out from her.

"Well, we dressed out in uniform carrying weaponry to the hilt, what we'd wear on a normal mission that would scare the hell out of an ordinary person. We had all intention for the kid to feel as if the wrath of God came down on his ass. In the middle of the night, we fast-roped down onto his roof from the Apache and stormed his apartment. We took him from his warm bed and hauled his sorry ass right back to the deserted country road he took you to. We stripped him down, marched him to a nearby cattle field, and tied him to a fencepost.

"Oh my heavens," she said, cupping her cheeks.

"Although we uttered not one word to him, he knew why we were there."

"Was he okay when you released him?" She looked at him incredulously, swallowed hard.

He leaned his head back and laughed.

"You guys released him, right?"

It was difficult for him to stop laughing, but he managed. "Yeah, after a few hours watching the cattle indulge in their new-found salt lick and witnessing his painful experience, we decided to release him. It was one hell of a show. He was in one piece, but I imagine he was mighty sore."

"Good grief! I never knew that!"

"Well, you were never meant to know, but it's too funny of a story to pass up. Now, that should give you a taste of our protective nature."

"Our?" she asked curiously.

His face suddenly sobered. "I meant your brother, of course."

"Of course," she said, her smile fading quickly. "I knew you only meant my brother. He's the reason why you're here to protect me," she said, turning her back on him. Mindlessly, she sliced the strawberries and felt strangely disappointed he couldn't admit he was the least bit protective of her even though she witnessed it firsthand, but now denied it.

He stood behind her still and silent, yet she could feel the tension radiate from his body. She placed the last few strawberries on the block and sliced them probably a bit too vigorously. The knife handle shifted and the blade nicked her. She jerked back her hand.

Blood dripped from her thumb.

"Damn!" She dropped the knife, walked over to the sink, and placed her hand under the cold water to see the damage.

Suddenly, he appeared at her side and cradled her hands inside his. He grabbed paper towels and gently patted dry her hands, concentrating on her bloody finger.

She backed away from him, shunned his help, walked back over to the island, and held pressure to stop the bleeding. Out of the corner of her eye, she saw him place his hands on his hips.

The woman was driving him crazy.

He walked up behind her, right up against her, molding himself against her body, and then flattened his palms on the countertop on each side of her.

"Let's you and I get something straight," he growled over her shoulder, into her ear. "I arrived on your doorstep at your brother's request to check things out because he was worried about you. I've checked it out. Now, I could've easily reported to him and then left, but I didn't. I'm here because I want to be, not because your brother asked me but because I care what happens to you."

"Really?" she whispered hopefully over her shoulder.

"Yeah. I can't deny that. Yet I also realize I'm sending you mixed signals, telling you one thing and my actions are proving another. I know it confuses you because it's confounding the hell out of me. The worse part, I can't guarantee it won't happen again. We have to keep our relationship on a safe, hands-off level."

The stove timer beeped insistently.

Slowly, he backed away from her.

She closed her eyes, reminisced the feel of his warm hard body against hers. She cursed the stove timer for taking him away from her. Perhaps her choice in clothing danced a bit on the dangerous side, just what he hinted at.

"I'm sorry," she managed to squeak out.

He turned off the timer.

In the next second, he spun her around and sat her on top of the island.

She looked up at him startled.

"Let me see," he asked with his hand out.

"It's nothing," she muttered as she stared down at her hands.

"Please," he pleaded.

She laid her hand in his, palm up. "See, it stopped bleeding. I don't need a bandage either." She wiggled her thumb for good measure.

His thumb swirled in the center of her palm and that little action made her heart do a somersault.

"You do such amazing things with your hands," he whispered. "I've heard over the years what you're capable of, how you've saved lives, yet today I saw it. It was impressive."

She positively beamed.

"Thank you. I do what I love," she replied. She looked up at him curiously. "My brother talked about me to you?"

"He did," he admitted with a smirk.

She frowned. There was something behind his sly smile.

"I probably know you better than you know yourself. I'm sure he never told me *all* the intimate tidbits about you, maybe just the funniest or the quirkiest."

"Oh no," she muttered and felt her cheeks blush.

He reached over, grabbed their wineglasses, and handed her glass to her while he downed the contents of his. He sat his glass down and pushed it aside.

When she finished hers, she set it down beside her then looked up at him through her lashes. Again, he laid his palms flat on the island on either side of her legs. He stared deep into her eyes for a long moment.

"You only wear pink panties, no other color," he told her, giving her a knowing smile.

She was mortified.

"You hate operating on knees."

She shook her head, grinned impishly at him.

"And, last but not least, you love butterflies," he revealed smugly.

Her reply was an open-mouthed gasp. "He told you about my tattoo?"

"Yes, he wasn't happy about you getting that butterfly tattoo, but then that was the only impulsive thing you've ever done so he couldn't complain too much."

"I swear, when I see him next…"

"You've had a rough day, Summer," he said, pushing her hair away from her cheek, "but it's about to get better."

He brought his cheek to rest against hers. In her ear, he whispered thickly, "I'm hungry."

She nearly fainted hearing those two words seep so erotically from his lips.

The next instant, he snatched her off the island and thrust a plate in her hands where he dished a heap of steaming spaghetti onto her plate. He ushered her to the dining table laden with crisp white linens and subdued candlelight. She was sure it wasn't his intention to make it look and feel so romantic.

The choice of spaghetti for dinner was a mistake.

Soon after she took that first bite, he knew he was in trouble. How in the world could she make eating spaghetti look so sensual, so erotic?

She stabbed her fork into the spaghetti, twirled it against her spoon, and then lifted it slowly to her mouth. Her pink lips opened wide in anticipation where she slipped a forkful in her mouth. A few spaghetti strands dangled from her lips past her chin. She glanced up at him under her lashes and slowly sucked the spaghetti through her pursed lips, making a loud slurping sound. She closed her eyes as she slowly chewed.

"Oh god, this is delicious," she said in a half moan, leaning her head back against the tall chair back.

His fork full of spaghetti was halfway suspended from his plate to his mouth. His mouth turned dry having witnessed the suction power of her lips.

She smiled coyly at him then dipped her fingertip into her spaghetti sauce and brought it to her lips where she slid half of her finger into her mouth.

He watched her eat for a number of agonizing minutes.

He nearly fell out of his chair.

It made his cock stand to painful attention, the hair stand up on the back of his neck, and a sheen of sweat on his forehead.

"Your spaghetti sauce is incredible," she complimented before raising another forkful to her mouth where she paused and looked up at him innocently. "Why aren't you eating? You said you were hungry."

He barked out a dark laugh and then took a bite of his cold pasta.

He wasn't hungry any longer.

For food.

He poured them more wine, anything to dull his senses.

They drank greedily.

Then she reached for her garlic bread and took a crunchy bite. He watched her lay her half-eaten bread back down onto her plate, chew, and proceed to lick the butter and garlic off her fingertips slowly, tantalizingly. Her tongue lathered against her thumb and forefinger, way too enthusiastically for his peace of mind.

God, he wished she'd stop tormenting him.

"Why aren't you eating?" she asked innocently again.

She should know why. He was too enthralled with her every movement and absolutely lacked the willpower to look away. She wore down his defenses and now he was utterly petrified with what she'd do with the dessert.

Not a good choice.

Strawberries and cream.

She plucked up a large ripe strawberry covered with cream and placed it between her lips and took a bite of its center. Cream and the strawberry juice seeped from the corner of her lips.

Any other woman would have used her napkin to wipe her mouth, but not her. She was out to make him suffer.

She looked directly at him, her gaze unwavering, as she swiped the corners of her mouth slowly with the tip of her tongue.

He was at the end of his rope.

The second strawberry had cream dripping off it when she lifted it to her lips. A dollop of cream landed on the curve of her right breast.

Again, she looked across at him under her lashes.

Intently.

A smug smile lifted the corners of her mouth and made him squirm in his chair.

He looked down at his barely eaten plate of food then glanced up at her, his eyes full of warning, "You're messing with fire, Summer."

"Storm, I've accepted our friendship. I admit it's difficult, but you are right, anything more would cause complications. It's nice to know I can be myself around you. I haven't felt this relaxed in a long time."

He groaned. Yes, that was exactly what he told her. Now, his very words were choking him.

All thoughts escaped him as he watched her swipe her fingertip across her breast and plop the cream in her mouth. She sucked her fingertip.

He blinked and his mind went blank.

"Do you feel relaxed?" she asked him innocently.

He dropped his head in defeat.

"You seem tense," she said, smiling playfully as she leaned forward and refilled their wineglasses.

He downed the contents in one gulp.

"You're thirsty," she commented, sitting the bottle down on the table. "Can you believe we're out of wine?"

"I can believe just about anything right now," he muttered.

She struggled to keep her face composed and not burst out laughing. She looked over at him and gave him a smug smile. Her night was successful after all!

Suddenly, his eyes narrowed on her. His lips were unsmiling as he stared at her in contemplation.

He figured out her game.

A game of seduction.

And she won hands down. He'd give her credit. But the night was far from over.

Now, it was his turn.

He rubbed his chin thoughtfully and smiled back at her.

"You don't know me very well, Summer," he informed her. "I don't play to lose."

She was in trouble now.

She wanted to run to her bedroom and lock the door. The look he gave her was all about the danger he warned her about.

Storm would show her who was in control now. How no one played with fire without getting burned. He would use this innocent game as a way to quench his thirst of her.

But no sex.

He rose from his chair and walked over to the refrigerator, opened up the door, and pulled out the chocolate syrup and a can of whipped cream.

"We've played your game, and now we're going to play mine," he said, laughing tauntingly over his shoulder. "Follow me and bring the empty wine bottle and the strawberries."

19

Her heart set to the tune of beating at least two hundred beats a minute.

He walked straight into the living room to her round wooden coffee table sitting centered upon a white fur rug. He set down the chocolate syrup and whipped cream on the table while she sat down the bowl of strawberries and the empty wine bottle. He picked up the table and carried it forward a few feet from the sofa. He glanced over at her trying to gauge her reaction and saw she looked thoroughly perplexed seeing the new setup. He arranged all their items on the table in a circle with their wine bottle sitting in the center. He sat down on the rug and leaned his back against the sofa, his legs outstretched before him. He pointed for her to sit but with distance between them.

"We're watching a movie?" she asked curiously, glancing toward the flat screen television on the wall.

He laughed, but he wasn't smiling. "No movie. We're going to play a game, you and I."

"A game?"

"Spin the bottle," he informed her with a devilish smile.

She gulped.

"Spin the bottle? I've never played before," she stammered.

He looked at her dumbfounded. "Seriously?"

She gave him an anxious smile, silently answering his question.

"It's a kissing game of sorts," he said, laughing under his breath.

Her mouth dropped open at the thought of them playing a kissing game. It definitely went above and beyond her expectations for the evening.

Alarm was written all over her face. "So how do you play?"

"That bottle there," he said, pointing at the empty wine bottle. "If you spin it and it lands on me, then you get to kiss me and vice-versa.

If you spin the bottle and it lands on the whipped cream for instance, then you can take the whipped cream and do whatever you please with it to me."

The look on her face was priceless. This would prove a pleasurable evening with very high stakes, an evening she'd never forget.

He wagged his finger at her. "Thirty seconds is the time limit," he said in sultry voice as he glanced at his thick black timepiece on his wrist. He initiated his stopwatch by pushing a side button resulting in a few beeps.

His hot gaze swept over her. She had the most radiant blush on her cheeks. He could've easily grabbed her right then and there and tossed his watch aside and to hell with a time limit.

Restraint. Patience. Resistance.

He *would* abide by them.

"And then there's the seven minutes in heaven," he informed her.

Her eyes widened. She never heard about the heaven part. "Seven minutes where?" she squeaked out. "Did you say in heaven?"

"I did," he added with a nod. "But ours will be only four minutes in heaven," he said with a smirk. "If the bottle lands facing that mirror," he pointed to the opposite wall. "We get four minutes in heaven with each other."

God help him, surely he couldn't get into that much trouble in four minutes. But since it involved her, nothing would surprise him.

"What do we do in heaven?" she asked timidly, suddenly, feeling like a breathless girl of sixteen.

"Anything," he said, rubbing his hands together.

Her mouth dropped open.

"Now, to add some excitement to this," he said, his gaze smoldering over at her and narrowed on her pearl buttons. He crawled toward her on his hands and knees.

Hesitantly, she shrunk back from him. He looked like a lion on the prowl. "May I?" he asked, nodding toward her tank top.

She nodded hesitantly, glancing down at her tank top wondering his intention.

His warm lips grazed her skin, the hollow area where her breasts met. She swallowed her gasp watching his teeth fasten over her first pearl button. He tugged and jerked his head back with a quick snap. When he leaned back and smiled at her, her pearl button was clamped between his teeth.

Her mouth gaped open, and her hand fluttered anxiously against her chest as she watched him crawl over to the table and lay the pearl button between the whipped cream and the chocolate syrup.

"What happens if the bottle lands on my button?" she asked curiously.

"One of us has to remove a piece of clothing," he answered over his shoulder.

Her face caught on fire.

He chuckled. "Okay, we'll leave on the bare necessities."

She found herself speechless since he told her it was time to play his game. Everything about him was wild, reckless, and out of control, the very attributes she loved above him. She pledged absolutely no sex, especially because he made his feelings known. Yet if tested, she knew she'd be incapable of stopping. Far be it for her to play the responsible one.

"Ready?" he asked.

She smiled back at him and took a deep shaky breath. She already knew she'd be on the losing end of this game.

"Lady's first," he advised.

On her knees, she walked over to the table, reached for the empty wine bottle timidly, and laid it on its side. With a flick of her fingertip against the neck of the bottle, it twirled lazily in a circle, spinning.

Quickly, she scrambled back to her spot on the rug, gave him a sideways glance to see him lean back casually against the couch, his arms folded across his chest as he watched the bottle spin.

She held her breath waiting for the bottle to stop spinning.

It stopped.

It pointed at him.

She stared at the bottle and realized the implications.

With a press of a button, the sound of a beep, his watch counted down from thirty seconds.

She gave him another quick look. He stared forward at the bottle. His face gave nothing away as she nervously crawled over to him.

Time was ticking.

Her body quivered with nervous excitement and anticipation. Yet at the same time, she was scared out of her wits. She edged closer to him, her lips hovered mere inches from his cheek. He smelled like her strawberry soap. She could've easily spent her thirty seconds only inhaling the mesmerizing scent of him.

He glanced at his watch. "Ten seconds."

She pressed a lingering kiss on his cheek and then quickly retreated to her side of the rug. Instantly, she regretted not kissing him fully on the lips.

"Thank you," he said softly as he turned off his watch alarm. He stared down at his watch for a long moment then looked over at her and smiled. "We don't have to do this. I don't want you to feel uncomfortable."

"It's your turn," she advised him, lifting her chin a notch suddenly feeling her confidence build.

His face broke out into a breathtaking smile as he scrambled over to the table and twirled the bottle. It spun and spun and then slowed, landing on the chocolate syrup.

Her breath caught in her throat.

She watched him set his watch. There was no hesitation on his part as he reached for the chocolate syrup. On his knees, he walked over to her. He wound his arm around her waist and slid her onto her back, careful of her bandaged arm and tender shoulder. He straddled her body and leaned over her, his eyes dancing devilishly as he grinned down at her.

She never felt such exhilaration in her life.

He turned her head aside, brushed back her hair, and exposed her throat. He drizzled the cold syrup along the slim column of her throat.

She gasped, jerked, and felt his body rumble with quiet laughter as he set the chocolate syrup aside. She squeezed her eyes shut as she waited anxiously, anticipated for only God knew what; either way, it was guaranteed to knock her socks off.

He leaned down and grasped her neck in both hands, lifted her, opened his mouth wide, and clamped his lips hungrily against her throat where her pulse throbbed wildly against his lips. He ravaged her with his mouth. He suckled and licked away every droplet of chocolate syrup.

"Oh!" she moaned as she squirmed under him. She felt a couple of nips from his teeth.

Time was up.

"Done!" he said triumphantly as he smiled and licked his lips. He went back to his side, laughing all the way.

He left her still lying on the floor, breathing harshly. Her body had dissolved into a puddle of water. She staggered back up into a sitting position. Dear God, she'd never experienced anything so seductive in her entire life.

Her inhibitions quickly took flight and flew out the window. It was her turn. She couldn't wait to spin the bottle. She pounced back on her knees and hurried to the table to give the bottle another spin.

It landed on her pearl button.

She glanced over at him. He set the timer on his watch and then reached to pull off his tank top.

"Wait!"

His hands stilled while his lips curled with a challenge.

"Isn't it my choice what clothing you remove?"

She was losing her inhibitions, and this was a good thing. His smile grew broader.

"Why of course. What would you like me to take off?"

Everything.

She decided to get down to business quickly.

"Shorts. Take your shorts off, please."

He got to his feet and looked expectantly at her.

"Rule is that you remove them," he informed her smugly.

Her eyes widened. She gulped hard, so much for being assertive. She got to her feet and walked over to stand before him very much aware his heated eyes watched her every move. She faced many challenges in her life, felt the exhilaration of her heart racing uncontrollably in a trauma room where her hands never wavered as she made confident split-second decisions as she tried to save someone's life, never stumbling, hesitating. Yet as she stood before him tonight, her hands shook like an almighty, and she couldn't unsnap his top button. It was horrifyingly embarrassing. Then when she finally got it unsnapped, determinedly, she grasped the zipper and slowly eased it down. She gently tugged them past his hips where they landed forgotten at his feet. He wore black boxers that molded his slim hips and hugged every inch of him with the most obvious, the thick bulge at his very center outlining the long length of him pulsing with life.

He was utterly breathtaking.

She was a recipient of his smug grin.

Time was up.

It was his turn.

He tossed his shorts aside and then reached over and twirled the bottle.

And wouldn't you know where it landed.

On her pearl button.

She'd just had her third heart attack of the night.

With his powerful hands, he yanked her to her feet.

This meant she made a very poor decision dressing skimpy. On wobbly legs, she stood before him. He was a man who knew what he wanted and went after it. Reaching for her skirt, he made quick work of it. With a quick snap, he'd released her top button then sliced her zipper down in less than a second. Her skirt dropped unceremoniously to the floor. His fingertips scorched her as they slipped under the thin strap of her thong. He wasn't quite finished with her.

He still had time on the clock.

His hand slid down her thigh where he hiked her thigh against his hip and massaged her backside bringing their sexes together so she could feel his hard arousal through her very thin swatch of fabric.

Time was up.

She was on fire and stretched on her tiptoes to kiss him, but he leaned back, shook his head, and wagged a finger at her.

"Time's up, baby," he said, releasing her.

A sigh of frustration escaped her as she walked up to the table, giving him a cursory glance over her shoulder to see him sit back down on the rug, his legs sprawled in front of him giving her a smug grin.

It was her turn.

The bottle twirled and landed on the whipped cream. She had thirty seconds to make his knees weak. Armed with whipped cream, she walked determinedly toward him. He was still heavily aroused when she straddled his body, resting the heat of her against him.

She avoided his eyes as she sat the whipped cream can aside. She ripped open her tank top, sending several buttons spinning through the air and giving him an ample view of her overflowing cleavage.

She heard his indrawn breath, a gasp, while his hands remained fisted at his sides. She reached for the whipped cream, and instead of spraying it on him as he undoubtedly expected, she filled the concave of her breasts with a large dollop.

Reaching for his left hand, she guided him, dipped his fingertips deep into the whipped cream, giving him a good feel of her breasts.

He clenched his eyes shut and moaned in response.

Their eyes held as she slid each of his fingers, one by one, deep her hot moist mouth, swirled her tongue around it, up and down the length of it, suckled until each finger slipped from her tight lips clean.

His eyes transfixed on her mouth; he was mesmerized. His jaw clenched and unclenched while muscles in his stomach jerked involuntarily.

"If I didn't know you so well through your brother," he choked out, "I'd swear you did this for a living."

Time was up.

Yet he wasn't ready to let her go. He grabbed her hips to stay her, thrust his hips up against the heat of her, grinded against her.

"Time's up, baby," she said, repeating his words, giving his hands a gentle smack and jumping off him quickly.

Dear God, give me strength.

He pulled his knees up and lowered his head. His body physically shook. Deep breaths were the only thing saving him from exploding. It was the most mind-blowing experience he'd ever encountered with a woman and only in thirty seconds. He couldn't imagine the explosion between them if there was no time limit.

She strutted back to her side of the rug.

After a long moment, his body under control, he sent her a smoldering look, a private message. He would show her no mercy the next time. He reached over and spun the bottle.

The bottle spun to a stop facing the mirror.

"Four minutes in heaven," he said with a smile in his voice.

Stealthily, he crawled toward her.

The hungry look in his eyes kicked her heart against her ribs painfully and thudded in her ears.

He grasped her ankle and tugged her toward him until she lay flat on her back once again, and he hovered over her between her legs.

You're mine now.

The anticipation was so great; she gasped when his fingertip brushed against her belly button.

His soft laughter rumbled above her as his hands sent a fiery path up her thighs coming to rest against her belly and ribs where he squeezed and massaged. He crawled up her body not wasting any time as he lowered his body onto hers, nestling himself between her legs.

She entwined her legs with his.

He cupped her face in his hands and caressed her cheek while his eyes searched hers for any sign of resistance. When he saw none, he trailed a scorching path of kisses against her throbbing neck and along her jawline. He moved to her lips and sucked her bottom lip into his mouth. His tongue swiped deep as he gave her a slow smoldering kiss. She sunk her fingers deep in his hair, clutching him tightly against her as blood boiled under her skin.

"Would you stop squirming," he rushed out in a harsh laugh.

"I can't help it," she whispered against his neck as her hands feathered down his sculpted back coming to rest against the waistband of his boxers, which she tentatively slid her fingertips. She wanted to peel them off.

"You're not making this easy," he murmured against her ear.

"Easy for what?" she asked as she reached a trembling hand up and stroked his broad shoulder, reveling in the power underneath her fingertips, the bunched muscle.

"Easy to walk away," he said, gritting his teeth and trying to gain control.

"You can stop," she offered. "But I don't want you to."

He drew a ragged breath. "Can you just help me a little bit tonight? I'm trying to keep your virtue intact, and you're making this pretty damn hard."

"You chose the game, remember?" she subtly reminded him.

He laughed abruptly then and started slowly moving against her, rotating and swiveling his hips until it turned into frenzy.

Time was up.

He stilled his movements.

"Oh no, you're not stopping?" her question came out as a frustrated half moan, half gasp.

Touching her trembling lips with one finger, he smiled down at her. His face was a mottled red, sleek with sweat across his forehead. His chest rose and fell as if he'd run a marathon.

"You can't be serious," she said with disbelief clearly outlined on her face and in her voice as she stared up at him.

"That was your four minutes in heaven, babe," he said, giving her a nod and another smug grin.

"It's supposed to be seven minutes in heaven," she argued. "Besides, how can you just stop cold?" Her gaze dropped to his midsection. It was rock solid. If she had to guess, it was much more difficult for him to walk away than for her.

"There was a reason why I set the limit at four minutes, Summer," he said knowingly.

She raised an inquiring eyebrow.

"Well, seven minutes would've been too much for you. You wouldn't have been able to handle it," he told her as he returned to his side of the rug.

Her mouth gaped open. "Well, of all the ridiculous notions," she exclaimed, choking back a laugh as she jumped to her feet, grabbed the can of whipped cream, jerked off the cap, and pointed it threateningly at him.

Guessing her intention, his eyes widened; he leaned back and pointed at her, laughter welled up inside him. "Summer Benson, you better not," he warned her.

"Are you daring me?" she asked, giving him a wicked grin.

"Are you prepared for the consequences?" he challenged.

In answer, she sprayed whipped cream across his broad chest.

She tossed aside the empty can and took off running as if her life depended upon it. Behind her, he landed on his feet in one lithe motion, a lot quicker than she anticipated, and came after her with a vengeance.

Good grief, she temporarily forgot she dealt with a Navy SEAL.

20

She laughed hysterically as she rounded the dining room table.

He was on her heels.

Around and around the table she ran breathlessly, upsetting chairs, pushing the table off center. She ran into the kitchen where she dodged him back and forth around the island until she made the fatal mistake thinking she could escape into the living room, but he was a step ahead of her.

His arm shot out and snagged her around the waist where he turned her around in his arms. She looked exhilarated and was very much out of breath. Playfully, he tossed her against the nearest wall, imprisoning her body with his while his mouth worshiped hers.

She reached up, curled her arms around his neck, and parted her lips without hesitation, starving for his hungry kisses. She drowned in his passion, sank deeper with each kiss, each stroke of his hand. Her lips slid from his mouth to the hammering pulse at his neck.

"By the way, I've never seen anyone eat spaghetti like you," he added with a groan then suddenly gasped when he felt her teeth nip his neck. His passion for her became intense with need as his fingertips skimmed over the swell of her hip, the curve of her belly. His hungry lips found hers, and he gave into a need he knew only she could fill.

She reached for the hem of his tank top, bringing it up over his head, only breaking off the sultry kiss a few seconds as he tugged it over his head. She used it to swipe off the whipped cream from them and then winged it across the room.

He reached for her tank top, ripped it open the rest of the way fully exposing her breasts to him; and this time, she made no effort to shield them. He lifted her while she wound her arms back around his neck and wrapped her legs around his waist.

His lips were smiling against hers as he carried her to her bedroom.

To hell with the rules.

A part of him wanted to drive hard and fast inside her; his need was so great. Yet the logical, most rational part of him wanted to remember and savor every single passion filled caress, every spellbinding kiss of their lovemaking. He wanted to embed the memories in her mind so she'd never forget him.

He set her down at the foot of the bed.

She reached for him and slid his boxers off.

Mind blowing.

His hand skimmed her waist as he guided her and carried her with him to the center of the bed.

She felt the mattress dip beneath her then the additional weight of him lying on top of her. His heated body covered every inch of hers and more. She marveled at the heat of his skin and the acute sensitivity she felt as her breasts rubbed against the silky hairs of his chest and the hard pressure of his belly against hers.

His hot, searing mouth slid torturously slow down the length of her neck and stopped at the base of her throat where he felt her pulse beating erratically against his tongue.

"I wanted you from the very first moment I saw you," he whispered against her skin.

His thickly whispered confession sent her pulse racing; her body spiraled out of control with wanting him. Nothing else existed, only the two of them as they explored one another.

His fierce eyes caught hers as he slid down her body between her legs.

She licked her lips nervously, watching his every move with anticipation.

His lips curled up in a slow predatory smile.

With a feather's touch, he trailed his long fingertip down the channel of her belly, coming to rest at her belly button where his fingertip swirled around the rim lazily and seductively.

Her body lunged in anticipation as he leaned down. The whisper of his warm breath blew across her belly made her body lunge and made her suck in a gasp.

He wasn't done with her quite yet.

His hot tongue dipped and swirled inside her hollowed belly button.

She screamed and clutched his shoulders.

Her body arched like a bow while goose bumps raced across her skin. Her breathing did double time coming in harsh gasps while he was mercilessness and took no prisoners.

As his tongue blazed a path from her belly button up to her breasts, his eyes hungrily feasted. Her nipples were instantly erect and begged to be sucked, teased, and lavished upon.

She stared at him in utter fascination as his warm, wet lips closed over her breast and teased her pink nipple, tormenting her with his swirling hot tongue, sending incredible sensations all through her body. She strained high against him, giving him a silent message, an appeal to covet her other breast with the same degree of wonderful torture he displayed upon the other.

His lips moved to her other breast, the most incredible, painfully intense feeling she'd ever felt.

He slid farther down her body where his hand hooked under her knee and raised it where he skimmed his hand across her shapely thigh followed with his mouth, leading straight down the path to her lacy thong, her only barrier against him.

Trembling with need, Summer closed her eyes. The feelings and sensations were unbearable.

Ragged breaths claimed him as his brazen fingertips skimmed her inner thighs.

"You're one hell of a beauty," he whispered huskily.

He slipped a lone finger behind her lace thong, winding through her curls, stealing within her sleek, damp flesh, stroking, skimming the outer and inner pink folds, and then dipping again. Exploring further, he found the very heat of her, a tiny flange of flesh hidden high in her cleft. The caress was shockingly intimate and very bold. The slickness of her drenched his fingers and made him want her with madness beyond his control as he felt her writhing, tightening all around his finger. He squeezed his eyes shut imagining him inside her as it glided through her, creating an explosive friction against her tight, swollen walls.

"Storm!" she cried.

He pulled aside the flimsy lacy thong and buried his face between her parted thighs. His hot, moist tongue flicked out and relentlessly teased her cleft, making her hips lunge wildly against him.

She gasped, writhed, strained, and let out a strangled scream as she tried to escape his sweet torment; but there was no such escape as he held her against him. He wouldn't allow it as he suckled and licked. She clutched his shoulders. Within minutes, a scream tore from her throat as shudders of passion washed over her heated, shivering body.

She was speechless and couldn't utter a coherent thought if she tried.

He climbed back up her body and kissed her chin.

"I want you, all of you," he confessed as desperation edged his voice. "Are you ready for me?"

She nodded eagerly. Storm took his knee and widened her legs. His hands cupped her face, kissing her softly as he settled between her legs.

She wrapped her legs around his hips, arched against him, and felt the round swollen head of his cock lay insistently against her slick opening with just enough pressure to make her gasp into his mouth.

He laid his forehead against hers, his breathing harsh and unsteady. It took every bit of control he could harness not to totally spill his seed that instant. He bent his head and kissed her hungrily and greedily.

God, how many years had he dreamt of this very situation with her, dreamt of possessing her fully, mind, body, and spirit.

Making her his.

He broke out in a cold sweat, his body trembled like a sixteen-year-old, and he wasn't even an inch inside her.

Yet.

"Storm, it's…it's been a very long time for me…," she squeaked out, avoiding his intense gaze.

He smiled down at her. "Relax," he whispered fiercely, raw against her lips as he massaged himself against her slickness.

With incredible restraint, he entered her and spread her open an inch at a time; he stretched her to the brink. He squeezed his eyes shut because the incredible urge to storm her and thrust hard deep inside was intensely great. Yet he fought the urge. Her opening was tight and fought against his size, and he was far from being fully inside her.

Slow and easy.

Perspiration clung to his forehead as he tried to calm his body.

Oh god.

She placed her trembling lips against his shoulder and tried to relax her body. He was a big man in many ways.

"Am I hurting you?" he asked in a ragged breath.

"No," she breathed.

"You'll tell me if I do? I don't want to hurt you," he said as he lowered his mouth onto hers, giving her a slow drugging kiss, making her forget her own name while he entered her a bit more. Raising his mouth from hers, he gazed down into her eyes.

He whispered her name.

Her eyes glittered fever pitch as she lay there, memorizing every feature of his face, even down to the huskiness of his voice as he once again whispered her name. How sultry her name sounded as it rolled softly off his tongue.

Oh god, she was in love with him.

"I need you now. I can't wait," he groaned. He paused then, his mouth covered hers hungrily, silently sending her the message he fully intended to deliver her right to heaven's door.

"Look into my eyes, Summer," he said as he held her hips and sunk deep and shoved his full length inside her until he touched her womb. His body bowed over as he gasped, felt like he sunk into warm molten hot juices, an incredibly intense feeling, leaving him breathless.

He savored the pleasure, bared his soul to her, as their bodies melded into one knowing all the while he'd never be the same again.

Swallowing her gasp, he swept his tongue inside and mated with hers, deepening the kiss. He held himself still for as long as he could inside her, giving her body time to adjust to his invasion, but he couldn't hold back any longer.

He had to have her.

Now.

His hips began to rise and fall, slowly, ever so slowly at first.

Summer churned in a frenzied storm of passion that threatened to consume her.

He was frantic with wanting her. She tightened herself around him, making him pump hard, driving deep inside her. His thrusts jolted the bed and slammed the headboard against the wall as they found the tempo bounding their bodies together. His breathless mouth united with her sobbing moan as he angled his hips so each plunging stroke brought him to bear against the hidden flange high in her cleft.

As he pierced deep into her body, Summer gasped, moaned, and scrapped her fingernails desperately against the hollows of his back.

His last driving lunge sent an explosion of pleasure through her.

Hoarsely, he whispered her name against her lips.

Storm felt her shudder and contract deep, squeezing the length of him. It triggered a white-hot heat to thunder through his veins sending a shock current down his spine. He gritted his teeth, a harsh groan escaped his throat as he erupted, flooded her with his heat. It spurted hot and thick inside her as he surrendered both his seed and his soul into her safekeeping.

"Oh god," he whispered breathlessly as he laid his head on her shoulder.

In his time, he made love to a staggering amount of women. Yet none ever felt as intense and mind-blowing as what he experienced now. He knew why. His heart was fully engaged with Summer whereas before it was fleeting, a way to seek his relief.

He rolled onto his back, bringing her with him, feeling her heartbeat rumble at a maddening pace against his side.

"I think I've just experienced heaven," she said, sighing and snuggling against his heated, shivering body.

After a few minutes, their harsh breaths and pounding heartbeats quieted; they fell asleep in each other's arms.

He didn't want to let her go.

21

She had seduced him.

The sun crested high in the sky when she rolled over against him. He was already awake, already in full force regret mode. He could easily blame the wine on his weakness for indulging in Summer, or if he was truthful with himself, he knew it was for purely selfish reasons why he took her—a buildup of a number of years hearing about Summer, this wonderful young lady Reaper wanted him so desperately to meet. And she proved to be just as incredible as he knew she would be.

What happened last night wasn't supposed to have happened. His willpower weakened considerably when she was around. Scratch that, he had no willpower.

Storm exhaled heavily and wondered what the hell he'd done. The consequences of his actions collided with his conscious. He wasn't there to ravage her but to protect her. He knew if this occurred between them, it could put her life in danger, and he took her anyways. And it never stopped him from indulging in her numerous times during the night when they reached for each other.

He knew exactly what he needed to do. He had to distance himself from her, become emotionally detached so it wouldn't happen again. He was good at this, had done it all his life when he became a SEAL because certain situations forced him to.

He swung his legs over the side of the bed and hung his head in his hands. A second later, the bed dipped toward him; she scrambled to sit next to him. He felt her eyes on him.

"Good morning," she said, her voice was full of happiness. "I hate to remind you, but I still need to find a gown for the gala tomorrow and your parent's anniversary party."

He glanced over at her, and she blessed him with the most beautiful smile he'd ever seen. It knocked the wind from his sails. Her eyes were anxious as they scanned his grim face and then her smile slowly faded.

"I don't believe you're looking at me that way just because you have to take me shopping." She paused and held her breath as she braced herself for his reply to her next question. "Do you regret what happened between us, Storm?" she asked barely above a whisper.

"Yes," he answered truthfully. He rubbed his eyes wishing he could turn back the hands of time.

She jerked off the bed, but he was quicker and caught her in two steps, his hand cuffed her wrist.

"I'm not asking you for marriage, Storm. We spent a great night together, that's it, nothing more," she lied.

He waved toward the bed of rumpled covers and tossed pillows. "This shouldn't have happened, Summer. I'm here to protect you, not sleep with you. It's because I've let all this go on it has made me totally lose focus. You could've been easily killed twice now under my watch."

"How can you say that? You had no control over those men on the highway or the gunman walking through those hospital doors."

He disagreed vehemently, "I should've been more alert, better prepared, blocked the door. Instead, I couldn't keep my eyes off you. I failed to get up and escort you to the hospital."

She argued, "Only because I kept you up all night trying to seduce you in my sleep. That's my fault, not yours."

"It doesn't matter what happened the night before. That accident could've easily killed you. God, if it would have." He let out a harsh breath. "I couldn't bear it. I've lived with enough guilt to last me two lifetimes because I failed to protect a little girl whose death is the blood on my hands. I can't endure that again."

"Storm, you're doing a great job protecting me."

"You're so very wrong. I'm so distracted I can't even think straight around you," he confessed.

"That's a good thing, isn't it?" she asked, smiling.

"Hell no, it isn't! We can't do this again, no matter."

"Maybe you can discount the numerous times we made love last night as something that shouldn't have happened, but I can't. You held me in your arms, remember? I saw the raw emotion, the feelings that poured from you. You wouldn't have allowed me to witness them if you didn't trust me."

"I trust you. I just don't trust myself. Like I warned you before, I'm not the kind of guy you want to get hooked up with because I'll only hurt you in the end."

"You won't hurt me," she said defiantly, her eyes imploring as they gazed deep into his.

"Yes, I will. It's inevitable," he said, raking his hand through his disheveled hair.

"No, you won't."

"It would never work between us."

"I don't believe that. You need me as much as I need you," she argued and felt her hot tears build behind her eyes.

"No," he simply said.

I have too many black secrets.

"Why are you doing this?"

"It's the way it has to be. When you're trying to protect someone and you allow emotion to get involved, you lose your gut instinct. Instinct tells you when something isn't quite right, keeps you on your toes. Without it, you lose all the advantage on your side, and you can't think straight. I've been through this, and I've reaped the results a thousand times over. It has to be this way, Summer, because if not, I need to arrange for someone else to protect you."

She exhaled a shaky breath.

"You win because I don't want anyone else protecting me," she whispered forlornly, looking around her bedroom at the disarray of clothing on the floor, the same clothing he tugged off her body before he made passionate love to her.

"Get ready and I'll take you shopping," he offered as he walked toward the bathroom. He went to shut the door and caught a glimpse of her staring dejectedly at the floor. Her face was pale, distressed, and once again full of rejection. God, he hated himself for causing her pain.

It took everything he possessed to not go to her and sweep her up in his arms.

If only the circumstances were different.

While Storm took his shower, Summer walked with leaden feet into the living room and saw the table pushed back with the empty wine bottle they used for spin the bottle. The large white rug lay askew, and she couldn't help but remember the times he gave her such delight with his mouth, his hands, and his body. She'd never played spin the bottle, and it turned out a most satisfying adventure. Her body still felt the riveting effects hours later and something she'd never forget. She filed past the dining room table still littered with dishes from their spaghetti dinner and couldn't help the small smile that crept on her lips remembering how she ate the spaghetti so boldly, so wickedly, trying to get a rise from him.

And it worked.

Pots, pans, and silverware littered the counter tops, which included two empty wineglasses. She ran her fingertip across the rim of one, remembering.

She gazed around her house in wonder. It looked like a bomb had gone off. Or maybe it looked like she actually had a bit of excitement for once. Furniture here and there sat askew where he chased her after she sprayed him with whipped cream. She could still feel the anticipation, the excitement, her laughter overflowing, the pure joy she felt.

Because of *him*.

This wasn't how she expected to start her day after spending a glorious night in his arms.

She experienced the start of her day not with a joyous uplifted heart but with solemnity. Yet as she gazed around the room surrounded by such strong memories, so much passion, she knew last night would go down as the most incredible night of her life.

The memories overwhelmed her, consumed her.

Storm was towel drying his hair when he strolled quietly into the living room. He stopped dead in his tracks.

She stood across the room, her eyes closed, and she was smiling. She was far away, and if he imagined, she was remembering the night they shared. Her hand hovered over her heart then it slowly lifted where her fingertips brushed softly across her bottom lip.

Regret filled him.

He had only shifted his gaze for a second or two to look across the room; when he looked back at her, their eyes collided. And just as quick, her smile vanished, and she gave him her back as she collected the dishes so she could start loading the dishwasher.

Storm felt like a heel. The look she gave him was void of all emotion. She looked right through him. He would've felt better if he saw anger or frustration, anything was better than nothing. Shame on him for sending her mixed signals with one minute telling her he couldn't become involved and the next enticing her to a game knowing where it would lead.

There was so much more he wanted to say but dared not to, dared not to give her hope for a future with him. He wasn't good for her, no matter how much she believed differently, no matter how much he wanted to believe differently. She deserved better.

He took full responsibility for the outcome. Now he didn't know how to get her smile back nor did he know how to subside the urge to pull her back into his arms and relive the most breathtaking experience of his life.

Dejectedly, he draped the towel around his neck and returned to the bedroom to get dressed, her silence ringing in his ears, her sadness tugging at his heart.

She never looked back, only listened as his steps faded.

After a moment passed, she glanced over her shoulder toward the bedroom and the memories nearly buckled her knees.

He branded her entire body with his mouth and hands, yet she was supposed to forget, act as if it never happened, act as if she didn't look forward to the next time when he leaned in and gave her a drugging kiss. Or when he'd look at her, stare at her with his simmering eyes a minute or two longer than normal, fully capturing her curiosity, and leaving her with the feeling she was hyperventilating. It was that powerful.

Now, looking back, she realized her too hasty decision wearing scantily dressed clothing in front of him, her teasing led up to what happened between them.

He made it perfectly clear he wanted nothing to happen between them giving her valid reasons why, but she continued to ignore his request and provoke him.

That's what you get for playing with fire.

Now he had to escort her to buy a couple of gowns. Mentally, she shook her head, even more uncomfortable situations he'd have to endure with her.

If she thought the strain and the tension between them would be unbearable, awkward, now it was intolerable, and she had only herself to blame.

What had she done?

She took a deep, calming breath. She needed to make things right. Just as she did before she walked into any trauma case, she wiped away all emotions, focused on what was most important. In this case, she would abide by his wish so he would continue to stay by her side and protect her. Whatever it took, she would do it because he *was* right. Her life hung in the balance of his hands.

Opening a cabinet drawer, she pulled out a telephone book and rummaged quickly through the pages to find the directory for furniture stores. She chose a high-end store close by she patronized in the recent past and dialed the phone number.

In less than five minutes after speaking to the manager and advising him of her urgency, they were set to deliver Storm's new bed in less than an hour.

Storm and she worked quietly side by side placing the house back in order. They were cordial and pleasant to each other as they should be. When she began moving the smaller pieces of furniture around in the spare bedroom, she found him standing in the doorway.

"Do you need help?" he offered.

"No, but thank you," she replied.

The doorbell rang.

"Right on time," she replied.

"You're having furniture delivered?"

"A bed for you so you're comfortable staying here, Storm," she replied as she walked around him and headed to the foyer. She reached for the doorknob when suddenly his hand covered hers.

"Remember, you never answer the door," he reminded her softly.

She jerked back her hand.

As soon as he opened the door and she gave the orders to where the bed needed set up, she busied herself getting dressed for the shopping trip.

He was still standing at the doorway, in shock, when three deliverymen walked around him and headed into the spare bedroom and began setting up his new bed.

What the fuck?

He knew for a fact the bed wasn't purchased out of spite. She was simply making an effort to carry out his wishes. The thought of sleeping without her was suddenly unsettling.

Yes, it was the sensible thing to do since they couldn't seem to keep their hands off each other, but he still didn't like it.

Once she heard them leave, she placed a few final touches on her hair and walked over to the spare bedroom. She glanced over and saw him sitting on the couch, not watching television, just quietly waiting for her, preoccupied with his thoughts.

The black wrought iron bed dominated the bedroom. It looked extremely comfortable with a thick camel-colored comforter and fluffy pillows. She wanted him comfortable, yet the bed resembled a divider between them, and she hated it. She *loved* him sleeping beside her.

He looked up and saw her staring at his new bed.

Suddenly, an uncontrollable sob escaped her. She slapped her hand across her mouth to stem the onslaught of emotions spiraling through her.

He was on his feet in an instant coming to her side.

The phone rang.

She waved him off, pointed at the phone. He looked at her torn, wanting to console her instead. Finally, he walked over and picked up the phone after the fourth ring.

"Hello," he said.

She watched his face split into a half grin. "Going fine, man. Yes, hold on a sec." He handed the phone to her. "It's your brother."

She shook her head. "Tell him I'll call him when we return please," she begged, her voice cracking.

He relayed the message to Reaper.

"Is she okay?" Reaper asked.

Long pause. "Yeah," Storm replied as he watched her stand by the front door. He witnessed her wipe away a stray tear from her cheek, and it made him hesitate in his step.

"Sure?"

"Yeah, I'll make it right," Storm said and quickly hung up.

He made her cry.

He pulled out his remote and started the car then escorted her to the passenger side because he wanted her sitting beside him so he could comfort her, but she walked around to the driver's side.

"I think it's best I sit in the backseat behind you. You're right, it's probably safer."

The warm breeze swept up and swirled the heady scent of *him* as he walked around her and opened her car door. She inhaled it deep in her lungs, that clean-smelling fragrance yet not overpowering, very subtle cologne she imagined a man wearing who wore custom-made suits. The euphoria made her want to peel her clothes off; it was so intoxicating.

He opened the door wide for her. A rush of chilly air swept across her sandaled feet.

"Whatever you want," he told her softly then swung the door closed.

His response sent her reeling.

Whatever she wanted.

She lived by that phrase actually for as long as she could remember when going through medical school. She blazed through the classes, grasped her career by the horns, and took control. Whatever she wanted, she went for it and usually accomplished it.

But her love life was on a totally different hemisphere. She struggled at it. It sure as hell wasn't something that came easily and naturally for her, contrary to popular belief. She'd likened the understanding of the male species to rocket science.

Whatever she wanted.

She wanted *him.*

She sighed as she slid into the backseat wishing she were more like *him*, unfazed by raw lingering memories so sensual it made her blush with the barest memory, like when he swirled his tongue inside her belly button. She reached for her shoulder harness and was about to buckle up when memories assaulted her once again where she was thrown back in time when she and Storm were in the hospital garage. He buckled her seat belt for her, and it ended with their first kiss.

An unbelievable kiss.

Her fingers curled around her shoulder harness as if she tried to grasp and keep the memory of their passionate moment alive a bit longer. She gazed out the midnight-black window and felt her stomach tie in knots. Her resolve sifted away the moment she got into the car with him. It was hard not to conjure the erotic memories in their short span of time together.

This whole business of acting as if he was nothing more than a bodyguard to her wasn't going so well, not at all as she planned. In fact, this whole ordeal hadn't gone as planned when her brother told her he sent Storm to protect her. From the first moment she laid eyes on him, the air between them sizzled with such intensity it blindsided her, and she believed Storm felt the same.

Unknowingly, he became her rock.

Her gaze slid to the seat next to her, empty. It was much different when she rode in the front seat with him. His presence was so powerful it enveloped her in a cocoon, made her feel safe. Now, she never felt more alone and suddenly very claustrophobic in such close quarters with him.

Under her lashes, she glanced up at him through his rearview mirror. He wore sunglasses, his mouth set firm, unsmiling. Those glasses protected all emotion pouring from his eyes. It wasn't fair. She forgot her sunglasses at home. Her eyes were the windows into her soul, bared for all to see.

For *him* to see.

She studied the roadside rushing past her and kept her gaze averted.

His wary voice broke through the silence. "Any particular store at this mall you'd like to visit first?"

Her head shot up, his voice startled her. She caught his reflection again in his rearview mirror.

"The boutique at the end will be fine. It won't take me long," she promised warily.

"Take as long as you need," he said softly.

She'd make this the fastest shopping trip she ever undertook because she was dying to get out of the car, get some space between them, find those damn gowns, and get back home where she could lock herself up in her bedroom.

The bedroom where he made love to you, her conscious sneered back at her.

Everything suddenly felt so overwhelming. She had the urge to jump from the car, start running, and never look back. Her heart thundered in her chest. She swallowed hard as she tried to push away the lump forming in her throat.

Her heartbreak suffocated her.

As soon as he pulled into the parking lot and rolled into a parking spot, she hit the unlock button and tried to open her car door, but it wouldn't open.

She glanced up again in the rearview mirror to see his head lift to look at her.

"Safety feature," he informed her with a small smile. "Why are you in such a hurry?"

She never responded.

He took his sweet time getting out of the car, she noted. He opened her door and held his hand out before her as if to keep her close to the car while he shut the car door.

"Can you please just give me some time to myself?" She clutched her purse against her middle and looked away from him, across the parking lot, at the ground, anywhere but at him.

She started to step away from him, but he blocked her path. He whipped off his sunglasses; his eyes narrowed on her.

He tipped her chin up to look at him.

Her eyes swam with tears.

A tear escaped and slid unheedingly down her cheek.

He sighed heavily as he reached up, swiped away her tear with his fingertip, brought it up to his lips, and tasted her tear.

Hell.

He kept his distance yet entrapped her against the car, making her sink against the car door. He planted both hands on either side of her shoulders.

For a long moment, he looked into her eyes intently.

"Summer, we're going to work through this, you and I," he promised her.

She looked at him with such longing it took his breath away. "Why did you make love to me if you knew you'd regret it later?" she asked, staring down at her feet.

He laughed darkly as he glanced around them, surveying the cars pulling in and out of the parking lot, ensuring it was safe for her. He looked back at her thoughtfully.

"I couldn't help myself. From afar, I've wanted you since the first day your brother spoke of you. You're everything a man could dream of and more. You're smart as hell, you're fun to be with, and you're very courageous. You're an incredible woman. You can't even imagine how difficult it is for me to push you away. It goes against what I've always desired. Believe me, baby, it's tossing my guts far worse than you think it is."

"So you don't regret it?"

"God, no, I don't regret it. It's just the circumstances and timing I regret. It couldn't be worse. I'd rather arrive on your doorstep and ask you for a date like normal people do. But instead, we've been thrown into a very volatile situation we can't control."

She finally found her voice. "Yes, we'll get through this," she said, smiling up at him.

He leaned into her, reached up, cupped the side of her neck, and pressed his lips against her forehead.

"Thank you for sticking it out with me," she whispered.

"Always," his lips whispered against her skin.

They entered the boutique, and she watched his eyes scan the small store, noting the exit door in the back and the two-middle aged sales clerks dressed elegantly who walked toward them and three younger ladies at the far end of the store who browsed the clearance racks. She also noted their approving gazes in his direction.

He stood by the door, his eyes settled on her, never wavered, watching her every move.

Calm, she told her beating heart.

Four hours later, they left the last store with Storm carrying a dainty bag containing jewelry she purchased. He had absolutely no idea what she even bought no matter how many bags he carried to his car. He was too preoccupied watching her. Not to mention, he was on fire today with memories from their lovemaking. He could still taste her on his lips, could feel how she felt beneath him, inside her heat. It was exhausting keeping his distance from her today.

All he could think about was having her close to his side and touching her. He lost count how many times their hands brushed as they walked and he had to impose his will to not reach for her.

"Now, what do we need to do about your suit?" she asked him as she held the trunk lid up while he stored her bag.

"I have a suit at my house to pick up. Hungry?"

"Famished."

"Do you like fish?"

"I love fish. What's on your mind?"

"My place for dinner," he said as he shut his trunk.

22

The sun, like a celestial fireball in the sky made its descent shortly upon their arrival to Amelia Island after picking up Apollo. He showed her inside his home and instantly flooded it with light. Besides the warm light and exquisite wood, the home felt cold, void of life, and very empty.

Her heart ached for him. He must have been living in a roller coaster of hell. She glimpsed over to Calypsia's photograph on the barren side table and knew it had everything to do with her death. She wouldn't pry. He'd tell her his story if he really trusted her.

"I know I've said this before, but I really do love your home. It's beautiful," she said, gazing out at the sunrise-gold beach. "You have a breathtaking view of the ocean."

"It does have its amenities," he said as he pulled out his two guns and laid them on the counter and shrugged off his shoulder harness. He looked around at the warm wood, all the glass. The house in all its beauty bellied doom and gloom and barrenness without furniture and curtains, yet that wasn't how he felt now. He found it very odd walking back into his house tonight. He wasn't the same man who walked out almost a week ago feeling the burgeoning weight of guilt crush his shoulders, beat down his every broken step.

He glanced over at her to see she had her nose pressed against the window. It was because of her that hope surged in his heart. He experienced not a single nightmare about Calypsia since he met her.

She calmed his soul.

Her movement caught his attention. She backed slowly away from the windows, her face apprehensive.

"What's wrong?" he asked, frowning, walking toward her.

She laughed nervously. "I was thinking if someone wanted to make another attempt on my life it could happen easily with me standing in this glass house lit up like a Christmas tree."

He walked over to the massive windows and tapped his knuckle against the thick glass. "Protective glass. Nothing is coming through these windows to get you."

Still, she backed away from the windows.

He left her side, walked across the room, and opened a wall compartment covered by tinted glass and jerked down a lever. The next second, steel shutters slid down from the ceiling to conceal the windows. Exterior doors echoed across the house being sealed and locked with deadbolts.

She whirled around and laughed shakily. "You take your security very seriously."

"I do," he agreed. "I have something very precious to protect."

His words made her heart soar on wings.

She gave him a brilliant smile. "I feel safe already. But then again, that's how I always feel when I'm with you."

"Good, it's how it's supposed to be."

"When do you think this will be over, Storm? When will Malone give up on his vendetta and leave me alone?" she asked, folding her arms across her chest and rubbing the chill spreading down her arms.

He slowly walked toward her. "I don't know, but rest assured, he'll have to go through me to get to you."

"Please don't say that. I'd die if something happened to you."

She desperately wanted to fling herself into his arms and feel his heat, the security, but resisted the urge.

He sensed the direction of her thoughts.

Keep your distance.

Even a hug between them could easily catapult them to full-blown ripping each other's clothes off and going at it. Yeah, he laid out the rules about them keeping their distance, yet he couldn't help himself. He planned to bend the rules a bit tonight. She was right; he needed her as much as she needed him. Plus, when she looked up at him with those hero worship eyes, his knees turned liquid and it stirred a tickling, an excitement in his gut he'd never felt before.

He reached for her and held her tightly against his chest. There was no resistance on her part. She clung to him as if he was her lifeline. There was something pretty heady about her trusting him so inexplicitly.

After a few minutes, she lifted her head and looked up at him. "See, I feel better already. That's the effect you have on me."

He tossed his arm across her shoulder and kept her close to his side as he led her down a corridor then down a staircase to the basement.

"Where are you taking me?" she asked when he opened a wooden door.

"Another amenity," he drawled.

Low light eased on, shined down around the circumference of a wine cellar with gorgeous floor-to-ceiling cabinetry overflowing with wine bottles nestled in their coves.

"Choose some wine for us, milady," he invited as he drew her into the middle of the room. "I'm going to make us fish tonight for dinner."

"You're such the cook," she teased.

"Well, I'm anxious to see how erotically you can eat fish," he teased. "If it's anything like the way you eat spaghetti, I'm in deep shit."

She blushed furiously recalling her wanton behavior and quickly gave him her back while she investigated his wine selection.

"There's so much to choose from," she said as she pulled out several bottles. Finally, she settled on a white chardonnay. She heard him chuckle behind her as he reached above her and grabbed another bottle of wine.

"You think we need two bottles?" she asked.

"Most definitely," he replied as he followed her up the steps. It would be that kind of a night.

"But how will you drive us home, my dear bodyguard?"

"You're not going home. I'm keeping you," he informed her with a smug smile as they both sat down their bottles of wine on the kitchen island.

"You are?" She liked his way of thinking. She wanted him to keep her.

"Yeah, since you're off work tomorrow, you need a change of scenery and some relaxation."

"I could easily prescribe the same therapy for you. So you're going to provide the entertainment?" she asked, quirking her eyebrow at him seductively.

He gave her a smoldering gaze mixed with a silent warning.

"Storm, we do have a bit of a problem," she informed him.

"I see no problem," he said with a quick shake of his head.

"You only have one bed."

"I have a plan actually," he told her, his lips curving into a sinful smile.

"And what exactly is this plan?" she asked curiously, leaning her hip casually against the counter.

"Get you drunk and then sneak into bed with you."

She swallowed hard, poorly hiding her excitement. "I'd know."

"And if you knew?" he asked silkily.

Her smile eased up, turned contemplative. This was the part where she needed to remain levelheaded and not banter back and forth with him using sexual undertones.

"No worries, I know the rules. I promise to stay on my side of the bed," she taunted.

The look she gave him questioned his confidence.

"I can do it," he said.

I think.

"So when will you offer me a tour?" She smiled up at him hopefully.

"How about right now?"

He motioned her to walk before him. At the same time, he realized he opened himself wide open for her questions. But this time, he was ready.

They toured sixteen rooms and found themselves standing before a closed bedroom door.

She watched him pause as if stilling himself for whatever lied on the other side. She reached and entwined her fingers with his and gave his hand a reassuring squeeze. At the same time, she realized how much at this very moment he trusted her, allowing her a bit more into his world.

"Storm, are you okay?" she asked.

He took a deep breath. "Yeah," he said as he reached down, grasped the brass doorknob, and swung the door open wide.

He held his breath.

The bedroom walls were the color of pink cotton candy with a thick carpet a shade darker. A large white canopy bed with all the trimmings of white satin and lace a little girl could ever ask for dominated the room. The bedcovers were still rumpled. Stuffed teddy bears, miniature purses, and little girl's clothing littered the floor. The closet on the far side of the room was filled to the brim with floral dresses, colorful shorts, T-shirts with tags still hanging from them untouched.

He put a death grip on her hand. She was sure he never realized it. A quick glance up at his face revealed anguish and misty tears in his eyes.

Without hesitation, she slid her arm around his waist, leaned against him, and placed her head against his chest while her hand softly feathered across his back.

"Calypsia's room," he whispered his strangled confession. "I haven't been in this room since her death two years ago."

"A child's death is the most difficult to overcome. They're not supposed to die young," she consoled.

He released her, took a deep breath, and placed his hands on his hips, stared into the room.

"May I?" she asked hesitantly, indicating to enter the room.

"Of course," he said, ushering her inside the room while he stood by the door.

She walked straight over to the nightstand and picked up another photograph. Calypsia and Storm. It was very similar to the photograph downstairs, both at the beach, the sun to their backs and both smiling so happily. While Storm smiled at the camera, Calypsia smiled at Storm.

Summer nodded down at the photograph in her hands. "She loved you, you know. It's so very evident in this picture."

He gave her a brief nod as he walked farther into the room.

They stood in silence and looked around the room. Everything was just as she'd left it, even down to her hairbrush lying on the floor next to her nightstand, even to her fluorescent green flip-flops lying haphazardly by the door. She wasn't good about picking up, but it never bothered him. It was why he had Rosalinda come clean weekly.

He walked farther into the room, coming to stand behind her, looking over her shoulder at the photograph.

"I haven't had the courage to walk back into this room since the day she died," he confessed.

She set the photograph down and reached for his hand. "You found the courage today," she told him, looking up at him with a teary bright smile because the vulnerability on his face was so telling.

"I found the courage, Summer, because of you."

"No, it wasn't because of me. It's because Calypsia and your heart is telling you it's time to start living again. She loved you. She wouldn't want you to be sad."

He never needed anyone or anything.

But he needed Summer.

Once again, he pulled her into his arms and held onto her for dear life. He'd opened one tortured chapter in his life to her, bared his soul for her to peek inside, but there was more for her to see.

After a few minutes, he turned them toward the door and down the long corridor where they walked downstairs.

The moment of truth arrived.

He would reveal the story of Calypsia to Summer and let her be the judge. She needed to know about his dark side.

"Want to take a walk on the beach?" he asked.

"Yes, I'd love to."

"It's late, and we shouldn't have any problems, but just in case," he said as he shrugged on his shoulder harness again and slipped his two Glocks in his holsters.

The look she gave him wondered if it necessary.

"Yes, very necessary. I won't take chances with you."

She watched him walk over to the bar, open a door, and produce a tall shot glass. Next came a crystal decanter full of honey-colored liquid undoubtedly with the power to light your world on fire she guessed. He filled the shot glass to the brim and tossed the contents back in one gulp.

She eyed him carefully as she walked over to the bar. He seemed unfazed. Either because he was accustomed to drinking strong liquor or the liquor wasn't as strong as it looked.

He was about to put away the decanter when she picked up his shot glass and rattled it against the counter.

He gave her a startled look.

"You want a shot?" he asked humorously.

She nodded.

"You're one brave lass," he said as he picked up the decanter and hovered it over the shot glass. "This is Scottish whiskey, mighty strong," he forewarned with a wide grin.

She gave him a nod to proceed. Suddenly, her backbone produced itself.

He filled her shot glass while his lips slid into a smile as if it beheld secrets.

She cringed, seeing he filled it to the brim and then some. A bit of her backbone faltered.

He slid the shot glass toward her and braced his hands against the counter. He watched her, giving her a skeptical look as she picked up the shot glass with a slight tremor.

"Slow and easy," he instructed with a velvet voice.

She lost all concentration with those three sexually highly charged potent words.

"Blow out deep through your mouth when you're done," he instructed.

Slow and easy.

She followed his instructions to the tee, sat down the shot glass, and slid it toward him, smiling with victory.

Why was he looking at her so expectantly?

Wait, there was one final instruction he gave her. It was about breathing out afterward. She forgot that part.

Her lungs were on fire! She opened her mouth but couldn't breathe. Tears tumbled from her eyes.

He came around the counter and smacked her on the back.

It worked. She coughed and felt much better.

Laughter rippled up from his throat as he picked her up in his arms and hugged her against him.

"Good girl!" he complimented.

Their mingled laughter echoed through the corridors of his once somber home. He stopped and listened to the welcoming sound. He looked back down at her; she still giggled while her face blushed from the strong drink.

"What?" she asked as she smiled up at him.

"You've brought laughter into my home, Summer."

"I bed to differ. *We* brought laughter into your home."

He crushed her tighter against him. His lips lingered against her forehead where he planted a couple soft kisses.

"Ready?" he asked.

She was ready for sex, forget the walk, or maybe sex on the beach. Good Lord, this man had a way about revving her engine to full steam without even knowing it. Again, she looked at him with amazement. He was unaffected.

His body nearly exploded from the pressure he built up inside. With every touch, every caress, every look she gave him tore down his defenses by leaps and bounds. He practically tossed her outside the door, a race to get her out of the house before he ripped her clothes off and carried her up to his bed. Suddenly, he wasn't all too sure he made the right decision bringing her to his house knowing he planned sharing his bed with her.

No sex, he reminded himself.

They walked a short distance down the shoreline in silence, listening to the ocean roar, the chant of a distant seagull flying overhead, all the while she waited.

She waited for him to pour his heart out to her.

He took a deep breath.

Here goes everything.

23

"Her name was Calypsia Garraci." He sighed.

"A very unique name she had."

Dreaded silence filled the air. Soon, he would reveal his blackest secrets to her, and it scared the hell out of him her reaction.

"I had recently retired from the SEALs having my own set of misfortune with a bum knee. I was rambling, unsure where I wanted to settle, so I agreed to take the assignment of protecting Calypsia from another retired SEAL who was getting married and moving to Canada. It was supposed to have been a temporary assignment in Spain until the Garraci family relocated to Greece."

"Calypsia was intelligent and inquisitive, and whether or not I liked it, she made me open up about myself. There was no topic off limits with her." Storm chuckled softly. "That included her attempt to introduce me to nearly every single female I came in contact in hopes I'd marry and start a family.

"What I learned while with the Garraci family for a little over a year was they never had any time for their only child. She was always left behind, whether sent off to a fancy boarding school in France, which she despised with a passion, or home alone with her nannies and her bodyguard, me. A classic scenario of a couple who shouldn't have had a child. Sofia was a former model and jetsetter who traveled around the world to attend fashion shows and parties while Gerard constantly traveled promoting their many business ventures that inevitably couldn't seem to keep up with their lavish lifestyle. I learned they were in debt up to the hilt and borrowed money from the wrong kind of people, and when those people didn't get return on their money, the situation got very ugly. Their target became Calypsia. After a couple kidnapping attempts, I approached the Garracis with an alternative solution of me adopting Calypsia."

"They just let you take her?"

"Oh no," he answered, shaking his head. "They wanted me to pay for her."

"They agreed to sell their own daughter?" Summer asked, taken aback.

"They did, to the tune of twenty million dollars, but Calypsia never knew."

She looked at him incredulously.

"My inheritance," he confessed to her unspoken question of how he obtained the funds.

"Wow," Summer muttered. "Calypsia was okay coming to live with you then?"

"Yes, I brought her back to the States, and she and I got on rather well. She was actually much happier. We both were. She loved Amelia Island and came to love the sea. She'd never swam in the sea before, never had swimming lessons, which she made me promise I'd teach her how to swim."

"You realize her name is associated with the sea. Calypso was a Greek nymph who captured a prisoner, held him against his will on her island."

"Yes, I'm aware." He chuckled.

"So you immediately set to building your gorgeous home."

"I did. She even helped me design it. We made enough room for four bedrooms. Her only request was her bedroom to be located between her new brothers and sisters."

"That's so sweet," Summer said. Tension crawled up her neck as she waited to hear how the innocent child met her demise.

"We arrived here soon after the house was finished. She was so fascinated with the sea. She reminded me of my promise to teach her how to swim. For two weeks, from dawn to sunset, we consumed ourselves with swimming lessons. We had no time for furniture shopping, only enough time to buy two beds and a couple of televisions and food to eat. The one thing I did was have my home secured like Fort Knox so no one could get to her."

"Calypsia's photograph downstairs was taken earlier the same day she was kidnapped," he revealed. He could easily close his eyes and recall everything about that picture. It haunted his memory every single day, memories for the past two years that unsettled him, made him hate himself, made him feel like he could never climb out of his cesspool of guilt that threatened his sanity.

"Calypsia and I were on the beach when my cell phone rang. It was Gerard. I was expecting his call. We were set to finalize the money transfer for her adoption, and since I didn't want Calypsia to overhear our conversation, I walked away, up to the house, still glancing ever so often over my shoulder to see her building her sand castle. There wasn't another soul on the beach for at least a mile away in either direction. I never felt she was in immediate danger. I stepped in my house, walked immediately to the windows, and looked out. She was gone, disappeared into thin air."

"I bet you were beside yourself."

He laughed darkly. "I followed two sets of footprints that led me farther down the beach into hundreds of other footprints that led in every direction."

"Probably an hour later, I received a phone call from the kidnappers. They told me when Gerard turned over the money to them they'd release Calypsia to me."

"The Garaccis turned over the money to them, right?"

"No, they didn't. They were much greedier than I gave them credit for and pretty much hell bent on saving their own asses. They fled with the money."

"How did the kidnappers react?"

"They were enraged. I tried to soothe things over by offering them more money, which they agreed. We set up a meeting location, which turned out to be a deserted warehouse. I brought the money with me for the hand-off only to find them not there. They left a note behind for me to leave the money behind and to go to yet another location and wait for further directions forthcoming in a phone call."

"How long did you have to wait?"

"I waited six long exhausting hours until they finally gave me the location to pick her up."

"Where?"

"A nearby cemetery."

Summer's eyes widened.

"When I arrived, the cemetery was deserted. I searched while Apollo set out to tracking her scent. The sun was setting quickly, and I started to panic. Thankfully, shortly thereafter, Apollo found her. They buried her in a small coffin deep in the cemetery. They left her with only a small hose for her to breathe through. She stayed alive just long enough for me to hold her in my arms one last time and tell her how much I loved her. I felt her last heartbeat beneath my hand."

"Oh my god, Storm," Summer cried. "I can't even imagine," she said, her hand clamped over her mouth in disbelief. "Did the kidnappers get away?"

Here came the moment of truth.

"Only temporarily," he confessed.

"You went after them?" Her question was more in line of a statement.

He nodded slowly while his eyes leveled on hers as he tried to gauge her reaction.

"You found them?"

He nodded again at her, his gaze unwavering. "It took me almost two months, but I tracked down everyone involved, and I got my money back."

"What did you do to them?" she asked quietly, knowing he'd never let something like this go unanswered.

Again, dreaded silence.

"I killed them," he confessed in a voice void of regret.

"What happened to her parents?" she asked.

He stared at her incredulously. Why would she care about what happened to Calypsia's lousy parents? Did she just hear what he confessed? He confessed to murdering those involved, some seven people whose lives he ruthlessly took, and worse, he never regretted it for one instant.

Regardless, the fact remained. He was a murderer.

She tapped him softly on his chest, prompting his answer.

"I read in the paper about two weeks after Calypsia's death that Gerard and Sofia were found in a cemetery in Spain and hung side by side from a tree."

"You had no involvement in the parent's deaths?"

"No, but they were on my list. If I would've found them, it would've been much worse I can tell you that."

"I'm so sorry, Storm," she said as she walked into his arms and laid her head against his chest while she gazed out into the ocean, unable to take away from her mind the little girl who was snatched on this very beach. It sent shivers down her spine.

He set her away from him.

Confusion flickered in her eyes.

He planted his hands on her shoulders and got eye level with her. "Do you understand what I just confessed to?"

She paused for a moment, exhaled a deep breath, and stared deeply in his eyes. "I know exactly what you just confessed to. You protected the life and memory of a child. If that were me, I would've wanted to do the same if only I were as fearless as you were. What you did was make this world a safer place. You eliminated those criminals. You can't blame yourself, Storm. What happened to Calypsia was completely out of your hands. Had it not been on that beach where they took her, they would've waited until the perfect opportunity arose for them. So see, it would've happened anyways. She loved you. She'd hate to know you're suffering because of her."

His heart sang knowing he'd bared his soul to her, and she accepted him, hadn't judged him.

"Sounds like you've been through some pretty tough times these past couple of years, Storm."

"Yeah."

"Kyle was really worried about you."

"Hell, I was worried about myself, and things came to a crashing halt the day I received Reaper's phone call about you."

Her eyes beckoned him to tell her more.

"I'd reached the end of my rope," he said, coming to face the churning sea.

"What happened?" she asked, coming to stand beside him.

"The nightmares were getting ugly," he confessed.

"Nightmares about Calypsia?"

"Yes. That particular morning I decided I couldn't take it anymore. I was determined to swim into the sea and never return."

She gasped.

"Just before I left the house that morning, Reaper called and left a voice message about you being in trouble. I still left, turned my back on him. I swam out deep, but Apollo wasn't so set on letting me get off the hook so easily. I tied him to a pole just outside the front door so he wouldn't run in after me, but he did. He tore down that damn pole and came after me. I was torn about leaving behind Reaper having a problem with his baby sister, the young woman I still hadn't had the pleasure to meet. Not to mention the heartache I'd cause my family and friends, so I swam back, picked up my dog, and here we are."

"Thank God," she breathed.

He tossed his arm over her shoulder and pulled her tightly against him. They followed the moonlit path back to his house.

His heart felt a thousand pounds lighter.

A good hour later, they were sated from their fish dinner and on their second bottle of wine. She helped him clear away the dishes.

"Ready for the gala tomorrow night?" he asked as he rinsed off the plates.

She rolled her eyes as she set to the task of filling his dishwasher. "I'm not much of a party reveler. I like the quiet life. I'm sorry I have to drag you along with me."

"We'll make the most of it," he said, smiling over at her.

"Yes, I imagine you'll die of boredom, so I'm giving you my apology up front. Kyle planned to attend, but with the baby coming early…," she trailed off, turning on the dishwasher.

"I really don't mind, Summer. I'd never die of boredom with you around." He tossed aside his dishtowel and walked slowly, purposely, toward her.

She put her hand out to ward him off, but instead he reached up and planted his palm against hers, looped his other arm around her waist, and dipped her slowly over his arm.

"You can dance?" she asked breathlessly as he brought her upright.

"I was just testing the waters," he said as he raised his wrist to glance at his watch. He whistled low. "Almost midnight. We should hit the sack."

She waited for him by the staircase, watched him set the house alarm, and then walk toward her.

Her hesitation prompted his eyebrow raised at her.

He gave her a slow knowing smile.

"I know what you're thinking, Summer, us sharing my bed. I've been thinking of nothing else since I took you shopping this morning, knowing as I formulated the plan to bring you back here, you'd be a great temptation to me."

"So why did you bring me here?"

He laughed under his breath. "I wanted to sleep next to you. You see, I'm a very selfish creature. Even knowing I shouldn't have contemplated bringing you here, I did anyways because the effort to keep you at arm's length is mentally exhausting me. I can't do it anymore," he confessed, raising his hands in surrender.

"I feel the same. I hated the thought of going home and us sleeping apart."

He reached for her hand and together they walked up the steps to his bedroom. His large bed loomed, taunted them.

"I don't have anything to sleep in," she said, looking at him expectantly as he pulled down the covers on his bed.

He walked over to his closet, switched on the light.

"What's mine is yours," he whispered, waving her into his walk-in closet.

In the bathroom, she glanced at her reflection through the mirror. Her face was flushed and her stomach giddy. She tugged the white T-shirt over her head to find the shirt landed about mid-thigh and the sleeves fell to her forearms.

She walked quietly into the bedroom to see him sprawled in bed. Good God, she wished he didn't look so damn appetizing. "You sleep to the sounds of the ocean each night."

"I do," he said as he rolled onto his side and patted the place next to him. "I'm used to the sound, but I'm hoping it doesn't keep you awake."

He looked at her as if he were contemplating.

"A penny for your thoughts," she asked walking toward him.

"Do you really need to ask? You may need to be the strong one tonight and kick my ass away if I get too frisky."

"You've got the wrong person for the job," she forewarned him. "Kyle always said I lacked backbone."

"Yeah, you're right, you'll definitely be a hindrance."

She lay down next to him with at least a foot between them.

Not going to happen.

He reached for her, tugged her up tight against him on her side, and curved his hand over her hip where it suddenly stilled. He reared up. "Jesus, Summer. Seriously? You actually came to bed without panties on?"

"Easy boy," she said huskily as she turned around to face him, shoving him on his back, and kneeling between his legs. She slipped her fingertip under the waistband of his boxers, giving him a knowing smile. "Tonight, it's about you. You need to relieve a bit of tension, keep your mind clear. I think I can help you," she said as she slowly peeled down his waistband.

He covered her hand, stilled her. "That's not necessary."

She batted away his hand, slid his boxers down over his hips, over his muscular thighs. He lay before her in all his glory.

He was hard and pulsing when she wrapped her hand around him, bent, and took him in her hot mouth. He gasped, feeling her moist tongue swirl across his tip, down the long length of him, feeling her envelope him in her mouth, feeling the suctioning power of her tongue and lips, feeling his head caress the back of her throat repetitively. It was enough to shoot spasms through his body.

She felt his big body tremble, heard him groan deep through his gritted teeth while he sunk a fist deep in her hair begging her not to stop.

Slow and deep.

He tilted his head back against the pillow and thoroughly enjoyed her repetitions of *slow and deep.* It built this frenzied storm until his breathing came in harsh gasps, his body stiffening, and his heart palpitating, all because this woman's mouth was relentless against knocking down his defenses and he couldn't take it anymore.

He had to have her.

In an instant, her blouse came off, and he positioned her on her knees in the center of the bed. He mounted her, entered her from behind, sliding his full length inside her. He curled his large body over hers, his hands planted outside hers. His first stroke went deep inside her, filling her up then pumping with short thrusts, setting a rapid rhythm pace to ensure a quick fever pitch. His lips slid to her neck where he nipped and suckled the throbbing column of her throat.

His hand slid over the curve of her hip, over her belly, moving down where his slickened finger massaged her cleft.

She moaned, cried out, and arched her back against his thrusting hips. He rode her until she screamed, until her body spasmed with the explosion of her orgasm. His was fast coming, the sensation turning intense nearly blinding him as silver stars danced before his eyes. A moan tore from deep within him as he thrust one last time into her. His body jerked and heaved as he poured himself inside her.

He rolled over to his side, taking her with him. "Good God, woman. I think you nearly killed me. Your mouth could easily be labeled as a weapon."

Their harsh breaths and laughter filled the room.

"Night, baby," he purred in her ear, effectively sending goose bumps down her neck and wondering how the hell she proposed to stay on her side of the bed all night without trying to ravage him again.

"Storm?"

"Yeah?"

"Thank you for telling me about Calypsia. I imagine it was very hard for you, and I'm happy you trusted me enough to tell me your story."

"Thank you for listening," he whispered, hugging her tighter against him. This girl had proven very easy to fall in love with.

The night, however, would prove not to be about erotic dreams but nightmares.

Deep in the night, Summer stood before the windows and watched the ocean curl back and forth and the shrimp boats in the distant horizon flash their light beacons.

She glanced again over at the bed. Storm tumbled back and forth in bed so much so she couldn't sleep.

The poor soul was having nightmares.

In one of his dreams, Storm ran frantically down the lone beach and couldn't see her in any direction, not a soul. He fell to his knees, the pain in his gut hit him like a grenade. He couldn't bear the thought of losing her just when his life had taken on some semblance of order. She meant everything to him. Now, she was gone.

The next dream consisted of him trying to find her.

Under freezing black water.

And he couldn't.

Sheets were clenched in his fists when he rolled over in his bed and found it empty.

He jerked upright. His chest was heaving, exhaling harsh breaths, gasping for air.

"Summer!" mingled with fear and rage, he screamed her name in his sleep.

"I'm here," she said, running to his bedside. His eyes were clenched shut.

"Summer," he gasped, reaching his hands out to her. He found her and dragged her down on top of him, tucked her by his side.

She wiped away his tears.

"It's okay, I'm right here," she whispered, holding his face in her hands.

He opened his red-rimmed eyes and stared all the way into her soul. "Don't leave me," he replied with a shaky breath.

"I'm not going anywhere," she assured him as her hand reached up and delved her fingertips into his hair.

The next minute, he rose on his elbow and looked down at her, leaned in, and kissed her thoroughly.

"I can't live without you," he said, his words smothered against her lips.

"You won't."

He tucked her back against his side and held her.

The premonition ate away at him.

For it wasn't Calypsia's face but Summer's face now claiming his nightmares.

The showdown was coming. He felt it in his gut.

24

She looked like hell the next morning, exhausted when he rolled over in bed and reached for her. She stared back at him with concerned eyes.

Then he realized, he remembered.

His nightmares kept her awake.

"I stopped having nightmares when I met you," he acknowledged. His lips turned up in a heart stopping smile as he nuzzled his nose against hers. "I'm sorry I kept you awake."

She reached up and caressed his cheek. "Don't apologize. I was just worried about you. You couldn't have slept much."

"No worries," he said as he pulled her tightly against him.

"How about I make it up to you?" he asked, looking into her eyes. She was someone he'd never take for granted, never get used to, feeling reborn every time he looked at her. He sunk his hand deep into her tresses. The early morning sunshine cast a blazing path across her pillow likening her hair to spun gold.

"Hmm," she said smiling, running her tongue over her lips. "It's going to have to be something big."

He nearly choked on her words. He laughed darkly, his eyes focused on her soft sensual lips, very talented lips.

"Believe me, you don't know how much I'd love to give you something big right now, but I'm thinking my mind better stay more focused on the lines of food."

"Your mind is so in the gutter," she exclaimed teasingly. "I thought only of food," she lied.

"Yeah, right. Well, I can make a mean omelet. Do you want to give me a try?"

"I'd love to give you a try," she replied seductively.

Flashing a tolerant grin, he suddenly jumped on her, straddled her, and captured her wrists above her head.

His eyes roamed her face. "Aren't we just full of innuendos this morning, you sexy little tease. Today is the only day you'll get away with making them. From this point on, I plan to make you pay dearly with your words."

She squirmed beneath him while he tickled her relentlessly, had her laughing, gasping for air, her face flushed.

He hauled up her out of bed, hefted her effortlessly over his shoulder, playfully smacked her backside, and carried her downstairs to the kitchen.

It amazed him how easily they moved into this domestication business of preparing meals together, cleaning the house, and going shopping together. He could easily become accustomed.

But technically, their life was far from normal. Had it been normal on her part, she'd be working far more.

The problem was he knew he could never accept the idea seeing her on a part-time basis and sleep alone on his bed at night for days on end. As he looked over at her chopping the green peppers for the omelet, he let himself imagine her well rounded in her belly carrying his child. He wanted a family desperately, right now, and he wondered how it would fit in her busy life. Hell, he hadn't a clue her thoughts on marriage, having kids.

He decided to feel her out on the subject.

"Reaper's got him another fine baby boy," Storm said, glancing over at her as he cracked the eggs in a bowl.

"Yes, very handsome little fella that they haven't named yet that I'm aware," she said, looking up and giving him a broad smile.

"Do you want to have kids?" he asked curiously.

"I used to believe that a too far fetching possibility with my career, but yes, I do want kids. My life has flip-flopped since the day that young bride died on my table. The turn of events since has been unimaginable, the good and the bad. I recall looking at that bride after she passed and realized the same could happen to me. In an instant, my life could slam to a halt, and if that happened, all I'd have is material possessions and financial security from my job that never gives me the time to spend money. Kyle says I've been missing having a family and he's right."

"What about your career?" he prompted because this was an obvious concern for him.

"I'd shift gears and make new priorities," she answered with a quick, confident smile.

"Would you now?" he asked skeptically. "I've witnessed firsthand you working at the hospital and you're at your element there. It's where you belong. It's your passion. I can't deny that, not to mention God gave you your uncanny intelligence for a reason."

"I've realized a few things. I can't save every life. I worked those long exhaustive hours so I could always be on the front lines. Yet now I realize those bodies will show up regardless if I'm there or not. That doesn't mean I haven't lost my passion because I'll fight to the very end to save a life, but I have my own life to live too."

"What are your thoughts?"

He walked over to her, leaned his hip against the island, pushed back her hair from her cheek, and tucked it behind her ear.

"When I marry, it's for keeps. I don't believe in divorce. I want a good-sized family. That's the good stuff. The unpleasant part is I come with baggage, nightmares, and I never know when they'll creep up. I've done things in my past I'm not proud of, but I believe I'm a good man with a good heart and I'd never hurt you. I'd never leave you. I'd protect you until my dying breath."

She reached up and cupped his cheek. "Do you know I've heard your name most of my life, heard of your heroics, and how you saved my brother's life? But it's not about the hero you were over in Afghanistan and all the places you've been around the globe with my brother, it's about the hero you are to me. Your name is fitting because you literally 'stormed' right into my life and took over. I realize I haven't done such a swell job at following your rules, but I'm working on it. I know the danger is real, and I have someone hell bent on wanting to kill me, but I'm not afraid anymore. I know if I get into a fix, you'll save me. And if it doesn't work out that way, I already know you tried your best."

He pulled her in his arms and tucked her head under his chin. "Baby, you're not to worry. I'll handle the situation when it arrives."

Again, his gut kicked him, giving him a trickling of foreboding inking down his spine.

There was no fucking way he was going to lose her.

No fucking way.

They ate breakfast and then headed back to her house, rounding close to two o'clock in the afternoon to discover they had a visitor.

Kyle walked out her front door to greet them. Wearing his familiar attire, wearing a black SEALs cap backward, aviator sunglasses, a blue embroidered T-shirt with NAVY stretched across his broad muscular chest and tucked into a pair of faded jeans with his usual snakeskin boots.

"Kyle's here!" she cried as she tried to get out of the car before Storm had the car stopped.

Storm parked the car and watched Summer rush into her brother's arms, excited to the extreme.

When Storm looked at Reaper, it brought forth a rush of memories that spanned the past twenty years that began during BUD/S, Basic Underwater Demolition/SEAL training in Coronado, California. Midway through the eight-week training program was Hell Week. Neither imagined the pure hell they'd endure that week, the grueling five days of constantly moving, constantly being hungry, ice cold, wet, and covered from one end to the other with mud and sand. And sleep, there was no sleep, or else he never remembered it. They kept each other awake and motivated. Motivated by the ringing of a shiny brass bell that hung in the middle of the camp for all to see one's disgrace. A bell they refused to ring because it signified giving up. Together, they defied the 80 percent dropout rate and been together ever since. And now, Reaper was a BUD/s instructor, he did the same taunting shit those men did to them, urging them to ring that shiny bell when they felt they couldn't go on.

"Hooyah!" Storm grasped his hand, his arm, pulling him in for a hug. "Reaper, I'm happy as hell to see you, but what brings you here?"

"Her hospital gala thing," Kyle said, chuckled.

Summer cringed when someone called her brother Reaper, a name synonymous with death, a name given to him by his SEAL team for his talent as one of America's most deadly snipers with a record of accuracy and high body count, something she didn't even want to contemplate.

Summer gazed at the baby picture Kyle handed her, a replica of Kyle in every way. "So what name have you decided upon?"

Kyle looked over at Storm thoughtfully. "We named him Storm."

Storm swallowed hard, felt a huge ass lump grow in his throat. He swallowed hard again and saw tears blur his eyes, which he hurriedly scraped away as he looked down at the picture Reaper handed him from his billfold.

"Seriously, man?" Storm asked in a rough voice. "You're giving the kid a wrap before he's even a week old."

"Seriously," Reaper nodded somberly.

When Reaper looked upon Storm, he couldn't help but recall one particular night in Afghanistan when they were called in to rescue a reconnaissance team pinned down by militiamen. Upon arrival, a rocket grenade shot down their helicopter. Many had life-threatening injuries and were incapacitated; he was one of them suffering a back injury. Storm suffered a severe knee injury but risked his life by single-handedly facing down the militants and crossing enemy lines to call in air support while they riddled his body with bullets. His heroism awarded him a Navy Cross for actions he refused to acknowledge going beyond the call of duty.

Reaper considered it an honor to name his son after Storm. He tried to make light of the situation. "I wanted to check things out for myself."

Summer smiled at her brother. The name of her new nephew couldn't have made her happier, and from the looks of Storm, he was as proud as a peacock. The two of them needed some privacy, and Kyle obviously wanted an update on the psycho person after her.

"When did you get here?" she asked. "How did you get here? I could have picked you up from the airport," she said, walking up the steps to the front door.

"I arrived about thirty minutes ago. I hitched a ride with the training squadron, the kind that doesn't land on airport strips. I can't stay the night. I've got a deadline to meet."

She frowned at him.

Kyle blew her a kiss as she closed the door behind her.

This was their time to catch up, and she decided she could use a shower and a change of clothes.

He turned around and nodded toward Storm's holsters. "You've always carried one holster."

"That went out the window with your sister."

"I'm sure it did. Even carrying Glock 45s I see. Impressive." Reaper gave a low whistle.

"Not as impressive as your 308, believe me."

"Yeah, you're right. I'm kind of partial to my sniper rifle," Reaper teased. "So what have you found out so far?"

"Derek researched our man. We're dealing with a Green Beret by the name of Mark Malone, a Silver Star recipient who did a tour in Afghanistan. As of a few months ago, he's been walking on the dark side. Evidently, this chump believes your sister is to blame for his fiancée's death and even came back to the hospital later that same day and put a gun to her head and told her he wouldn't kill her until she suffered properly."

"What the fuck?" Reaper bellowed. "She never told me that."

"I can't imagine why." Storm gave him a sardonic smile, indicating his temper. "The scoop I got from Derek is he's been busted for his bad temper. Now this is good and bad. From what has happened with your sister, I can pretty much determine on target what this guy has and has not been responsible for."

Reaper looked at Storm incredulously. "Are you saying what I think you're saying? That we have two fucking psychos terrorizing my sister?"

"Affirmative," Storm replied with a definite nod. "My gut tells me someone is using Malone's anger and twisting it into their own terror game on Summer. For instance, the day I met her at the restaurant, she was stopping by on her way to the dealership to get another car because someone wrote the word *killer* with acid on the hood of her car."

Reaper's eyes blazed furiously.

"Yeah, this Malone guy called her a killer at the hospital when his fiancée died. Yet I honestly can't believe he poured acid on her car. It's too trivial for a Beret."

"At the restaurant, she saved a guy from choking. We later found in this guy's SUV a gun, rope, duct tape, and a knife. Now, I can't say for sure he was after her but pretty damn coincidental and the way he looked at her. We both know a Special Forces guy isn't going to hire someone to kill a person he's sworn revenge."

As Reaper paced back and forth, Storm continued.

"Afterwards, when I arrived at her house, I checked out her mail and checked out her newspaper. Someone took blood and wrote *killer* across the headlines. Again, trivial petty shit if you ask me. As for the car accident, I still can't wrap my mind around Malone being responsible. The page from the hospital was bogus. I can't help but wonder if someone affiliated with the hospital has a death wish against her."

"Son of a bitch!" Reaper swore.

"Later that same morning, I visited Malone's home and talked to his younger brother who said they hadn't seen Malone in well over a week, and they were very concerned about him. Now, get this, the DUI suspect who hit Malone's fiancée posted bond, and he's suddenly disappeared. This guy's family is searching for him. In my opinion, that's something I could believe Malone doing, kidnapping him and doing God only knows what to him."

Kyle agreed. "Yeah, if he wanted her dead, she'd been dead before she even called me. He's planning right now and that thought scares the hell out of me."

"I asked her if she had any enemies, and she says she doesn't. So right now, I'm basically swinging my dick in the dark trying to figure out who is coming next bearing God only knows what means to harm her."

"Well, I'm pleased to see I have the right man on the job," Reaper said.

"It's not over yet, Reaper. I hope you can say those words after all hell breaks loose and the dust settles because I feel it and it's coming."

25

She dressed for *him* tonight.

She gave herself one last glance at the floor length mirror and sent a couple fervent prayers heavenward that Storm would like her gown, and secondly, she'd not turn into a stumbling fool wearing her new sandals.

Kyle and Storm were at the kitchen island when she rounded the corner. Kyle was dressed in his navy blue suit and sitting on a barstool facing her. She grinned at him and felt her heart burst with pride knowing he would be by her side tonight.

Storm had his back to her wearing only his black dress pants and a crisp white shirt with creased sleeves that hugged his broad shoulders and culminated down to a narrow waist. Muscles rippled under his shirt as he shrugged on his shoulder harness. It quickened her pulse.

Kyle was the first to react; he jumped off the barstool, cocked his eyebrow up at her, giving her an appreciative smile as his eyes swept across her gown. He glanced over at Storm who was in the process of situating his harness and just picked up one of his guns from the counter. Kyle tapped him on the shoulder and gave his head a slight tilt behind him indicating Summer.

Storm, a bit distracted, gave a quick glance over his shoulder.

He lost his breath and his reflexes.

His gun slipped through his hands.

Easily forgotten.

"Whoa!" Kyle scrambled and caught the gun. "Brother, let me help you," he said, laughing under his breath as he slid Storm's gun into the holster against his ribs.

Storm never heard him. He was too mesmerized by the stunning beauty standing before him, the perfect picture of elegance.

Her hair was piled high in a woven set of riotous curls with teasing wisps against her neck. Her emerald silk gown, the color of the bottomless ocean just after sunrise, intensified her blue eyes, hugged her soft curves, and showed ample tantalizing cleavage that electrified every nerve ending in his body. Diamond straps draped over her shapely shoulders. A thin diamond choker and matching earrings completed her ensemble. He continued his perusal a bit more down south to reveal a shapely thigh and diamond strapped sandals exposed by a thigh high slit up the side of the gown.

Mouthwatering.

Kyle's gaze flitted back and forth between Summer and Storm. It was as if he stood between two sticks of dynamite about to explode, the atmosphere combustible and so powerfully charged.

That all-consuming look Storm gave his sister revealed a few things. One, Storm never followed his instructions about sleeping with his sister. Secondly, he was in love with her. His glance swiveled back to Summer. She beamed, positively glowed, and all that happiness was directed to only one man.

Storm.

She was in love with Storm. It was so easy for him to see, any stranger would see it for that matter. The question was, did they both know it? Ever since his arrival, the both of them had been polite to each other, almost too polite, almost as if they walked on eggshells. Something wasn't right. He planned to find out from Storm soon enough, but for now, he planned to have some fun with it.

"Sunshine," Kyle said, walking up to her taking her by the hand and twirling her slowly around in a circle. "You look positively stunning. If I didn't know any better, I'd say you took some extra care dressing up for this event tonight. Have you decided to put yourself back on the market?"

"Kyle!" she shrieked.

Kyle looked over at Storm, still in a trance. "I bet we'll have to take numbers just to get a dance with her tonight."

Kyle's gaze then landed back on Summer. "Or is that doctor guy… what's his name? I bet he plans to occupy plenty of your time. Hmm,

I can't remember his name." He snapped his fingers a couple of times, definitely over exaggerating.

Kyle received a stare from Summer that could've easily burst him into flames reminding him of their youth and how he relentlessly pushed her buttons as only a brother knew how. He could feel Storm bristle beside him, and it made the situation even more comical.

"Oh yes, I remember now. Dr. O'Malley, yes, that's his name," he said, grinning innocently at Summer.

She groaned and felt a sudden throb against her temple. She leaned into Kyle and whispered in his ear, "Shut up please."

In return, she received a playful smack across her bottom from Kyle, earning him another glare from her. Kyle turned around and looked at Storm expectantly. "So what do you think?"

Storm's mouth had turned as dry as the desert since he took his first glance at her.

"He's speechless," Kyle said, laughing, cuffing Storm's shoulder.

"Damn," Storm finally managed.

Summer leaned over, pulled up the hem of her gown, and wiggled her foot in her sandal.

Storm's jaw dropped when she leaned over; her breasts nearly spilled out.

Kyle reached over and tapped Storm's bottom jaw upward with his fingertip.

"I hope I don't trip in these sandals. The heel is a bit higher than what I'm accustomed to, and my ankle is still a bit weak."

"I won't let you fall," Storm said huskily as he tugged on his black suit jacket, his eyes unwilling to release her.

"I know you won't," she said, straightening up to look at him. He looked so incredibly handsome in his suit. Just as swiftly, her cheeks exploded with heat because her thoughts ventured to another night when they used up all their energies on each other's bodies and laid in bed breathless.

Even though they swore no physical involvement until the crisis ended, the emotions were uncontrolled inside her and in his eyes. The heated look he gave her melted her and made her feel like she was levitating.

Tonight, she'd be with the two men who meant the world to her. The evening would prove interesting if she could concentrate long enough on the other guests and the festivities without looking and thinking of *him* every second. Secretly, she prayed it ended quickly so she could once again be alone with him.

"Oh, I forgot my purse," she said, turning around and leaving Kyle and Storm alone.

Kyle slapped his hand against Storm's shoulder. "Hey, man, can I have a word with you outside?"

Storm followed him outside where they walked for a short distance and all the while Storm waited; he knew what was coming. He could feel it already.

A bird fluttering overhead to a low branch captured Storm's attention and caught him off guard as did the solid punch that landed against his right jaw, staggering him back a step. He rubbed his jaw, gave it a test, nothing was broken.

Reaper leaned against the palm tree and pointed at him, smiling. "That's a love tap, my friend, for sleeping with my sister after I warned you not to. God damn it!" He shook out his hand, wiggled his fingers trying to relieve the burning, tingling sensation. "Is your jaw made out of steel or what?"

Storm smiled in answer and then shrugged his shoulders knowing Reaper waited for an apology, an explanation he couldn't offer. "Man, if you're looking for an apology, I guess I could give it, but I'd only be half giving it because she's…she's…," he said as he paced slowly back and forth in front of Reaper.

Words failed him.

"Well, she's just quite irresistible," he summoned out.

"Storm, just be careful. She's very vulnerable right now."

"I know," he said, coming to stand next to him, leaning his hand against the tree trunk.

"You are too," Reaper acknowledged, giving him a worried glance.

"I understand your concern especially when you know all the skeletons in my closet, but rest assured I'm on it. I'll protect her with my life."

"That's not even a question. I know that. How can you fully protect her if your mind is clogged?"

"She and I have an understanding," Storm confided.

"An understanding?" Reaper's brow rose.

"I expressed the same concern to her about me needing to be focused when I protected her, and we're going to chill out."

"Buddy, who the hell do you think you're fooling?" Reaper looked at him incredulously.

"Seriously, we did," Storm said, lifting his right hand.

"I saw the way you looked at her. Worse, I saw the way she looked at you, like no one else in this world existed. If I hadn't been standing there taking up space, you guys wouldn't have even shown up at this gala tonight. Now, you both can tell each other you've sworn off sex but you're only fooling yourself."

Suddenly, Reaper groaned and started laughing. He smacked his hand against his forehead.

"Oh hell, here I'm the one to talk. You gave me this same lecture when we rescued Sibella in Afghanistan. Yes, I remember now. You slugged the hell out of my jaw. You told me to stop thinking with my dick, but I told you it was so much more than that." He whirled around, looked at Storm, frowning. "Is it so much more than that?"

"Yeah, it sure the hell is," Storm confessed.

"I told you she was hands off."

"That's what I told myself too, but I made the mistake of making her spaghetti for dinner one night and that was all she wrote."

"What the hell?" Reaper was staring at him, his arms folded across his broad chest.

Storm smiled and let out a loud sigh. "Hell, I'm going to have to marry her, aren't I?"

"I'm afraid so." Reaper turned around to see Summer standing at the door. Her face was red, and her eyes spat fury.

"Kyle!" she yelled, pointing at him, marching toward him.

Both men took a step backward.

Storm gave Reaper a nudge forward.

"You had no right to hit him," she said sternly.

"Does it look like I hurt him?" Reaper looked over his shoulder at Storm who smiled arrogantly back at him.

"Well, it wasn't his fault," she said, giving Storm's jaw a glance, seeing it reddened with an imprint from Kyle's fist. "It's my fault. I seduced him."

"You?" Kyle asked incredulously.

"Yes, me!" she said indignantly, placing her hands on her hips.

"I didn't think you capable of seducing a broomstick." Kyle chuckled, looking down at her, raising a quizzical brow.

"I've been around a block or two," she replied, exasperated.

Both men bowled over and started laughing.

"You can stop any minute, both of you."

"I guess I find it hard to believe he didn't seduce you first," Kyle confessed. "He's got a lot of shortcomings."

Storm gave a slight punch to Reaper's back. "I've cleaned up my act since way back, thank you. Now, if you'll excuse me."

Summer received a secret wink from Storm as he walked around her. She wanted to follow him into the house and lock him up in her bedroom. Her brother's words interrupted her wayward thoughts.

"Wonders never cease," Kyle said to Summer as they watched Storm leave to go back inside the house.

"You've been a trooper through all this," Kyle said, pulling her into his arms and holding her tightly against him.

She kissed his cheek and then laid her head against his chest. "I wished we lived closer to each other. I miss you."

"I know you do, honey. That's why we share those phone calls several times a week. It's so you know I'm only a phone call away."

"Yeah, I got that, but it's still not the same as having you here in person. I'm so happy you are here."

He hugged her tight again and set her away from him.

"My boy seems like he's taken a new stance on life and her name is Summer Benson."

Her face broke out into a bold smile.

"I was worried about him for the longest time. Did he end up confessing anything to you about Calypsia?"

"Yes, he did," she admitted as she turned her head and watched Storm pull his car out of the garage.

"Everything?" he asked curiously.

"You mean about him taking justice into his hands and killing those people responsible?"

He nodded.

"Yes, and it doesn't change how I feel about him."

"Yeah, I didn't think so, but I'm glad he finally got it off his chest. That tells me how much he trusts you."

Her eyes narrowed on him. "Speaking of trust, can't you keep a few things private between us?"

A mixture of confusion and humor flitted across his face.

"Like I only wear pink panties. You talk way too much, Kyle Benson," she gently admonished him.

He lifted his hand up, laughing way too hard to speak, much less apologize.

"He told me about you guys terrorizing my lab partner, scaring the wits out of him when you kidnapped him from his bed in the middle of the night."

His laughter faded into a curious smile. "Did he now?"

"Yes, how you guys hitched him up against a field post while animals did things to him that I can't even allow myself to think about," she said with a shudder.

He looked at her odd.

"What?" she asked as he crossed his arms over his chest, rocked back on his heels, giving her a smug grin.

"He was only telling you a half truth, sister. It was *his* idea, *him* who wrenched that poor little lamb from his bed, *him* who we had to control. Hell, we thought *he* was going to shoot his ass. It was *him*. Believe me, I would've done all that and probably more to that little mutant. It was *Storm* who delivered the very personal message to that kid. Not me."

She smiled to herself.

He loves me.

26

The hospital gala took place inside a large two-story historical building on the grounds of a local art museum.

Summer, Storm, and Kyle arrived and was directed off the entrance, down a long corridor leading into a sprawling ballroom. Massive crystal chandeliers glowed overhead reflecting down on the gorgeous snow-white linen draped tables outlining the perimeter of the ballroom. The centerpieces were silver bowls overflowing with plump fragrant red roses. A lady directed them to the center of the ballroom to some very advantageous seats.

Summer prayed it went by fast. This wasn't her cup of tea.

She felt a tap on her shoulder and turned around to see Mariann dressed in a flowing blood-red gown that hugged her slender figure.

Mariann hugged her tight. "I've been so worried about you, Summer. Your life has been in an upheaval lately. I hoped you were coming tonight, and just in case, I brought you a little something." She presented her with a clear carton containing a corsage of pink rosebuds and baby's breath.

Summer smiled at her as she opened the carton and retrieved the corsage. "How very thoughtful, Mariann. You shouldn't have." Her gaze then flickered over Mariann's gown. "You look so gorgeous. Red definitely suits you."

Kyle pinned the corsage on Summer's gown.

Summer reached up and felt the silky petals between her fingertips. "My gown is complete now."

Mariann stood back and looked at her and gave a low whistle. "Are you sure it's complete? It looks like it's missing a few strips of material. I wouldn't have imagined you wearing something so provocative."

Summer looked startled, glanced down at her figure-hugging gown. It showed a bit more cleavage than she was accustomed, and she suddenly felt terribly exposed. She was starting to discount her choice of gown until she looked up at Storm. He gave her a wink, turning her knees to mush.

All was right with her world.

"Did you come alone, Mariann, or did you bring a date?"

"Dr. O'Malley," she replied and gave a look over her shoulder toward the door. "He's parking the car."

"Great," Summer replied, hoping to keep the surprise from her voice.

Mariann glanced enviously at Summer, flanked by two extremely handsome men with killer bodies and sinner smiles. They stood so close to her. Their arms brushed her body as if to protect her. She imagined her body rubbing against one of them. They easily made Dr. O'Malley look like a park hobo in her opinion. She pledged by the end of the night that she'd dance with one of them.

"And while many of us struggle to find a date, you bring two," Mariann teased as once again her eyes slid enviously over Summer's escorts.

Summer immediately set forth introductions yet couldn't help wonder if Mariann's tone was underlying sarcasm. She surely hoped not; she never imagined Mariann being the jealous type. Yet considering her struggling love life, there was always the possibility.

The cocktail hour and the prime rib dinner went by in a blur as did the number of people who greeted her. Summer found herself having a good time.

As the large video screen peeled down in the center of the ballroom floor, guests took to their seats, the lights lowered, and the documentary began.

Storm positioned Summer between him and Reaper. Their chairs angled her direction, unbeknownst to her, more for protective measures.

Her face flashed across the screen.

The very first scene showed her caring for a stabbing victim, showing her holding two fingers against the patient's neck wound to stem the flow of blood. It showed her giving orders to her team while blood dripped off her face mask, off the front of her apron. It showed everyone working in perfect precision together, and it made her burst with pride for her team.

The next scene showed the aftereffects of a trauma case, the room minus the trauma cart. Pools of blood along with opened packages, gloves, scissors, bandages, and tubes littered the floor. Various machines jutted at odd angles around the perimeter of the room. The chaotic scene gave gravity to the situation showing the professionalism and courage it took to save a patient's life that an average person would never witness.

Another scene showed her and her team trying to revive a five-year-old child severely beaten by her drunken father. It showed Summer with the heart paddles jolting the child's body while the child lay before her motionless.

Summer turned her face away from the screen. She felt Storm reach for her hand under the table where he pulled her against him, stretching his arm across the back of her seat.

Gladly, she sunk against him, letting him support her.

She glanced back up at the screen to see a cameraman had captured her on film shortly afterward leaning against the wall, sobbing in a deserted hallway over the child's loss. There were multiple scenes as such, similar scenarios. It made her uncomfortable to watch seeing how they exposed her private feelings for all to see.

Storm looked over at her and watched her unconsciously twist her hands together. He reached out and caught her hands in his.

Thankfully, there were some funny scenes where the staff played tricks on each other, the cute birthday cake surprises, the holiday gift exchanges, and carry-in meals.

Watching the film made her realize something. She spent her birthdays and all her holidays at the hospital. She allowed the hospital to rule her life.

She'd lived more in the past two weeks than she's lived in almost ten years. That was a startling discovery.

Once again, Summer was featured when the film crew interviewed her, asking her what she loved about her job. She listened to her tell them how she loved working with her team, a very talented team, and how this was her dream job, her passion, and she couldn't imagine doing anything else.

As she stared at the screen, another realization came to mind. She was passionate about her job, but more passionate about the man sitting next to her.

She loved Storm.

She thought about his kindness, his intelligence, his sultry voice, his hypnotic eyes, the magnetic force of his personality, and the blow-your-mind sex, not to mention he would be a great father one day; and the thought of her sharing a life with him, having his children, overruled everything else.

Storm brought her hand up to his lips, gave her a lingering kiss there, never taking his eyes off the screen. Across the room, her eyes landed on Mariann who looked directly at her smiling having caught Storm kissing her hand.

Summer smiled back and then gazed back up at the screen. Out of the corner of her eye, she saw Storm look Mariann's direction, but only for a fleeting second as if to see what held her attention, then he focused back on the documentary.

After showing pictures of the hospital and plans for renovation, the documentary finally concluded.

Thank God.

The screen disappeared back into the ceiling and in its place sat a podium and a microphone.

The president of the hospital spoke briefly, thanking everyone for attending. Then he called out her brother's name, waving him forward.

Shocked, Summer turned to Kyle. "What is this about?"

"Hush. Now, sit back and enjoy this," he said, getting up and walking toward the podium.

She glanced at Storm. "Did you know he was coming here? What exactly is he doing?" Her apprehensive glance flitted back and forth between Kyle and Storm.

Storm shook his head.

"Sit back and relax, baby," Storm ordered, effectively tucking her against his side.

Kyle stood at the podium, looked around at the sea of faces, every bit of one hundred and fifty people. God, he hated making public speeches, but because it was for his baby sister, he'd make the exception. He had no speech prepared, not as if he really needed it. It was all in his head and his heart.

He braced his hands on both sides of the podium and went for it, looking at Summer.

"Good evening, my name is Kyle Benson and I'd like to tell you a few things about a wonderful talented young lady who doesn't see herself as special," Kyle began.

"The *she* to whom I'm referring is my sister, Dr. Summer Benson," he said, giving a wave of acknowledgement in her direction.

"She started reading books when she was five years old, specifically, our father's medical journals."

The guests whispered.

"On a particular Saturday afternoon, our parents took us to the local bookstore where I headed to my usual comic book section while my five-year-old sister went her way, which I assumed was to look at her princess books with our mother. An hour later, my father and I found my mother and her sitting in the corner of the bookstore. Summer had a large thick book sprawled across her lap, the title of the book, *Surgical Techniques for the Twenty-First Century*.

"I remember my mother sitting there, telling us how she couldn't get the book away from Summer. My father bought Summer the book because she was bound and determined she wasn't leaving without it. For one month, she read the book diligently. We thought she was enthralled with the colored photographs, but we soon learned it was so much more.

"Approximately a week later, our mother received a phone call from Summer's school nurse. Summer was running a fever and needed to be picked up from school. When my mom arrived, the nurse pulled her aside and assured her Summer would be perfectly fine after some rest. Then she confided something extraordinary. It seemed Summer had the ability to cite the name and location of all 206 bones in the human body. She could also recite the names and locations of the organs, some sixty, and their function.

"Let me remind you, at the age of five."

The guests erupted in whistles and applauses.

Summer shrunk down in the seat wishing she could crawl under the table.

"She took off from there. She shot through elementary school, finishing the material for six grades in one year. The school officials advised our parents to send her directly to high school where she completed the curriculum in the blink of an eye.

"At the age ten, she graduated from high school and earned a perfect score on her SAT. My parents then sent her to a school for gifted children. All too soon, she outgrew the paces. At the tender age of fourteen, she graduated summa cum laude from Johns Hopkins University and went on to study medicine there.

"She was midway through her surgical residency here at Regional Medical when tragedy struck our family. Our parents died in a car accident. While I was on the other side of the world battling terrorists, she was here alone. With the help of this community, she stayed strong and found a home here. Her thirst for knowledge hasn't been quenched yet, and I don't think it ever will.

"Yet she doesn't see herself as special. Well, I beg to differ. I say she's pretty amazing. Thank you." Kyle left the podium to return to the table.

She received a standing ovation.

Summer watched Kyle walk toward her, his arms already opening wide. A sob broke from her as she threw her arms around his waist and hugged him, burying her wet face against his chest.

He wrapped his beefy arms around her, lifted her several inches off the ground then set her down and brushed his hand softly against her cheek. As he escorted her back to her chair he wiped away a lone tear dashing down his cheek.

Storm knew of Summer's many accomplishments yet to hear it announced by Reaper caused a lump in his throat at the intensity, the love he felt for his sister. Storm thought about his sister, Caro. She had a law degree yet decided on a career as a wedding planner, which totally dumbfounded his family, even him. She actually made more money being a wedding planner than a lawyer and seemed to get a hell of a lot of enjoyment out of it. Never again would he give her a rough time about it, and when he saw her at his parent's anniversary party, he planned to tell her just how much he loved her.

Summer's limelight was far from over she realized with dismay.

The chief of trauma walked to the podium and announced her many accomplishments, which she listened to with only half an ear, feeling the eyes of her colleagues on her. She felt like a tiny ant under a blazing microscope.

"Her participation in numerous medical groups, her serving on various medical boards, named Outstanding Physician Champion last year, received the teaching excellence award, presented award winning lectures…"

On and on the chief droned.

She sighed with relief when he finally finished.

Next, the hospital president stepped up to the podium and indicated a special donation presentation.

In the hazy darkness across the far side of the room, Summer watched a familiar-looking man walk toward the podium. He was a tall man with thinning mousey brown hair and black-rimmed glasses. When he stepped directly beneath the light, she recognized him.

Then she remembered.

"Last year when they brought our Matthew, aged sixteen, into the trauma center at Regional Medical because of a car accident, my wife and I were devastated, so unprepared. You see, we heard he died twice in the ambulance on the way, and we knew his golden hour was already up because of the length of time it took them to extract him from his mangled car. But that young woman," he said as his voice broke tearfully as he pointed across the room at Summer, "never gave up on our child. At two o'clock in the morning, she took his life into her competent hands. After several hours of grueling surgery, she pieced him back together and saved his life."

Applause thundered around her.

He raised his hand effectively quieting the guests. "There's more to this, more I'm ashamed to admit as I stand before all of you today," he said quietly and then he paused for a long moment as the guests waited in silence.

After exhaling a harsh shaky breath, he continued, "She came out to talk to us after surgery. At first, I refused to talk to her, refused to believe she was the one who operated on my son. In my mind, I envisioned this surgeon being a man having weathered hands, gray hair, done thousands of operations, someone my age, and certainly not a young woman the age of my young daughter. She was stern when she stepped forward, toe to toe with me, glared into my eyes, and asked if I wanted to know about my son's condition or not. It made me think how often she probably had to defend herself, possibly even on a daily basis, her career choice. After hearing her brother tell us about her attending medical school at such an incredibly young age, I can now only imagine the heartache she endured to be equal. Now, I thank God she became a trauma surgeon because if she hadn't been there on that fateful night, we may have lost our Matthew.

"In closing, when I heard about the foundation gala and the documentary featuring in part Dr. Benson, I requested an invite. After watching this documentary, it has enabled us to see her compassion for her patients and therefore because of her intense dedication, her competency, her commitment to every patient, no matter their background and because she saved our son's life, we've decided to give a donation of one million dollars toward the hospital's renovation project. Thank you."

Another standing ovation.

The man left the podium and walked directly toward her, followed by his wife and her patient, Matthew.

Summer tearfully rose from her chair with open arms and hugged the family.

"Speech!" the guests chanted.

Summer groaned. She hadn't prepared a speech.

The guests were insistent.

She walked to the podium. She had to wing it.

"What you've witnessed in this documentary is how a highly skilled medical team works together with one single goal in mind. Save lives. It's not because of one person but because of a team who has committed themselves to excellence. We, as a team, share in jubilation when we can do the unimaginable and save a life. We, as a team, share our grief when we've exhausted all efforts. We stand united as a team."

"My dream for this hospital is it be accredited to a Level I trauma center where no matter how grievous the injuries of our patients, they remain here under our care and protection while we try to save their lives.

"In addition, I would like to see this hospital collaborate with our local universities and colleges to enhance the education of our medical students because they're our future and because we must strive to stay a step ahead of tomorrow's technology and research.

"Last, we should encourage the collaboration of our community. They need to be involved in what we do at their hospital. Let's open our doors, and you'll see the financial support pour into this hospital, ladies and gentlemen, because they'll know what we do here is for them, our community. Thank you."

She stepped away from the podium.

The guests gave her a thundering applause.

Soon after, with the lights lowered and candlelight filtering across the room. The pianist sat down, a small statured Asian woman who made wonderful music dance off her fingertips. The dance floor filled with couples.

"Sunshine, will you do me the honor?" Kyle asked as he rose from the table and reached for her hand.

"Yes." She gave Storm a quick glance. He sent her a wink.

Kyle led her onto the dance floor, took her in his arms, and gave her a swift kiss on her forehead. "Did I embarrass you by telling everyone your secrets?"

"Sort of," she admitted. "People don't take me seriously the way it is sometimes and for them to now know extra stuff about accelerating through school, they'll tease me mercilessly now."

"Only because they're jealous. They all seem to genuinely love you here, so if they tease you, I'm sure it's just for fun," he consoled.

"You made it wonderfully special coming tonight, Kyle. I can't thank you enough."

"Isn't that what big brothers are for?" he asked, rubbing his nose against hers.

"Yeah, I just wish there was something I could do for you."

"Well, there is. You can follow Storm's orders and no longer question him. No exceptions," he ordered.

"I promise," she said, giving him a nod.

"I love you," he said, standing still. He brought the back of her hand up to his lips. "Always remember how much you mean to me. How much the both of you mean to me."

She gulped, hugged him tight, and felt foreboding slither down her spine. Hot tears raced down her cheeks. She hated that their song ended.

He glanced up his wristwatch. "I've got to roll. They're here to pick me up."

Receiving a nod from Reaper, Storm rose from his chair. As he walked toward them, Mariann stepped in front of him, placed her palm against his chest, and pressed her body against his. Her body weaved back and forth like a reed blowing in the wind.

"You and me on the dance floor. What do you say?" she offered in a slurred voice. Potent whiskey laced her breath, making him take a step back. Her eyes were glazed over and focused hungrily on his lips. She reminded him of a barracuda circling him in a tiny fish bowl. She was one desperate woman.

"Sorry, but no thank you," he said and set her quickly aside.

He strolled toward Summer and Reaper and saw Summer looking over his shoulder at Mariann, a concerned look on her face.

"Storm, perhaps you should dance with her. She looks upset."

He raised his brow at her. "She's too drunk to dance."

"Mariann's drunk?" Summer asked. Now, that was surprising.

He nodded. "Where's her knight in shining armor, O'Malley?"

A quick glance across the room showed him sitting at another table chatting with three eager, pretty nurses.

"I feel sorry for her," Summer said, frowning.

"Feel sorry for me, brat. I'm the one having to leave," Kyle said, giving her a fierce hug.

She cupped his cheek. "I love you. Thank you for coming. Give everyone my love."

Kyle hugged Storm. "Take care of my sister. Call me if you need anything." He left, exiting out a side door.

Summer looked up at Storm and gave him a flirtatious smile. "What do you say we blow this joint? I won't even make you dance with me," she said and reached for his hand to tug him off the dance floor.

Storm pulled her up against him. Moving slowly, yet sensually, his eyes never wavered from hers.

"I thought you didn't dance?" she smiled up at him curiously.

"I said I didn't dance, that doesn't mean I can't dance. I guess you're stuck with me," he said, smiling down at her.

"Oh, believe me, I'm the lucky one. As a matter of fact, I believe I'm the envy of this gala by some of the hungry glances you're getting from the lady guests."

"Ditto, babe, you're looking like a hot commodity. These men can't seem to keep their eyes off your breasts and your backside. I'm thinking you're right. If we don't leave soon, I'll have to beat them off with a stick."

She looked up into his eyes and realized she could dance forever in his arms. "Thank you for bringing me tonight. I've had a wonderful time."

"I did too, actually. Wow, you're one special lady, so young, yet you've accomplished so much."

They danced another three slow songs and discovered the dance floor was empty with only a few couples left in the ballroom.

"Where did the time go? For that matter, where did the people go?" she asked, laughing up at him.

Storm curved his arm around her waist and escorted her back to the table to retrieve her purse. A white envelope sat next to her purse. She opened it and pulled out the snow-white card. In typed bold letters, the color of crimson red was the words:

Your time is up.

She gasped. The card floated to the floor.

Storm glanced over at her and saw her pale face. He bent down and picked up the card, read it. He tucked it inside the pocket of his suit jacket. He reached for her hand.

"It's okay, baby. No one's going to hurt you."

He led her to the front door and looked at her over his shoulder. "I'd like to go get the car, but I don't want to leave you alone. So you're going to walk close to me, in step with me, if something should happen, follow my orders."

She shuddered and suddenly felt violently ill as her stomach twisted with fear.

With his other hand, he unbuttoned his jacket to have access to his guns if needed. The hair on the back of his neck stood up, a chill swirled down his spine. He didn't have a good feeling glancing out into the dimly lit parking lot.

Before he opened the door, she pulled him back. She leaned in, kissed him hard, with fervor. She stared into his eyes for a long moment. "I love you."

"Don't worry. I'm not going to let anything happen to you," he whispered, giving her another swift kiss against her lips. His jaw tightened, but he kept his smile in place with some effort. He opened the door, and they walked out.

She placed a death grip on his hand.

They were approximately twenty feet away from his car when suddenly from the side of the building a loud engine roared to life and flooded his shining lights across the parking lot. A large truck careened around the corner, its tires squealing, burning rubber, and bearing right down on them.

Storm recognized it as the same truck that shoved Summer over the embankment.

You're a dead motherfucker.

"Stay down!" he shouted as he pushed Summer aside and brought both guns out of his holsters.

In the middle of the parking lot, he stood, feet braced apart with the truck barreling right at him full throttle. He aimed, fired his Glock 45s into the driver's side of the cab, riveting the cab with massive gunfire. Suddenly, the truck lost control, veered hard left, and slammed into a large oak tree head on.

Steam poured beneath the truck's hood.

He jogged over to the driver's side and opened the door. A young man, light blonde hair, late twenties to early thirties, spilled out onto the ground at his feet, bloody from gunshot wounds to the face and chest. He bent and felt for a pulse against his neck.

Dead.

The remaining guests poured outside to witness the scene.

He glanced over at Summer; she was still on the ground and now gazing at the dead man across the parking lot. He quickly jogged over to her and got her settled inside his car then met the blaring police cars rushing into the parking lot.

After answering the police's questions, filing a police report, he headed back to his car. He found her staring off into space.

"You with me, baby?" he asked.

In reply, she grasped his hand, entwined their fingers, and clutched them against her chest. She looked over at him unsmiling. "Take me home."

He put the car in gear.

"Take me home," she repeated, squeezing his hand against her heart. Suddenly, she started trembling uncontrollably.

He broke every speed limit getting her to his home in record time. He set the full alarm on his house. Steel covered every window, locks slid into place, exterior lights exploded on. He pulled her from his car and carried her in his arms up to his bedroom where he sat her down on the edge of the bed. He walked across the room, slid aside a large panel to reveal a bank of twelve screens, cameras capturing every inch of his property.

He hunched down before her, never taking his eyes off her as he unfastened her sandals and slid them off her feet. Then he unzipped the back of her gown now with a gaping hole at the knee from where he pushed her aside to get her out of danger. The dress and the rest of her attire pooled at her feet.

Gently, he picked her up in his arms and laid her in the center of his bed, watched her shiver uncontrollably.

He watched her while he undressed, kicked off his shoes, slowly pulled apart his tie, shrugged off his jacket, unbuckled his belt, slid off his pants, and peeled off his dress shirt but kept on his boxers.

He'd feel better if she cried but she couldn't; her emotions were locked tight inside her.

Traumatized.

He lay next to her and covered them up with blankets. He held her, giving her his warmth, yet she still shivered. He draped his leg over her and then finally just settled his big body over hers, lending her heaps of his body heat. He cupped her chin tenderly in his warm hand and caressed her cheek. He stared down at her for a long moment trying to decipher her bottled emotions. He cradled her head in his hands, kissed her chin, each cheek. His lips lingered against her forehead.

"I need to know what you're thinking," he said in a low, rough voice full of anxiety. "If I know what you're thinking, how you're feeling, I'll know what to do to help you. I'm at a loss right now, baby."

A sound emanated around the room, a strange keening wail making her eyes dart over at the windows now shielded with steel. She heard it again and cowered against his chest. She couldn't tell where it was coming from. It was getting louder and louder. She clenched her eyes shut.

"Shh…Summer, you're safe," he coaxed her.

Summer understood then, the frenzied noise, the sobs came from her. Her eyes beckoned him.

"You sure about this?" he asked, knowing exactly what she wanted from him.

She nodded, reached up, and caressed his cheek. "Please."

He rolled onto his back and tugged off his boxers. He was hard, throbbing, and more than ready.

Slowly, he eased inside her then tenderly rocked the length of his body against hers with long, deep strokes. "You're everything to me. Do you understand? We're going to get through this."

She nodded as tears slid down her cheeks. In his arms, she felt safe; he kept away the bad people, he kept away nightmares, he helped her keep her sanity, and he helped her believe this ordeal wouldn't last forever. He made her believe they had a future together.

"I love you, Summer." His eyes were gloriously intense as he uttered those three words to her.

She suddenly couldn't remember how to breathe.

She wrapped her arms around him and sobbed against his neck.

There was no rush to complete the act, to feel the orgasms he knew he'd eventually bring them to. It was about making passionate love to her, warming her back to life. It was about making her feel safe and protected and nothing would come between them, making her feel he wanted no one but her for the rest of his life.

She reached up and cupped his face in her hands.

"You scared me to death, Storm, the way you faced down that truck. He could've killed you, and I would've lost the love of my life tonight. I can't lose you," she cried again.

The woman lying under him puzzled him to the extreme. His eyes widened; he opened his mouth to speak but couldn't. That would've been the last thing he thought upset her. She wasn't upset with the fact someone tried to kill *her* tonight, but him risking his life to save hers.

He shook his head slowly.

"Woman, I've been dropped in the middle of raging gun battles, gone singlehandedly against terrorists aiming to hang my ass at high noon, and had bombs thrown at me. I've parachuted over oceans in the middle of the night with sharks waiting on my ass. I've detonated grenades and roadside bombs. I've done mission impossible more times than I care to remember. I've seen and done it all. Now, that doesn't mean I don't get scared shitless just like any other guy, but having a truck trying to run me down in a parking lot is kid's play compared to the hell I've been through in my lifetime. I wish you'd have a bit more faith in my abilities."

He was highly offended.

She giggled.

She laughed!

His heart sang; now it was time to make *her* body sing.

He played her body like a well-honed violin, stretching, taunting every cord within her, teasing her, pacing her to a crescendo, then back down, nearly stopping, over and over again, while she begged him to stop his sweet torment and give her release. His final act pulled out gut-wrenching groans from the both of them when their orgasms finally claimed them.

As he laid there holding her tightly against him, he couldn't imagine being anywhere else.

27

Today was her last day of call rotation before she, Storm, and Apollo headed to his parent's home for their anniversary party. The location was kept a secret in part to surprise her and part for her protection. She was excited to meet his family, yet it worried her. What would they think of her? She fell in love with Storm in two weeks. How credible can she seem in their eyes? Yet in her eyes, it was very credible, just as Kyle and Sibella's passionate love. She absolutely adored the man walking beside her.

As the glass doors slid aside, they walked through the hospital entrance. The past two days, entering the hospital took on a whole new meaning considering the new package of security detail accompanying them. They were stopped frequently by patients, guests, hospital personnel giving praise and needing to pet the dog, especially when they'd see his slight limp.

Apollo was in his element; he enjoyed the attention. He was a standout dressed to the hilt wearing his ballistic body armor. A very disciplined hound, he stood for only a few seconds for his fan's gratification and then looked back up at Storm to take the lead. He was back on duty and had little time for socializing.

She never asked Storm why he suddenly decided to bring Apollo along but gathered the threat against her was still very real. She did an Internet search on military work dogs and found her answer.

Bombs.

Apollo's photograph surfaced on the first hit, and he was labeled a hero. She recalled leaning over and looking down at the dog snoring at her feet, the same she secretly smuggled treats. The article stated he was discharged early from his military duties due to being wounded in action. In Afghanistan, he went into a building to snoop out bombs to clear the way for Storm and his team when a bomb exploded and injured his hip with shrapnel. She pledged Apollo would live in a lap of luxury until his dying day.

When Storm spoke directly to her trauma team a few days ago about the possibility of an explosives threat, they never retreated, the brave souls. He explained he was there to protect them and the patients.

Her team likened Storm to James Bond hearing accounts of him taking down the lone gunman who stormed the trauma room and the tales circulating from the evening of the gala where he killed the driver who tried to run them down.

The three of them had just sat down at the coffee shop when she was paged to the trauma center.

While she scrubbed, Apollo scouted the room, outer corridors, hidden corners, sniffed door handles, anything that could contain hidden bomb residue. Satisfied, he took his position just outside the door to the trauma center. He was on the front lines while Storm stood just two feet away with a door separating them.

She looked over at Storm as she finished scrubbing. He was quiet the past few days, not saying overly much, but he held her at night while she slept. They refrained from making love to her great frustration. He remained utterly focused, yet underneath the façade, she could see him ready to explode.

Mariann came in to assist Summer with her protective gear. "We've got a forty-year-old male with a gunshot wound to a shoulder." Hearing no response from Summer, she looked across the room at Storm.

"You two having a tiff?" she whispered in Summer's ear.

"Oh no," Summer replied distractedly, looking away from Storm.

"This is a bit nerve wracking the thought someone could come here to harm you," Mariann admitted.

"Yeah, tell me about it," Summer said, slipping on her gloves.

"You know, Summer, I'm here for you if you need to talk. We need to have a girl's day out, just the two of us to get your mind off things."

Summer smiled grimly in Storm's direction where he stood in complete silence.

"That sounds like fun, and I'm hoping I can take you up on the offer. But unless Mark Malone is found, I'm attached to his hip, which translates to no girlie fun."

"No worries, friend, if he pops up, your man will take care of him," Mariann said, nodding over to Storm as she dried her hands off. She added her protective gear then walked tentatively up to Storm.

"Hey, about the gala, I got a bit too tipsy and made a complete fool of myself. I'm sorry."

"Not a problem," Storm replied and kept his focus on the room.

Mariann looked over at Summer, rolled her eyes, and shrugged her shoulders.

Summer watched Storm's jaw clench. She wasn't about to begin dissecting everyone's mood swings and personalities today. She felt frazzled and ready to burst into flames at any given moment.

Her patient arrived drunk and belligerent.

In less than two minutes, her male patient vomited on her, spit at her, urinated on the table, and last but not least, punched her in the neck while she tried to clean the debris from the stab wound in his shoulder. His arms flailed and twice nearly fell off the trauma cart. She was too tired to battle. She stepped back from the table and gave a nod to Mariann.

"Put him under," Summer ordered.

Mariann had the needle ready and proceeded.

Summer straightened to relieve the ache in her shoulders and looked up at Storm through her protective visor.

Wariness and fury was hardly contained in his expression.

He shook his head.

She could read his thoughts loud and clear. He wondered why the hell she put herself through it day in and day out. In her current state of mind, she strongly questioned it herself.

A few hours later, she finished up and changed into fresh scrubs. She rounded in ICU for almost two hours where he never spoke to her. His eyes searched every person they encountered. Wherever they walked, he put himself between her and that person to protect her while all she could think of was someone harming him and how she couldn't bear it.

They went back down at the coffee shop, and she tried to make conversation with him.

"So you're anxious to see your parents?"

He nodded, not looking at her, not elaborating as he glanced around the large seating area and the sea of faces.

She looked away. Her fingers drummed distractedly on her crossed knee.

It caught his attention. He looked back at her, nudged her leg with his leg, a silent question wanting to know what was wrong with her. She stopped smiling a few hours ago.

She shook her head, unable to stop a tear from sliding down her cheek. She swiped it away and turned away from him.

He sat forward, reached for her hand, smiled apologetically at her. Even a seductive wink he sent her direction that always earned him an immediate sexy smile was no longer in place. He had to make amends and make it quick.

"Stay," he ordered Apollo who lounged under his chair.

He got up, tugged her from her chair, and led her down the corridor until they came to a door leading down a stairwell. He opened the door and pulled her behind him. He flattened her up against the wall, his lips drifted to her cheek, skimmed across her jawline, making several slow sensual passes while her legs suddenly turned boneless.

"Mmmmmm…," he breathed.

His lips found hers, an urgent and needy kiss, as he pressed his lips hard against hers. He thoroughly tasted her and teased her with his tongue while his hands slid up her ribs to cup her breasts, massage them.

Her hands tangled in his hair as she crushed herself against him not wanting the moment to end. But all too soon, he stepped back, his hands in the air, breathless like her.

"Sorry, I got carried away, and I'm sorry for being an ass these past few days. I just want you out of danger," he admitted warily. He ran a distracted hand through his hair.

"I'm sorry. I know it's wearing on you," she admitted with a shaky breath and gave him a seductive smile, trying to get him to smile back at her.

He smiled faintly and then his face sobered.

"How do you seem to make it through each day, through each catastrophe trying to save lives, have people who want to kill you, and still manage to smile the majority of time?" he asked with a trace of disbelief in his voice.

Her face broke out into a warm smile. "You, it's because of you," she said, tapping his chest with her fingertip.

He took her face in his hands, bringing on another round of kissing and completely oblivious to the three doctors running past them down the stairs.

When he pulled back from her, he placed his fingertip against her smiling mouth and pointed upstairs. She stopped laughing.

Harsh whispers filled the stairwell above them.

Familiar voices.

Dr. O'Malley and Mariann.

"I've told you, and I won't tell you again!" Dr. O'Malley whispered fiercely.

"You'll change your mind soon," Mariann swore and then broke out into hysterical laughter.

"No, I won't. It was a mistake," Dr. O'Malley vehemently replied. "By the way, stop stalking me and driving by my home at all hours of the night."

Footsteps shuffled. The door above them opened and shut then silence.

Storm and Summer walked out of the stairwell and headed back to the coffee shop where Apollo waited for them.

She looked up at him, her eyebrow raised. "What exactly was that about, I wonder?" Mariann's behavior sounded so very out of character. The situation with her and Dr. O'Malley seemed surprising.

"With O'Malley involved, who the hell knows," Storm muttered.

"After today," Storm said, "you need to chat with the chief and advise him you need to take a leave. I want to take you away until we fix this problem."

Summer inwardly groaned. She knew how difficult it was for him to protect her at the hospital, knew he'd bit his tongue and held back his current request, and knew any objection on her part would undoubtedly create distention between them. "I'm going away with you to your parents, but I can't take a leave. We're too short staffed."

"Yes, you will," he said, brooking no argument.

She wanted to argue with him yet knew he was right. If she had to admit to herself, she knew herself incapable continuing to work under such strain and the fear of one of her coworkers getting hurt or even killed because of her.

They'd just finished their drinks and sandwich when she received another page to the trauma center.

Summer scrubbed, donned her protective gear, and waited for her patient to arrive. Minutes passed and she found herself pacing, eventually coming to stand beside Mariann watching her unwrap the sterile instrument trays.

"They should've arrived by now, don't you think?" Summer asked her.

"You'd think but maybe they got stuck in traffic," she replied.

The next instant, Storm heard Apollo's ferocious bark and a scuffle just outside the door.

Apollo would never engage someone unless he smelled explosives. Whoever stood on the other side of the door had an agenda.

He drew both guns.

"Go!" Storm ordered her team. A few days earlier, he instructed them to exit into an adjoining room if a threat existed. Summer gathered her team in the room. Her face, frozen with fear, not for herself, but for him, was the last face he saw before she shut the door.

He rushed out the door.

A gurney carrying a large rotund man covered with a white blanket up to his chest suddenly met him, plowed through the double doors, but never made it more than two feet with Storm's body absorbing the impact. He pointed one gun at the deathly pale patient who lay quivering on the cart. His eyes squeezed shut.

The patient's hand shot out to Storm. "Get it out of me!"

Storm shoved the gurney back through the doors, finding Apollo in a vicious fight with a tall broad-shouldered man dressed in a navy blue uniform and matching cap pulled down low over his eyes.

Storm knew his identity before he even turned around.

Mark Malone.

Apollo attacked Malone's right hand holding a handheld device, a black box with a white button resembling a garage door opener.

Storm's heart stuttered and went double time.

Now he was scared shitless.

He was sure it was hitched to an IED (Improvised Explosive Device) a homemade bomb usually containing fertilizer, gunpowder, hydrogen peroxide, sometimes wrapped in metal, glass, and nails to cause the most impact and damage when it exploded. He had dealt with a number of these in Afghanistan. They were hidden in buildings, along roadsides, hidden in sacks, buried, disguised in a number of unimaginable ways unsuspecting to the enemy with its only intent, to kill.

Again, the patient screamed hoarsely. "Get it out of me!"

Storm never took his eyes off Malone and Apollo but knew then what the patient wanted to get out of him.

A bomb.

Blood dripped from Malone's wrist, and Apollo was going back for another lunge.

"Call him off, or I'll blow this place up!" Malone shouted, his body shaking uncontrollably with fury.

"Stop!" Storm ordered and immediately Apollo stepped back, crouched low, continued to growl and bare his teeth.

"Killer!" Malone bellowed.

He called for Summer.

Storm kept both guns drawn and aimed at Malone.

"Take me to her," Malone ordered.

"No way," Storm growled, shaking his head. "Put the device down or someone's going to die today, and I guarantee it will be you."

"You realize I have the upper hand here," Malone taunted, nodding at the device he held in his hand. "I have the remote and the IED in that son of a bitch's stomach, the same man who was drunk and hurt my Lisa. I have all the key players here, those people responsible for my beloved Lisa's death."

He nodded over Storm's shoulder. "I want *Killer* to remove the bomb. I want to see her hands deep in his body when I hit this button," he said, nodding again at the remote clasped tightly in his trembling hand.

This was one messed up situation.

Storm kept his composure. "You've got it so wrong, man. She fought to save her life, but she was too far gone. Is this really how you, a Green Beret, would want to end his life, kill innocent people?" Storm inched closer to him, never taking his eyes off the remote.

"They're not innocent, damn it! They're going to die today. Besides, I don't have any reason to live," Malone said, pressing a trembling fist to his temple and squeezing his eyes shut. "Take me to her, God damn it!"

"No fucking way."

The patient wrenched out another hoarse, weak scream.

Malone suddenly lunged, running toward the gurney, and stormed the doors as he tried to get to Summer.

In a split second, Storm made a decision.

He holstered his guns and leapt on Malone's back. He threw a heavily muscled arm around Malone's neck stifling his breathing while he tried to wrench the remote away.

In their struggles, the remote fell, skidded across the sleek, shiny floor.

Malone fell to his knees and screamed with fury and scrambled to grab the remote.

Storm punched Malone's neck, knocking him off guard long enough for Storm to pick up the remote.

A growl erupted deep from within Malone. He staggered to his feet and charged toward Storm with blazing fury.

Without hesitation, Storm pulled his Glock 45 and blasted two bullets into Malone's temple at close range.

Thunk, thunk.

It wasn't a pretty sight.

With Malone's blood splatters dripping off his clothes, Storm hunched down beside Malone's body and checked for a pulse.

No pulse.

With his eyes on the remote he carried, he walked slowly in the direction of the patient.

The patient wasn't there.

He heard a bloodcurdling scream.

Summer.

Fuck!

Storm ran into the trauma room to see everyone standing around the patient.

Summer looked up and couldn't hide the relief she felt seeing Storm walk through her doors.

Storm looked over a resident's shoulder to see the patient now uncovered, his rotund stomach exposed. The word *killer* was engraved across his abdomen. Blood seeped from each crudely drawn letter. Right above it was a six-inch incision running horizontal across the man's stomach. The man begun to shake, going into shock.

Summer felt a nauseous swirling, rolling in her stomach. "He says the bomb is in his stomach," she said, glancing at Storm and then back over at the red puckered incision. "I have to get it out," she replied, resigned.

"No you're not!" Storm shouted.

"I have to, Storm!" Summer looked back over at the patient. The situation was grave. Tremors began to rock her body as she thought of a dismal outcome, blown to smithereens. Now, her life was in the balance of her hands.

She looked over at the anesthesiologist. "I need him out in an instant," she stammered. She looked around the table at her team. "Everyone needs to leave please."

"We're not leaving you," a third year resident replied and seconded by the anesthesiologist and the rest of her team who began prepping.

"Someone else can remove the damn bomb. Now step away from the table, Summer," Storm ordered her, pointing at her. "Don't you even think about it!"

The anesthesiologist looked over at Summer. "Dr. Benson, he's gone."

Summer sighed down at the patient whose eyes were open wide and staring lifeless up at the ceiling. She reached over and closed his eyes. Malone tortured, maimed him for several days, and planted a bomb inside him. She bet this man never in his wildest dreams would have imagined he'd die such a horrific death.

It was far from over.

Officer Havilan was the first to arrive on the scene. Storm walked over to talk to him.

Summer looked around at her team. They worked together for a long time, side by side on so many cases, and today, placed in this life-threatening situation because of her. It was time she stopped living in fear. She refused to let them die today because of her. She was brutally tired of being scared of her own shadow.

Mariann reached over and held her hand. "You're shaking like a leaf, doll. You're normally so serene, so composed. Today, you look actually human instead of a robot. I bet you never thought you'd have this kind of excitement today when you walked in the door?"

Summer and the team paused and looked over at Mariann incredulously. She had the strangest sense of humor at the oddest times. The way her eyes sparkled with anticipation as she looked around the room then back at Summer, as if she was on one hell of an adrenaline rush; either way, she looked crazy scary.

Mariann handed Summer her scalpel.

Summer hesitated, looked closer at Mariann's face, particularly her nose. Her nostrils had traces of a white powdery substance. Surely, that wasn't what she thought it was.

Cocaine.

Summer had no time to deliberate. She had to act now.

By the time it took Storm to walk over to Officer Havilan and his security team and discuss the events, he turned around to see Summer lift out what resembled a pack of cigarettes wrapped in bloody white sterile material from the man's abdomen. Her hands trembled like an almighty.

Storm stopped short and shook his head in utter disbelief. He pointed at her from across the room.

"Don't move," he ordered. "I'll come to you. Whatever you do, don't drop it."

The woman's tenaciousness and grit was going to get them killed. She was too valorous for her own good.

Sirens shrilled in the background as well as the shuffling of feet just outside the door.

Everyone backed away from the table as Storm walked up to stand beside her. He held out his hand, palm up, keeping his eyes focused solely on the IED.

"Gently," he said. "Lay it in my palm gently and then get out."

She laid it carefully in his palm. "Everyone get out," she told her team.

His gaze flickered at her. "That means you."

She shook her head. "I'm not leaving you."

He swore vehemently under his breath. "I swear, Summer, when this is over—"

"You're going to marry me," she provided, laughing shakily.

He couldn't help smiling at her quip. "Yeah, I'm going to marry you."

"Just to clarify that wasn't a marriage proposal because you can do better than that," she mimicked, reciting his words from earlier.

"Yeah, I can do better than that," he said, smiling over at her. Here they stood in the middle of the trauma room joking while he held an IED and a remote in his hands that could easily detonate at any given moment.

A tall man dressed in black bulky armor from the top of his head to the bottom of his feet walked up softly behind them.

"You lovebirds ready to hand over that bomb?"

Relieved, Storm handed him the IED and remote and watched him walk cautiously across the room.

The unthinkable happened.

The man tripped, sending the IED and remote sailing through the air.

You've got to be fucking kidding me!

Slow motion began.

Storm hurtled over the man's body sprawled on the floor and leapt in the air. He kept focused on his two targets. He snatched the IED out of the air with his right hand in less than three feet of clearance from the floor. He twisted his body so he landed on his back, in a cradle position, his body absorbing the jolt. The remote landed between his legs.

Storm laid his head back against the floor and exhaled a shaky breath. He looked up to see the bomb squad guy standing over him, smiling.

"The work of a SEAL is never done, hmmm, brother?"

After Storm and Summer finalized the paperwork on the patient, answered questions from the police, and changed their clothing, Storm looked over at Summer. "I'm ready to get the hell out of here and take you on an extended vacation."

"Me, too." Her eyes twinkled back at him. "A much needed vacation."

It was finally over.

Mariann walked up to them. "So where are you guys going? Someplace exotic I can imagine."

"It's in Florida someplace, right?" Summer turned and asked Storm.

"It's a secret," Storm repeated.

"I was just curious," Mariann replied, smiling thoughtfully at Summer. "Well, I hope you two have fun."

"Thanks, Mariann," Summer said as she walked up and hugged Mariann.

Summer whispered in her ear, "Don't ever walk into my room again under the influence. Is that understood?" Summer released her.

Mariann stiffened and gave her a somber nod.

Summer watched her walk away. Her glance swiveled over by the door where Apollo sat, keeping guard. She walked over to him, hunched down, and hugged him around his neck. "You saved our lives today, fella. I'll always be grateful to you."

His response was an enthusiastic lick across her right cheek.

Five minutes later, she and Storm walked hand in hand while Apollo trailed, greeting his many admirers. Storm kissed the back of Summer's hand.

"You showed a lot of bravery back there and a lot of stupidity," he advised, giving her mocking smile.

"Really? How else was that bomb going to get out of that man's stomach unless I removed it?" she countered.

"I swear you're going to make me gray before my time."

Summer looked up to see Jacob Howard's mother walk toward them.

She was sobbing.

Alarmed, Summer approached her and laid her hand on her shoulder. "Mrs. Howard, what's wrong?"

Mrs. Howard looked up at Summer, her face anguished as tears raced down her cheeks.

"Jacob just passed," she cried.

Summer took a step back, stunned, and felt a jolt shoot through her heart. She operated three times on him, and he was improving. "He was fine two days ago."

Summer glanced up to see Dr. O'Malley walking toward them, his head was down while he wrote on a notepad.

"That doctor." Mrs. Howard pointed at Dr. O'Malley as he passed them. "He operated on Jacob maybe he can tell you."

Dr. O'Malley whirled around, his eyes glaring and defensive as they landed on Summer and Storm. "He had an infection, and there was nothing I could do for him."

"He was my patient, and you should've consulted with me first!" Summer replied coldly.

Dr. O'Malley stormed off.

Summer hugged Mrs. Howard. "I'm so sorry for your loss."

"You did the best you could. You gave me more time with him than I ever expected, and I'll always be grateful for that," Mrs. Howard cried.

Summer watched her walk slowly down the corridor, her shoulders slumped and defeated, overcome by grief.

Fury tore through Summer. She took off jogging in the other direction down the corridor.

Storm followed her. "What's going on, Summer?"

"I need to have a word with the chief," she replied over her shoulder.

She pointed at Storm just outside the chief's office. "Storm, I won't be long. You may hear arguing, but please don't intrude."

Summer never bothered to knock when she walked through the office door of Dr. Christopher Chabott, Chief of Trauma. Dr. Chabott was a tall willowy thin man in his midsixties with a deeply lined face and sunken aquamarine eyes who wore a wiry toupee, usually sitting askew. His prestigious career with Regional Medical spanned almost twenty years serving as the trauma chief.

He stood beside his desk, gazing out the window, and from the look he gave her, he expected her.

"Why is Dr. O'Malley still doing surgeries?" she demanded.

He walked around his desk quietly, sat down heavily in his chair, and looked up her with a resigned expression. "He's a good surgeon."

"He *was* a good surgeon. I thought you spoke with him."

"I did," he exhaled heavily, arranging a few documents on his desk.

Summer slammed her palm down on the documents.

"And?" she demanded.

"Be careful," he warned her as he stared down at his littered desk, avoiding eye contact with her.

Recklessly, Summer replied, "Evidently you didn't get through to him. My patient Jacob Howard has died under O'Malley's trembling hand."

The chief's head bobbed up. He gave her a startled look.

"He's taken three lives already, and Jacob's makes four. Your job is to protect the patient, remember?" she angrily reminded him.

"As you know, I'm retiring in a few weeks with a benefit package that will see me out to my dying day."

"What?" Summer leaned up and folded her arms across her chest. "One minute we're talking about the unnecessary death of four patients and now you're spouting garbage about your retirement benefits. Are you telling me you don't want to make waves because it might affect your benefits, Dr. Chabott?"

"Dr. O'Malley's family is very wealthy and influential in this community and particularly this hospital," he defended quietly.

"I never thought you'd turn your cheek in the face of a crisis because of greed, but I was wrong. I always had so much respect for you."

"I have great respect for you, Summer, or else I wouldn't have recommended you to be the new trauma chief, but it seems I didn't have any influence over the final decision."

"Let me guess. Dr. O'Malley is our new chief?" Summer asked with disgust lacing her voice.

He nodded, avoiding her gaze.

"Then Dr. Chabott, I resign my position effective immediately," she replied and walked to the door. She had her hand on the doorknob when the door suddenly burst open.

Storm paced down the long corridor when from a distance he saw Dr. O'Malley rush into the chief's office. From the look on Dr. O'Malley's face, Storm didn't have a good feeling. He took off running toward the chief's office with Apollo keeping pace.

Enraged, Dr. O'Malley entered the office and locked the door behind him. He confronted Summer.

"You bitch! You need to learn to keep your mouth shut!" He swung his body putting the full force of his backhand across her left cheek.

The strength of the blow sent her reeling back against a large wooden bookcase where she slid precariously to the floor seeing stars and feeling a throbbing pain in her lower jaw.

Suddenly, the doorway literally exploded.

Pieces of wood splintered from the doorframe and landed across the room. The door hung completely off its hinges.

The chief had no choice but to duck to miss the flying debris and took that as a good opportunity to grab the phone and hide under his desk while he called for Security.

Storm kicked the door aside.

Apollo stayed at the door and growled low.

Storm searched for Summer. He found her lying across the room on the floor with blood seeping from her lips, her cheek reddened with a visible hand imprint.

He roared with fury.

His focus was on Dr. O'Malley and blocked the door so he couldn't escape.

Dr. O'Malley whirled around and was met with Storm's foot landing a solid strike against his chest. It sent him spiraling across the room skidding across the chief's desk, landing haphazardly face first in the chief's chair. He never had time to get up on his own. Storm had his coat front scrunched between his fists dragging him back across the desk where he held him with one fist and pummeled his face brutally.

"Storm, stop!" Summer pleaded across the room, but too late, Dr. O'Malley lay limp in his grasp, unconscious.

Officer Havilan and his fellow officers walked through the door, took in the busted door, Dr. Benson injured on the floor, and Dr. O'Malley unconscious in the clutches of a man who looked like he was ready to commit murder.

The chief crawled from under the desk. He stood with this phone clutched against to his chest as he tried to rearrange his toupee. He looked upon the chaos in his office with wide eyes. He pointed to Dr. O'Malley whom Storm slammed furiously to the ground.

"It's all Dr. O'Malley's fault," the chief reported. "He walked right in here on me and Dr. Benson's conversation and hit her in the jaw, poor thing," he said, looking at her as Storm brought her up in a sitting position. He then pointed at Storm. "That man knocked the door down just in the nick of time."

Storm bent and picked Summer up in his arms and turned to leave when Officer Havilan stepped in front of him.

"Sir, you and Dr. Benson will need to complete a report."

When met with Storm's thundering expression, Officer Havilan stepped aside. "I guess I could use his statement," he said, indicating the chief.

Summer raised her head off his shoulder as he carried her away and looked into his eyes. They were stormy and dazzling with fury. His neck, chest, and fist were splattered with Dr. O'Malley's blood.

Could this day be more bizarre?

Doctors and nurses met them and escorted them to a treatment room.

An hour later, and thankfully after no broken bones, no busted teeth, only abrasions, they left the hospital with only an icepack to place against her jaw and a bandage on Storm's hand.

This time Storm sat her beside him in the front seat and Apollo in the backseat. As soon as he started driving, he reached over and held her hand.

She glanced over at his profile, his jaw was locked, rigid, and his eyes piercing as he focused on traffic, giving a concentrated effort to tamp down on his rage. She remembered the look on his face so vividly in the chief's office. It was his eyes. They held such ferocity, a frightening intensity. He was in combat mode when he grabbed Dr. O'Malley, and a wonder he didn't kill him.

"I'm sorry for getting you involved in this mess," she said quietly.

"Don't you apologize," he said, guessing her train of thoughts, tugging her against him so she could lay her head against his shoulder.

"I've just resigned my position, Storm. I don't have a job," she informed him grimly.

"You're such a talented lady you can do anything you want. Also, remember my dad wanted to talk to you if you ever decided to leave Regional. You have the world at your feet. Take some time off and think about what you really want to do."

"I think I will take my time and think about it. But honestly, I've had enough excitement to last me a lifetime, Storm."

"We've only just begun," he whispered, giving her a swift kiss against her forehead.

She fell asleep with a smile on her lips.

His smile faltered and turned grim. He dreaded morning where he'd have to tell her it wasn't over.

It was far from over.

28

A storm was brewing.

Summer stood before the windows and peered out onto the ocean's churning waves then up at the dark clouds beginning to gather in the sky and saw the first splatter of rain against the window.

Storm, barefooted, padded up softly behind her, slid his arms around her waist, bringing her back against his chest where he nuzzled his lips against the silky column of her throat.

Her lips curved in a slow smile as she tilted her head aside and allowed him full access.

"This is the kind of day you spend indoors, in bed," he growled suggestively in her ear.

"I was thinking the same, but I really need to get a few things done before we leave tomorrow. Do you mind taking me home?"

She waited for his response. There wasn't any, other than him pulling her tighter against him. She sighed and turned around in his arms.

"Take you home?" he said hesitantly, his brow rose. Earlier, he observed her for several minutes across the room without her knowing, and she reminded him of a bird trapped in a gilded cage. He knew this was coming. She was very independent, and he knew once she believed the danger cleared, she would want to strike back on her own. He understood and what he loved about her. The problem was he believed danger still lurked.

"I'd like to go shopping and pick up a few things," she explained, smiling up at him.

She watched uncertainty flicker across his face.

"You want some time alone, I can understand that," he said carefully.

"But?" she inquired.

He shrugged his shoulders. He had no plausible explanation to give her other than his gut screamed to keep her close. Something still didn't feel right. All his life he'd lived by his gut instinct, it's what saved his ass on many occasion. He refused to worry her. She'd suffered enough.

She cupped his face in her hands and pressed her lips against his and looked him in the eye.

"Storm, I'm out of danger now. No more boogeyman hiding under my bed," she said, smiling up at him.

As he looked into her eyes, he could see she had no worries and was confident the threat passed. He wished he felt the same.

"Summer, I don't think you're out of danger yet. I don't believe Malone was responsible for the acid on your car or those two trucks that ambushed you. I can nail down the behavior of a guy like him from our similar backgrounds. If I were out to harm you, I'd do it before you could blink an eye or I'd make a huge production out of it just like Malone did with the IED."

She frowned up at him, worry creasing her brow. "So who's after me?"

"I don't know. I'd almost venture to say someone at your hospital, but I don't know."

She shook her head adamantly. "There's no one at the hospital who would want to hurt me, Storm. If they did, they would have done that by now."

"I hope you're right," he replied grimly.

"I feel perfectly safe," she reiterated again. "Maybe Malone did do those things. Either way, we'll never know. We really need to put this behind us and move on. I don't want to dwell on the past, only our future."

He pulled her against him and held her tight. Maybe she was right, and he worried needlessly. But she was absolutely his world and just the thought or the idea of someone still lurking in the shadows to hurt her threatened to send him over the edge.

As it was, Derek still hadn't found any tangible connection with the truck driver he killed the night of the gala and Malone. Derek was diligent; if there was something to be found, he'd find it. Not to mention, the second driver involved in her car accident was still in hiding. That was the needle stitching his side, the threat. Moreover, he had other suspicions he couldn't bring to her because he had no foundation, only his gut telling him the puzzle wasn't quite ready to fit so snugly.

She tapped his cheek playfully. "I'm going to be just fine, Storm. Besides, if I need you, you're only a phone call away."

By the look on his face, her argument wasn't wholeheartedly convincing him, yet his face softened.

"Okay," he said reluctantly, loosening his hold on her.

She looked up at him hopefully. "Do you want to meet up for dinner tonight?"

"I like that idea. You'll be my dessert," he said, sealing his smiling lips against hers.

She blushed as she stared into his mesmerizing eyes. How in the world did she land a guy like him? He was handsome as sin, her protector, and everything she ever wanted.

"Pick me up for dinner at six o'clock tonight? We'll celebrate a night on the town," she suggested with a seductive smile.

"I'll be there," he promised her, leaning down and claiming her lips once more.

He drove her home an hour later and insisted on checking her house. Satisfied, he looped his arm around her waist as she walked him to his car. He noted the temperature dipped all of a sudden.

"Six o'clock sharp," she reminded him, curling her arms around his neck, standing up on her tiptoes, leaning into him to meet his lips for a good-bye kiss.

When she went to release him, he held on to her, and the look he gave her was so very vulnerable. His eyes scanned her face as if entrusting it to his memory. She leaned back into his arms, her eyes narrowed on his face.

Firmly, gently, she promised, "Storm, you *will* see me at six o'clock. I *will* be right here waiting for you with open arms. I'm *not* going anywhere."

He exhaled a shaky breath.

"I love you," she whispered, pressing a fierce kiss on his lips.

He squeezed her against him for a long moment. "You're the best thing that's ever happened to me, Summer Benson. I love you too," he murmured against her forehead and then released her. He got into his car and left, all the while looking back at her through his rearview mirror, watching her wave good-bye to him as distance separated them.

God, please let me be wrong.

The sky was stirring itself into a frenzy with pockets of gray-black clouds colliding. Overhead, it thundered, crackled furiously shooting a scintillating lightning bolt in the shape of a mandrake root across his windshield.

An omen?

A chill of foreboding shot up his spine.

Fifteen minutes dragged by.

Storm counted every minute since he'd left her, watched his dashboard clock, until he couldn't stand it a moment longer. He picked up his cell phone and called her. He just had to be sure.

It rang twice.

"Hi, stranger," she said, answering breathlessly.

"Hi," he said, relief flooding through his voice. "You sound out of breath."

"Are you checking up on me?" she sighed, loving the sound of his husky, velvet voice. She'd never get tired hearing it.

"Maybe," he chuckled ruefully.

"I was just leaving. I've made a list longer than my arm today of errands I need to run. By the way, I'm very excited about meeting your family, Storm. I hope they'll like me."

His heart picked up a beat. He smiled into the phone. "They're going to love you." After a pause he added, "Be alert, okay?"

"I will," she dismissed his overly cautious warning with a soft laugh. "Remember, six o'clock and don't be late, young man. I love you."

"I love you," he said and hung up.

She grabbed her purse, car keys, slid on sandals, and headed to the garage.

A soft knock sounded at her front door.

She frowned, stopped, and looked back at her front door. She could do without visitors today and spun on her heel and quickly walked to the front door and peeked through the window.

Mariann. She waved at her, smiling.

Summer opened the door with a ready smile. "Hi, Mariann."

Mariann's gaze flickered over her. "Looks like you're heading out the door. I wanted to bring this by to you," she said, handing her a DVD in a clear plastic case.

Summer took it and looked down at it hesitantly.

"It's the documentary's uncut version, an extra copy. I've seen it. I thought you might like to watch it if you haven't already."

"No, I haven't seen it. Thank you."

"That's not the real reason for my visit," Mariann confessed. "I wanted to apologize about yesterday. I am seeking treatment. I've had some problems lately. I do hope we can keep this between us," she replied hesitantly. "You haven't reported yet, have you?"

"No, I haven't. You are seeking treatment?" Summer clarified.

"I am. I've got plenty of things to work out, but rest assured, I'll be top of my game in the trauma room."

"Good. I'm happy to hear that. Is there anything I can do for you?"

"No, I'm good. I'm actually on my way to a couple nearby boutiques and thought I'd stop by to see if you'd like to go shopping before you ride off in the sunset with your sweetie."

Summer really wanted to go alone and have a day to herself.

Sensing her hesitancy, Mariann added with a hopeful smile, "I have a confession. I'm horribly lonely today. It must be the weather. It's on days like this that my willpower goes by the wayside. We could hang out for an hour or two and then you can shop on your own."

Mariann was really struggling, definitely needed a friend, a support mechanism right now. It was the least she could do considering she was a close, dear friend.

"Sounds good. Let me put this up," she said, signaling the DVD. "I'll be right back."

Summer walked over to the kitchen island and tossed down the DVD, crossed the room quickly, and shut the front door behind her. She walked out to Mariann's black Honda Accord. "I'm looking for another summer dress to take with me."

"You mean the kind that will thrust his heart rate into overdrive?" Mariann teased.

"The very one," Summer sighed, smiling as the opened her car door. On the passenger seat sat a tray container holding two drinks.

Mariann got in and picked up the tray. "I picked up iced tea for us at Jerry's Restaurant, the very best in town," she said, handing Summer her drink.

"Thank you. Now, what if I hadn't come with you today?" Summer asked, quirked a humorous eyebrow at her.

"Then my plans would've fallen through. I would've been very lonely and drunk way too much tea. So I'm very happy you came," Mariann said, sipping her iced tea and smiling over at her. She put her car in gear and drove down the driveway.

Summer sipped her tea. "This is very good tea."

"It's going to be the best you ever had," Mariann informed her. "I'm looking for some new sandals. I'm thinking we could head to Bella's. They have some eye-popping dresses right up your alley," she said, flashing her knowing smile. She glanced out her window as rain pelted against her windshield. "And I don't care if it's raining. Today's going to be a great day."

"Even if we get caught in the rain and look like two drowned rats." Summer laughed, sipping her tea as they drove toward a small outdoor strip mall located about twenty minutes away.

Mariann laughed. "You're remembering when we went Christmas shopping and I locked my keys in my car, and we had to stand out in the rain and wait for my car to be unlocked. That was miserable if I recall. And yes, we looked like two drowned rats."

Fifteen minutes into the drive, having finished her iced tea, Summer stared out the windshield. Rain pelted viciously against it and made her vision hazy. She felt groggy as she watched the wipers race back and forth making an eerie rhythmic pumping sound.

Summer looked away from the windshield, out her window, thinking it would clear her vision. It became worse. She concentrated on the passing scenery—the sidewalks, palm trees, and the houses with gated driveways but they soon took on distorted, blurry images.

She reached up to rub her eyes and could barely lift her hand, no strength. Her hand dropped back down in her lap, useless. She stared at it, confusion clogging her mind. She went to turn her head to warn Mariann something was terribly wrong. Her head refused to turn. Instead, it dipped as if it weighed a hundred pounds, just like her hand. The more she fought it, the more her chin tilted toward her chest as if the bones in her neck dissolved into liquid and could no longer support her head. Her head dropped for the final time. There was no lifting it. She opened her mouth to speak, but her words were paralyzed.

She panicked.

Her mind reeled as she tried to determine what happened.

The iced tea.

And with that, a realization.

She'd been drugged.

Sadistic cackling laughter echoed, swirled around her, and taunted her inside the confines of the car.

Summer heard the faint chime of her cell phone ring. Her eyes landed on her purse lying on the floorboard between her feet. She stared at it forlornly knowing she missed Storm's call. Here, she dismissed his obvious concern believing him to be a bit overprotective. He was right all along. Now, he was no longer just a phone call away. He'd spoken about following his gut instinct. She prayed he followed his instinct and find her before it was too late.

Irrevocably, a trauma patient Summer tried to save three years ago, a young lady, barely twenty years old came to mind. Summer remembered her vividly. Brutally raped and tortured by her brother's best friend while on a date, she confessed on her deathbed to Summer that the incident blindsided her. She wouldn't have dreamt it in a million years, not by the person she trusted so explicatively. Summer felt the same. She trusted Mariann explicatively and didn't see it coming.

Oh god, Storm was right.

The black abyss finally swallowed her.

Her nightmare had only just begun.

29

Time stood still for Storm without Summer by his side. He wondered where she was, what she was doing.

Please let her be safe.

How many times had he picked up his cell phone to call her since he'd left her house? Each time, his restraint overrode his actions.

At least a dozen times.

Now, he had a plan to keep busy. He pulled into the small parking lot of Gerard's, an exclusive jewelry house on the west side of Jacksonville. The place bespoke of opulence with the molded hunter green canvas umbrellas shielding each window of the two-story brown-bricked building along with its stunning landscape.

Only the best for my lady, he thought as he got out of his car into the steady rain. Normally, places such as these preferred appointments, but he was sure he could skirt around their preference considering the amount of cash he carried in his billfold. He chuckled to himself. He'd always shied away at the idea of marriage, but he was a changed man, now sprinting down the aisle.

Clad in jean shorts, a shirt, and sandals, he strolled into the sprawling plush lobby bedecked with thick carpets, marble floors, overflowing crystal chandeliers, and sparkling glass cases containing countless, rare gems winking back at him.

A tall, distinguished fair-haired man, midforties, wearing a crisp black suit greeted him with a confident smile, a solid handshake, and led him over to his private office.

Close to an hour later, the jeweler slid across the counter to Storm a medium-sized black bag blazing with the embossed golden emblem of Gerard's, an elaborate cursive *G*.

Storm left Gerard's and walked into a virtual downpour; he tucked his precious bag protectively under his arm like a running back and sprinted to his car. His hair and shirt was soaked through, but his bag was dry and that's what mattered. He started his car, glanced at his watch. Time flew by, but time well spent.

He was very pleased with his purchase, took his time, and received sound advice from the jeweler who thoroughly asked about Summer and her occupation to determine the best style engagement ring suited especially for her. He felt uplifted, having made a purchase directing his life down a far better path than it headed just a few weeks ago.

He pulled out his cell phone and checked for missed calls. There weren't any. He stared thoughtfully at Summer's phone number. He hit the call button. By God, call him a demented overprotective guy but he had to hear her voice, ensure she was okay.

It rang five times.

No answer.

His breath left his body.

His heart raced as he hit the call button again.

It went straight to voicemail.

Calm.

He took a deep breath. Maybe she was on another call. He stared at his dashboard clock clicking off the seconds and never allowed for the full rotation of a minute before he hit the call button again.

Still, no answer.

Rising panic stifled him and sent shivers of cold dread through his limbs.

He blew through stoplights and stop signs, squealing tires as he careened around corners, the back of his car fishtailing on the wet pavement as he drove back to her house. He was anxious to get there but terrified what he might find.

His car slid sideways coming to a screaming halt in her driveway. He barreled up to the front door, nearly knocking the door down. The house was empty.

He ran through the kitchen and jerked open the door leading to the garage. It was pitch black. His breath held as he flipped on the garage light.

Her car was still there.

And then he knew.

Oh god, I was right.

No notes were left behind. Who would have taken her and why? Were they watching her home, lurking in the shadows waiting until he wasn't around to protect her? Would they request a ransom? Maybe it evolved solely around revenge for whatever reason and they only wanted to kill her.

Scenario after scenario twisted in his mind.

He had to get answers quick.

However, he had one dreaded phone call to make.

To Reaper.

Nine seconds, that was how long the phone call lasted.

Reaper was coming.

Something caught his eye on the kitchen island, something he hadn't seen when he dropped off Summer earlier. He quickly walked over and grabbed the DVD. He headed toward her living room, turned on her television, and then quickly slid the DVD into the DVD player. Did it belong to Summer? Did someone, possibly her kidnapper, give it to her? Was it meant for him to see, maybe a ransom notice? Unanswered questions swirled viciously in his mind, all the while his heart pounded as he waited for the disc to play. Summer's smiling face flashed across the screen, her interview with the documentary team. His knees nearly buckled.

No particular scene struck him as odd or questionable as he fast-forwarded the DVD. He was about to stop the video when his cell phone rang.

Glancing down at the phone number, it was Derek. He answered not waiting for the courtesy words. "Please tell me you've got something. Summer's been kidnapped."

Storm pushed fast forward again and suddenly saw Mariann's face in the background of a trauma case.

"Oh shit," Derek rushed out. "As a matter of fact, I dug up some stuff on the truck driver you neatly disposed of."

"Hey, man, can you hold on just a sec?" Storm asked. He focused his attention on the scene unfold on the television with Summer finishing a trauma case and talking to Dr. O'Malley. Unadulterated hatred mimicked Mariann's expression as she looked at Summer from across the room. When team members reappeared back in the room, Mariann placed a mask of pure serenity on her face.

"Sorry, something caught my attention. Can you check out a lady by the name of Mariann—" Storm trailed off. "Shit! I don't know her last name."

"Would that be Mariann Haley who works at Regional Medical?"

"How did you know?"

"She's why I'm calling. I snooped through the dead truck driver's phone records and saw where he's contacted her three times the past two weeks and just minutes before he was killed at the gala. I kept digging and found another caller linked to her, another male. She spoke to him three times this morning. The last call between them was fifteen minutes ago."

"Can you get a fix on them using the GPS in their cell phones?" Storm asked. "I'm thinking they're together," Storm said, as again, his gaze once again flickered over at the television to see the hatred on Mariann's face. It was more than just this revealing scene; there were many more like them.

Now, she had his attention.

"Yes, I'm triangulating between cell towers right now, basically trying to circle in on the areas to get a solid location. I'll call you in one minute. Be in your car and ready to roll," Derek instructed.

Summer was in serious danger.

Mariann had an obvious mental imbalance. It sent chills down his spine. This woman wouldn't want a ransom, her only agenda was to kill Summer, and God only knew why.

He thought it odd Mariann's behavior at the gala, seeing a twinge of jealousy as she mentioned to Summer about her revealing gown, the way she stared at her through most of the documentary yet would turn away when he'd look over at her and her erratic behavior lately with Dr. O'Malley.

He'd tucked those observations under his cap to save in case something prompted further investigating, which he hoped in Summer's case wouldn't bear fruit. Now, this made perfect sense why Mariann was so persistent wanting to know their vacation plans, and when she never got her answer, she knew she had to act fast and kidnap Summer.

He had to save her.

He got into his car and called the police to report Summer's disappearance.

And then he waited.

It felt like a lifetime before Derek called him back, but it was less than two minutes.

"I've got a location tapped for Summer's cell phone. Get on A1A and head south toward Ponte Vedra Beach. I'm sending the GPS coordinates to your car as we speak."

"Is it a moving target or stationary?" Storm asked as he headed his car that direction.

"Stationary," Derek replied.

"What about Mariann?" Storm asked and glanced at his dashboard seeing the GPS coordinates Derek sent to him pop up on his navigator.

"Mariann's a moving target heading toward St. Augustine. I'll keep track of her. Let me know what you find out."

"I will." Storm tossed his phone over onto the passenger seat and slammed his foot down on the accelerator passing through small beach towns in a blur.

He came upon the coordinates Derek gave him. No vehicles sat off the side of the road, nothing, but traffic passing through.

His heart trembled as he got out of his car and searched the roadway for Summer; instead, he found her cell phone tossed in a nearby ditch. He picked it up and jogged back to his car. His cell phone rang.

Derek.

"I've got coordinates on Mariann. Just a few minutes ago, I pinpointed her at St. Augustine beach area, and now, she's over the Atlantic. She's in a boat I'd imagine."

Static came over the line, something garbled.

"Derek?" Storm exhaled as he waited for Derek to return on line.

"Hold on a sec, Storm. I got someone cutting in."

"Storm?" a familiar voice said.

Storm paused for a second. "Reaper?"

"Get to the St. Augustine airport. We have air asset waiting on us."

"I'll be there," Storm finished and hung up.

Summer was slumped over, lying on her side, disoriented, and staring at the back of a black car seat. She tried to sit up but couldn't move her hands; she had lost feeling in them. A tilt of her head to look down at her hands sent explosive pain to her temple. Thick plastic tie wraps bound her hands so tightly she couldn't move them. Her wrists were bloody and raw.

Then she remembered.

Mariann drugged and kidnapped her. She squeezed her eyes shut, willed herself not to panic but knew she was in a world of hurt now.

It took three attempts to levy herself up into a sitting position using her weak legs and that small action caused brilliant white stars to twinkle behind her eyes.

Mariann's smiling eyes lifted to her rearview mirror. "Welcome back, doll."

Summer stared back at her. How could someone keep his or her tone of voice so level yet with a hint of exhilaration while in the process of kidnapping someone? Mariann definitely had mental issues. She glanced at the dashboard and saw an hour and twenty minutes had passed since she got into the car with Mariann.

"Mariann, why are you doing this?"

Mariann laughed darkly.

"I can't imagine anything I've done for you to do this to me," Summer confessed.

"No, I can't imagine either. You're so perfect," she replied snidely.

"I'm not perfect," Summer admitted, exhaling a shaky breath as she glanced out the window wondering where they were. They drove south down A1A parallel with the Atlantic Ocean and no longer in Jacksonville. They passed through small beach towns. It no longer rained but gray skies loomed overhead and the wind kicked up.

"Oh yes, you're perfect," Mariann disagreed viciously. "Everything is effortless with you. You have brains, beauty, and guts. You received all the glory for the documentary. They focused everything around you as if we never existed."

"It wasn't just about me," Summer argued.

"Yeah, right." She laughed darkly. "Your speech was convincing."

"Mariann, why are you doing this?"

"Because it has to be done," Mariann replied somberly.

"No, it doesn't," Summer pleaded. "We can forget this happened. I won't breathe a word of it."

"With you out of the way, Dr. O'Malley will belong to me. You're the reason why he can't love me. Plus, I'll get the recognition I deserve at the hospital."

It was all about jealousy; Summer realized as she stared back at Mariann.

"He thinks I'm just a mindless robot who hands him instruments, does his paperwork, and a body to have sex with at his whim. I see the way he looks at you. He's in love with you."

"I'm in love with Storm, Mariann. I don't love Dr. O'Malley."

"I'm still going to kill you. I won't allow you to steal him from me," Mariann said as her hands clenched tight around the steering wheel.

"Mariann, if you loved Dr. O'Malley, then why did report his tremor to me? You knew the outcome once I discovered it. You knew I'd have no choice but to report it to the trauma chief. Don't get me wrong, you were right to report it, yet I would've thought if you loved him, you would've protected him."

"Love?" She laughed harshly. "It was payback for how he's treated me. I knew if I brought it to you, you'd confront him because you'd have the patient's welfare in mind. I also knew how furious he'd become at you for bringing it to light and jeopardizing his career. I told him you applied for the chief job and that really got his fury going. I never realized just how much of a coward he was when he never retaliated against you, only until yesterday when I told him you were going to the chief to report him."

Mariann paused.

"You know what, you're hard to kill," Mariann revealed, shaking her head.

Summer looked at her with disbelief.

Mariann nodded at her. "When I saw how Mark Malone threatened you, I knew I had my opening. I could do anything I wanted to you and it be blamed on him. Then he had to get stupid and impatient and try to kill us with a damn bomb. As predicted, your handsome protector killed the bad guy and saved us.

"Yeah," Mariann confessed with a laugh under her breath. "I hired people to kill you but obviously that didn't work. The first guy was pathetic. It was planned it down to the tee. He was to meet you at the restaurant, abduct you, that simple. But it wasn't so simple. The idiot choked on his food, and you, the doctor, saved his life. The guy fled to Canada and refused to carry out the job. So I hired a couple guys. Again, it was very simple, a car accident should do, I told them. I paged you to the hospital because I knew you'd come. And you did, all by yourself. It was set up perfectly until your knight in shining fucking armor showed up. Nothing has gone as I planned, even the night of the gala. Now, I'm going to kill you myself to make sure you meet your demise."

"Then it was you who poured acid on my car?"

"Yep," Mariann said gleefully. "And all along you thought it was Malone. Hilarious."

"I remember," Summer said. "I worked with you that night and distinctly remember you asking me when I planned to go home. Here, I thought it was out of concern. Instead, you wanted me to see your handiwork. You knew it would upset me and that brought you some kind of sick pleasure. I suppose it was you who wrote *killer* on my newspaper and left me the card at the gala."

"Yes, I did," she said, laughing.

A few minutes later, Mariann's car slowed to a stop as she parked alongside the roadway. Traffic passed them but otherwise there wasn't a soul around to help her, Summer dismally noted.

Mariann turned around in her seat and pointed a small handgun at her.

"Don't make any quick moves because I won't hesitate to shoot you," she warned. She tossed a sweater over her arm to hide her gun and got out of her car. She jerked opened the door and wrenched Summer out of the backseat, her grip hard and biting while she pressed her gun painfully against her ribs.

A perfect time to escape in Summer's mind, but her body was sluggish and her legs weak. There would be no escaping.

A white speedboat fast approached the beach with a young man behind the wheel.

Summer's heart instantly swelled with hope.

"Your chariot awaits you," Mariann informed her.

Her relief was short-lived. Summer shuddered. Mariann had an accomplice to kill her. She knew once she boarded the boat, her fate would be sealed.

I love you both so much.

She closed her eyes and sent her words to Storm and Kyle wherever they may be. She boarded the boat.

She was one step closer to death.

In the distance, she heard the faint roar of a jetfighter. She smiled inside and felt comforted by the sound as she thought of Kyle even though she knew she imagined it. Perhaps that's what happened to one when at death's door; they imagined, hallucinated, and wished things were normal, wished they weren't one step away from death.

30

Storm heard him before he saw him.

Reaper.

In the distance, he heard the shrill thrust of pure muscle roar across the skies above him. Glancing up through his windshield, he saw a visible jet wash in the gray sky with a flare of afterburners from a jetfighter.

Minutes later, he pulled into the small airport and drove straight to a sleek black Seahawk, a search and rescue helicopter waiting at the end of the airstrip.

A jeep pulled up behind Storm's car.

Reaper got out of the jeep, dressed in full fatigues, carrying a duffle bag and a rifle case. He slapped Storm on the shoulder. "Let's kill this bitch, shall we?"

They boarded the helicopter, met the crew, discussed their plan, and lifted off. While Storm changed into a wet suit, Reaper set up his 308-sniper rifle.

Summer was at the mercy of a mad woman.

Those were Summer's thoughts as she sat on the boat, her hands turning a bluish hue and unable to escape. A few times, she nearly became unsettled as the speedboat collided and ripped through the waves as they headed out to sea. The cool wind picked up, diced against her icy cheeks, lifted her hair, and whipped it violently against her face and neck.

She looked over at Mariann sitting beside her, prodding her with her gun. It was time to face her fate. Would she die of a gunshot wound or drowning? Gunshot wound preferably, a quick death. She gazed out at the wind-tossed sea lashing the sides of the boat and felt a shiver of pure terror rip up her spine.

Please don't let me drown.

Mariann grinned over at her guessing her thoughts. "I remember one time we talked about dying. You said you hoped you'd go peacefully. Your idea of a horrific death would be drowning since you couldn't swim."

Mariann motioned with her gun, ordering Summer to stand.

"They'll mourn your death and won't know I had anything to do with it. The lady genius could do everything besides swim. Imagine that!"

Slowly, Summer stood, her legs unsteady. She glanced over the rail at the bludgeoning waves.

She would die today.

The boat suddenly slowed down to an idle. The young man twisted in his seat and got up. His eyes focused on Summer as he walked toward her.

Summer's heart nearly burst from fear, his intention was obvious.

He planned to throw her overboard.

His eyes flickered over at Summer's face then down at her bound hands. He shook his head at Mariann.

"What the hell are you doing?" Mariann demanded.

"I can't go through with this," he sighed, raking a trembling hand through his windblown hair.

Mariann pointed her gun at his chest. "Like hell you're not! Get back and man the boat or else you won't live to tell about it."

The man shook his head and looked over at Summer again.

"Now!" Mariann shouted, glaring at him.

"I don't know why I got mixed up in this in the first place. I guess I was desperate for the money and wanted to leave the country. Now, I'm more interested in staying alive. The newspapers say her guy is a Navy SEAL for God's sake, and I can only imagine he's hot on our trail as we speak."

"Shut up!" Mariann bellowed. "I'll give you two seconds to get back over there and start the boat."

"You're right you know," Summer said soberly to him. "He'll hunt you down and kill you if you go through this. If you release me, I'll forget about this."

"Bitch, you're not going anywhere!" Mariann screamed, coming to her feet, her face masked with unbridled rage.

Her gun exploded.

The young man shuddered and collapsed, falling backward. The center of his chest was bloody. His body twitched once. Mariann shot him again, ensuring his death.

Summer screamed and squeezed her eyes shut.

Mariann kicked his body aside and slammed her hand against the gearshift, sending the boat lurching forward nearly dislodging Summer from her seat. Once again, her gaze flickered over at the dead man. She was about to look away when she noticed a mixture of water and blood gushed under the man's body.

The boat was taking on water, sinking.

Oh god, could this get any worse?

The sound she heard next was *not* her imagination.

Helicopter.

She whipped around in her seat and looked behind her, a black menacing helicopter glided low against the water coming directly at them. She glanced at Mariann who was oblivious, her attention held by a speedboat intercepting her in the distance.

Storm adjusted his binoculars.

"You got eyes on anything?" Reaper asked Storm as he pulled his sniper rifle from his case.

"A speedboat, one hundred and ten yards out, traveling at a high rate of speed. It has to be them."

Reaper went down into a kneeling position in front of the open door of the helicopter with his rifle in his hands, the air rushing against him. He saw the speedboat in the distance and broke out into a cold sweat. Suddenly, he dropped his head and his shoulders slumped. Christ, how many times in his life had he prepared for such a maneuver, to aim and shoot his target a football field away, normally a cake-walk for him.

But today, he wasn't killing for his country. He killed to save his sister's life.

Storm cupped his shoulder. "Relax, brother, deep breath."

"Storm, this is my sister we're talking about. One wrong move and I'll kill my own damn sister," he said grimly. "As soon as I got on this helo, my heart started banging against my chest. I guess the gravity of the situation became clear. There's no allowance for mistakes here."

"There never is, and you won't make one either. Focus. You can do this. I imagine once you place that scope on your sister and see the danger she's in, it's going to piss you off, and suddenly, all your fears will subside because your sister's life is hanging in a balance and you're the only one right now who can help her."

Fuck!

Again, Storm stared through his binoculars.

"Another search and rescue boat is closing in on them," Storm noted. "Hopefully, she'll slow the boat down."

Again, Storm's lens settled on Summer sitting at the back of the boat while Mariann drove erratic. His binoculars weren't strong enough to clearly see Summer's face.

Reaper looked up at Storm. "You're very calm, my friend. I envy you. I now understand why you were our platoon leader other than the obvious reasons. You can keep a level head in times such as this while I would definitely struggle."

Storm wanted to laugh. Inside, his heart was ripped to shreds. But right now, he was in combat mode; he had one focus, to bring his girl back alive.

Reaper repositioned the rifle's butt firmly against his shoulder, just above his armpit and settled his cheekbone against the butt stock, positioned behind the scope. He zeroed his weapon, dialed in his scope so the bullet's point of impact was at the scope's crosshairs. Shooting downward at a moving target, a boat bobbing on the ocean and traveling at a high rate of speed was difficult especially when trying to factor the range to the target, wind direction, and velocity.

Reaper peered through the scope to get a quick sweep of the situation. Fury erupted inside him. He lowered his rifle.

"Storm?"

Storm hunched down next to him.

"That bitch has a gun. There's one man dead. Summer's hands are bound, and the boat is taking on water, and now, she's slowing down."

"Time isn't on our side, brother. With her slowing down, the boat will sink faster taking on water quickly. Do what you do best, play God, and kill the bad guy while I do the rescuing."

Reaper aimed his rifle back in the direction of the boat. The situation turned from bad to worse in less than ten seconds. Mariann no longer sat in the driver seat but beside Summer.

Game on.

His eyes focused on his crosshairs, not on his enemy.

One hundred yards out.

He was going for the headshot.

He eased the trigger back with the ball of his finger careful not to jerk the rifle sideways. He concentrated on his breathing and then held his lungs empty as he lined up the shot against the back of Mariann's head. Next, he focused on his heartbeat to minimize barrel motion. He aimed low to compensate on his moving target. He waited between heartbeats, waited for the rhythm, the downbeat of his heart.

Waited for the perfect shot.

He fired.

Storm jumped from the helicopter to rescue Summer.

Mariann never knew what hit her.

Her gun clattered to the floor, and she slumped against Summer.

Summer looked over to see the side of Mariann's head missing and blood splattered against her; she screamed and jumped from her seat, causing the boat to become unstable and dip farther into the ocean. Water gushed through the leaks. The boat creaked from the pressure.

She lost her footing on the wet surface, fell to the floor, slid on her back, and collided against the dead man at the front of the boat. The bloody water gushed in, pooling around her, filling the boat, causing the boat to dip and pitch forward into the ocean. She got to her knees and staggered to the back of the boat. Her sudden movement sent the boat careening over onto its side with her body hurtling over the railing.

The front of her blouse caught the railing.

She was at its mercy.

The force slammed her hard against the body of the boat.

With her hands still bound, she couldn't save herself.

She barely had enough time to open her mouth and gulp in a large breath before the boat rolled, dragged her down, tumbling her in the murky cold depths of the ocean.

She was going to drown.

Storm relived his nightmare.

As soon as she went under, he went under with her. Where he thought Summer would land, she didn't. He searched for her but couldn't find her. He tried not to panic, but the boat was slowly rolling, nose first, and twirled like a drill sinking deeper and deeper. He could hold his breath under water for eight minutes, but he couldn't afford to take the luxury because he knew Summer couldn't swim and was probably panicking at this very moment. This was how the ocean ripped your life away, by stealing your breath in moments of panic.

Out of the corner of his eye, he saw a glimpse of her blonde hair, a long webbed sheen, floating in the water barely visible on the other side of the boat. He sliced through the water toward her.

She wasn't there.

Then it dawned on him somehow she was attached to the boat. The boat tumbled another turn, still not seeing her, he waited for another full turn.

He found her.

Her terror-filled eyes were open when he got to her. She was still trying to hold her breath. Releasing his knife, he sliced down the front of her blouse and freed her from the boat and not a moment too soon before the boat crashed to the ocean floor.

She fell into his arms. He placed his mouth over hers, gave her his breath, and kicked hard to shoot them back up to the surface.

She kissed him as soon as their heads were above water.

"I prayed you would find me," she sobbed against his lips. "You were right, Storm. I should've listened to you. It was all about jealousy with Mariann. I didn't see it coming. It's hard to believe."

Storm snipped the ties binding her wrists and held her in his arms. "It's all over, baby."

Moments later while Storm watched Summer being airlifted into the helicopter and into the arms of her brother, his heart pounded fiercely against his chest with pangs of relief. This time, the hands of fate was merciful. He had been too late to save Calypsia but he sought his redemption in saving Summer and received it.

Thank God.

31

The anniversary party was delayed for a week so Storm and Summer could attend.

Summer gazed out the window of the airplane as they flew over the Atlantis-blue water. Palm trees, its leaves rustling and swaying in the breeze, flanked the sand as white and pure as the snow. The plane began to bank, circling above a sprawling whitewashed home that sat upon a hillside sprinkled liberally with cabanas on the oceanfront side. Balconies wrapped around the second story undoubtedly giving breathtaking views of the Atlantic. With the lush sprawling landscapes and tropical gardens, it was peaceful, a paradise.

"Are you going to tell me where we are now?" she asked anxiously, looking over at Storm who looked back at her with a secret smile. Dr. Maddox's private plane picked them up at the airport, and they'd been flying for almost five hours.

"Montego Bay, Jamaica."

"God, it's beautiful," she breathed, glancing again out the window.

She pointed out the window. "Is that your parent's house?"

He nodded. "It used to be a sugar plantation, sits on three thousand acres. It's been in our family for well over one hundred years."

Together, they peered out the window; he pointed to a hidden cove on the east side of the property, pointing to an old wooden ship that resembled a pirate's ship.

"I'm going to take you on a sunset cruise on that ship," he promised her.

"You definitely have all the amenities one could ever want here," she said, shaking her head in awe. "It's breathtaking."

Then something caught her eye on the beach as the plane lowered.

A fire.

Orange flames arranged in some sort of strange pattern were lit stretching across the beach.

Storm leaned over and nuzzled her neck, reached for her left hand.

She held his hand, gave it a gentle squeeze, and distracted, once again glanced back down at the beach.

"Honey, the beach…there's a fire down below…"

Her eyes widened as she read the words.

Startled, she read the words again.

Will you marry me, Summer?

She gasped.

Storm pulled her toward him.

She whirled around and looked into his eyes, now locked with hers and intense. He reached up, cupped her face, swirled his thumb lazily against her cheek.

"Will you marry me, Summer Benson? Will you share your life with me, have our children, and grow old with me?"

He had his usual effect on her. Her heart stuttered, kicked against her ribs, and she was speechless. She swallowed hard and bit back the rush of tears.

"Yes!"

He eased onto her left finger a thick brushed gold band encrusted with dazzling diamonds.

She stared down at the ring's brilliance. "It's perfect. It's exactly what I would've picked. You really couldn't have done any better than this," she breathed, laughing excitedly.

Together, they both glanced out the airplane window to see a crowd of people walking onto the beach, standing by her fiery proposal and waving up at them.

"Are you sure you didn't get help from a close, personal wedding planner, like your sister, maybe?" she asked skeptically.

He started laughing. "Okay, I confess, she helped. But most importantly, she also helped gather our family and close friends together. We have much to celebrate."

"Yes, we do," she said, leaning over and kissing him softly. "We have our life to celebrate."

Later that night, he was lying on his side in bed reading when he heard her walk across the floor. He never looked up.

After a minute when she didn't approach the bed, he looked up, across the room. With the door open, the warm tropical breeze floating inside their cabana and the full moon looming at her back, he saw the outline of *her.*

His fantasy.

Wearing a skintight doctor's coat that landed just above her knee and red high heels, she was leaning against the doorframe.

Please don't let me be dreaming.

She walked slowly, deliberately, seductively toward him carrying an empty wine bottle in her hand. She gave him a sultry, mystical look, a come-hither look.

"Interested in a game called spin the bottle?"

Suddenly, buttons popped and cascaded against the floor.

He fell off the bed.

About the Author

Dawn Williams grew up in Muncie, Indiana and lives in her hometown with her husband, Dave and two adorable cats that are on occasion, sworn enemies and need refereed. She attended Ball State University and majored in Business. Currently, she works for IU Health Ball Memorial Hospital. When she's writing, she indulges in her unhealthy addiction to caffeine. When not writing, she enjoys chick flicks and listening to 80's music. Growing up, she went from reading massive amounts of romance novels to writing them and feels incredibly blessed to do something she feels so passionately about.

She's a member of the Romance Writers of America.

Note from Author: Thank you for buying this novel. Knowing how busy you are, I appreciate you letting me sweep you away for a few hours from your work or your loved ones.

CPSIA information can be obtained at www.ICGtesting.com
Printed in the USA
LVOW11s0237020115

421155LV00001B/142/P